# CRAVING
## IN HIS
# BLOOD

# ALSO BY ZOEY DRAVEN

### Warriors of Luxiria

*The Alien's Prize*

*The Alien's Mate*

*The Alien's Lover*

*The Alien's Touch*

*The Alien's Dream*

*The Alien's Obsession*

*The Alien's Seduction*

*The Alien's Claim*

### Horde Kings of Dakkar

*Captive of the Horde King*

*Claimed by the Horde King*

*Madness of the Horde King*

*Broken by the Horde King*

*Taken by the Horde King*

*Throne of the Horde King*

### Warrior of Rozun

*Wicked Captor*

*Wicked Mate*

### The Krave of Everton

*Kraving Khiva*

*Prince of Firestones*

*Kraving Dravka*

*Kraving Tavak*

## <u>Brides of the Kylorr</u>

*Desire in His Blood*

*Craving in His Blood*

# CRAVING IN HIS BLOOD

## BRIDES OF THE KYLORR BOOK TWO

ZOEY DRAVEN

# CRAVING IN HIS BLOOD

*She's the fated mate he never wanted...and the human that will bring him to his knees.*

As the daughter of a traveling chef, I grew up flitting around different galaxies, immersing myself in fascinating cultures, and rubbing shoulders with socialites. Coming to Krynn was a new chapter, a permanent place to finally call *home*.

But when tragedy strikes and I'm suddenly alone, broke, and desperate, I take work at a *dyaan*. An establishment where the Kylorr—blood-drinking, winged, fearsome aliens with berserker-like rages—come to feed on willing necks to satisfy their fierce hunger.

That's where I meet him. Kythel of House Kaalium, the ruler of Erzos, with his mesmerizing eyes like fractured ice and a sinful voice that captivates me.

We're polar opposites. I'm a hopeful optimist who always looks for silver linings. He's guarded and mistrustful, a wealthy heir to a powerful legacy, who thrives on rigid, unbending control. Yet he craves my blood with a frenzy that maddens him, and he'll stop at nothing to claim me.

But when the forbidden desire between us becomes too tempting to resist, I fear it will destroy us both...especially when an impossible choice threatens to be our ruin: Duty or love?

# CHAPTER 1

## MILLIE

That starry, inky evening, Raana *Dyaan* was bustling with activity. As I bobbed and weaved through the growing crowd in the common room, my arm was beginning to wobble under the weight of the heavy goblets perched on the even heavier black steel tray.

"Millicent," Lesana said, touching my shoulder when I passed her in the main entrance hall with the Drovos wine for the group of Kylorr in the lounge. Her tone was slightly distracted, a serene smile pasted onto her full, gray lips. "*Tassa*. Did you take it tonight? They're smoking *lore* in the lounge."

"Already took a vial," I told her, flashing her a small, reassuring grin even as the tray began to shake. "Don't worry. I need to get these to them before the wine ends up all over your new rug."

Lesana had had it imported from Dumera, the crafters' colony. And it was exquisite. A deep bloodred with threads of silver and gold woven into an intricate, swirling pattern. It reminded me of tattoos I'd seen inked onto Dakkari males. Or of the tapestries I'd seen hanging on the walls of Bartutians' extravagant atriums, meant to impress their guests.

"Go," she ordered, waving me off, her eyes already landing on the next client who'd just entered the darkened establishment. "Ah, Jaan—welcome, my friend. What would you like tonight?"

"Quick feed. Is Bryna here?" Jaan of House Nu replied, shaking off her wings in the entry, sending drizzly little drops onto the walls from the rain. "I need to get back to my son. My mate is away in Laras for a barter and..."

But I didn't stay to listen. Repositioning my grip on the tray, I continued into the quietest room, the lounge, which was right off the main entrance hall. Behind paneled steel doors, the large, elegant space was lit by Halo orbs swirling overhead, casting a gentle, golden light on the—mostly horned and winged—patrons below.

The silver smoke of *lore* floated gently in the dim lighting. The *tassa* I'd taken earlier ensured I didn't have any, *ahem*, adverse reactions, as were common of humans, but out of the corner of my eye, I still caught a pointed stare, a lazy smirk from a dark-horned Kylorr male drinking and eating alone in the corner. Waiting for the expected *enthusiastic* response from a human? I adverted my gaze, striding forward to the group of four Kylorr and one Keriv'i male, chatting and ribbing among themselves.

One of the Kylorr I recognized. He was a regular of Raana *Dyaan* and was Lesana's own cousin.

"Still working in this hovel, are we, Millicent?" the male in question asked, a wide grin stretched over his face, exposing sharp incisors that poked into his dark gray bottom lip.

"Well, you're still coming here, aren't you, Hanno?" I teased, sweet relief spreading through my arms when I set the tray down on their table. "Can't be that bad of a place for your discerning tastes."

The *dyaan* was a blood establishment. A place for Kylorr to come and feed from a wide array of willing blood givers.

Raana *Dyaan* was well known as one of the most exclusive and select establishments not only in the province of Erzos but throughout the entirety of the Kaalium—for its upscale ambience dripping in quiet extravagance; for its location so close to Erzos Keep; for the attentive, meticulous service. Lesana demanded the best from her workers and only gave the best to her patrons.

Two months prior, she had employed me, though not as a blood giver. For now, I was cleaning after prime hours and serving food and wine to patrons to go along with their blood givers' necks and wrists, in my pristine and pressed uniform, not a speck of dirt or dust on my face.

Had I ever thought that when Father and I had landed on Krynn that I would be working in a *dyaan*, alone with no one else in the entire universe, in difficult financial straits?

Never.

But Father's body was on Horrin. In the First Quadrant. And it would take many, many credits to bring him back to Krynn. Credits I didn't have. Not yet, at least.

And so I pasted on smile after smile at wealthy patrons who frequented Raana *Dyaan*. Though I'd broached the topic of being a blood giver with Lesana last week, she hadn't given me her answer yet. Being a blood giver paid more credits per night, my own personal reservations about it be damned. Gifts were not unheard of from the wealthier patrons if they liked the way you tasted. Gifts I could sell to further pad my savings.

Did I like this woman I'd become?

No.

But as I deposited the Drovos wine goblets in a neat circle around the table, I couldn't stop thinking that in two months, my father's uncollected body would burn and his ashes would be spread among the stars. I couldn't allow that to happen.

Two months.

I was running out of time.

To the group of males, I grinned, though it felt too widely stretched across my skull, and said, "Are you here to feed as well? Would you like me to have Lesana make arrangements for you?"

The Keriv'i at the table, with his gray-blue skin, took a swift drink from his goblet.

"I'll be the only one who needs to feed tonight," Hanno said. "I have a long journey to Salaire in the morning."

"Of course," I said, placing a hand on his shoulder and giving it a brief squeeze. "I'll let Lesana know. Enjoy your wine."

Before I left, Hanno asked, "Can you have the cook prepare those tarts we had last time? The ones with the *kanno* spice?"

"Culinarian," I corrected softly, on instinct. I blinked at him, tilting my head to the side. "Of course. It might be a little while. They weren't on the menu tonight, but I can put in a special request for you. Will that be all right?"

Hanno lounged back in his chair, tipping his goblet up at me. He grinned around at his friends. "We'll be here all night. And I've been craving them almost as much as blood this last week."

Pleasure warmed my belly—a feeling I'd never get used to whenever someone praised my food. "Anything else?"

"Just a heaping platter of those tarts, if you will, Millicent."

"You got it," I said, grinning again—though it felt genuine this time around.

When I left the lounge, I passed Lesana again.

"Are you going to stand here all night?" I asked.

"We're expecting some special guests this evening," she informed me. Ah, that was why she seemed so on edge. "I don't want to miss them."

"Anyone I know?" I asked, hugging the empty steel tray to my chest.

She gave me a tight smile but didn't answer. "How is your group in the lounge?"

"Hanno wants to feed tonight," I told her.

She inclined her head, reaching over to tap on her Halo Com, one of the many screens she'd had installed throughout the *dyaan*, including in the private rooms. "He prefers Kian. I'll see if he's up for one more feeding tonight. He's already been with two other patrons."

I shifted on my feet, waiting for her to finish putting in her request for Kian's presence on the Com. "And, um, they requested the *kanno*-spice tarts I made last week."

She started to frown before her gaze ever left the screen. When Lesana met my eyes, she asked, "They did?"

"Yes."

She let out a long-winded huff that I'd learned was a Kylorr version of a sigh. "You know Draan doesn't like to share his kitchen, Millie. He'll skewer me with his favorite knife."

Most culinarians—and gods knew I'd met a lot over the years —were fiercely, fiercely territorial over their kitchens. Once, when my father had come to serve at a party in Potri, I'd literally watched the head culinarian piss on the floor in front of him, splattering the kiln in lime-green urine. My father had merely stepped over the puddle to lay out his knives, sharpening them deliberately and with thoroughness as they'd stared one another down.

My father had been calm, level headed, and very rarely confrontational—a rarity among culinarians, truthfully. Except for that night.

"He's your mate," I argued, shooting her a sweet, sweet smile. "So afterward, he'll kiss your wound to make it all better."

Lesana huffed again.

"Very well. But don't get in his way, Millicent," she warned, wagging a long, tipped finger at me. "Make them quickly. Then get out. Oh, before you go, can you get Grace? She hasn't responded to my Com message. She should be finished with her patron. I need her in the common room tonight. And soon."

I scurried away before she could change her mind, already making a mental list of the ingredients I'd need to poach from Draan's stores for the tarts. They were a recipe I'd cobbled together quickly, taking inspiration from a similar dish my father had created for a Bartutian family when we'd lived on Bartu briefly. Only, instead of crackling spice—a Bartutian favorite, which popped and fizzed on the tongue when eaten—I'd used *kanno* spice, a Kylorr staple. Spicy and earthy, it melded well with the tart sweetness of the *ito'nag* plums I'd found in Draan's cellar. I'd been delighted over the surprising discovery, unable to stop myself from popping a small black fruit into my mouth, savoring the juicy spill over my tongue as I'd avoided the spiked pit.

They'd been beautifully ripe last week, and I only hoped he had more. I knew it was an expensive import, but then again... this *was* Raana *Dyaan*.

Only the best for Lesana's patrons.

First, I needed the blue-pepper compote from my room. I was loath to use it, truthfully. Carefully stored in pressurized silver flasks and bottles and jars, nestled in a padded case within the depths of my heavy trunk, were the last of my father's stores. But the compote complemented the *kanno* beautifully, bringing out its best qualities and softening the sharp spiciness. It was necessary. It was what my father would have done.

*But first, Grace,* I remembered, beginning to ascend the winding staircase, heading up one level to the private feeding rooms. My own room was on the third, uppermost floor.

Treading down the hallway on the second floor, my footsteps falling silent on the velvety stone, I stopped in front of a black wooden door. Grace's room.

Just as I raised my fist to knock, I heard a moan come from within.

I stilled, my fist raised but motionless.

Another moan, breathy. *Hers.* It was quickly muffled, as if a hand had snapped over her mouth, fastening into place.

My heart began to hammer.

"Grace," I called out.

Shit. What was she *thinking*?

Silence came from inside. I rapped my fist across the black

wood, quickly looking down the hallway to make sure no one was around.

"Grace, open up."

*Please don't make me open this door while you're doing what I think you're doing in there*, I pleaded silently.

I heard something topple from within the room and then the scurry of small feet. A moment later, the door knob turned. The rooms couldn't be locked from the inside, a safety feature Lesana had insisted on.

Grace's red hair was mussed, her cheeks even redder. Her dress was loosened, untied at the back, baring her smooth shoulder. She peeked out of the crack, her eyes glassy and wide. The smoke of *lore* drifted from within the room, but I didn't so much as blink.

"Is someone in there with you?" I asked quietly, studying her. "Did you not take *tassa* tonight? Did he start smoking *lore* when you weren't—"

She bit her lip. "No, nothing like that. Millie, just—"

I pushed at the door, and she stumbled back, letting it fall open. A Kylorr male—a regular who came a few times a week, one who I knew had a mate because he'd brought her once—was naked, though he was hurriedly trying to shove his stiff cock back into his black trews.

Looking back to Grace, dread curling in my belly, I breathed, "Lesana will have your head."

The *only* strict rule in Raana *Dyaan* was that *no* intimate relations with the blood givers were allowed.

I didn't truly understand the severity with which Lesana implemented the rule, considering most *dyaans* in Erzos—at least from what I'd heard through salacious gossip—had *private* private rooms for such things.

"But you're not going to tell her, are you, Millie?" Grace asked, pressing her lips together briefly. She was one of two human blood givers employed in Raana *Dyaan*. She glared, an expression I'd never seen overcoming her features. "I know you won't."

To the Kylorr, I croaked out, "You need to leave. *Now.*"

Grace had the good sense to keep her mouth shut as the Kylorr male strode past me.

"Get yourself cleaned up and take some *tassa*," I told Grace. "Lesana needs you in the common room tonight."

Not waiting for a response, I followed the Kylorr male down the stairwell. He didn't say a word to me, likely worried that I'd tell Lesana and he'd have his membership revoked.

We passed the Kylorr female in question, right where I'd left her mere moments before, but now I felt a ripple of unease when her demure smile turned to one of confusion. The last thing I wanted to do was lie to her...but I knew Grace desperately needed the credits. Like me, she had no one else.

"Did you enjoy your night, Vraad?" Lesana asked, shooting me a narrowed-eye assessing stare before turning back to her patron.

"As always," Vraad said gruffly.

"Bring Lynara next time you come," Lesana said, ever the charming hostess. "Tell her we just imported her favorite *slew* from Bavia."

"Yes," Vraad said, his voice hitching higher when he shot me a brief look. "Yes, I will."

Then he scurried through the main entrance, nearly hitting his outstretched wing on the steel.

"Grace will be down soon," I told Lesana, eyeing Vraad's back as he gusted his wings, about to take flight, eager to leave. "Do you mind if I get some fresh air? I'm still mentally preparing for Draan's wrath," I teased, hoping my voice didn't sound too strained.

"Go," Lesana said, still eyeing me in a way that told me she knew something was wrong. Shit.

All my excitement over making the tarts had evaporated. Grace was my closest friend. We'd begun working at Raana

*Dyaan* around the same time and had both clung to one another as we navigated these halls. But the look she'd given me tonight… I hadn't recognized that woman.

Outside, the cool night air felt wonderfully soothing over my heated cheeks. Seeking some privacy, I walked around the front entrance, settling my back against a tall black tree, which smelled comfortingly like cinnamon. It was called a bleeding tree. Because when the weather warmed at the height of summer, it oozed a thick, black sap that was used in many types of perfumes and soaps and oils on Krynn.

But now its bark was dry and rough. I plucked at a piece of it, turning my gaze to the sky.

Thousands of stars greeted me. For a moment, I felt so lost in them. I wondered which direction Horrin lay at this time of night, during this time of the season when the days were beginning to warm. I thought of my savings. I thought of all the permits I needed to apply for, all the transport depots I would need to navigate, all the stern-eyed beings I would need to face just to reach my father.

I felt so incredibly tired. Lost. Lonely.

It had been four months since Father had died. And *still* I wasn't used to these feelings.

Three Kylorr were flying toward Raana *Dyaan* in the distance, coming from the South. I watched as they zoomed over Stellara Forest, the great flaps of their wings almost in sync with one another. Males, I knew, when their thick horns became silhouetted against the night sky.

Blowing out a breath, I looked over Stellara Forest again. I scraped the pad of my fingertip over the piece of bark prodding into my back. The forest was pitch black this time of night. Most Kylorr didn't venture inside Stellara. Superstition, I'd determined —something about an ancient war, though my long walks beneath her trees were nothing short of a peaceful reprive.

A breeze kicked up, blowing back my hair. For a moment, I

closed my eyes, savoring it, drawing in another deep breath, scenting the breeze of the nearest sea. We weren't that far from the ports. It was why we'd come here. Because *she* had lived near the sea. *She* had lived in Erzos. This was where they'd fallen in love.

*Boom.*

When the three Kylorr males landed on the cobbled stone that spread out like a fan from Raana *Dyaan*'s front entrance, I nearly gasped in surprise, my eyelids popping open.

"I don't think I even need to feed," came a gruff voice. "I just want some *lore* and some brew."

Twin blue eyes were watching me in the darkness, reflecting off the golden light pouring out from the window of the lounge.

Stunned, my breath whistled out of my lungs, my back straightening against the bleeding tree.

The Kylorr male's black wings were still stretched wide from his flight. Sharp curved talons made peaks on both, like spikes over his broad shoulders. His horns were arced, hugging closer to his skull than most Kylorr I'd seen but no less deadly. His ears were pointed, jutting beyond his black hair, which he kept short and trim, neat.

His pants looked perfectly pressed, and every silver latch on his intricate vest was bone straight. The long-sleeved tunic he wore underneath it was skin tight, molding to his thick arms and broad shoulders. The light gray skin that was exposed—his large hands, his wide neck, his beautiful, beautiful face—gleamed in the warm light.

Then there were his eyes.

Hard and glinting, his eyes reminded me of a winter sea: harsh, brutal, merciless.

A sapphire sea I could drown in.

Kythel of House Kaalium.

High Lord of Erzos.

I recognized him as easily as his beautiful, spired, gothic keep jutting beyond Stellara's borders to the south.

He frowned as he studied me. Then the sharp cut of his square jawline slashed away like a blade when he turned to regard the first male who'd spoken, a male I couldn't see beyond the corner of Raana *Dyaan*.

"You're more than welcome to return to the keep, Kaldur," came Kythel's voice. "But stay far away from my own stores of *lore* and my cellars."

"Stay away from his keepers too," came a third voice, a husky laugh accompanying it. "Didn't you fuck one when you were last here?"

"Enough," Kythel said sharply. My breath turned to ice in my throat when he turned his gaze toward me again. I watched his brow furrow briefly.

I should greet them. Smile. Lead them to Lesana, who was waiting eagerly just inside the door. Instead, I was frozen solid in place, pinned by that gaze.

Kythel finally turned away. To his companions, he said, "Come. I need to feed, and we already have so much to discuss tonight."

Then he strode from sight. Their heavy footsteps retreated. A few moments later, I heard Lesana's calm and confident voice as she greeted, "*Kyzaires*. We are delighted that you can join us tonight."

When I was alone once more, my body sagged against the bleeding tree like I'd been a puppet...and he'd been controlling my fraying strings.

# CHAPTER 2

## KYTHEL

*T*he Kylorr female's brief flash of nerves sparked at me from across the room the moment I stepped inside. I'd fed from her before. I couldn't remember her name, though Lesana had remembered that I'd liked the taste of her blood last time.

Like a mask settling in place, erasing that brief glimpse of vulnerability I likely hadn't been meant to witness, she smiled. Like an ocean wave sliding over sand, polishing it smooth, her nerves disappeared.

"Where would you like to feed from this evening, *Kyzaire?*" she asked me, voice husky and quiet, though her smile felt plastered on her face. A practiced smile, I knew. *Professional,* even.

"Wrist," I told her gruffly.

*She remembered,* I thought as I watched her nod and turn away to look into the hearth, where an orange fire was blazing. Her long, graceful arm reached out, straight and still.

Stepping up behind her, I took hold of her wrist. She didn't look at me once, which was why I preferred Raana *Dyaan* over the rest. Other females in other houses would be vying for my attention, trying to entice me in other ways that went beyond the taste of their blood.

Lowering my head to her wrist, my pupils dilated, the room growing brighter. My body hummed in anticipation.

At the first spark of her blood on my tongue, my grip on her tightened. My eyes closed. Rich and decadent but not too thick or tart, her blood began to satiate that gnawing, aching hunger that I'd felt ringing through my bones. It had been a few days since I'd last fed, from a blood giver in Vyaan, when I'd been in my brother's territory. I needed this.

I got lost in her blood for a brief moment. I always hated that —that brief loss of control when I was *this* hungry. That was why I didn't like to be watched as I fed.

The discomfort, however, ebbed the longer I drank. When I'd had my fill, I released her wrist, not wanting to touch her for longer than absolutely necessary, and then backed away. The heavy fatigue I'd felt, the tightness at the base of my neck, the weighty feel of my wings, lifted. I felt better than I had in days, though I knew I desperately needed sleep too.

"Thank you," I told her, though my words sounded hollow.

She swiped her finger over her own fangs, catching venom, and pressed it to the small wound I'd left behind. Her practiced smile greeted me when she faced me and asked, "Would you like me to escort you back to the lounge, *Kyzaire*?"

"No," I told her, the walls of the room suddenly feeling much too close. "That won't be necessary."

I felt her eyes on me as I left, returning to the dimly lit stairwell and descending to the main floor. There was a scent in the air, one that made my fangs ache and my venom flow, which didn't make sense considering I'd just sated myself on the giver's blood. I stilled on the landing, trying to determine where it was coming from, nostrils flaring.

*Strange.*

Deciding to forget it, I shook it from my head. It evaporated like afternoon mist, and I strode forward into the lounge, spying my two brothers drinking from shining goblets in a private corner, nearest the window that overlooked the front courtyard.

The lounge was quiet tonight, though I'd heard quite a crowd in the common room of the *dyaan* when we'd entered. The moon winds were approaching. Sometimes, the week leading up to them could feel frenzied, the need to feed much more pinching.

I slid into the black high-backed chair, my wings slipping easily around the velvety spine.

"Better?" Thaine asked, a knowing expression on his features as he sipped from his goblet.

I gave a brief nod, the taste of the giver's blood still lingering on my tongue. There was a goblet waiting for me, and I quickly reached for it, taking a long draw. Perhaps unintentionally, most of the Drovos wine variants paired beautifully with the thick, earthy richness of Kylorr blood. The Kylorr had our own wine-makers—though most lived in the South, nearest Salaire—but the Drovian winemakers were consumed in their art. They lived and breathed their craft, their strides toward perfection almost obsessive. Drovos was a small planet on the outskirts of the Third Quadrant.

Otherwise unremarkable...except for their wines. They'd made a name for themselves throughout the universe because of them. As such, it had made their race—not just the winemakers—very wealthy indeed.

I savored the bite on the back of my tongue. A full-bodied wine with high tannins from the extended aging in their under-water casks. As always, there was a slight tang from the Drovos sea. Perfection. I'd always wanted to journey to Drovos—to see their forested vineyards of *brol* berries, smell the fermentation process in their highly acidic soil, and watch their ships pull up their casks from deep below the sea.

"It's good," Kaldur drawled, tipping up his goblet. "But I prefer the brew from Vyaan."

He said it just to vex me, but I flashed him a small smirk from across the black circular table. My goblet landed on the shining surface with a harsh thud.

"Did you learn anything from the port master today?" I asked him. "About Maazin?"

Kaldur's wings rustled before he let them relax again. I'd been kept in meetings all day and figured my brothers might as well make themselves useful while they were visiting from their respective provinces.

"There's little in the records in your library, but Thaine found his name in an old port ledger. I left it in your office," he said. "I asked the dock master personally about him. He said he remembered Maazin but that he didn't dine or socialize with the rest of the dockhands—he kept to himself. He thought he might have been living somewhere in Raana."

"Here? I find that strange," I murmured. "Why work at the ports only to travel so far inland to sleep? They have accommodations specifically for port workers."

Kaldur took another sip from his goblet, his gaze straying to the other patrons within the lounge. There was a group of four Kylorr and one Keriv'i on the opposite side of the room. A Kylorr couple. A lone male in a darkened corner, eating voraciously from a shadowed platter. Another group of three Kylorr females, one laughing musically at something that was said.

I knew all of them. Sena and Jerr of House Kraan were the couple. Two of the females I recognized as vendor owners from the food market. The third female was the one who organized the entire market. Three of the male Kylorr worked in the high offices of the export port of Erzos. The Keriv'i, whose name was Makav, owned an apothecary down the road—oils and salts and stimulants. The last male of their group was Hanno, a noble from House Arada.

I knew everyone except for the male in the corner. In the lounge of Raana *Dyaan*, which typically only catered to those who could afford its high price, I usually recognized everyone. Perhaps he was a traveler passing through. Judging by the expensive material and cut of his vest, I thought he might be from Laras.

"So Maazin was as much of a mystery in Erzos as he was in Laras," I said quietly, meeting my two brothers' gazes.

"What is it that you hope to find, Kythel?" Kaldur asked, piercing me with those silver eyes. Mother had always said looking into them was like looking into a mirror. Or a *zylarr*. His eyes reflected souls back. "He was one male."

"He was a spy," I said, my tone clipped. "Not just a male. A *Thryki* male. Sent from across the seas to the Kaalium. To...what? To create division between the Kaazor and us?"

War was coming.

We were in a time of peace, but already fractures were fissuring through it like broken glass.

It could've been years away, but I knew deep in my bones that war was coming to the Kaalium. Again. And we needed to start preparing. The Dyaar were ruthless barbarians from across the sea. The Thykri were no better, though they were more cunning. Would the Koro ally with us? Would the Kaazor to the north?

*Zyre has no reason to come to our aid,* I thought. My twin brother, Azur, wasn't worried. He wasn't worried about the Kaalium standing on our own. We had the best armies on Krynn, after all. Legions of soldiers. But if all the other nations turned against us, it wouldn't matter how well-trained our soldiers were, we would be outnumbered four to one.

Many Kylorr would die. On all sides.

"Have you considered it possible that Maazin was working alone?" Thaine asked quietly. "He was close with Gemma. He didn't seem violent to her. All we can say for certain was that he was stealing shipments of *lore* and trying to blame the thefts on the Kaazor. That's hardly a cry from across the seas for war. Maybe it was just greed."

Gemma was Azur's wife. He'd married her under...less than ideal circumstances. But now the two were so besotted with one another that it was nearly sickening. She'd trusted Maazin, until she discovered what he'd been doing with the *lore* accounts.

"Then why did Zyre find him and kill him in the North? Why did Maazin try to flee to the very people he was trying to frame?" Kaldur asked.

"I need to meet with Zyre."

The words left my lips like heavy, falling stones. But the truth of them was becoming more and more apparent to me.

Zyre was the leader of the Kaazor. Their king, who'd taken over rule from his father after his death. It was no secret that our relationship was strained, hanging by a thread. The merest flinch could sever that tentative peace completely, and I had worried that Maazin's death had done just that.

"We *all* should meet with him," Thaine argued. "Not just you alone. You don't have to take on the weight and burden for the entire family now that Azur is...occupied."

Occupied? He was married. He'd married the daughter of the human male who'd killed Aina. Our beloved aunt. My mother's twin sister. Her death had fractured my family beyond repair.

Azur had married for revenge...until he'd fallen in love with our enemy's daughter. And truly, I was happy for my brother. He deserved the peace she brought him.

I took a long, long drink from my goblet. The last few months had been difficult. I felt both stretched out so long I couldn't see where I ended and curled so tight into myself that I wondered if I could disappear.

*Nothing* would shake that sensation. Not blood. Not drink. Not *lore*.

*Perhaps a female, then,* I thought idly. The last thing I hadn't tried.

Thaine and Kaldur exchanged a look, one that sparked my irritation.

"What?" I growled softly.

Kaldur's tone was carefully nonchalant when he asked, "Is it true? About Lyris of House Arada?"

I cut him a sharp look, narrowing my gaze on him. "What did you hear?"

I had only told Vadyn, my head keeper, what I'd decided because I'd had him manage all correspondence between House Arada and myself. Just this morning he'd informed me that I was invited to their House for the moon winds celebration.

"*Raazos's blood*, Kythel. You would keep this from us?" Thaine asked quietly. "We're your brothers."

"Don't take it personally. I haven't even told Azur," I murmured, not missing the hurt that flashed over Thaine's feature. I added, "You know I don't mean it like that."

"We all know Azur is your favorite," Kaldur said, a sly smirk on his face, but it felt slightly cutting.

This conversation again.

"Actually, Kalia is my favorite," I argued, glaring at all of them. "Because at least she answers my Coms. Azur doesn't even do that these days, much less you two."

"Jealous of Gemma?" Kaldur drawled. "Don't think you can squirm out of what I asked you. Is it true or not?"

"Yes," I said suddenly, my claws curling into the silver steel of the goblet, scraping the metal. Thaine glanced down at the marks before he met my eyes. "It's true. I've decided to make Lyris of House Arada my wife. The *Kylaira* of Erzos."

Again, Kaldur and Thaine exchanged looks at one another. They gave me shit for Azur when they were obviously connected like twins themselves? Though, perhaps they had bonded because of necessity. I had Azur, and Azur had me. Lucen and Kalia were next closest in age and had always been attached at the wing. That left them. Two was better than one in a large family like ours.

I didn't move. I leveled them a cold stare, waiting for them to cast their judgments, not like it would matter. My mind was made up.

Now that my twin had married, now that Laras had a *Kylaira* once more—in Gemma of House Kaalium—I knew it was my duty to marry for *purpose*. Azur had married for revenge. Then he had married for love. Both forms of it happened to be performed with the same human female.

But I didn't have that luxury.

House Arada was a wealthy family. *Lore* was House Kaalium's export. But *drava*, Kylorr black steel, mined from the Three Guardians in Erzos itself, was House Arada's export—they alone controlled its production. My ancestors had gifted the mountain to House Arada after their undying allegiance in an old war.

And *drava* was one of the strongest metals in existence. It made the sharpest and most durable of weapons. The best shields. The best walls. The best armor. The best ships and vessels.

We would bleed money during a war. The only thing we had that the other nations of Krynn did not was *wealth*. An abundance of it.

With House Arada tied to House Kaalium, we would have the amount of wealth necessary to easily crush a war in its early stages. Loss of life would be minimal, especially throughout the Kaalium.

My decision was made.

I only needed to announce the union between the two Houses.

So why hadn't I yet?

Why hadn't I even told Azur yet?

I'd barely spoken two words to Lyris, but I supposed that didn't matter. She would agree to the union because it was expected of her.

Duty. Responsibility to one's family. Responsibility to the Kaalium.

*At least we will have that in common,* I couldn't help but think, ignoring the sting of bitterness that tightened my throat. I didn't have a right to feel it, after all.

"Mother never wanted arranged marriages for any of us," Thaine finally said, his words chosen carefully. "They aren't necessary."

"That was before..." I trailed off, my throat tightening. "That was before Aina."

Kaldur's expression darkened.

"That was before the Kaazor broke their peace agreement. That was before these ripples of unrest started pushing toward our shores from the Thryki. From the Dyaar," I finished. My gaze went to Hanno across the room. Lyris was his niece. "House Arada is the second-wealthiest family in the Kaalium. It would be logical and wise to shore up our defenses now *before* war comes. Despite what you think, with Azur married, it *is* my responsibility. I—"

There was that scent again.

My venom began to drip on my black tongue.

That intoxicating scent made me straighten as my nostrils flared. I scanned the small, dimly lit room, my eye catching on Lesana coming in through the door. *Lesana?* I wondered, brow furrowing.

"What is it?" Thaine asked, confusion in his voice.

"You don't smell that?" I asked, my own words sounding far away.

A human female stepped out from behind Lesana's statuesque figure.

*The female from the courtyard,* I realized, standing from my chair without thinking, my gaze pinned on her.

She was nothing special to look at—not that I'd ever been particularly attracted to human women before.

Her hair was cut just past her shoulders. Bone straight and the color of straw during the harvest season. Her full brows were unnaturally dark for her hair color, giving her a severe expression. Her mouth was wide, her lips the color of *haana* blooms, a softened pink. The bridge of her nose was sloped, giving the very tip an unturned appearance.

She was small and short, whereas I preferred my females tall and strong. She would barely come up to the center of my chest.

The sleek, black uniform of Raana *Dyaan* flared around her breasts and hips. I watched as Lesana hurriedly wiped a smudge of something tan—a dusting of flour, perhaps—off the material. The human woman gave a sheepish smile in return before she strode forward into the room.

From across the quiet lounge, our eyes met. There was a clash of calm and oddly charged ferocity, all bundled into one singular moment that made me hold my breath.

The human's eyes were hazel and primarily gold. Shimmering streaks of it ran like rivulets through her irises. I'd never seen a color quite like them. I'd caught their shadowy depths outside in the courtyard when we'd first arrived, though the darkness had kept much shielded from me. Now, with the Halo orbs glowing and moving overhead, she had nowhere to hide.

*She has sad eyes,* came the unwanted thought. Sad but beautiful. For the first time in years, my hand itched to draw them, but I wondered if I could even capture them properly. I wondered if I even wanted to—because surely it would be a waste of paper when I could look into their living reflection.

She was ugly *and* beguiling, a study of strange proportions and even stranger beauty.

And she smelled divine.

Though I'd just had my fill, I wanted to feed from her. I wanted to taste her blood, sweet and lush like sin.

I wanted her *now.*

# CHAPTER 3

## MILLIE

"*M*illicent," Lesana hissed through a calm smile that she gave to her patrons. I felt her hand press to my shoulder, urging me along.

*Right.* Her voice brought me back, piercing through the sapphire haze I'd found myself trapped in.

Jolting, I scurried toward the table where Hanno sat, mercifully breaking the *Kyzaire* of Erzos's consuming gaze. My heart was thundering in my chest, and I felt like I couldn't catch my breath.

*What just happened?* I wondered, dazed, even as I leveled the group a small, soft smile.

"The tarts are baking right now," I assured them. It had been a mad dash to slip them into the kiln oven under Draan's huffing and pointed, grumpy glare. "I'll have a whole heaping platter for you soon, all right?"

Hanno didn't smile. His gaze strayed past me. "You know the *Kyzaire?*"

"No," I said, keeping my smile in place. "I do not."

"Hmm," Hanno grunted, though the expression on his face had taken on a curious edge. One I was confused by. "Another round of the Drovos wine would be appreciated. Is the room ready yet for my feeding?"

I blinked but said hurriedly, "It's being prepared right now. I'll let you know the moment it's ready. And of course I'll get more wine for you all. One moment."

A little taken aback by Hanno's sudden briskness, I strode to the Halo Com screen and placed the order for the wine. Lesana was speaking with the *Kyzaire* and his two companions, who, in the gentle golden light of the lounge, I realized were his brothers.

Three *Kyzaires* in attendance at Raana *Dyaan* this evening. No wonder Lesana had been on edge.

Kythel, the High Lord of Erzos, was still standing. His gaze still flitted to me every other word that Lesana spoke. Hesitantly, I approached, and I watched his nostrils flare, those winter-sea eyes fastening themselves to my every step.

Lesana noticed where his attention lay, and she turned to me. I saw her look between us. I didn't miss the brief frown that flashed over her usual expression, one meant to be approachable yet distant from her patrons.

I took a deep breath, ignoring the *Kyzaire*'s stare, and looked only at Lesana. Quietly, so the *Kyzaires* wouldn't hear, I said, "Hanno is getting impatient for Kian."

Lesana's eyes flickered to the group across the room. "I'll take care of it," she said. Then she hesitated—and I very rarely saw her hesitate. She raised her voice, her smile dropping back into place. "Serve our honored guests tonight, will you?"

Nerves shot through my belly, but I didn't let them show. All my life, I'd spoken and served and complimented and rubbed noses with all sorts of beings from across the universe, most of them in very powerful and influential stations. I'd lived in all Four Quadrants. I'd lived on seven different colonies and planets and visited dozens more.

Yet over two months ago, before Lesana had taken pity on me, I'd barely had enough credits to pay for a single night at the nearby inn. I'd worried that I'd have to beg for food, unwilling to part with a single credit because I needed every last one to reach my father.

Lesana had never asked about my past. About why she'd found me, dirty and hungry, on the streets of the Raana food market. About where I'd been before I'd come to Krynn. But I sensed that she recognized that part of me—that part of me that could speak with *anyone*. It was why she had me working in the lounge most nights and why, I suspected, she didn't want me to be a blood giver.

"Of course," I replied.

Lesana nodded and then strode away, heading to Hanno. I watched her touch his shoulder, offer him a wide smile, and then he stood, following her out of the lounge. I didn't miss the way Hanno looked back, however. Not at me. His eyes were settled on the *Kyzaire*.

"Who are you?"

The High Lord of Erzos's voice was nothing more than a rasp. Like a harsh whisper dragging across my flesh.

There was a tight band slowly constricting around my chest when I looked up into his eyes. Shockingly blue. Bright like crystal stars, they were *too* beautiful. There was such a thing as *too beautiful*. Because they almost hurt to look into.

"My name is Millie," I said, grateful my voice sounded no different than it had when I'd spoken with Hanno. "I'm honored to serve you tonight, *Kyzaires*. If you need anything at all while you're at Raana *Dyaan*, please let me know."

I didn't know how I did it, but I managed to break Kythel's gaze to look at his brothers, inclining my head in respect. It didn't truly dawn on me that these males were responsible for a large portion of the Kaalium. Perhaps later it would, but for now, I kept that knowledge locked away in case it threatened to choke me.

I looked down at the table and took note of the Drovos wine.

From the blue hue in the silver goblet, I knew they were drinking the R-09 variant, possibly R-10 from the western region. Kythel's was nearly gone. But the other two goblets were virtually untouched.

To his brothers, I asked, "Would you like something different to drink tonight?"

Kaldur of Vyaan and Thaine of Kyne. It took a while to place their faces, but I remembered seeing a portrait of them in Erzan's archives. I'd wanted to learn everything I could about Krynn, more than what my father had told me.

Kaldur's gaze was on his brother, careful and watchful. Thaine's was on me, the sudden intensity of his stare making me want to look down to the floor.

"Brew," came the sharp word from Thaine. Then he seemed to make an effort to soften his words when I jumped slightly. "For my brother and me. Anything from the South. For your *Kyzaire* here, he will continue with the wine."

I feared Lesana and I had interrupted a strained moment between the brothers because the tension pouring off each one of them was extremely palpable.

"I'll get those straight away," I assured them, my smile beginning to feel like a wide caricature-version of itself. "Anything to eat from our kitchens? Draan is—"

"Are you a blood giver?" came the words from Kythel. My gaze flitted to him, pulled, shocked. His tone was strange—oddly lifeless and controlled except for the way he was looking at me. There was nothing lifeless about *that*.

It was my turn to be confused, my brows furrowing. My heart was a frenzied little thing in my chest, beating out a pulsing, erratic rhythm.

"No. I'm not."

"Then what do you do here?" he asked next, slight frustration dripping into his tone.

"Kythel," came Kaldur's deep voice, cutting through the thick air like the whistle of a blade.

It was his brother's interruption that finally seemed to shake him. He blinked, then took a step back, his wings finally relaxing.

"My apologies. I'm being abhorrently rude," Kythel murmured, a mask falling into place. A part of me was fascinated as I watched the subtle transformation—the smoothing of his features, the careful way his eyes watched me, the deepening and strengthening of his voice—and I wondered how often he needed to wear that mask. "You were out in the courtyard when we arrived."

"Yes," I said, my neck craned back to meet his eyes. The lounge seemed ten times smaller with him in it. "Yes, I was. And to answer your question, *Kyzaire*, I am not a blood giver here. I help wherever I am needed."

Kythel's swallow was palpable. A little knot in my chest loosened when he finally took a large step away and sank back into his chair, tucking his wings comfortably in the cutouts along the high spine.

He looked away from me, his gaze going to Thaine across the table. Silence dropped into place.

"Well," I chirped, my voice hitching too high with my nerves, "I'll go get your drinks."

"*Lore* too," came Kythel's harsh tone. I stilled. "K10092 if you have it."

I processed the number. "We do."

"And something from your kitchens. I don't care what," he finished, still not meeting my eyes.

"Of course," I said, my smile widening. I knew when I was dismissed, but here, I needed to act happy about it.

Quickly, I strode away, through the steel doors that separated the lounge from the entrance hallway, done up in gleaming silver and gold, its quiet hall a wonderful reprieve.

Lesana was waiting for me at the end of it.

"Do you know the *Kyzaire*?" she questioned me immediately, the question identical to Hanno's.

"No, of course not," I said, my hands trembling at my sides, so I pinched the soft material of my pants. "I saw him out in the courtyard when he arrived, but I've never spoken to him before now."

Lesana huffed. A Kylorr sigh.

"Is Hanno in with Kian?" I asked when the pause lasted too long.

"What?" she asked. "Oh. Oh. Yes, he is."

"And...Grace came down?"

"Yes." Her gaze flickered between my eyes. "On second thought, I think that I should serve the *Kyzaires* this evening. What did they request?"

I wouldn't deny that I was a little relieved by her words, even though I worried I'd done something wrong.

"K10092 of *lore*. Two brews for Kaldur and Thaine—anything from the South, they said. And Kythel will continue with his wine. I think Illaira must've served him R-09 or R-10, but you might want to verify that. Oh, and they wanted something to eat from the kitchens."

"Your *kanno* tarts will be done soon?" she asked.

"Yes."

"Then get back in there. After they're done, why don't you take the rest of the night off. You deserve a break, Millicent. You look tired."

"No," I said quickly. Then I bit my lip, embarrassed. "I—I need the credits. From a full night's work."

"And you'll have them," Lesana said, reaching out to smooth her fingers over my cheek.

It embarrassed me that I soaked up her kind touch like a sponge and savored it like a steam cake, which melted on the tongue and was gone much too soon. It made tears prickle the backs of my eyes, and I thought that I should tell her about

Grace, about what I'd discovered earlier. Lesana valued loyalty over anything.

Yet…my tongue was stuck to the roof of my mouth. The words never came. Grace's secret was safe. And I knew that I'd never tell.

"You did enough tonight. Get the tarts ready, and then get some rest."

Hesitantly, I said, "If you're sure."

"I am," she said, taking her hand away. "Oh…and Millicent?"

"Yes?"

"Stay away from the lounge tonight," Lesana told me, her lips pressed together in a slim line.

Uncertain, I nodded.

"Good," she said.

Then Lesana grinned, whatever concern I saw in her eyes wiped away. It felt like relief to me.

"Good," she said again, exhaling a sharp breath.

Still, I felt her yellow eyes follow me as I made my way into the depths of Raana *Dyaan*.

# CHAPTER 4

KYTHEL

"*W*hat was that?" Kaldur growled softly, pinning me with a hard stare from across the table.

Turmoil was building inside my chest, tight and hard. An awareness, an energy was thrumming through me as I dragged in lungfuls of smoky air, trying to dispel the human woman's scent in my nostrils. It didn't work. I could taste her floating softly over my tongue before I swallowed her down. Deeper and deeper inside me she burrowed.

A female had never smelled so *fucking* good to me. Not once. Not ever.

Trepidation bloomed like spilled ink in my mind, spreading. Spreading. Consuming.

"Nothing," I rasped, taking a long swig of my wine. But it tasted like ash in my mouth, lifeless. "It was nothing."

Thaine's watchful green eyes looked so much like our mother's—and like Aina's—that I had to look away. Green eyes were the mark of House Sorn. Those green eyes had haunted me for years. It was likely why Father could barely look at Thaine.

Thinking that, I made an effort to meet my brother's eyes and

29

hold them. It wasn't his fault he'd inherited so much of our mother.

"What do you think of Lyris?" I asked them then.

"Does it matter what we think?" Thaine asked, frowning. *No*, I thought, my hand clenching around the goblet. "You've already made up your mind."

"Azur won't be happy," Kaldur told me. "Kalia won't either."

"There are plenty of arranged marriages within the Kaalium, especially among the noble Houses," I scoffed. "Don't act like this is anything new. Our own parents, for example."

"Lyris is certainly beautiful," Thaine said. "But everyone knows that she's as bland as *baanye*. She would bore you within a month—I guarantee it. War will not last forever, Kythel. But I know you. You wouldn't dispel the marriage after a war. You would stick to your vows even if they ate you up inside for the rest of your life."

There was a pressure pushing at the bones of my chest from the inside out. I knew that Thaine spoke the truth. It wasn't anything that I hadn't thought myself.

"The Kaalium comes first," I finally said, my voice quiet. I hoped they didn't hear the bitterness I felt dripping off my tongue. "Always."

Kaldur huffed. Thaine took a swig of the wine that he hated.

"Have you told Father?" Kaldur wondered.

My jaw tightened. "No."

"Will you?"

"Eventually," I said, meeting his silver gaze, giving him a hard look that had him sinking back in his chair.

"When will you announce the union?" Thaine asked after a tense silence.

"After the moon winds," I said.

In less than two weeks' time.

I DIDN'T SEE THE HUMAN WOMAN—MILLIE, SHE'D SAID HER NAME was—again for the rest of the night, though I was frustrated to realize that I'd been looking for her. Every time the door to the lounge opened, my eyes flicked to it, my legs tensing.

But it was Lesana who served us for the remainder of the evening, bringing us our drinks and *lore* and addicting little tarts from the kitchen, steam curling from them, perfuming the air with *kanno* spice.

I had inherited my mother's and Aina's appreciation for food. Something disappointingly rare among the Kylorr, I'd found.

"These were delicious," Kaldur complimented with a wide grin, gesturing to the empty tray when Lesana came around to check on us. He was in a much better mood at the night's end, having had his fill of brew and *lore*. "Give Draan our compliments."

Lesana gave us a small smile, her expression unreadable.

"I will," she said, watching us rise from our seats. Most of the lounge's occupants when we'd arrived were still here, with the exception of Sena and Jerr of House Kraan. She told my brothers, "I hope you will join us again before you both return to your territories."

Kaldur was all charm tonight as he said, "Raana *Dyaan* has always been my favorite *dyaan*. Not even the ones in the South can compete."

Lesana's eyes sparkled with pleasure. Kaldur might've been in a better mood—Thaine too, judging by his relaxed wings—but I only felt more tension building the longer the night went on. I nodded at Hanno of House Arada as we passed him on the way out of the lounge, trailing Lesana as she chatted with Kaldur about the brew they imported from his territory.

"I will see you at the moon winds celebration, *Kyzaire*," Hanno murmured to me when I paused close to his group. "My brother told me you accepted his invitation just this morning."

I didn't like that he announced it to the entirety of his group.

Then again, I'd always known House Arada were more lax about their private affairs, especially if it involved members of other noble Houses. A flaw. A large one. One I would speak with them about once the union was announced.

I said nothing. Merely inclined my head, holding Hanno's gaze, then I left. Outside in the courtyard, I told my brothers, "I need to speak with Lesana. You go on ahead."

Thaine's knowing gaze felt smug, but I turned my back on my brothers as they departed, letting the wind catch the whistling whip of their wings, flying back toward my keep, beyond Stellara's borders.

Lesana was still lingering on the front steps of her *dyaan*, and her slippered feet were nothing more than a whisper as they padded down the smooth gray stone.

We were alone. The night was beautifully quiet. I deliberated over my next words as she stopped in front of me.

Her yellow eyes glowed, her beautiful features carefully sculpted into an expression of gentle patience. I wondered what expression her husband saw most nights. If it was this one, or if it was her true one. I knew how tiring it was to put on a carefully filtered mask. Every single day. Every single moment, except for the ones when you were alone.

"The human female," I finally rasped.

For a brief moment, I saw her hand laid bare. Her mask slipped. Nerves sparked beneath it.

"Millicent," she said softly. "Yes?"

"She said she's not a blood giver," I said. "But would she consider being one for me?"

I was playing a dangerous, dangerous game. Toeing a line I wasn't sure I *could* uncross.

Her smile widened. Her tone was too high pitched when she said, "I can ask her for you, *Kyzaire*. Certainly. But like all of our blood givers, it is their choice if they wish to serve—"

"Of course," I bit out harshly. "I wasn't suggesting otherwise."

Her eyes widened, perhaps finally realizing that her words could be considered insulting. Her head ducked. "My apologies. I did not wish to offend you. They were careless words on my part."

I let it slide, though my mood had darkened at her implication.

"How long has she worked here?" I asked after a tense silence.

"Two months now," she told me.

"Do you know how she came to be on Krynn?"

Lesana shook her head. Residency contracts were rare to come by in the Kaalium for outsiders. Though more and more were becoming available every year, we were still incredibly selective on who we allowed onto our planet. She must've had connections in high places...or perhaps her family did. Or maybe she'd just gotten lucky, in the right place at the right time.

"Ask her," I said, making an effort to gentle my voice. "Ask her what it will take. Send her answer to my keep tomorrow."

"I will, *Kyzaire*."

As I flew over Stellara that night, I couldn't shake the feeling that I'd just made the second-biggest mistake of my life.

# CHAPTER 5

## MILLIE

"He...*what?*" I asked, breathless, shaken.

Lesana was watching me carefully. I was in my dressing gown, had just been about to crawl into my bed when I'd heard a knock on the door.

Downstairs, Raana *Dyaan* was quieting. Guests were trickling out, judging by the flaps of wings I caught every now and again and their traveling shadows in the moonlight that shone across my floor.

"He requested you as a blood giver," Lesana repeated. Her hands were folded in front of her, but I caught the way her gray skin lightened around her knuckles as she twisted them.

I sank down onto the edge of my bed.

The wages for a blood giver were nearly twice what I made now. But I would have to eat what was required of me, drink *baanye* multiple times throughout the day to help with the blood loss, and mentally prepare myself to be *fed* from multiple times a night. Was I ready for that?

*Anything,* I thought. I would do anything. I had already asked Lesana weeks ago if I could. I needed the credits. There was no choice.

"I will," I told her. "I'll do it."

Her hand twitched. Behind her, she carefully and quietly shut my door until we were alone in the darkness of my room. I straightened on the plush mattress.

"What is it?" I asked.

"When we first met at the market," Lesana started, "what I remember most about you was that even though life had obviously been unkind, there was still a bright strength within your eyes, Millicent. A bright strength that I admired. And I respected you for it. Do you respect me too?"

I was confused by the direction this conversation was taking, which was evident in my tone as I said, "Of course I do. You know that."

"We've grown close these last two months, have we not?"

"Yes, we have."

Lesana's neck straightened, her chin tipping up. She leveled me a steady stare as she said, "Then I will ask you this once. Turn down his offer."

I jolted. "What?"

"When a male looks at you the way he was looking at you tonight, Millicent...it won't end well." She walked toward me, taking my hand in her warm grip and kneeling on the floor so that we were eye level. "I'm doing you a favor, my dear. I'm trying to protect you, trying to protect that strength I saw in the market that day, as I would my own *daughter* if I had one."

"I don't...I don't understand."

"He's a *Kyzaire*, Millicent," she said, her tone hardening. "Of House Kaalium itself. I am trying to protect you from a male like that who, I'm sorry to say, will only ever see you as a commodity. Your heart is much too open for him not to completely break you."

I laughed, the sound strained and disbelieving. "I'm not going to fall in love with a *Kyzaire*, Lesana. I'm not a fool. He's asking me to be his blood giver, not his wife."

Did she truly think me so impressionable and naive and *young*?

Then again, she didn't *really* know me, did she?

"Kylorr can be highly possessive over the things we covet," she told me. Her tone sounded distant as she said, "And he certainly covets you."

She dropped my hand and rose from her knees. There was a shift in the room, a subtle change in the set of her shoulders. I could practically *hear* her thinking as she gazed unseeing around my meager belongings. The room she'd given me was small, but it had been the last one available at Raana *Dyaan*. Most of the blood givers didn't live here. Most had families, homes of their own. It was just Grace, Illaira, and me living under Lesana and Draan's roof.

"Will you turn down his offer?" she asked.

"I need the credits, Lesana," I said quietly.

"For what?" she asked, her voice sharpening, pinning me with a frustrated gaze that I had only ever seen her reserve for blood givers she'd fired from Raana *Dyaan*. My heart gave a treacherous little lurch at the realization.

I hadn't told anyone about my father. Not even Grace. I wasn't entirely sure why either. But there was this strange fear I had. Like if I spoke about his death, it would make it true. It would make it real. Sometimes I had this twisted fantasy in my head that he was only living on Horrin. That he was waiting for me there. That once I reached him, everything would be right in the universe. I would feel safe and loved and *home* again.

When I said nothing, Lesana dragged in a sharp breath.

"Turn down his offer, Millicent," she told me. My brow furrowed, hearing the order in her voice. "I'll raise your wages. You don't even have to be a blood giver."

"You will?" I asked in disbelief. "But why?"

"I want to help you. Just don't tell the others," she said. "But if I do this, you have to promise me something."

"What is it?"

"Promise that you will never let him feed from you," she said softly. "He will only taint you. House Kaalium has too many demons. And one of them lives in that keep beyond Stellara."

I stared at Lesana, processing her words.

"Millicent," she prompted when the silence stretched too long.

It didn't feel right. Taking more credits for a job that I wasn't doing...

Then again...

I *needed* them. I wasn't in a position to question her generosity. I was just desperate enough that I wouldn't debate the morality of the situation I'd found myself in.

Lesana seemed to have her reasons for not allowing me to be a blood giver within her establishment. Perhaps she found me lacking. Perhaps I wasn't beautiful like Grace. Perhaps she found a flaw in me.

"All right," I finally said, my voice hushed as if I were speaking a blasphemous thing. "I promise."

Another huff left her. Her shoulders relaxed.

"Good," she said. Reaching out, she squeezed my shoulder. "I'll have your credits adjusted. But this remains between us, yes?"

"Yes."

Lesana turned to leave. I studied her back, my eyes pinned onto her form.

After she opened the door, I heard her say, "And Millicent?"

"Yes?"

"Don't break my trust," she warned softly. "If I find out that you let him feed from you...I'll have no choice but to let you go from Raana *Dyaan*."

I stiffened, shock making my spine straighten.

Over her shoulder, as if she hadn't just threatened me, she smiled and asked, "No walk tonight in Stellara?"

"No," I croaked, still reeling. The word tumbled from my lips, my mind catching on the ease with which she'd said she could discard me. It felt like there was a stone lodged in my belly. Clearing my throat, I said, "No, not tonight."

"What is it that you're looking for inside the forest?"

Quickly, I schooled my expression into one of calm, focusing on relaxing my lips so the bottom one didn't tremble. Had she asked a handful of moments before...I might've told her the truth.

My father's letters were soft and worn, hidden in the secret compartment of my trunk, my most prized possessions. The Forest of Stellara was vast. I wondered if I would *ever* find it.

"Just walking," I told Lesana. "I like the fresh air."

"But not tonight?" she asked.

"It's been a long week," I said, hoping she would take the hint and leave. "And I always forget how tiring a hot kitchen can be."

Mercifully, she inclined her head, squeezing her wings through the door. "You did well tonight. Rest, my dear."

Then she shut the door behind her. I listened to her heavy footsteps as they retreated down the hallway. Her room was on the opposite end of Raana *Dyaan*. Grace and Illaira stayed on the floor below.

I had always considered myself to be a good judge of character. I had met plenty of beings from all across the universe, after all, and had only been wrong about one or two.

But one thing was abundantly clear to me.

I'd misjudged Lesana.

Tears sprung into my eyes, but I furiously dashed them away. Then, taking a deep breath, I padded to my trunk, still half-packed in the corner of the room.

Sliding the metal latch on the inside of the trunk, the top compartment sprung open, and I reached inside for the buttery-soft parchment. Luckily it was Kesren-made and guaranteed to last three thousand years, or else surely the paper would've been in tatters in my hand, the inky words no longer legible.

Curling up on the bed, I carefully unfolded the letter. One of dozens. This one was my favorite, however. Much shorter than the rest. My father had been a romantic. And this letter was his very essence.

---

*Ruaala,*
*I dream of Stellara this night.*
*I dream of our quiet place, where the world falls away, a secret realm of our own making.*
*I dream of your whispered, sweet words pressed to my lips, promises we know will be broken.*
*All I wish to see are your starry eyes reflecting mine.*
*All I wish is for your hands to entwine with mine because it means we are together once more.*
*I wait for that day.*
*I dream of that day.*
*I will wait a thousand lifetimes.*
*Even as I wish that this lifetime was only ours.*
*Joss*

---

I READ THE LETTER TWICE MORE BEFORE I CAREFULLY FOLDED IT into its original creases. I hadn't even needed to read it—I had every last word memorized.

My father had told me of Ruaala all my life. He'd never kept her a secret. He'd believed love was a sacred thing. A beautiful, cherished thing. But it was only later in my life that I'd begun to cry after he'd told me stories of her. Because it was only later that I'd realized how unfair and tragic their love had truly been.

*This* was my father's last wish.

Her.

Ruaala of House Loria.

Only…we'd found no trace of her within Erzos. The House was long gone or had moved to a different province of the Kaalium.

I hoped—and prayed—that a hint of her whereabouts might be hidden in their *quiet place*, which was so often referenced within these letters. A cottage made of wood and stone nestled deep in Stellara.

Did I even know if it was still there?

No.

But I had made a promise to my father, on our last Halo Com call with one another before he'd died.

With that thought, though my eyes were heavy, though my legs ached from flitting around Raana *Dyaan* all day and night, I climbed from bed and stored the letter. I raked back my hair, tying it up. I pushed my feet into my thinning boots. I pulled on thick trousers and a long-sleeved shirt, tying a scarf around my neck.

*I will find her,* I thought as I slipped down the stairs, thinking of another path of Stellara I hadn't taken yet. One that led south.

*I must find her.*

# CHAPTER 6

## KYTHEL

"*A* letter for you," Vadyn announced, sweeping into my dim office. I hissed out a small breath when he threw back the curtains, which had kept the bright morning sun at bay. "From Raana *Dyaan*."

Ire forgotten, I took the letter from his grip. Smooth, thick parchment with a shining red seal.

Quickly, I scanned its contents, my lips pressing together at the flourish of Lesana's signature, inked in her blood, at the very bottom.

Truthfully, I didn't know if I should feel relieved or frustrated or bewildered.

The human woman—Millie—had turned down my offer.

*Who turns down a* Kyzaire *of House Kaalium?* I griped, turning from Vadyn to step toward the arched floor-to-ceiling window that overlooked Stellara. My whole wing of the keep overlooked Stellara. I much preferred this view to the one of the sea.

I hadn't expected to be refused.

*It's for the best,* I reasoned. Being intrigued by a human female —one without noble blood, presumably—was beneath me. As callous as that sounded, it was the truth.

"And there's a report that just came in through the Coms," Vadyn continued, either ignoring the dark, brooding mood that had descended in the room or perhaps he was entirely too used to it lately.

I couldn't get that human female's scent out of my mind.

"What is it?" I asked, distracted.

My keep backed up into the southern border of Stellara Forest. Every year, we had to cut down saplings that were attempting to encroach onto my property. I wondered if in a hundred years, Stellara would eat up my keep, so slowly and so deliberately that I hadn't even seen it happening.

"A protest near the archives. About the South Road being built."

"*Vaan*," I cursed, feeling a tightness creep up the back of my neck.

"A small one," Vadyn added. "Kaldur left just now to disband it."

For his quick temper, my brother was surprisingly calm and levelheaded when it came to diplomatic and political matters such as these. Some residents of Erzos, specifically in Raana, were wary of the construction of the South Road, which would connect Erzos to the small villages on the outskirts of the territory before winding south, ending in Vyaan, Kaldur's territory. Most were in support of it, reasoning that it would be a safer option from raiding parties for merchants and travelers, that it would be easier to sell and import goods to and from the South.

Some, however, thought it would bring an influx of new residents—including raiding parties—and that it would threaten the quiet life that this province was known for.

Erzos was the largest territory of the Kaalium by far, based purely on the spread of land. We were made up of small villages, spread along the coast and the forests and the mountains to the north. Our largest village was Erzan, the village closest to the ports.

Their fears weren't unfounded. Erzan was already close to capacity. New homes would need to be built to support a growing population. More food would need to be caught from our seas and grown in our fields—or it would need to be imported.

But the Kylorr had always faced a weakening population. Females were rare. Males outnumbered them four to one. Our population was aging, growing older with each passing year, and was one of the oldest in the Kaalium. It was why we were opening up our borders to more and more residency contracts. Because we *needed* to.

An increase in population wouldn't be unwelcome.

"I'll leave right now," I informed Vadyn, turning from the window and chucking Lesana's letter into the fire smoldering in the hearth on my way out. I tried to shove the frustration from my mind. "If you see Thaine this morning, tell him we still need to discuss that import contract. I haven't forgotten, even though he might hope I have."

"I will," Vadyn said, his face ever-patient and impassive.

---

THE PROTEST WAS SMALL. AND BY THE TIME I REACHED IT, KALDUR had a wide grin on his face already, his hand clasped on the shoulder of the female that I knew was the most outspoken about the construction of the South Road. Marr was her name, from the coastal village of Savina. I'd spoken with her at length over the last few months, and simply *seeing* her brought a sharp pinch between my shoulder blades.

"Marr," I said, landing with a heavy thump next to her and my brother. "We had an agreement, did we not?"

The aging Kylorr female tilted her head back to meet my eyes.

"Everything is handled," Kaldur said easily, shooting me a

warning look disguised by a disarming smile. "She disbanded the protest already."

I looked around the village's center, noticing the Kylorr who lingered. It was a small square, cobbled with aging black stone, most cracked. On the north end lay the village's shrine. To the south were the archives. To the east lay the ports—the salted breeze of which I could smell from here. To the west was the forested road to Raana, which resembled a smaller version of Laras with its pristine, glittering shops and steam cake carts on nearly every corner. It was where most of the noble Houses were located.

"You promised me, *Kyzaire*, that you wouldn't be encouraging southerners to make their homes in Erzos," Marr said, her tone nearly acerbic, which made my jaw set in stone. She forgot her place. "And then what do I hear? Another village is being built along the South Road, close to Erzan, minutes of a flight from here."

"I made no such promise," I said, the harsh clip of my tone and the cool glare in my gaze temporarily tying her tongue. "I made you *no* promises actually. Do you know why, Marr?"

"Kythel," my brother warned. Since when was *he* the cooler head of the both of us?

I leaned down until I was eye level with the Kylorr female who had been nothing but a headache these last few months. "Because I don't need your permission to build within *my* territory. Do you understand?"

Her lips pinched even tighter.

"When your father was in charge of Erzos," she started, her age filling her with a courage that most would not dare to have, "he would never have *attempted* to disrupt our village this way."

I nearly snorted with derision.

It was on the tip of my tongue to say, *Because he didn't* fucking *care about this black hole of a place.* Laras had been his glittering jewel. The main source of our family's wealth. All the other provinces under his rule had fallen to the wayside, and it had been my brothers and me to build up the territories once more, especially after our mother's death.

*I care more for Erzos than he ever did,* I thought. But I didn't voice it. I wouldn't ever, not to a stranger outside of my own family.

"I've had patience with you, Marr. Don't test that patience again," I said, my tone low. "I am still your *Kyzaire*, after all. I still own this land. And House Kaalium still owns all of Erzos. I can take your worries about the South Road into consideration. But that is *all* that I am obligated to do."

Across the courtyard, my eyes landed on a familiar human female.

I straightened, my jaw setting tight. The sea wind was blowing the opposite direction, which was likely why I hadn't scented her first. Immediately, venom began to drip onto my tongue, the ache of my fangs making them elongate.

She was walking toward the archives, seemingly lost in her own head since she didn't even register the crowd in the village's center, especially this early in the morning. I watched as she slipped inside the tomb-like doors, disappearing from view.

The words from the brief letter flitted into my mind.

*Millicent has decided to refuse your most generous offer, Kyzaire, citing personal reservations. But if you ever have need of another blood giver, Raana Dyaan will be more than happy to accommodate you whenever you wish.*

*Personal reservations*, she'd claimed?

Meaning...the human found it abhorrent to be fed from.

When my gaze came back to Marr, I watched her shrink a bit. My fangs were pressing into my bottom lip. I wondered what it was she saw in my gaze.

*Good,* I thought. A fortunate accident.

Marr's nostrils flared, and she started, "You still need to—"

My patience snapped.

A animalistic growl rose from my throat—a *berserker's* warning—harsh and angry and violent. My muscles bunched, tightening until I could swear I felt every last straining tendon in my back.

I was strung together like a chaotic tapestry, but I wondered what it would take for me to unravel completely. I was the ice to Azur's fire. I was the calm brother. The logical twin. But lately…I had felt like something was clawing inside my chest, needing to break out.

Marr's face blanched and she backed away quickly. The rest of the crowd in the courtyard wisely left too, until there were only a handful of unsuspecting beings cutting through the village's center on their morning journey.

Kaldur and I stood like sentinels within the courtyard. My brother's expression was surprised when I caught his gaze. Wary too.

"Kythel," he said pointedly.

"I'm tired of her getting in the way," I told him, feeling the muscles in my back slowly relax. My eyes went to the door of the archives. "It's been endless for the last three months, ever since I announced the South Road."

Kaldur blew out a breath. He glanced around the mostly empty courtyard. "You need to be more careful. Don't forget our family's history here. Or in Salaire. You don't want to be lumped in with Jynaar, do you?"

"Of course not," I grated, shooting him a glare. "Raazos's blood, Kaldur, telling a female to back down is a hell of a lot different than public executions. Why would you even say that to me?"

"Perception," he told me, his brow furrowing as he scanned my features. "Here more than anywhere else. I don't envy you, Kythel."

I looked away from my brother because I had the strongest urge to punch him right in his scarred face. Instead, I stalked a few paces away from him for good measure, feeling the thrum of energy in my body vibrate the damn cobblestones beneath my booted feet.

"Let them protest," he told me. "But we all know, even Marr, that it won't make a difference. The South Road needs to be completed, especially with war in our periphery."

At those softened words, I glanced over at my brother, nostrils flaring.

"They don't understand that. But we do," he finished. "You're doing the right thing."

Some of the tension leaked out of my shoulders. Sometimes Kaldur could really fuck things up with his words. Other times he knew exactly what to say.

"Just don't go berserk trying to explain that to an elderly Kylorr female, all right?" he continued, exasperation in his tone. "I'm heading back to the keep. I haven't slept yet. You coming?"

I turned my head to regard the doors of the archives.

"No," I said, already knowing that this was a foolish decision. But right then, I was feeling reckless. I just needed to escape the buzzing underneath my own skin, if only for a moment. "You go. I need to find something in the archives."

# CHAPTER 7

## MILLIE

Since arriving on Krynn, the Erzan archives building had been one of my favorite places. It reminded me of the grand, gothic cathedrals on Bartu with their sweeping stark lines, echoing the haunting reverberation of the Bartutians' chants in the evenings.

The archives were quiet that morning, which wasn't strange in itself. They'd been mostly deserted every time I had happened to visit in the last few months—which, admittedly, had been often.

Obviously, I didn't read the Kylorr language, but the archives had translator pods, though they were terribly out-of-date and always pixelated every third word as I ran one over the parchment of the books and scrolls.

There was no one to offer help either. Or to monitor or even protect the texts here. Anyone could freely walk in, steal a whole trunkload of books, and no one would be ever the wiser. I thought that was incredibly reckless and foolish…and yet Erzan had never seemed to have a problem with it considering the archives were packed to the gills, stuffed with more texts and tomes than it seemingly knew what to do with.

I found comfort in the quiet and the maze of stacked books that sometimes resembled small, haphazard skyscrapers on the revolving colonies of Injit. I ran my translator pod over any spines that had writing on them. I was looking for maps of Stellara. Maps of Erzos, even. And, especially, histories of the noble families that had once resided here—or continued to. Surely there should've been record of them somewhere.

Anyone who I had ever asked about the noble House of Loria had gone strangely mute. I knew that the residents of Erzos were a superstitious people, but they always pressed their fingers to their chests when I spoke the name *Loria*, their wings rustling with an unfelt breeze. Every single time it happened, it made dread curl tighter and tighter in my belly.

I scanned my pod over the spine of one book, which translated to *Erzan Ports...something*. The third word was illegible. I hit the pod with the back of my hand a couple times, trying again, but it yielded the same results.

I heard heavy footsteps from the next shelf of books over. Another patron to join the handful who were inside the archives.

*Erzan Ports...*what?

"Are you looking for something in particular?"

I jumped, whirling around when I recognized the voice.

Kythel of House Kaalium stood there, his wings wedged between two book skyscrapers. His expression was fixed on me, and with a surprising grace, he turned his body in such a way that he slid into the aisle without rustling a single piece of loose parchment poking out from the tomes.

Immediately, my tongue felt glued to the roof of my mouth. I had thought that, perhaps, his eyes hadn't been as...*consuming* as I'd remembered them from last night.

Unfortunately, I found that wasn't the case. Not at all. If anything, they were even more fatally beautiful in the daylight, with sun streaming in through the wide, arched window, spearing through the black steel bookcases.

I clenched my hand around the small translator pod.

"Oh, I was…" I began, my voice sounding too high pitched, nervous to see him considering Lesana's warning from last night was still running through my mind. I cleared my throat and forced a small smile. "I'm looking for maps of Erzos. Of Stellara specifically."

I had the impression that Kythel was holding himself perilously still. Was he even *breathing*?

"Why are you seeking maps of Stellara?"

"Curiosity," I said, my smile widening. I began to turn away before second-guessing myself. Was it rude here to turn one's back on a *Kyzaire*? It was rude to do so to a royal family member on Hop'jin, after all. A high insult indeed. It could mean one's death if the rank of the royal member was high enough.

To be safe, I angled my body in such a way that he could still see the profile of my face as I navigated the aisle.

*He wants to feed from you,* I reminded myself, feeling my throat get strangely tight. Should I have felt…honored? Complimented? How did a Kylorr go about choosing their blood givers? Was it something that they specifically searched for, or was it more of a spontaneous whim?

"I lived in a forest once," I told him. "On Gwytri. Its forests are filled with these little insects that spray you with this *foul* liquid. It made my skin burn. Humans are allergic to it, we later found out. I hated it there, but the people as a whole were incredibly welcoming and kind. Though they would try to pluck strands of my hair as I passed because they were fascinated by it."

I swallowed down the other rambling words that threatened to surface. I was used to making idle small talk with strangers. I prized myself on my ability to speak with anyone, and yet… Kythel of House Kaalium was exceedingly intimidating.

*Slowly, Millie,* I thought. It was something I told myself when I felt uncertain. When I felt nervous. It reminded me to take one moment at a time. A *single* moment. It made *everything* feel more manageable.

In that single moment, I took in a long breath through my nostrils, imagining my lungs expanding. I caught a hint of leathery musk—spicy and earthy and oddly calming—only to realize it was *him*. That was his scent.

"Who are you?" he asked. I had the strangest realization that he had memorized every last word I'd spoken of Gwytri, that he was filing it away like he had the mind of Halo tech.

"Millie," I said, my tone edging on uncertainty. "I told you last night. Millie Seren."

"And how did you come to be in Erzos, Millie Seren?" he asked, those winter-sea eyes unyielding.

My name on his tongue made a shiver trail up my spine, like ghostly fingers were tracing my skin. "I have a residency contract, if that's what you're asking."

His brow furrowed. "No, that's not what I'm asking."

"Oh."

I cleared my throat. My gaze went to the stacks of books in front of me. A few titles were written out in the universal tongue. My language.

"By caravan," I answered, giving him a sly smile as I edged farther down the aisle. "After landing in the transport depot. The one that borders Vyaan."

His left wing twitched.

"You know what I meant, little one," came his gravelly voice. "I did not mean how you physically came to be here. I want to know *why* you came here."

I shrugged one shoulder, unable to get a read on him. He reminded me of a cyborg in some ways. A pillar of a machine. Stoic. Unemotional. Cold.

*Yet he'd asked for you,* I thought. *He wants you.*

"My father used to live in Erzos," I finally told him, sliding my gaze to him to see how he'd react. "He was a culinarian. He...he worked for a noble family here. House Loria. Long ago."

If Kythel reacted to that name, he certainly didn't show it.

"Perhaps you know them?" I asked hopefully, studying his expression.

Was it my imagination, or did his jaw tighten?

At least he didn't touch his heart, nor did his wings rustle.

"Not many humans were allowed within the Kaalium back then," he said instead, and I heard the unspoken question in the comment. Tactful, yes...but present.

I huffed out a small breath, deciding to take my chances by turning my back on a *Kyzaire*. I walked ahead, navigating down the next aisle, this one wide enough to allow a Kylorr to walk freely. Behind me, I heard his footsteps follow.

"My father was half-Kylorr," I said softly. "He was born in Erzos."

"*You* are part Kylorr?" came the roughened question. Surprising enough that it made me turn to regard him. His eyes scanned me head to toe. "You don't look it."

"No, I don't," came my sharp reply, sharper than I'd intended, but this subject had always made me a bit defensive—and likely always would. "Because I am not a Kylorr. But he was my father nonetheless."

Kythel studied me carefully, his chin dipped down.

"I understand," he finally said, his tone oddly soft. "My apologies. I didn't mean to offend you."

"You didn't," I said, though they were just polite words. Words I didn't truly feel. I was used to it. The speculation. The wary glances cast my father's way, especially when they'd seen a Kylorr traveling with a young human girl. The looks had always been the worst on the smaller transport colonies. Little had they known, my father had been my *everything*. My whole world. He hadn't *needed* to love me. He had *chosen* to. "You couldn't have known."

An uncomfortable silence descended between us. I felt the time stretching and stretching, scratching over my skin.

"Come," Kythel ordered. Then he turned his back, sweeping down the aisle and disappearing around the next corner.

Hesitantly, I followed. For one so large, he moved silently. So much so that I feared I'd lost him within the aisles until I heard him say, "Here."

I found him standing next to one of the only bookcases in the archives that held stacks of scrolls, all bound in brown leathery twine, the edges of their parchment frayed and torn. He plucked a scroll straight from the middle of the stack, one that looked, to me, like any other.

He handed it to me. It was surprisingly heavy and made a pleasant papery sound as it transferred from his palm into mine.

"Stellara," he said gruffly. His eyes strayed past me, the line of his lips taking on an impatience that struck me as irritated. "At least, one of the attempts at mapping it."

"Thank you," I breathed, surprised that he'd helped me. He had no reason to. "Why...why did you—"

"Why did you turn down the offer I made you?" came his sudden question. Cold. To the point. One moment, he'd seemed impatient to leave. The next, I had his full attention, and I wasn't quite sure what to do with it.

My spine straightened. My lips parted.

*Because Lesana made me a better one,* I thought. *And then threatened me.*

But I couldn't say that.

"I'm not interested in being a blood giver," I told him instead. Quietly. Lowering my voice even though the other patrons in the archives were aisles away. They likely didn't even know the *Kyzaire* was in here.

It was a half-truth. But I had to tell him something.

He wasn't satisfied with that answer.

"You think it would be painful?" he asked.

53

"No," I said, shaking my head.

"You think it would be demeaning?"

"No," I said sharply. "My father was half-Kylorr—how could you ask me that?"

He seemed surprised by my words, which had been unguarded by politeness. I swallowed down my apology, however, which clung to the tip of my tongue.

Then he did something I hadn't expected.

He smiled.

It was more of a smirk, truly. But I saw that his fangs were elongated as if he was hungry even now. Our eyes connected and held.

And then they *held*.

For a moment, I felt like we'd been transported back to last night. Out in the courtyard of Raana *Dyaan*, with the stars bright overhead, golden light gleaming off his wings from the Halo orbs in the lounge. I swore I could smell that cool breeze coming from the South. My breath felt caught in my throat. My heart was jolting out a strong, melodic beat. Kythel's eyes traced the lines of my face. His feet drew closer. Mine must've too.

His smile slowly died.

"What will it take?" he asked me quietly.

I nearly closed my eyes, feeling the *pull* of that voice. Hearing him speak made the hairs on my arms raise, made the back of my throat tingle like I'd eaten something too sweet. Rich and resonant, his voice made the world tilt sideways.

I'd listened to bards across the Quadrants recite stories and poetry in languages much more beautiful than mine. I'd listened to symphonies composed entirely with instruments I would never be able to learn, simply because I didn't have enough hands or fingers or mouths to play them with. I'd listened to mournful crooners on street corners, spilling their souls onto unsuspecting strangers as they passed.

Still, nothing had ever felt so beautiful as his voice.

I didn't understand it. In fact, I felt a little fearful of it, a skitter of trepidation spiraling up my spine.

"What?" I breathed. The archives rushed back in. I smelled dust and parchment again. I realized I'd stopped breathing for a moment as I dragged in a greedy lungful of air.

Dazed, I turned and walked a few paces away. Kythel allowed me to leave the tight circle we'd—unconsciously—made. I felt like I could breathe again. Something was clenched in my fist. Ah, yes. The scroll. The map of Stellara. Why I'd come.

His voice followed after me when he continued with, "What will it take for you to be my blood giver, Millie Seren? Name your price, and it is yours."

My breath froze in my lungs.

"I—I have to go," I told him in a rush. "I can't...I can't do this—"

"No," he said. Frustration ate at his tone. He looked away from me, his jaw clenching. Then he donned that familiar mask. I watched his face transform. He met my eyes again, but this time, there was a clarity to his gaze. "My apologies, little one. You gave me your answer. I will not ask you again."

I didn't know what else to do but nod. Lesana was already raising my wages. If she found out that I was even speaking with Kythel outside of Raana *Dyaan*, what would she do? Surely she trusted me enough to know that I wouldn't break our agreement. I couldn't afford to lose my job. And one fleeting moment with the High Lord of Erzos threatened that.

One payment for a feeding was not enough to make up for *months* of nightly credits.

"You never told me," he said.

"Told you what?"

"What are you looking for in Stellara?" he asked.

I looked down at the scroll.

*Ruaala, I dream of Stellara this night.*

*I dream of our quiet place, where the world falls away, a secret realm of our own making.*

Briefly, I closed my eyes.

I was looking for a memory. A lost one.

A lost love.

"I'm looking for...a quiet place," I answered, meeting his ice-riddled, faceted gaze.

He frowned. I didn't know how long we stood there, regarding one another. But he didn't ask me what I'd meant. Somehow...I'd known he wouldn't. Which was why I'd told him. Another half-truth, held suspended between us.

"Then I hope you find what you're looking for, Millie Seren," he finally said.

Then Kythel turned away. His heavy strides retreated until he left the archives entirely. The *boom* of the door as it closed behind him made me sigh. He wasn't anything at all like how I'd expected.

Just like last night, I felt raw in the aftermath of that sapphire gaze.

# CHAPTER 8

## MILLIE

"Stay out of the lounge tonight," Lesana ordered me, her shoulders seemingly tight though she smiled at a patron as he slipped past us into the common room.

"Why?" I asked, brows furrowing. "I was meant to—"

"You'll be in the kitchen tonight with Draan," she told me, spearing me with a long look.

Excitement made my breath hitch and my smile widen. "Really? He'll allow that?"

"Yes," she said. "Now, go."

I watched her for a few moments more, my smile slowly dying. She'd been in a strange mood all day. Impatient. Sharp. But only with me.

I wasn't a fool. There was only one reason she wouldn't want me in the lounge.

"Are you truly so worried that I'll break my promise to you?" I asked softly, hurt that she would think so.

Lesana's nostrils widened briefly, her yellow eyes finding mine on the threshold of the bustling, crowded room beyond. Uproarious laughter and a cacophony of voices spilled from the open door. Synthetic strains of music were pouring from the

Halo orbs which floated overhead. *Lore* smoke made the room seem perpetually filled with silver fog.

"Of course not, my dear," she told me, her features smoothing. She reached out her hand to tuck a stray strand of hair behind my ear that had loosened from the gold clip. Softly, she added, "I know you won't."

There was an edge to her words that made me step away, forcing a smile. I thought of Grace. We hadn't spoken all day because I'd been uncomfortable keeping her secret from Lesana. But right then, all I could remember was that Grace didn't like Lesana. She kept her distance from her. I wondered what it was she saw that I hadn't before.

"If I give you my word, you have it," I told her, restless at the thought that she would question my loyalties. "I hope you know that."

"And *I* know desperation well," Lesana whispered, holding my gaze. "I know that you would do anything to get what you want, no matter the cost, no matter who you hurt."

I frowned.

She smiled.

"Kitchen," she told me after a lengthy pause. "Draan is expecting you."

On hollow legs, I turned and left, her words following me down the stretch of hallway to the back of Raana *Dyaan*.

When I reached the smoky kitchen, Draan scowled at me from over his prep table.

"Chop those," he ordered me, gesturing to a pile of multicolored wild roots with a sharpened blade. "And stay out of my way."

"Yes, Draan."

THE COOL AIR FELT GLORIOUS ON MY PINK CHEEKS WHEN I FINALLY escaped the kitchen for a short reprieve.

I'd forgotten.

I'd forgotten a full night in a kitchen.

I'd forgotten the heat, a sweat-slicked neck, and a furrowed brow. The bustle, which sometimes felt like the frantic, intoxicating, humid streets of Qapot'a. The *life*—a frenetic pulse, a running current, a constant sparking of energy.

The singular state of mind where distractions melted away and I knew every millisecond of what would come next. Every fraction of a moment carefully spliced and then sewn back together into something new. With ingredients I was familiar with, I knew how many moments I had with a glance at the sear, by the flip of a fish, by a singular curl of steam rising from a simmering sauce.

I was out of practice, I knew. But I thought I'd surprised Draan tonight. So much so that he'd asked, "Where did you train?"

I'd only smiled. "I'm not a culinarian," I'd told him, wiping up a spill of *onu* cream on the prep table.

Because I wasn't. My father had been. And I'd trained with him all my life—but just as an extra set of hands.

A lifetime in a kitchen, however, had made for a very good education.

Now I slipped from Raana *Dyaan* and went down the alleyway. We were situated at the end of a row of shops in this village. Right next door was a clothier, though their windows were currently dark, as was the entire street. The bleeding tree was the only thing within the wide alley, a remnant of a seed that had floated from Stellara and hadn't been plucked from the earth before it had taken root.

I blew out a breath, tempted to slide to the ground since I'd been on my feet for most of the day. Instead, I merely leaned back, letting the tree take most of my weight as my gaze slid to the edge of Stellara.

There was a rustle of wings and heavy footsteps in the court-yard beyond, but the wall blocked them from view. Not many lingered on this side of Raana *Dyaan*. On the opposite side, at the common room exit, was where most gathered for fresh air.

I saw the curl of *lore* smoke before I saw him.

I'd known he was here, after all.

My breath stilled in my lungs as I watched him come fully into view. He had his back to me, and he was lingering near the edge of the road that separated the shops from Stellara.

He was alone. Smoking, the tip of his *lore* pipe a bright blue in the darkness.

*I guess his brothers didn't join him tonight,* I thought.

Though I shouldn't have dared, my gaze traveled down the stretch of his back, admiring the span of his wings, even relaxed. He was in a dark green fitted vest, sleek black pants with silver catches, and pristine boots. Not a hair was out of place, and even alone, he held himself stiffly, his movements measured and controlled.

I wondered what he would look like *untamed*. A little feral. I wondered what he looked like in his berserker state. A state I had never witnessed before—at least not in real life. Only in research and from what my father had told me over the years from his own experiences.

Simply, I couldn't imagine it. Not him.

It looked like the High Lord of Erzos was just leaving Raana *Dyaan*, smoking the last of his *lore* leaf, when a breeze blew from the North, funneling down the alley like a whisper. The same strands of hair that Lesana had tucked behind my ear escaped.

It only took a moment. He'd been walking away, turning off his pipe, unfurling his wings...

Then he stiffened. Freezing in place.

Until he finally turned. I saw the silhouette of his horns

against the dark backdrop of Stellara before his crystalline blue eyes connected with mine.

For a long moment, we regarded each other from a great distance away.

Then Kythel turned, and every step he took closer to me made my heart thump more forcefully until they matched his heavy strides in tandem.

He slid into the dark alley with me. He smelled of *lore*, but thankfully I'd taken a vial of *tassa* earlier in the evening. Or else I feared I'd be trying to nuzzle against him like a desperate whore on the streets of Gharata.

"Good evening, *Kyzaire*," I greeted quietly when he didn't speak.

Kythel leaned back against Raana *Dyaan*, his wings spreading to keep his vest from getting dirtied. He crossed his arms over his chest as he regarded me. Only a couple arm lengths separated us. I scratched at the bark of the tree at my back. The scrape felt *good* —perfectly distracting.

"You weren't in the lounge tonight," he said, the words nonchalant but I heard the question in them.

I smiled, slipping into an old skin. The one I wore at parties or socials, the one I'd worn whenever we'd arrived to a new colony or planet or town or home.

Teasing, I said, "Were you looking for me? And were you disappointed when you couldn't find me?"

Kythel frowned. A small slip until he caught himself. Then he slipped into an old skin himself, one he'd likely worn since he'd been a child.

The small upturn of his full lips made my blood rush.

This was a game I wasn't sure I could win, against a player who was much more experienced than I was.

Suddenly I was aware that sweat was cooling on my skin, the sharp prick of it icy as I shivered. I likely had grease stains on my vest and flour in my hair. I likely smelled like the *wylden* we'd been braising for Draan's stew, which I truthfully thought could use more *kanno* spice and a squeeze of bluestone fruit for acidity.

"It was a mere observation," he informed me. "Any disappointment I felt was fleeting, I assure you."

"Ouch," I said with a smile, purposefully sliding my gaze away as I rolled my neck, hearing a sharp crack. "You sure know how to charm a woman."

"I don't need to charm anyone," he replied softly. We both knew the truth in his words. He was a *Kyzaire*, an heir to the Kaalium. He had nothing to prove. No one to impress. "Though you're right. Perhaps I should make more of an effort with you, little one."

"Because you want something from me," I guessed.

He didn't deny it. He said nothing.

"Why? You can feed from anyone. Anyone in there," I added, nodding to the stone building he was leaning against. "Why do you want to feed from me?"

"Because your scent is unlike any I have experienced before," he answered, surprising me. "I am curious. It is...quite maddening."

I hadn't expected him to be quite so honest. "Ah."

His eyes narrowed. "What is that sound for?"

I slid him a small smile. "It means I understand."

"Understand what?" he asked, frustration creeping into his tone.

Licking my lips, I weighed the words carefully. He was still the *Kyzaire* of Erzos. I couldn't afford to anger him. Then again, I wanted to be truthful. I didn't want to lie.

"You want something you've never had before," I told him. "You're an heir to the Kaalium. All your life—and I hope I'm not overstepping here—you've never wanted for material things, right? Things easily attainable?"

He frowned.

"You've fed, you've feasted, you've been surrounded by the

best tech and tutors and high-society nobles and parties," I said softly. I'd been too, but I was always on the outskirts of those things, pretending that I belonged. "And now you're presented with something you want but cannot have."

I felt the exact moment Kythel bristled. He straightened from the wall.

"You know nothing about me."

I swallowed, darting a quick look over at him, brow furrowing.

"I'm sure I don't," I murmured, smoothly. "I apologize, *Kyzaire*, if I offended you. It's just…I've known people like you my whole life. I *understand*. Just like I understand that there are unfathomable pressures and experiences you've had *because* of your upbringing. Your life isn't easier because of who you are. If anything, you're more shackled than all of us. But in matters like this, simple matters with simple solutions," I started, gesturing to myself, "like wanting to feed from a specific person at a *dyaan*, I understand why *this* frustrates you."

Silence dropped between us, heavy like a stone.

I cleared my throat. Thinking of Lesana's words about desperation.

"My answer, however, still remains unchanged," I added.

"I didn't ask, did I?" he replied, his tone clipped. Grumpy.

My lips lifted. My gaze turned to Stellara, highly aware that his eyes were fastened to me.

"No," I said quietly, swallowing the lump in my throat. "No, you didn't."

"Where did you come from?" he asked. "Before Krynn? Have you lived here before?"

His questions held an edge of demand, but I took my time answering.

"We came to Krynn five months ago. It's the first time I've been here. We'd just come from Drovos. Before that we lived on Qapot'a for a few seasons."

"Drovos? Is that why you knew about the wine?" he questioned.

My brows furrowed. "The wine?"

"Never mind." He shook his head. "We? Just you and your father? The culinarian?"

"Yes."

"Where is your father now?"

My chest twisted, my heart a tangled, mangled thing.

"Dead."

I'd never said it. Not out loud. Such a simple, common word. Yet it felt like a blade, scraping my insides.

Kythel's lips tightened, briefly. Still as a statue, he stood tall in the darkness, staring down at me with that faceted gaze. Like broken glass. "So you're alone here."

His words struck a nerve I hadn't thought would sting as much as it did. Likely because no one had ever said it to me in that way.

"No," I argued. "I—I have...I have Raana *Dyaan*. Lesana. Grace. Draan."

"Of course," Kythel said, his tone smoothing. Diplomatic, even, and that irritated me, though I ignored it. "But you don't truly have anyone to depend on. Because most people are selfish and only loyal to themselves."

My breath wheezed out from my lungs. I didn't know whether to laugh or cry.

"Has anyone ever told you that you're terrible at comforting people?" I asked, keeping my tone light. "You were supposed to say, 'I'm sorry, Millie. I'm sorry that your father is dead. How terrible.'"

"You don't want that," he said, stepping closer, making me swallow. "Hollow words. Do you?"

"It's only polite," I said, grappling for words as his nearing presence made my nerves spike. My neck craned back when he stopped mere feet away. "An heir to the Kaalium should know better."

A gruff laugh tumbled from his lips, unexpected and surprising.

Then, when that laugh slowly died away, for a seemingly endless moment, we regarded one another.

I jumped when a loud burst of laughter poured out from the entrance of Raana *Dyaan*, a couple guests leaving, chatting amicably on the front courtyard. Then I heard the gust of their wings. Silence came again. A breeze blew between us, and I watched Kythel's nostrils flare.

I shrank back into the tree. A slight movement. But he noticed.

He turned his gaze sharply away, the profile of his regal features on display as he regarded Stellara.

And perhaps it was the soft quiet in his voice or the darkness of the alleyway, but I admitted, "I'm looking for a cottage within Stellara's borders. Do you know of one?"

If anyone did, it would be him.

His only reaction was a brief tightening of his lips. My heart sped in hope.

"You do, don't you?" I asked.

"No," he said, meeting my gaze, his eyes hard like flint. "No, I don't."

I was certain I'd seen otherwise, however.

There was a lengthy pause.

"You do know that there are many places in Stellara where the realm is thin, yes?" he asked.

"Yes," I answered. I'd heard stories of the realms all my life from my father. But experiencing them was an entirely different thing. The first time I'd felt a soul brush against me in the forest, I'd nearly jumped out of my skin.

"The forest is pocketed with thinning veils. From an ancient war. The living realm never rebuilt itself. Never healed," he informed me. "It's safe. They cannot hurt you. But go carefully. It wouldn't be the first time someone lost their way in Stellara."

The ominous words hung like a whisper between us.

"Good night, *sasiral*," Kythel said, finally turning away.

His words hung in the air long after he was gone.

# CHAPTER 9

## KYTHEL

*Pathetic,* I thought, slumping into the plush black chair in the lounge at Raana *Dyaan.* My third time in three nights. I couldn't stay away.

Rolling my tight neck around my shoulders, I caught Kaldur's look from across the table. His smirk irritated me. Luckily Thaine wasn't here tonight. He'd left for his province just this morning. Kaldur would be departing tomorrow.

"What?" I growled, the warning evident in my tone.

A silver goblet of Drovos wine, thick and blue, slid in front of me by a server who was not Millie. My mood only darkened.

"Where is the human woman tonight?" Kaldur asked the server over his own goblet of brew, flashing her a charming grin. "She was in here a few nights ago."

The Kylorr female bristled with the sudden attention but smoothed her expression quickly. "Millie? She was serving earlier. But now she's working with Draan in the kitchen."

That was curious. She'd told me her father was a culinarian but not that she was herself.

"Does she typically work in the kitchen? Or in the lounge?" I asked.

"In the lounge," the server answered. "Most nights."

Across the lounge, my eyes caught on Lesana, who was laughing with Hanno, a broad grin on her face, her arm perched on his shoulder. Cousins, though Lesana was not of House Arada. Not anymore.

My eyes narrowed. I murmured under my breath, finally understanding. When Lesana caught my gaze from across the room, I dipped my chin. She straightened and came at my beckoning.

"I'm so delighted you were able to join us again, *Kyzaires*," she said, her smile demure, though I knew it hid bite. "Would you like a blood giver this evening? I can make arrangements for both of you. Any of our givers can be available for you."

"No," I said, holding her gaze. "Just food and drink will suffice."

I didn't like to be maneuvered. Not in my own province by a noble House that thought it could guide my hand.

"I hear your husband has extra help in your kitchen tonight," I told her. Her left wing twitched. I grinned when I saw it. "How fortunate to have a culinarian's daughter working within your own establishment."

Her smile widened, but it felt jagged at the edges. "Millicent has many versatile talents. I was lucky to find her and even luckier that she chose to stay...for now."

"Oh?" I asked, snagging my goblet and lifting it to my lips. "She will be leaving?"

"That is my understanding," Lesana said. The admission made my jaw tighten. "Though I make it a point to respect my workers' privacy."

My hand paused, the goblet held suspended in the air, surprised that she would dare to lob a half-concealed barb at me.

Her grin widened to hide her slip of tongue. I saw the desperation begin to creep into her gaze, finally understanding what she'd done.

"Can I get you anything besides your drinks?" she asked quickly. "Would you like food from—"

"Yes," I bit out. "Everything."

"Everything, *Kyzaire?*" Lesana asked, her smile wavering for the first time.

"Everything," I repeated slowly. "We might need a bigger table."

---

"WHAT IN RAAZOS'S BLOOD WAS THAT?" KALDUR GROANED WHEN we stepped onto the courtyard. He knew better than to ask that question to me inside or to challenge the stream of plates and serving trays that had come our way. And we'd eaten every last bite. "I won't need to eat for a week."

Despite my full belly—filled with some of the best, most surprising food I'd had in a long time—I was still in a foul mood. When we were a fair enough distance away from the front doors of Raana *Dyaan*, I told him quietly, "House Arada knows."

"Knows what?" Kaldur asked. "That you'll make an arrangement with Lyris? That much was clear. Not much to know. Unless this is about the girl."

A joint in my wing popped with tension. The day had been long, one incident following the next. The only thing that had gone right was a shipment of stone from Vyaan that had arrived at the Syan Pass without incident. Construction would begin on that section of the South Road in the morning. Small progress, but progress nonetheless.

"I don't like to be controlled," I told him. "They should know better."

Kaldur lowered his voice. "Because the human female is your *kyrana?*"

More joints snapped. I didn't want it to be true. It would be a *nightmare* if it was true.

But Kaldur saw everything. He liked to disarm people with his smile, his easygoing demeanor, his charm. Underneath it all, he was as shrewd and perceptive as an inter-Quadrant officer.

"I can't be certain," I admitted just as quietly, holding his gaze. "But even if she is...it changes nothing."

Kaldur's gaze flickered. Disbelief threaded through his gaze. "You cannot be serious."

"I have a duty to Erzos," I growled. "A duty to the Kaalium. To you. To our family. I can't forget that."

Even if I wanted to.

"Do whatever the fuck you want. Like you always do," Kaldur told me—an easy, though mocking, grin sliding onto his features. "But whoever heard of a Kylorr turning his back on a fated one? Certainly not me. It's laughable that you think you can try."

"Don't," I warned.

"You don't want House Arada controlling you?" Kaldur continued. "The solution is simple. Show them they can't."

It was tempting. A seductive thought, one that would bring me a dark kind of joy.

But the truth was that I needed House Arada's wealth as insurance when a war came. I *needed* them. And I hated that.

"I can't," I said quietly. "You know that."

Kaldur shrugged. His eyes caught on something over my wing, gaze narrowing before they returned to mine.

"Like I said, you'll do what you want," he murmured. "You always have."

Irritation snapped in my chest. A brief flash of rage that *burned*. Disappointment and anger that I had thought long buried came rising to the surface, hurtling to my throat before I swallowed it back down.

"You think I do what I want?" I asked, the tight leash of my control near snapping. Perhaps Kaldur saw the flash of it in my eyes because he had the good sense to look ashamed. "I've never done *anything* that *I* wanted. Not once. Except...except when Aina..."

I trailed off, the guilt still suffocating all these years later. Kaldur's expression sobered.

"Look how that turned out," I finished softly.

"You know that wasn't—"

"Don't," I said. Though it almost sounded pleading. "Please. Let's not linger in the past. I shouldn't have said anything."

Kaldur inclined his head, his gaze flickering over my shoulder again. He gestured behind me. Just as I turned, he said, "I'll see you back at the keep."

Millie was in the shadows. I was confident she hadn't heard a single word of our conversation, as far away as we were.

Still, after I felt the gust of Kaldur's wings rustle my hair as he took to the sky, after I approached to where she was standing in her usual place against the bleeding tree, I asked, "Did you hear any of that?"

Her scent was overpowering, making my venom flow the closer and closer I drew.

*Raazos's blood.*

"No," she replied. And I believed her. "Kaalium secrets? I'm intrigued."

At her easy, teasing tone, I felt some of the tension in my shoulders loosen. Though a good portion of my mind was still on the conversation with Kaldur.

*You don't want House Arada controlling you? Show them they can't.*

Lesana was keeping Millie away. She'd seen my reaction in the lounge that first night. Hanno had too. I prided myself on my control, but I'd just been...stunned. I should've exhibited more restraint.

Now I couldn't help but wonder if Lesana had had a hand in Millie's refusal of my offer.

*Or maybe she just doesn't want you to feed from her,* came the thought, shaming me.

"You're back," she said, as if it weren't obvious. I heard the question beneath the words, however.

Her cheeks were flushed from the heat of the kitchens. She smelled like *kanno* spice, warm and earthy. Underneath...it was *her*.

I slid against the wall, leaning back against it, mimicking the position I'd taken the previous night.

"You're a culinarian too," I said. "Not just your father."

She started at the words, her arms uncrossing from her chest, straightening.

"No," she said. "I was never properly trained."

"Does that matter?" I wondered.

"Yes," she said without hesitation. "My father's training was rigorous. He was hungry when he was younger. That drive alone got him through the training, but just barely. But among culinarians...only the *obsessed* survive."

"Explain it to me," I ordered. I found I was achingly curious about this woman. About where she'd lived and traveled. The people she'd met. Who she was. Who she cared for.

Perhaps because she was everything different from me.

And everything I envied.

Her lips quirked at the order, but she still answered, "As he aged, his heart wasn't in it anymore. Culinarians are artists in their own way. It has to be your entire life. You have to be single-minded to the point of obsession, about every last detail. You spend weeks—*months*, even—perfecting a dish. Because it *has* to be perfect. To elevate yourself among the stage of the universe, everything has to be perfect. You have to be a peculiar person to live that life, and for so long. After a while, my father realized it wasn't worth it. He loved food. He loved creating. But he loved me more."

I marveled at her openness, discussing simple but sacred things like love.

"And I feel like that too," she continued. "I love food. I love cooking because it reminds me of my father. It reminds me of the first meal I ever served him. It reminds me of late nights in the kitchen, standing over a hot stove and being with him."

Her vision went a little blurry before she blinked the glassiness away, not embarrassed even though she shot me an apologetic look.

She cleared her throat, her tone shifting from its softened, intimate state to something I'd deem more appropriate when speaking with a *Kyzaire*. And I hated it.

"But cooking is not my whole heart. For many culinarians, you'll find it has to be for you to be great," she finished. She gave me an amused smile. "So no...I'm not a culinarian. Why do you ask?"

I'd never given much thought to the lives of culinarians. We'd always had one or two within the keep. I had one within my own now, though Telaana had never been properly trained.

What Millie had told me...it fascinated me.

"We ordered every last dish from the kitchen tonight," I informed her.

"Ah," she said, sliding me a tired smile. "It was you. I wondered. Why?"

*To make a point,* I thought.

Instead, I said, "Because I was hungry."

Her cheeks went a little pink.

"The *laak* eggs," I started. "Did you prepare them, or did Draan?"

"I did," she said.

I grinned. "I liked them."

"Yeah?" she asked, simple pleasure widening her own smile.

"Yes," I replied. "How did you get the *kanno* spice inside the shell? I've never seen that before."

"Kitchen secrets," she told me, her tone sly. "I can't tell you."

I grunted. "The *wylden*? Yours or Draan's?"

She looked smug, the expression oddly endearing, as she said, "Mine."

"What was the purple sauce with it?"

"Black pepper and *ito'nag* compote," she told me.

"*Ito'nag?*" I asked, brow furrowing.

"It's a fruit from Rupon," she told me.

"Rupon?"

I'd never heard of it.

"A small farming colony. In the First Quadrant," she told me, tilting her head to the side. "The compote? I have preserves of it. Preserves I made with my father."

Her dead father.

I frowned. "Why waste them on us, then?"

Her expression softened. For a brief, brief moment, she looked so sad that I wanted to reach out and trace the lines around her mouth, to try to erase them.

"Food is meant to be shared," she told me. "Plus, the *wylden* was fresh. Hunted just this morning beyond the Three Guardians, and Draan got the best cut. Why waste that life with some subpar demi-glace? The compote was right for it. It was what my father would've served."

I should've been alarmed by the startling warmth that bloomed in my chest at her perturbed expression, especially as she'd said "subpar demi-glace," whatever that meant.

*Dangerous, dangerous game,* my mind warned. Made even more dangerous with her sublime scent clouding my better judgment, a thick haze of everything I couldn't have.

"It was my favorite dish of the night," I assured her. "My favorite meal in a long time. Perhaps I should hire you for *my* keep, for *my* kitchen."

She laughed but didn't take my offer seriously.

"It's funny, isn't it?" she began. "Food is merely a supplement for the Kylorr, but it's blood that truly nourishes you. I thought maybe my father was different, but then I come here and find that most Kylorr appreciate food more than most species I've encountered. Food from the earth, from the sea, from the sky, from the forests, from the mountains. I've never seen a species enjoy food the way the Kylorr do. And it's not even what best strengthens you. I think that's interesting."

"We can appreciate it all the more because we do not *need* it," I told her. "Food is a fleeting thing. Beautiful…but then it's gone. Turned into something ugly inside our bellies as acid eats it away."

"I've never thought of it like that," she admitted, making a small face.

"I love food more than blood," I confessed to her.

Aina had once told me that she loved food more than blood too. Then, however, as a young child who'd had a steady supply of blood givers coming and going from the keep, as all my siblings had, I'd never understood the sentiment until I'd been older. Whenever she'd dined with us, I'd watched Aina savor. Taste. Enjoy. It had made me hungry, observing her.

"Why?" Millie asked, her shoulders relaxing into our conversation, her head tilting, baring her neck. My gaze trailed over the long, smooth column briefly before I swallowed the venom pooling on my tongue. I forced my eyes back to hers.

I knew the exact reason, the memory blooming in my mind like a starwood flower. One I hadn't thought of in years, truthfully.

"Once," I began, "my aunt gave me a piece of fruit at our morning meal. I'd just fed from a giver when I'd woken. I wasn't hungry for blood *or* food. But she ordered me to taste it regardless."

I could still see it in my mind's eye. A translucent orb tinged red with a black, marble-shaped pit in the very center. It had been firm but supple, velvety soft.

"She told me it was a gift from the Kaazor. I'd nearly recoiled when she told me, thinking it might be poisoned," I admitted, the corner of my lip quirking. "'Taste it. You'll never taste it again, Kythel.' That's what she told me. And I trusted my aunt, so I did."

I'd sunk my fangs into the plump fruit, my pupils dilating when a sharp tartness had suddenly softened into mellow sweetness, the two sensations tingling on my tongue as I'd licked my lips, hungry for more of the juice that had spilled from the ripe flesh.

"And it was the most delicious thing," I told Millie, holding her gaze. "My aunt had smiled as she watched me. And you know what she said?"

Millie shook her head, seemingly eager for more.

"'It tastes like peace, doesn't it? Isn't it the best thing you've ever tasted?'" I quoted quietly, remembering her exact words, even now.

Even with my full belly, I found myself craving that Kaazor fruit, which only grew in the northern region of our nation. I didn't even know its name. But my aunt had been right. That was the first and only time I'd ever tasted it.

"The fruit was part of a gift from the Kaazor king when my aunt had helped negotiate a peace treaty. A treaty that only lasted half as long as it should've," I added wryly. "But it was that morning that I realized food held a power all its own. It *did* taste like peace. However brief. However fleeting. One beautiful moment…and then it was gone. But I'll never forget it. Just like I'll never forget what my aunt wanted me to understand."

There was a gentleness dawning in Millie's golden eyes. A soft understanding.

Food kept me connected with Aina. How many conversations had we had over meals? How many memories had we shared? How many times had I watched her savor and enjoy, witnessing that small slice of peace and contentedness as she'd tasted a perfectly ripe berry because nothing would ever taste as perfect again than in that singular moment?

"Where is your aunt now?" Millie asked, the question

mirroring the one I'd asked her last night about her father, in this very place.

And so I gave her a mirrored answer.

"Dead."

*She is dead because of me,* came the thought, piercing and sharp and aching. It nearly stole my breath.

"I'm sorry," she said quietly.

And I knew she was. They weren't hollow words for her. I knew she understood loss. How it followed you like a constant shadow, sewn with bloodied thread to your heels.

I inclined my head in acknowledgment but said nothing more about it. Silence stretched, long but unhurried.

"You're different than how I thought you'd be," Millie murmured, a soft smile on her *haana*-blossom pink lips. One of her shoulders lifted. "Nicer."

Discomfort tangled like a hardened knot in my chest.

"I'm not nice," I informed her, my tone sharp. "Don't make that mistake."

Her smile died. It almost made me regret the words. Almost.

"I want something from you," I told her, pushing off the wall, knowing I needed to leave. And soon. "I'm selfish."

"And honest," she added quietly. "At least you're not a liar."

I looked at the column of her throat. I could see her heart thumping. I could practically *feel* her warmth. I could imagine the heat of her blood as it poured down my throat, the tingle and tang on my tongue. Venom once more flooded my mouth. My fists clenched at my sides. Since when did I fantasize about feeding from a *neck*?

But she'd be so warm there. I'd make her gasp as I sank my fangs deep.

*Vaan,* I thought.

I needed to leave before I did or said something I regretted.

I walked down the shadowy alley, stepping past the corner of

77

Raana *Dyaan*. Over my shoulder, I lowered my wing so I could meet her eyes.

"I haven't lied to you yet, Millie," I told her. Softly. Almost gently. "That doesn't mean I won't."

Before she could answer, I took to the sky.

# CHAPTER 10

## MILLIE

The Forest of Stellara was named after a warrior queen of the Kylorr. A warrior queen before the nations had been divided, before the land had been parceled and bordered. A *kyrana*—a blood mate—to a great warrior king whose name I'd, truthfully, forgotten.

But it was Stellara who'd brought victory during an endless war. Who was said to have felled a thousand enemy Kylorr singlehandedly.

Most of Erzos's villagers, who lived sprawled out across the land or along the blue coast or in the woods to the south of Erzos's keep, thought the forest was cursed.

They claimed that they could still hear the cries and roars from that war, that blood had soaked the earth beneath the shadowed confines of the black boughs and spindly branches. As such, no one ventured here. It was technically not part of the *Kyzaire*'s keep since the border ended at his land's wall. I'd not encountered a single soul within, living or otherwise, besides the scurrying creatures that made their homes within its quiet safety.

Truthfully, the forest was merely a place in the Kaalium where the barrier between the realms was thin, as Kythel had told me. Where Nyaan—the living realm, this realm—mingled with Alara —the after realm—and at times, Zyos—the lost realm. But the Kylorr were a superstitious people, especially those who resided in Erzos, I'd determined.

As such, Stellara was cursed. Haunted.

Yet the forest had always brought me peace. I'd found comfort within the cool embrace of her arms, under the shade of her bleeding trees after my father had been called away to Horrin. I'd found numbed calmness in the quiet after I'd learned of his death, gentle tranquility in the rustle of leaves and moss, the scattering of bark as a creature scurried up a trunk.

Stellara was the first place I'd come with my father when we'd arrived in Erzos. Still lugging our travel trunks, arms exhausted, clothes dirtied from the dust of the caravan, he'd brought me here. Not deep. Just far enough inside the forest for the village behind us to melt away, for the quiet to become loud.

That morning, I'd known he'd been remembering her, so I'd given him space.

But in the weeks we'd been in Erzos together before he'd been called away for a job on Horrin, I hadn't known if he'd sought out the cottage on his own.

I thought it likely, looking back on it now. There was one night he'd come back late, hair damp, his cloak gone. He'd been distracted. His smiles had seemed hollow. I'd been worried…but in the morning, he'd seemed perfectly normal again. I'd forgotten.

*Maybe he came here,* I thought. *Maybe this forest is haunted but for him, it was with memory, not souls from an ancient battle.*

Stellara was beautiful tonight.

Glittering stars of constellations I didn't yet know peeked through the canopies of the trees. A chittering cry of a flightless bird echoed in the maze of trees, and I heard its scampering feet retreat when I got too close. As I clamored over a fallen trunk, I felt an icy touch at my spine. I sucked in a sharp breath, looked over my shoulder to find nothing there, and then waited until it left. When my warmth returned, I hopped off the trunk, the rustle of the deep purple leaves above me like a thousand whispers.

Resting against a trunk, I wiped my hands on my pants to brush away dirt and pulled the scroll from the archives out of the satchel at my hip. I was heading south, toward Erzos Keep. There was a section of the forest I'd yet to explore, about two miles into Stellara from Raana *Dyaan*. I'd painstakingly memorized the map and brought my aging Halo orb with me, just in case I lost my way in the dark.

Still, the sheer vastness of Stellara was overwhelming.

I put the scroll away, then continued onward. At one point, I briefly spied a turret of Erzos Keep in the distance when the tree line cleared.

Just when I thought that it would be wise to retreat back to Raana, considering the late hour, I came across a beautiful tree.

A tree, truthfully, like all the others in Stellara, if not for the decorated trunk.

My heart sped as I crept closer. The trunk had been carved painstakingly with a blade-like tool, the carvings reminding me of woodworm markings on Gwytri.

These markings were beautiful, deliberate in their randomness. Curving lines and swirls wound up the trunk, deep gouges in the bark. And into the valleys of the carvings, silver metal strips had been fitted inside them until they were flush. It looked like an armored tree. A beautifully armored tree with its silver-carved trunk.

Looking around the clearing, I turned up the brightness on my Halo orb, and light flooded the forest. To my right, I spied the twinkle of silver. Another tree. When I reached it, touching the cool silver, I spied another, a stone's throw away.

*A path,* I thought, lips parting in hopeful realization.

A guide.

Next to me, my Halo orb hummed. Then it trailed me as I followed the path.

It didn't take long to find where it led.

*Show me,* I thought, heart quickening with every silver tree I found. *Please.*

The moment that the thought formed, I froze, my eyes widening. Because, as though the thought had willed it, as though the thought had magic infused within it, a clearing came into view, deep into Stellara, though perhaps only a couple miles or so from both Raana *Dyaan* and Erzos Keep's borders. A halfway point.

There was a cottage standing in the clearing. Dark and dead and overgrown.

The door had once been painted red, but the color had faded with time. The thick wood—inlaid with curving strips of decorative metal, the same as the trees—was hanging off its black metal hinges. There were two windows at the front of the cottage, one with broken glass as if someone had thrown a stone at it.

It was freestanding. Made of gray stone and wood, cobbled together in a style I'd seen in the coastal villages in Erzos, seams compacted tightly together to keep the salted sea breeze out. There were two windows that overlooked the front garden, though deadened blooms and blackened vines covered the panes, swallowing them up as if hungry. The door was a gaping mouth. Hesitantly, I took a step toward it.

I didn't call out. I knew no one was here. No one had lived here in quite some time.

My footsteps were silent as they padded over soft moss and rotting purple leaves. There was a stone pathway leading up to the door, though a few were loosened and I nearly stumbled over one protruding block when my boot caught on it.

I ducked into the cottage, a sharp chill in the air making me curl my arms around myself. It was dark and damp. The vines covering the windows let in little light, and there was white fungus growing on one stretch of the back wall.

The interior was simple. A single large room with a set of stone stairs at the back, leading up to a second floor. There was one table, a chair toppled over beside it, made for the bulk of a Kylorr. A hearth was pressed into the left wall, barren and empty. Nestled among stacks of damp wood, the color a bright mossy green, sat a rusted cauldron.

When I ventured upstairs, I saw a single bed. The smell was musty. The blanket strewn across it was riddled with mold. There was a washroom attached, complete with a small black metal bathing tub, which looked like the cleanest and most modern thing in this cottage.

When I walked to the stretch of windows of the bedroom, I could *just* make out the top of Erzos's brightly lit keep, but only if the wind blew a certain direction so the trees swayed in the clearing beyond.

Releasing a soft breath, I returned downstairs. I righted the chair beside the table and gingerly took a seat, breathing in the damp, listening to the quiet.

My eyes trailed to a dark lump on the floor. I stared at it, thinking it was a blanket, before I let out a quiet gasp when I spied something familiar twinkling on the material. Scrambling from the chair, I nearly fell onto the floor and lifted it.

My father's cloak.

The one I'd thought he'd lost.

The pin I'd bought him from the travel port ten years ago was still on the breast of the cloak. The pin of the two stars—me and him.

Seeing it now brought a rush of tears to my eyes, and I didn't bother to quiet my sudden sobs. I was alone here, deep in Stellara. No one would hear me, unlike at Raana *Dyaan*, where I muffled my cries into my palm under the weight of blankets late at night.

The cloak was damp. When I lifted it my nose, it smelled nothing like my father, another reminder of how long it had been since I'd last seen him. What had he even smelled like? I couldn't remember.

For the first time, I allowed myself to admit it.

"I'm afraid," I whispered, the words ripped from my throat, harsh and sad.

My shoulders shook with my sobs.

"And I miss you," I cried. "What...what am I going to *do*?"

I allowed myself to cry until I grew tired with the tears, until my eyes were swollen and my nose was running, thinking that last question over and over again.

I'd never been alone before. I'd always had him. But now... now I didn't. And I needed to learn how to live with that.

What was I going to do?

*What you promised him,* I thought next, the answer easy. *And once you do that, maybe you'll have a new answer to that question.*

That gave me comfort. One step at a time. One moment into the next. That was all I could do.

The hour grew late. After my tears had long dried and my nose felt raw from wiping at it, I sat with my back against the legs of the table, my father's cloak nestled in my lap.

I'd found it.

I'd found the cottage from his letters. He'd come here after all. Had he been looking for her? Had he discovered what I'd discovered now...an empty, rotting cottage? A melancholic, depressing shell of what it had once been?

I remembered the bleakness on his expression that night. It likely mirrored my own right now.

But as I looked around, my Halo orb making circles overhead, making the shadows dance in the open space of the cottage...

I knew what I wanted to do.

What I *needed* to do.

*I can see it,* I thought, my eyes beginning to prickle with the sting of longing, gazing around at the desolate space, imagining a fire, imagining the warmth. I could imagine this cottage cast in gentle light. My father would've imagined a kitchen of his own, drying his herbs along the windowsill, tied up with brown twine, once the encroaching vines were cleared away. During the day, shafts of sunlight would spear the floor, spreading gold in their wake.

I could imagine a garden in the front. Blooming bright with edible flowers in the warm season. A garden of his favorite things. *Kanno* spice. Winter weed for teas. *Varaam* for sweetener.

I could see myself here.

Disappearing softly into this magical, quiet place.

A home of my own making.

*Not my home,* I amended, feeling gentle determination rose.

*Theirs.*

It would be the last gift to my father once I brought his body back to Krynn and made his soul gem. I could bring him here. But only if it was restored to what it had once been. Their quiet place.

A home of *their* own making, the home they'd never gotten the chance to build together.

My breaths came quick. Tears rushed in my eyes. It wasn't quite a vision. It was a...hope. It was what could be.

Peace. Peace for both of them in the after realm.

Peace in Stellara.

With its haunted whispers and phantom touches. Where the wispy curtain between the realms was thin.

I pushed up from the floor, my legs numb and prickly as I gently laid my father's cloak on the back of the chair, and hobbled over to the damp pile of wood in the corner. I snatched the blackened logs, disrupting them from their place, leaving a darkened outline of muck and mildew in their wake.

It took eight trips to remove all the logs from the cottage. They lay in a strewn pile on the edge of the forest clearing, and my hands and arms and clothes were covered in grime at the end of it.

The moon was sliding over Stellara. It would be midnight soon.

But I was just getting started.

# CHAPTER 11

## KYTHEL

"*It what?*" I asked quietly, staring at Vadyn.

"The South Road was attacked by raiders," my head keeper repeated, ever patient, though his expression was grim. "Kaldur just sent a message through the main Com line. He's detouring there now on his way back to Vyaan."

My nostrils flared. I raked a hand through my hair and then stood from my chair.

"He's handling it, Kythel," Vadyn added. "It happened on his side of the border. It's not your responsibility."

"What was taken?" I asked quietly, going to the window and staring out over Stellara. The moon was sliding across the sky. It was late. How long had I been cooped up in my keep? The last I remembered…I had taken my morning meal.

My wing joints felt stiff, my back aching.

"Credits, mostly," he said. "The workers were robbed of anything valuable. They took some tools, all the rations and blood stores. They couldn't take the stone. Too heavy."

"Alert Dulan," I decided, turning to face my head keeper. Dulan was the keeper of the soldiers and guards stationed in Erzos, who oversaw their assignments, patrols, and training. "Tell him I want fifty soldiers sent down there in the morning. We'll get a rotation going until the road is complete. We can't afford any more interruptions. The workers will feel safer with soldiers at their backs. At the very least, it will keep raiders away."

"I will," Vadyn said. "Kaldur…"

"I'll Com him later tonight," I assured. Then, noticing he was hesitating, I asked, "What else?"

"Kaan of House Arada," he began, and immediately my shoulders tightened, "would like to meet with you. He sent a messenger earlier this afternoon."

My lips pressed. Kaan was Lyris's father.

"About?" I asked.

"He didn't say."

"Decline it," I told him.

Vadyn sighed. "Is that wise?"

I leveled him a sharp look. "I'll be seeing him in six days for the moon winds celebration regardless. Anything he'd like to discuss can be discussed then."

"Likely, he doesn't want to discuss business at a feast."

"Business," I repeated softly. More likely, it was that Hanno was in his ear, telling Kaan he needed a contract with me for Lyris's hand and *soon*. I'd made no such promises to House Arada. Hints, perhaps. But nothing written in *drava* black metal and blood. "My mind is made up. Tell him no."

"Yes, *Kyzaire*," Vadyn said before he left my office, sealing me shut inside again. He was displeased.

*One more thing*, I thought, tired. Restless. I slumped back down to my desk, scrubbing my hand over my throbbing eyes.

This mess with Maazin and the Thryki, of which I'd gotten nowhere. His trail had ended or was untraceable in Erzos.

The South Road construction. The protests within my own territory.

Two *kyriv* had been seen flying north, just past the Three Guardians. Yesterday, I'd sent up a small band of soldiers to protect the villages in case the beasts got restless. It was nearing their mating season.

*Lore* sowing season was nearly over. The seeds should've been planted last week, but the soil wasn't ready, too compact and hard from the harsher winter. Every day that we delayed risked the potency of the crop come harvest season, which risked the value of it once we exported it. Millions of credits could be lost.

The impending betrothal to Lyris of House Arada...a decision that I knew was logical and sound, a decision that was best for not only Erzos but the entirety of the Kaalium.

The only thing I was enjoying was creating the plans for the new village along the South Road, which I would name after House Sorn—my mother's House and Aina's House. The plans had poured from me, the sketches and schematics of buildings— some old creations, some new—taking shape. I planned roads. A gathering square. A market. Shops. Homes. Fields for crops. A shrine for soul gems.

A small village for now, but one that would grow long after I was dead. The infrastructure would be there for inevitable growth. Waste management. Fresh water. An *akkium*-power collector. Soldier barracks. It was a prime location along the new road. The potential was there.

*The one thing I enjoy,* I thought, sighing.

Well, Sorn Village and talking with Millie Seren. I enjoyed that too, even though I shouldn't have.

The hour was late, but I was restless. I needed a distraction, or I would spiral. I'd been within these walls too long. My wings needed a stretch. And though I felt frustratingly guilty for doing it when so much work needed to be done, I left my office, stepping out onto the balcony terrace that jutted from my window.

That first lungful of crisp night air was like the first drag on a *lore* pipe after a hellish day. It felt energizing.

I took to the sky, flying north. Flying toward Raana *Dyaan*, feeling the stroke of wind rush over the fine membranes of my wings.

I had no desire to go inside the *dyaan*. I didn't care for blood or wine this night, and so I landed a short distance down the road, in front of a darkened shop, an apothecary. The road was quiet. Deserted at this late hour. Walking toward Raana *Dyaan*, I veered right, cutting down another alley until I came up the backside of the one Millie took her breaks in. But she wasn't against her tree.

Yet...

I caught her scent, the pull of it *mind numbing*. She was here. She was—

"Sneaking around doesn't suit you, *Kyzaire*," came her voice, making me freeze.

She wasn't in the alley. She was in the forest, in Stellara, at the front of Raana *Dyaan*. Sitting on a stump of a tree, likely one whose boughs had grown too large and posed a hazard to the road just in front of it.

I walked toward her, keeping my gaze locked to her form. Her spine was slumped. She had dark shadows under her eyes that hadn't been there before. And a series of scratches along her hands and arms.

She was puzzled when I slipped into the forest too.

"What's that expression for?" I asked, inhaling her scent now that she was within arm's reach. Venom flooded on my tongue, but I swallowed the thick sweetness down.

"I'm wondering why you keep coming here," she replied.

I grunted. It was mortifying actually. And I didn't want to talk about it.

"What are those from?" I asked, reaching forward to touch the scratches, forgetting myself.

She smiled, though it was tired, when my hand touched her flesh. She didn't jerk or pull away. If anything, she welcomed the touch. Even seemed to savor it.

When I pulled away, she captured my fingers on the retreat, the movement surprisingly quick.

Her hand was cold. When she realized what she'd done, she let me go, a half-quirked smile of apology on her lips. It has been ages since someone had touched me so easily. When was the last time someone had?

I frowned, unable to remember.

But she mistook my frown for displeasure.

"I'm sorry," she said, ducking her head. "Forgive me. I—"

"No," I said, reaching forward to take her hand again. "It's not that."

"Oh," she said quietly, looking down at our hands. Gray against beige. Her hands turned pink with the cold.

"Where are the scratches from?" I asked again.

She replied, "I was moving wood logs."

"Why?" I asked. "I'm certain Raana *Dyaan* runs on *akkium* power."

"It does," she said but added nothing more, which I found supremely frustrating.

Slowly, Millie disentangled our hands before clasping her own together.

"Were you in the kitchens again tonight?" I asked.

"No," she answered. "In the lounge."

So my suspicions were true—Lesana didn't want her around me.

"Are you finished with your duties, then?" I asked, sliding my gaze to observe Raana *Dyaan* briefly. It was late. Most patrons would be gone by now. The lounge looked dark already.

She nodded. "I was going to go walking, but I just...I got tired."

"You look it."

"I had a late night," she admitted, sliding me a small smile I didn't think she felt. My hand twitched, wanting to cup her jaw. "Can I ask you something?"

"It depends on what it is. No Kaalium secrets, remember?" I answered, sliding my arms across my chest. "But try."

I was content to observe her as she deliberated her question. Her brows furrowed together. She blinked a few times, as if forming the sentence. I wondered about her upbringing. I wondered about her father, about the places she'd lived. She'd told me that she'd known *people like me* all her life. What had she meant by that?

"House Loria," she finally said. I felt the muscles in my thighs tighten, bracing, as if prepared to leap into the sky. Her gaze was watchful, but I kept my expression neutral. "Whenever I mention that name within Erzos, the village folk get uncomfortable."

"That's not a question."

She gave me an exasperated expression, one that had my lips twitching. "My question is *why*. I haven't found anything on the House, even though it was a noble one. Here in Erzos. I know that much for certain. Did you know them? What happened to them?"

"Why do you want to know?" I questioned. "Because your father used to work for them?"

"Yes," she answered. She met my gaze, the slivers of gold in them mesmerizing in the darkness of Stellara. "But also because he was friends with the daughter of House Loria. I'm trying to find her. Or find out what happened to her. I have letters he wrote to her that he never sent."

My gut twisted.

Ruaala.

I thought of her face, eyes closed. Lips nearly white, hair tangled in soil.

I hadn't thought of her for so long.

"House Loria," I said softly, "ended a long time ago. The Lord and Lady passed on. They only had one daughter, and she married into another noble House. House Loria's line ended. As sometimes happens."

"Yes, but the daughter…" Millie said, leaning forward on the stump, wide eyes fastened to me. "Ruaala. What happened to her? Where is she now?"

*Zyos,* I thought. The lost realm.

Was…was Millie's father who she'd been waiting for? Why she had forsaken everything, why she had done what she'd done?

"I'm sorry, Millie," I told her because they weren't hollow words. "Ruaala is dead."

# CHAPTER 12

## MILLIE

"What?" I whispered, a sad, deadened thump beating within my chest.

I couldn't say I was surprised, considering the reactions of the villagers whenever I'd asked about her. But there was heavy sorrow in my breast nonetheless.

"What happened?" I asked.

Kythel's jaw tightened. He only shook his head.

"Do you…do you know the House she married into?" I asked. Maybe they were still in Erzos. Maybe I could ask them about her.

He was quiet for a handful of moments. Finally he said, "House Kaalium."

I froze, my eyes rounding.

"My father's youngest brother," he explained quietly. "Thyri. He lives in Vyaan now. With his mate and children."

"He…he has children?"

"Not with Ruaala," Kythel said gruffly. "It's better if I show you. Would you want that?"

"Show me how?"

"At my keep. There's a book in the library with my family's

history and all those that comprise it. You can borrow it, if you'd like. There's a section on Ruaala and House Loria."

"Lesana..." I trailed off. "She wouldn't..."

Kythel's gaze sharpened like glass. "Lesana wouldn't like you away from Raana *Dyaan*? Is she your keeper? And you must not disobey her?"

"Of course not," I replied, spine stiffening.

"Then come with me."

We locked eyes. I thought of the number I'd read on my Halo orb earlier tonight—5,470 credits. Halfway to securing passage to Horrin, but not enough to return to Krynn, not to mention all the credits I needed for transfer permits. For food. For lodging.

*I'll figure it out,* I thought. The most important thing was reaching my father and claiming his body before they burned him and scattered him among the stars. If they did that, I would never be able to create his soul gem.

Lesana had wanted me to stay away from Kythel. If she found out...well, she might make good on her threat. I might be out of a job, a place to stay. I remembered that brief time when I'd been without a bed, without warmth and shelter, before Lesana had discovered me in the market. I didn't want to go back to that.

But the challenge in Kythel's eyes had me standing from the stump. I'd spent most of the night clearing out what I could from the cottage. My throat felt raw and swollen from the rotting damp walls. My legs throbbed, my back ached.

I raised my brow at his assessing look.

"Only for a little while," I informed him, peering back at Raana *Dyaan* briefly. "And I—"

The words died in my throat when Kythel stepped into me, the clasps on his vest brushing against my arm. Shockingly cool, though heat rolled off him in waves. He smelled like the spices we would dry in the summer. He smelled exactly like they had, swaying near an open window as a warm breeze perfumed the air with their fragrance. We'd lived on Rupon then, with its hot summers and perfectly lazy days.

My mouth watered. A heaviness bloomed deep in the pit of my belly before it sunk down…and down. Unthinking, I reached out a hand to touch his chest. Hard and firm. I missed touching. I missed being touched.

"What are you doing?" I asked softly.

His brow raised, but otherwise his features were expressionless. "How do you think we will get to my keep? By walking?"

"Oh," I breathed. "Right."

Kythel swept me up into his arms before I could take another breath. One arm went beneath my knees, the other supported my spine. I'd flown with my father before. And so I was used to the jarring leap as Kythel shot up into the air, the vibration that racked my body as his wings caught the wind, the way my belly dipped and swayed as he veered us south.

This also felt *unfamiliar*. Feeling Kythel's heat pressed against me, the light, distracting tickle of his hair when it swept against my neck, and the power I sensed in every gust of his wings…I was highly aware of our closeness in the strong circle of his arms.

The wind was loud and punishing above the trees of Stellara, but Kythel kept low near the canopies, I suspected for my sake. Any higher and it would be too cold at this time of night for me.

Still, I couldn't help but wiggle closer to his heat. His strong hands gripped me tight. I marveled that I truly didn't know this male at all. He could drop me, and I'd be dead in a matter of moments and no one would be the wiser for it. Everything would simply…end.

Yet…here I was. And I knew he wouldn't drop me. Perhaps I was foolish—to trust him so easily. My father would certainly say so, if he were still here. He'd always warned me that my heart would get me into trouble, even though he'd always said so fondly.

Erzos Keep loomed closer, coming up fast. Yet I tilted my

head back to look at the stars, tightening my hand into Kythel's vest. The view up here was always better. I caught him looking at me, those sapphire eyes gleaming. It was much too loud to speak, but I gave him a small, toothless smile nonetheless.

Then we dropped, hurtling down fast. I laughed, the sound breathless, surprised, and I caught the hard edge of Kythel's smile. Faster and faster we dropped, until the *Kyzaire* spread his wings wide to break the steep descent. A gust of wind blew my hair back, and we came to a sudden stop, the silence deafening as he lowered gently onto a cobbled path.

"Show-off," I teased under my breath, steadying myself with his arm as he helped me regain my footing on solid ground.

An amused grunt. "That is one thing I've never been accused of before."

"First time for everything," I said, but I was too distracted by the view in front of me to take in his reaction. I breathed, "Wow."

House Kaalium's keep of Erzos loomed before me, a towering guardian against the inky, starry sky. I'd never seen it up close, only ever from the distance of Raana *Dyaan*.

The keep mirrored the grand gothic architecture prominent in the capital city of New Inverness, with its tall spires and decorative glass windows. Or perhaps of the Drovians, who preferred their dwellings to be all sharp, stark lines and towering floors.

"This way," Kythel murmured. I felt his hand at my back, propelling me forward, and I sunk into the warmth of his touch, soaking it up like rays of the sun.

The closer we strode towards the keep, the larger it loomed. The main entrance stood proud before us, set well behind an extravagant black fountain with floating, glowing white orbs weaving in and out of a small waterfall as it tumbled into a decorative basin. The Halo orbs hummed, and I paused next to the fountain, tracking the pattern they made, before continuing.

Climbing up the stairs to the door—inlaid with silver strips of metal, much like the cottage's door—Kythel guided me inside.

The atrium of the house was stunning. I was used to beautiful places, beautiful homes, castles, fortresses. But *this*...I had never seen anything quite like it. It was extravagant even without a multitude of expensive furnishings. On Bartu, they crammed their entryways with the most grand of their possessions, to impress and preen for their guests.

But not Erzos's keep. It was stark. Cold, even. Quiet and still like a museum. But there was a delicate beauty in the glimmering black staircase stretched before me, winding up in a perfect circle overhead to the upper floors. The atrium was large and wide to allow for easy navigation to the higher levels of the keep, since Kylorr could simply fly upward to the open landings. In fact, I saw cutouts in the railings for that exact purpose.

Three stories above our heads, I saw a glass dome, revealing the night sky and the silvery, wispy clouds beyond.

The atrium was brightly lit from tall columns evenly placed around the entryway, light pouring out from a hovering diamond-shaped crystal on each. When I looked at Kythel, I saw him studying me.

"It's beautiful, *Kyzaire*," I told him honestly.

He inclined his head in quiet gratitude. I'd heard he liked beautiful things, after all, that he surrounded himself with beautiful things. Which made me wonder why he was spending time with *me*, considering I was no great beauty and had never lied to myself about that. Surely he could see that for himself.

"Oh," I gasped out, catching sight of an object on the far wall. Something I hadn't expected to see. I scurried closer, eager for a better view. "Is that *real*?"

"Of course," he told me. His tone sounded surprised when he asked, "You know it?"

"I met him once," I told Kythel.

"You did?" came the incredulous question. I'd surprised him again. I felt a little triumphant at that.

The artwork was a hologram, displayed within a rectangular

silver frame. The lines wavered in black, flickering before solidifying, constantly changing, a moving picture. But I would recognize it anywhere.

Ver Teracer was a universally famous artist who only created landscapes from his now-destroyed planet, Tirut. The frame itself was comprised of precious metals from the planet, remnants of it. As such, only a few pieces of the artwork existed.

Kythel must've paid a small fortune for it.

"He attended a party on Hop'jin a few years ago, one my father was hired for. In between courses, I would sneak out into the ballroom to watch the dancing," I told him, studying the shifting drawing. "Hop'jin dancing is very…theatrical."

Most of Ver Teracer's works depicted the ending of his homeworld, a product of war. This one, however, was beautiful. No destruction. No death. No pain. Just peaceful in its simplicity. A home as it had been. A meadow landscape melted into a moonrise. The moonrise became a wild sea. The wild sea became shadowy highlights on a sharp-faced mountain. The mountain melted back down into the meadow. The loop continued.

"He's rather grumpy, but I quite liked him," I told Kythel, shooting him a conspiratorial smile. "He told me I had a strange face, and it made my whole decade."

Kythel's wings rustled. He folded them against his back, leaning his shoulder against the wall where the artwork hung. "That is a high compliment indeed from an artist like Ver Teracer."

"It is," I agreed. "He was just sitting alone in a corner. He thought I was a server girl, so I brought him wine when he asked. We talked for a bit about the dancers, and then I had to return to the kitchen to help my father. But later that night, I saw him again. He said he would draw my face into one of his works. Then I never saw him again."

"And did he?" Kythel wanted to know.

I shrugged. "I have no idea. I never looked. And most of his works are unreleased. Only for him." I looked back to the shifting hologram. "If I owned one of these…I would keep it locked away. Aren't you worried it could get damaged out here in the atrium?"

"It seemed selfish," he murmured, "to keep it all to myself."

I nodded, understanding. Looking back at the hologram, I watched it loop twice more, admiring the way the lines faded and appeared, a dance all their own.

Then I cleared my throat, noticing the hushed quiet in the atrium and the weight of Kythel's eyes.

"The library," I prompted quietly. Ruaala. I couldn't forget why I was here.

"This way," he murmured, gesturing toward the staircase. The banister was cold and smooth, like black marble, beneath my palm as I started the climb, Kythel at my back.

"Where are your keepers?" I couldn't help but ask.

"Most are sleeping at this hour," he informed me. "We won't be disturbed."

The hallways were mostly dark on the second floor, the only source of light the moon streaming in through the plethora of windows. Kythel guided me to a set of arched black doors. When he opened them, I discovered a large room with floor-to-ceiling shelving and an open upper level with even more. Thick, dust-free tomes and pristine rolled parchment were carefully nestled within the metal bookcases.

There was a soft place in my soul that brightened at the sight. Moonlight streamed across the floor, but Kythel tapped a panel next to the door. Halo orbs hummed to life. Gentle, lilac-colored light illuminated the library, and I found myself wishing I could curl up on the chaise in the center of the room and just *stay*.

"Do you actually read in here?" I wondered. Kythel left the door open but guided me deeper into the room.

"No," he admitted. "I rarely have the time to read for pleasure anymore."

"Pity. I can imagine you in here so easily. It suits you."

He slid me an assessing look. "Everything in my keep suits me. I planned every last detail."

Confusion dipped into my tone when I commented, "I thought Erzos Keep has been here for generations."

"It has," he told me. "But no one in my family has lived here for nearly a hundred years. When I took over the territory, I had almost every room worked on. I kept the original structure in place, of course. It would be a travesty to tear down these walls."

I was...impressed.

"Where did you find the time?" I asked.

"I barely slept for two years," he confessed to me. The corner of his lip quirked. "Though I had been planning its renovation since I was a child, so I had long-held ideas for this place."

"You always knew Erzos would be yours?" I questioned, intrigued. I knew all the brothers of House Kaalium oversaw different territories, but it hadn't always been that way.

"My twin was always going to have Laras," he told me. "Erzos was practical for me. Logical. So yes, I always knew."

But there was a curious tone in his voice that had my ears perking.

"No," I said quietly, tilting my head to regard him. "You didn't. Did you want Laras instead?"

"No," he scoffed. "Never."

Another thought occurred to me, and it was out of my mouth before I could stop it. "Did you not want any territory at all?"

Kythel looked away sharply to regard the tomes of his library. He moved forward, sliding his long, thick finger down the black spine of a book before he plucked it from its place.

"I'm sorry—it's none of my business," I said quietly, his obvious silence prickling over my skin. "My father always said I was too nosy for my own good. But I like to understand people."

But there was something in my words that must've struck a chord. I'd never given much thought to the *Kyzaires* of the Kaalium. I'd never given much thought to their lives. It surprised me greatly to learn that the female my father had loved so dearly had been tied to House Kaalium. He'd never told me who she'd been betrothed to. It made sense now.

Kythel returned to me before proffering the black book between us.

"'People'?" he repeated softly, those jeweled eyes flashing in the dim light. "I'm not just any 'person,' Millie Seren."

Was he angry? Annoyed? I couldn't be certain. But I felt my own ire rise in response to the arrogance I heard threaded between his words.

Glancing between us at the black book, I reached forward to take it from his grip. I was surprised by the weight, convinced its pages were made of metal and not silken parchment. If I didn't *need* to peek within its pages, I would've left it in his grip.

"Neither am I," I answered, hugging the book to my chest.

There was a grimness in his expression at the soft words.

"Neither are a lot of people, in my experience. Strangers always have a way of surprising you," I informed him. "You think you're better than everyone else because you're a *Kyzaire* of the Kaalium?"

Now there was warning written in his features.

"Maybe you are," I said, shrugging my shoulder. "But many would say you're lucky. Lucky to be born into the family you were. Lucky to be the High Lord of Erzos. Lucky to live in this keep, which is perfectly suited to you. Lucky to purchase rare Ver Teracer art for your atrium."

"Careful, little one," he growled, stepping forward.

But I wasn't afraid of him. There was one thing I was afraid of in this universe, and it wasn't him.

"For what it's worth...I don't envy you. I know better," I said, craning my neck back to meet his flint-filled eyes. "They might call you lucky, blessed by your gods and goddesses. Me? I call you chained, like I told you already."

A small flinch, but one I caught nonetheless.

It made me soften. I exhaled a small puff of breath. My shoulders lowered.

Reaching out a hand, I pressed it to his forearm. His exposed flesh was warm, the muscles beneath solid, like marble. He was incredibly tense. I wondered how much more pressure would make him crack.

I trailed my hand down his forearm before I cupped the back of his hand, turning it over so his palm was exposed.

The intensity of his gaze nearly made me shiver as I ran my thumb down his palm's center. He had a large scar running across the length. Tracing it gently, I wondered what it was from but thought better than to ask. The tension beneath his skin, I noticed, slowly released.

*A little farther away from cracking now,* I couldn't help but think.

*He likes my touch,* I thought next, the realization heating my neck before it bloomed to my face.

"Seren," he said, the word gentle. Hushed in the sudden quiet between us. The throb of my heartbeat was loud, however. I could hear the leathery whisper of his wings when he stepped even closer.

"Yes?"

"You say your father was part Kylorr, but that is not a Kylorr name. Not one I've ever heard."

"It was his mother's name. His human mother," I said. "Back then, it was a common name given to orphans on Genesis, where she was born. In an Old Earth language, it means *star*. When she died, my father wanted to take a piece of her as he traveled among the Quadrants, so he took her name. Then it became mine when he found me."

"Found you?" he asked.

I was still stroking the palm of his hand, but I became careless. We both became careless. Because when I traced down his long fingers, I slid the pad of my thumb over a sharp edge of his claw, just as he curled it abruptly.

A sharp sizzling prick made me jerk away.

Kythel went deathly still. I watched little beads of red blood push through the cut flesh. It wasn't a bad cut by any means—hell, I'd nearly cut off my entire thumb in a kitchen once and still couldn't feel its tip.

Then I heard a rough rumble start up in Kythel's chest. I watched his nostrils flare, heard his deep inhale, watched his eyes slide shut.

"I—I should go," I said, squeezing my thumb against the material of my tunic to stop the flow.

"Yes, you should," he finally bit out, pumping his wings in one sudden gust, propelling himself backward toward a shelf. When he bumped it, the books rattled. "I'll have a keeper return you to Raana *Dyaan*. Wait for them out on the terrace."

"No need," I said. "I'll walk through Stellara."

"No," he growled. Across the room, his eyes burned into mine. There was no mistaking the order in his voice—he expected to be obeyed. "Wait on the terrace."

Exhaustion was beginning to pull at the edges of my mind. It had been a long day already. From Kythel's keep, it might take me an hour or more until I reached the cottage on foot. It could wait until tomorrow night.

"All right," I submitted, backing out from the room. "I'll return the book soon. I promise. Good night, *Kyzaire*."

But I didn't wait to hear his response.

The moment I was beyond the threshold of the library, I closed the doors behind me.

Then I fled.

Only when I was outside, sucking in lungfuls of cold air to soothe the burning in my chest, did I realize that I'd never been afraid of a Kylorr before.

Not that I was frightened that Kythel would *hurt* me if he fed from me.

I was afraid that I would like it more than I should.

# CHAPTER 13

## MILLIE

After Kythel's keeper—a tight-lipped, stoic female who looked like she'd been woken from a deep sleep—dropped me back off at Raana *Dyaan*, I entered the dark and quiet building, creeping up the stairs to my room.

I stilled when I saw a warm glow emanating from underneath my door. Frowning, I pushed it open, peering inside, wondering if I'd accidentally left on the glow orb.

There was a figure perched on the edge of my bed with familiar parchment in their hands.

Grace was reading my father's letters.

A surge of panic and angry disbelief propelled me forward. "What are you doing?"

"Who's Ruaala?" she asked, her voice soft, not looking up. "And Joss?"

Taking care not to rip the letter, I tugged it from her grip, trying my best to gather up the others lying strewn across the bed, while keeping a firm grasp on the book Kythel had given me.

My throat was tight. I couldn't stand the thought of *anyone* touching these letters. What if something happened to them? To even *one*? Even losing a single letter would be like losing another piece of him.

"You can't just come into my room and snoop through my things!"

"Millie, I—I'm sorry," Grace said, standing, biting her lip. Uncertain. "I was waiting for you. I saw them on your desk. I didn't mean to read them—I just...I couldn't stop. I'm sorry."

*She means it*, I thought, finding her apology to be genuine. I'd heard a lot of hollow apologies throughout the years, after all. Besides, Grace was my friend. One of my only friends in Erzos, though the tension between us since I'd discovered her with Vraad in the giver rooms had been prickly.

Depositing Kythel's book onto the small table in the corner, I was mindful of my thumb—though the bleeding had stopped already—as I gathered the letters into a neat stack. They were out of order. I would correct them later. The important thing was that the only *unopened* letter of the stack was still sealed. My father's last letter to me, the one I had yet to open.

Taking a deep breath, I placed them gingerly next to the book and turned to face Grace. She was taller than me, long and willowy, her deep red hair looking beautifully and effortlessly mussed in a pretty braid.

"Millie, I'm sorry," she said again.

I tucked a strand of my short hair behind my ear as I rushed out, "I know. I'm sorry I snapped at you."

"You forgive me for snooping?" she asked, her pink lips quirking hopefully.

My shoulders sagged. "Yes. Of course."

She smiled. She reached forward to take my hand, squeezing it before I could stop her, and I winced when she pressed on my thumb.

"What happened to your hand?" she asked, dropping it quickly when she noticed the drying streaks of blood.

"Don't worry—it looks worse than it is," I told her truthfully, skirting around her to go to the chest of tall drawers in the corner. I procured a clean cloth, dipping it into a goblet of water from last night before cleaning the wound and my dirtied hands. "I cut it in Stellara."

"Is that where you've been sneaking out to at night?" she asked, trying to infuse some playfulness in her tone, though it came out stilted and awkward.

We hadn't spoken in days, the longest stretch we'd ever gone. Not because we were ignoring one another in the hallways when we passed, but because we hadn't willingly sought one another out after the *dyaan* closed for the evening, like we used to.

We both knew this felt strange.

When my hands were clean, I tossed the cloth into a pile of clothes I intended to wash tomorrow. "Yes," I answered. "What are you doing here so late?"

Her luminous green eyes drifted to the letters behind me on the desk. Then she paced across the room. She turned to the dresser I'd fetched the clean cloth from, straightening my brush until it lay perfectly parallel with the hard metal edge.

I frowned. "Grace, is something wrong?"

She looked out the window. With her face in profile, I could see her nibbling on her bottom lip.

"I know things have been a little weird between us," I said, crossing the room to her before taking her hands in mine, "but you know you can tell me anything. I'm still your friend."

She met my eyes and squeezed my hands. She looked a little sad at my words. "I'm leaving Raana *Dyaan*."

"What?" I asked, taken aback. A thought occurred to me. "Did Lesana find out about—"

"No," Grace interrupted. "Nothing like that."

"You're *leaving*? But where will you go?" I asked, brow furrowing, feeling a little ball of loss begin to grow in my chest at the thought.

"Vraad…" she started, and my shoulders tightened at his

name. "He asked me to be his sole blood giver. Among other things."

His mistress, she meant.

"You know he has a mate, Grace," I whispered. "A *wife*. From a noble House."

"They have their own arrangement," Grace answered quickly, squeezing my hands again to keep me from pulling away. "Their own understanding. She knows about me. I even told Vraad that I can be her blood giver too, if she wishes. I've...I've been with them both. Before."

"Oh," I breathed, understanding what went unspoken. She scrutinized my expression beneath her lashes, her cheeks pink. "Oh, I see."

"There's a contract in place," she hurriedly added. "It's all very official. Vraad and Lynara are purchasing me a house on the outskirts of Erzan. I won't be far—it's not like I'm leaving Erzos, Millie. I'll visit you. Or you can come visit me."

I mustered up a smile because it was the only thing I could think to do. "Of course. Of course we'll still see each other."

But I wondered if she could sense the uncertainty in my words. Raana *Dyaan* had bound us. Would we still be bound when she left?

Clearing my throat, I asked, "And you'll be happy with this? Do you love him? Or...her? Or both?"

Her lips smoothed to a line. She dropped my hands, skirting around me to sink down on the edge of my bed.

"Love has nothing to do with this," she answered. Her voice was quiet but certain. We were nearly the same age, and yet I'd always held the impression that Grace seemed a decade older than me. For all that I'd experienced, she had experienced more. But we never spoke about it. "Maybe once, I considered myself a romantic. But not anymore."

I joined her on the bed. She played with the fabric of her white dressing gown, silky smooth and expensive. I wondered if it had been a gift from one of her Kylorr because I knew that Grace wouldn't buy something so extravagant for herself.

"I just want to be *secure*," she said. I felt those words reverberate in my own breast, and I released a long exhale. "I'm scared, Millie. I'm always so scared."

Placing my head on her shoulder, I wrapped an arm around her back in comfort. She leaned her head against mine.

"I'll do anything not to be afraid anymore. And Vraad... Lynara...they are being generous with their offer. Do you judge me for it?" she asked.

"Of course not," I said, my tone harsh in its earnestness. "I *understand*, Grace. I could never judge you for something like that."

"I know you understand," she said softly. "Out of everyone I've met here, I knew you would understand best."

We stayed like that for some time until my eyelids started to grow heavy.

"When do you leave?" I asked.

"I'll do one last night tomorrow. I'll leave the following morning," she said.

My expression sobered. "So soon?"

She nodded. "I'm eager to get away from this place. Though I'll miss you the most."

"Did you tell Lesana yet?" I whispered.

Her body tightened against mine. Briefly.

"Yes," she said. "This morning. She wasn't entirely pleased. I didn't tell her I was leaving due to a couple of her patrons. She doesn't need to know yet. She'll find out eventually, I'm sure, but I won't be around when she does."

A soft laugh left me. I straightened from her shoulder, feeling a tight crick in my neck from the prolonged position.

"The rest of us will face her ire," I joked. "Thanks for that."

Grace smiled, but it was only half-hearted. "Millie, I know you and she are close," she started, "but just...be careful."

"You never did like her," I pointed out, shrugging. Though I didn't let slip the side of Lesana that I'd witnessed this last week. A side of her I'd never seen.

"They're all cut from the same cloth," Grace said.

"Who?" I asked, brow furrowing. Laughing, I teased, "The *Kylorr*?"

"No. Nobles."

"Lesana doesn't come from a noble House," I said immediately. Then I paused when I saw Grace quirk a brow. "She doesn't. She told me her father worked the ports."

"You do know that her mother's line is House Arada, right?" Grace asked.

"What?" I asked in disbelief. "But Hanno..."

"Yes, Hanno is her cousin. He gave her the credits to start Raana *Dyaan*, but he's bleeding this place dry. I heard them arguing one night in her office. I almost feel sorry for her. He's a greedy little worm. And she's obviously desperate to get out from beneath him, given how successful she's made this place, but he owns nearly *everything*. Not Lesana. Not Draan."

I couldn't believe what she was telling me.

"You must be mistaken," I said quietly. "You *heard* all this? When?"

"A few months back," she said, shrugging. "Ask Illaira. She heard it too."

I didn't know what to say. How to respond. I was too busy processing the new information and having a difficult time with it.

Silence stretched between us again. Even still, distracted as I was, I noticed when Grace's gaze eventually turned back to the letters on my desk.

"Who are they?" she asked, voice hushed. "Your parents?"

I sighed. I followed her gaze to the letters. Softly, I said, "My father, Joss. They are his letters. He...died a few months ago."

"Oh," Grace said. She reached out, taking my hand. "I'm so

sorry, Millie. I wondered. Grief…it's easy to recognize, you know?"

I nodded. Clearing my throat, I added, "He loved a Kylorr female named Ruaala. He used to live here. In Erzos. A long time ago. They loved each other deeply, but she was from a noble family and was duty-bound to marry someone else."

"Oh," my friend breathed. "How terrible."

"Those are his letters to her after he left Erzos for good," I told her. "Letters he felt he didn't have the right to send to her."

"Star-crossed lovers," Grace sighed.

"What does that mean?"

"Shakespeare, my love," she said. "Haven't you ever heard of him?"

"Vaguely," I answered. "From Old Earth?"

"Yes. My mother would read us his plays when we were younger. The language is old, almost alien now. But I remember the stories," she said. "Romeo and Juliet. Ill-fated lovers. You know how the Kylorr have *kyranas*? Fated mates? Think of their opposites. A love never meant to be, even written in the stars, at the beginning of time. Thus star-crossed, not star-*aligned*."

She looked triumphant, even though I didn't dare breathe. Because if their fate *had* actually been written by the gods and goddesses of Krynn, long before they'd been born…then did they have any hope of reuniting with one another in Alara? In the after realm?

"I…I can't believe in that," I told her. "I have to believe that they are meant to find one another again. I *have* to."

Grace frowned. She placed a comforting hand on my back. "Millie, it's just a phrase. I'm being silly. It's not like these things *are* actually written by the gods. At least, I don't believe that."

"I know," I said quickly, standing from the bed, feeling jittery from her words. "Of course."

*Star-crossed.* The word wouldn't leave my head. I might be haunted by it until morning.

Grace mirrored my actions, straightening to her full height.

"Regardless," she said, "from what I read…he loved her very much. A love like that, it deserves a happy ending. Don't you think? I hope he finds it."

My throat went tight. "Me too."

"Maybe I am still a romantic after all."

I mustered a small smile at the sentiment. "I hope so," I replied. "I certainly am."

Grace embraced me. Then she walked to the door, her hand resting on the curved, silver handle. "See you tomorrow?" she asked. Her last full day at Raana *Dyaan*.

"Yes," I said, nodding. "Good night."

She departed, leaving me alone to my own thoughts. My gaze strayed to the book Kythel had given me. Had that just been tonight? It felt like so long ago now, but the throbbing in my thumb told me otherwise.

I felt weighed down just thinking about searching through its pages tonight. What if I didn't find what I was looking for? What if I never did?

*Another time,* I decided. Tonight I just wanted to curl up into a ball and sleep.

Before I did, I pulled my Halo orb from my pocket. I looked at my account.

5,470 credits.

The same as it'd been earlier. A strange sense of disappointment washed over me, as if I'd hoped—by some stroke of magic—the number would have gone up in the span of a few hours, when I'd done no work.

There was one thing I knew for certain.

I was running out of time.

# CHAPTER 14

## KYTHEL

The high afternoon sun was warm on my wings.

Stellara Forest was beneath me, the deep purple leaves of the trees a blur. At night, the whole forest looked ethereal blue. An otherworldly place with its phantom whispers and tragic memories. It stretched wide toward the coast. I knew the South Road would cut straight through it, cleaving it in two like a blade. I wondered if it would bleed.

As I drew closer to Raana, my gaze sharpened on a section of the forest I hadn't sought out in years. But talking with Millie brought up curious memories I'd long forgotten and, though I needed to be in Erzan soon to meet with a builder, I found myself tilting my wings, veering inland and dropping closer to the canopies. I circled overhead, my eyes sweeping, roving, until I found the telltale mark of a silver tree, following the path until I located the open clearing.

Landing with a gentle thud into the fuzzy, spongey, blackened moss that sprawled across the forest floor, I straightened to inspect the cottage I'd very nearly forgotten.

*Or chose to forget,* I amended silently.

I'd landed at the back of the cottage, where the shade of the canopies nearly blotted out the bright afternoon sun entirely. I went to the spot I remembered clearly. The secret thing I'd done —something Azur didn't even know—though it had been Ruaala's final wish.

Just beyond the decaying, crumbling wood fence of the cottage's back garden, underneath a bleeding tree, there it was.

The moss had smoothed with time. No one would know. Except me.

Crouching down, I touched the earth, spreading my hand wide. Even now, my belly roiled with dread and discomfort.

*Unnatural,* I thought. Even now, I still found it unnatural.

And for the hundredth time, I wondered if I'd done the right thing.

It wasn't my right to question it, I knew. Ruaala had made her choice. Shivering, I felt an icy touch crawl over the nape of my neck. I waited until it ceased.

With a sharp sigh, I rose. That was when I noticed the stack of logs tumbled into a pile at the edge of the clearing. I frowned. The undersides of the wood were exposed, revealing deep black wood not covered in moss. They'd been moved recently.

Rounding to the front of the cottage, I looked at it with an assessing, grim gaze. Looters? I didn't think bandits and thieves would dare to venture inside Stellara, especially this far. *Lyvins?* What would those hungry beasts care for wood?

Just beyond the front door, the interior furnishings had been placed outside. A table. Two chairs, one with a broken leg. A rusted black cauldron. A metal basin. A rotting rug. A bucket with a dirtied rag hanging off the edge.

"What in Raazos's blood…" I murmured quietly, my hand unconsciously reaching for the dagger at my hip.

Footsteps behind me, coming through the trees.

Immediately, my ears tipped toward the sound. A moment later, a growl reverberated up my chest, and I swung around to face the intruder—or the beast—dragging my blade out from its concealed sheath with a whispery hiss. My muscles tensed, preparing to leap.

My gaze widened, a curse falling from my lips, when I met shocked—and wary—hazel eyes.

"*Millie.*"

The human woman stood frozen on the edge of the clearing, staring at the dagger in my hand, which I hastily replaced at my hip.

"Fuck. What are you doing here?" I bit out angrily.

Only when the weapon was concealed did she meet my eyes.

"Kythel?"

My name on her lips made me shiver more than the icy touch of the soul on my neck. I didn't even think she realized she'd used my actual name in her shock.

"What are *you* doing here?" she asked, turning the question around on me, stepping from the clearing. Her hazel eyes gleamed in the sunlight. I'd only ever seen her in the archives during the daytime. Every other interaction had been at night.

Considering my frustrating and bewildering fascination with this slip of a female, I could do without knowing that the sunlight warmed her skin beautifully. I could do without knowing that her cheeks shone pink and that there were strands of molten gold shimmering through her dark yellow hair. Small details that didn't need to be imprinted into my mind that I would think about late into the night.

She was wearing a dirtied white tunic that hung past her hips and tanned brown pants that looked two sizes too big. The sole on her left black boot was loosened, flipping open at the tip with every step.

She had a bulky dark blue pack strapped to her back, and she looked comically small underneath it. Hanging from her hands was another bucket, one that had a hole in its side, and from this distance I saw it was filled with jars of varying colors and numerous gray cloths shoved along the edges.

Millie stepped toward me. The closer she came the further my neck tilted down to meet her eyes. I was still tense, an ancient instinct still prepared to battle, my hand itching for a weapon. Kylorr didn't like to be taken by surprise.

"What are you doing here?" I asked once more, the question clipped. I was still angry. Pissed off. She shouldn't be here. *Here* of all places.

"How do you know about this place?" she asked, ignoring my question yet again, which only made my hackles rise.

"How do *you*?"

She sniffed, setting the bucket at her feet and wiping a hand across her forehead. She grinned up at me. "Let's just continue asking each other questions and never getting any answers. I like this game."

My nostrils flared. She smelled so *fucking good*, and I had to take a step back when my mouth flooded with venom, nearly stumbling over an exposed root in my haste.

Turning from her, I forced myself to bite out, "This is your doing?"

I gestured toward the decrepit furniture and the door hanging off one hinge.

"Yes," she said behind me, finally giving in and answering me.

"Why?" I asked.

Millie's scent grew stronger as she approached, stepping up next to me, lugging the heavy bucket forward.

"Why not?" she asked, shrugging. "No one has lived here for years—that much is obvious. It needs care. Sometimes houses are like people. You need to love them even if it's hard. If you care for them, they will care for you. It just might take time and patience to get there."

Unwanted affection mingled with the hot irritation I was struggling to keep tightly leashed.

"Is this what you were looking for?" I pondered. "In the

archives? You said you wanted a map of Stellara. Was it to find this place?"

She cocked her head innocently. There was a brief narrowing of her eyes, and Raazos's blood, I felt my cock twitch at the sight. She was *calculating* this situation. She was calculating *me.*

"Why?" she asked, her tone deceptively breezy, her smile widening. "Would this cottage be of interest to me?"

We both heard my thick swallow.

She suspected that I knew why she would be here. But she wanted to hear me say it, and I refused to give her that satisfaction. This was a side of her I'd not witnessed yet, and it was stunningly...arousing. It *was* like a game.

We could both play pretend.

"I haven't the faintest idea," I said, my tone silken. "But you've obviously started to make yourself at home here when you don't have the right to."

Her smile dropped. Her jaw set.

"I researched Erzos law in the archives," she told me. "No one *owns* Stellara, not even you, though it borders your keep's land. Which means I can live wherever I please within its boundaries."

"Unless the structure itself and the immediate land surrounding it is owned," I informed her.

Millie froze. "What?"

Flashing my growing fangs, I gave her a sharp grin.

"Let's not play games anymore, little Seren. We both know who lived in this cottage," I rasped. Her lips pressed together. "As such, the home and the surrounding land belongs to House Kaalium. As it lies within Erzos, it belongs to *me.*"

Her own nostrils flared.

"Is that so?" she asked, tilting her head back to glare. If it could quite be called that. Her face was too round, too soft to be considered fierce or frightening. "I don't believe you."

I barked out a disbelieving laugh, crossing my arms over my chest. "You don't *believe* me? Why would I lie?"

When I stepped closer, her eyes narrowed, flitting briefly to the silver catches on my vest before flying back up to my face.

"I haven't the faintest idea," she repeated, throwing my mocking words back at me. And *vaan*, if it didn't make me want to push her back onto the black moss and rip those two-sizes-too-big pants off her.

Her spine was stiff. She *was* angry. Scared too, I realized, smiling like a predator who'd just scented the rich, delicious blood of its prey. She knew I could take this place away from her. What would she give me to keep it?

"You cannot intimidate me, *Kyzaire*," she emphasized. She tucked her chin closer to her chest. "I don't have to yield to you."

*Yield?*

Her words brought another hot spark of need. Unexpectedly, the dark fantasy rose. Of her *yielding* to me. Of her letting me do whatever I wished to her. I could drink from her until I was sated. Fuck her. Use her. Until I poured everything into her and let her break into a million pieces from the inside out.

My pants went tight, the knot at the base of my cock beginning to pulse, but I retained control, clenching one fist into my crossed arms so she wouldn't see.

"Your tongue is sharp, little one," I purred, my gaze traveling down her arms, "but your hands are trembling."

Her grip tightened on the rusted handle of the old bucket.

"My arms," she corrected testily. "Do you know how heavy this thing is? Do you know how far I've had to carry it? Of course they would be shaking."

I nearly smirked but allowed her that balm to her dignity.

"Of course," I said, attempting to take the bucket to relieve her of its weight, but she flitted away before I could.

I frowned, watching as she backed away toward the cottage's front door. But I was content to watch her, to see what she would do next. A tendril of amusement was chasing away my prior irritation.

"You are a terror," I commented softly.

Millie was walking backward up the cobbled path leading to the door, and so I saw when she stilled in surprised—albeit briefly—her pink tongue darted out to wet her lips.

"No one has ever called you that before?" I questioned, beginning to follow her, though I kept my pace slow. Lazy. "I find that hard to believe."

She took another step backward towards the door, leaving me at the end of the rocky path that needed replacement. Then she took another step. Slow and deliberate.

I wanted to laugh. Did she think I was some stray, wild beast that she could simply *trick* into leaving? Did she think she could slip into the cottage, with its broken door, and somehow manage to escape me?

Striding forward with purposeful determination, I followed.

Millie stopped, a huff of frustration punctuated by her dropping her bucket to join its counterpart next to the rusted cauldron, the jars of various fluids and pastes inside clinking brightly.

"You want to know what I'm doing here?" she asked. "I'm making this place a *home*."

"No," I said, shaking my head, thinking of what lay beneath the earth and moss at the back of the cottage. My mouth set in a grim line. "I will not allow it."

Millie actually laughed. A soft, decided sound. For a moment, I could only listen. Though it was tinged with incredulity, it was still beautiful. It rose from her throat, and I imagined that if I was flying, with a warm, gossamer wind stroking over my wings, it would sound like music floating up to me, cast in bright, enthralling sunlight.

"You don't have to allow it," she said when she ceased laughing. "Like I said, this is Stellara. This is…this is *their* place. Their quiet place."

My brow furrowed, remembering that she'd mentioned those words before. I'd thought it peculiar then, and I thought it peculiar now. Ruaala had mentioned those same words to me once.

"And if there is one thing you should know about me, *Kyzaire—*"

Why was I disappointed at the sound of my title and not my name dropping from her lips?

"—it's that I'm extremely stubborn. Most times I get what I want. Not because I'm lucky or pushy or mean. But because I don't *give up*. And short of posting a legion of soldiers here to keep me away, I will continue coming here to restore this place to what it once was for them. This is my last gift to my father. I don't expect you to understand."

Stellara went quiet, hushed, like the heat of summer dampening all sound. Not even the wind reached us as I wound my way up the dilapidated cobbled path to where she stood.

When I stopped in front of her, I reached forward. I gripped her rounded chin between my thumb and forefinger, tilting it up.

One of my first impressions of her had been that she was ugly. She possessed an odd, strange face—I could see why an artist like Ver Teracer would've been taken with it. Millie was no great beauty by far, and yet her face had been the only one I'd thought about this last week. Which should have been enough of a warning to keep me far away.

Now, however, I saw what I hadn't seen before. The weighted scales were tipping. She was growing lovelier by the day, becoming more familiar. With that familiarity, I was becoming more enthralled.

Millie's breath came softly as those hazel eyes darted around my own face.

Quietly, I ordered her, "Then help me understand."

## CHAPTER 15

### MILLIE

When my father and I had made the link jump between Horrin and the port of Jobar, we'd been on an old rickety commercial cruiser. The captain had needed to turn off the lights in the cabins to channel the spare power into the jump drive.

I'd never experienced a link jump like that before. It had been *frightening*. A flood of adrenaline had made me shake in my seat when the lights had gone out. My head had gone heavy. My mouth had gone dry. When we'd diverted enough power to the jump drive, it had felt like my stomach had bottomed out, and I'd felt like I was falling from the pointed tip of a mountain as space had seemed to shrink around us.

Looking into Kythel's faceted, icy gaze, I thought about that particular link jump because this moment felt eerily similar to it.

He wanted to understand?

Why?

What would a *Kyzaire* of the Kaalium care?

Then I felt guilty for thinking he wouldn't. There weren't any rules or limitations on the kindness of people.

"My father and Ruaala," I began. I backed away from his touch because it made my skin prickle. My shoulders ached from carrying the pack on my back. My forearm throbbed from the bucket, calluses beginning to develop over my palm. "They weren't just friends. They loved one another. Deeply."

Kythel's expression didn't even flicker.

"Star-crossed," I whispered, admitting that that word had flittered through my mind on a seemingly endless loop since Grace had spoken it two nights before. "You know that life took them in different directions. But my father never stopped loving her. Writing to her. Thinking about her. That's why he wanted to return to Krynn. He wanted to find her, but we found no trace of her in Erzos. One of the last places he visited before he left for Horrin was here. Right here. I found his cloak inside the cottage."

Kythel's gaze drifted to the open door, into the depth of darkness beyond it.

"I have letters he wrote her," I told Kythel, taking a deep breath. "In them, he referenced this cottage a lot. He called it their realm. Their private realm. Their quiet place. Where they could pretend—"

My voice cracked. I cleared it, my gaze straying past Kythel's wings.

"Where they could pretend to live a different life. The life they both wanted—together," I finished, my eyes going glassy. "All I want is to give this place back to them."

I gave him a wavering smile. "Do you understand now?"

We regarded one another for a long time.

Kythel finally inclined his head, and I felt hope seize in my chest.

"Will you let me?" I asked.

"For now," he clipped out. Relief spread. I grinned. "Against my better judgment," he added, his gaze narrowing on me. "If you intend to be here long, you need a *zylarr* placed nearby. It's not healthy to be surrounded by so many wandering souls—you need to channel them, you need to feed them."

"A *zylarr*," I repeated. "Right. Where would I get one? In Erzan?"

"I'll bring one," he said, tone harsh, like the words were being pulled from his throat.

"You will?" I asked, warmth spreading in my chest like runny honey.

His nostrils widened with his sharp exhale. He didn't answer me. Instead, he nudged past me and went to the crooked door.

"Why are you here anyway?" Kythel asked. "I thought Lesana would need you at the *dyaan*."

"It's the afternoon," I reminded him, lips quirking. "I don't work all the time, you know. I don't have to be back until a little before nightfall. Besides…"

"What is it?" he prompted when I paused too long.

Slowly, I slipped the straps from my shoulder and lowered the pack off my back. I placed it on the table I'd lugged outside the night before. The surface was dry, thanks to the bright, sunny day.

"My friend left Raana *Dyaan* this morning. For good," I told him quietly. "I didn't think I'd feel so sad about it. But it seemed quiet this morning. I didn't want to be there."

He grunted. "Where did your friend go?"

"She, um, got an offer from a regular client," I told him.

He was inspecting the hinges on the door, but at the admission, he turned study me.

"I see," he murmured. He huffed out a sharp breath. "I'd imagine that happens often."

"Why?" I asked.

"How much blood do you think an average Kylorr drinks a week? Or from moon wind to moon wind cycle? In an entire year?" he asked.

"A lot, I suppose," I said, smiling. My father had very rarely drunk blood. He'd subsisted on food mostly, unless we'd come across a *dyaan* in our travels at major ports. But those had been far and few in between. I'd never minded. But considering it was a faux pas to drink from a family member unless the circumstances were absolutely dire, it had usually been *me* to track down the *dyaans* for him. Or I'd ask around for willing givers if I'd seen my father getting too weak or tired or slower than usual.

"Yes," he said. "So when a Kylorr finds a source of blood they enjoy better than all the others, they usually do whatever they can to *keep* it. To secure it. Think of it like eating bread all your life and then having a meal prepared by a talented culinarian. It's difficult to go back."

There was a nudge of tension between us at the words. Because I knew that my scent alone enticed him. That he wanted me, my blood.

"Is it really like that though?" I asked, fascinated. My father and I had never talked about this. It wasn't even until we'd reached Krynn that I'd realized how much he'd been denying himself. I wondered if it was because he'd been half-Kylorr, if perhaps he hadn't needed the nourishment from blood as much. "Most Kylorr don't seem that picky about their givers."

"But they have preferences," he replied.

"Do you?" I asked, the question out of my mouth before I could stop it.

"Of course I do," he answered cooly, assessing me carefully.

What would that be like?

Had I envisioned being a blood giver for Kythel?

Yes.

I knew that the act of feeding was not a sexual experience—unless it was between lovers or mates. Males and females alike, of varying ages, of varying appearances all worked as givers at the *dyaan*.

Still…

I had envisioned what it would be like to have him feed from me. To feel his hot breath against the sensitive flesh of my neck or my wrist. To feel his heavy weight against me, pinning me. I'd watched Kylorr feed before. Sometimes they went mindless with the act. Not violent. Rather, *focused*. Every fiber of their being was consumed with feeding, and so, often, they wrapped their wings around the blood giver, to ensure they would get their fill.

The fantasy was…intriguing.

"At your keep?" I asked, picking at a hole in my trousers. "Or at Raana *Dyaan?*"

"I prefer to keep my feedings at a *dyaan*," he answered. "Not in my own keep, unless I send for a giver from the villages."

"Why?"

Kythel reached forward, turning his attention back to the door. I watched with parted lips as he raised the heavy metal of it with ease, hooking it back on its hinges. With a mighty pull, he jerked it down into place, and I heard the reverberating pound of the metal as it clicked. He tinkered with something on the hinge, then checked to make sure it swung.

When he closed it, it fit perfectly into place, though it creaked when he opened it once more.

"Because when you're a *Kyzaire* of the Kaalium," he answered, "people get strange. They always want something from you. Then they begin to expect things from you—promises you never made. It's easier to keep every facet of my life carefully confined. Even though I have preferences for my givers, I never drink from one more than three times."

Three times?

Had he only wanted to drink from me three times?

Walking to the door, I touched the metal, the beautiful swirling design it made.

"Thank you," I said.

"For a long time, I never knew this place existed," Kythel told me quietly, watching me trace the strips of silver metal hammered in. "She kept it a secret for years."

I blinked, looking at him over my shoulder. "It hasn't always been here?"

"There were old hunter outposts in Stellara, but all are abandoned now. This," he said, gesturing to the cottage, "was built recently. From the materials alone, I'd guess thirty, no more than forty years ago. Perhaps even by Ruaala. Perhaps even with your father. But it's obvious to me they weren't builders. The structure needs a lot of improvements. I hope you know what you're getting yourself into."

A breath wheezed out from my lungs.

"She did those. I remember her giving a wood carving of a *kyriv* with metal stripes to my sister once," he told me, his eyes glued to the way my fingers traced the doors. "You saw the trees?"

"Yes," I said. "Like she was marking the way. Like she wanted this place to be found."

His lips pressed into a grim line at the words. He knew more than he was telling me—that I was certain of. But I knew better than to press. With time, perhaps he would tell me.

"I need to leave," he informed me abruptly, turning to back down the path. "I'll bring you a *zylarr*. Tomorrow. Until then, be careful. Don't stay here after dark. There were once *lyvins* in these woods."

"No promises," I said. "Will I see you at—"

But he shot up into the sky, my hair blowing back from the sudden gust, and I didn't think he heard me.

I watched him fly over Stellara until he disappeared from my line of sight entirely. Then I turned to the cottage. If my father and Ruaala *had* built this place, then it only made me more determined than ever to restore it.

I looked at the door. I smiled.

At least now I could keep the critters out.

---

KYTHEL CAME THE NEXT AFTERNOON WITH A *ZYLARR*, JUST AS HE'D promised.

"The crystal will melt into a silver pool as the souls begin to feed on it," he informed me when he noticed I'd arrived for the day. He'd already set it up, curiously at the back of the cottage, next to a bleeding tree that had encroached close to the main structure of the house. "It needs to be replaced every month. Don't forget."

The *zylarr* was a shallow basin of white stone, perched on a columned pedestal that must've been heavy to transport here.

"You'll let me stay for *months* now?" I couldn't help but tease, silly pleasure rising in my chest at the sight of those broad shoulders and black wings. "Just yesterday you weren't going to let me stay at all."

"Don't tempt me," he grumbled, and I chuckled. His gaze swung to me, and he studied me until my laugh slowly tapered off.

"What is it?" I asked, tucking a strand of hair behind my ear, the back of my neck tingling with his intense assessment.

He said nothing. There was a single chunk of smooth crystal, the crystal I assumed was responsible for the molten pools of silver I'd seen within the *zylarrs* scattered through Erzos. I hadn't known they began in crystal form or that they needed to be replaced every month because souls *fed* on them.

"I haven't looked at the book you lent me yet," I admitted quietly, watching him straighten. The crystal clinked in the basin, and I watched as a stream of silver ran down the side of it, pooling beneath it.

*Already?* I wondered, though I didn't sense that familiar icy chill in the air.

"Why not?" he questioned. He placed his hand on my lower back, the warmth of it leaving me a little flustered, as he guided me around to the front of the cottage, away from the *zylarr* and the bleeding tree.

Every time I'd thought about cracking open the book's spine, something had stopped me. Maybe because I was scared at what I would find, which was foolish and ridiculous.

"Sometimes I'm angry with her," I admitted, something I'd never voiced. "A lot of the time actually."

"Why?"

"Because she haunted him," I answered, leaning back against the strongest stretch of fence of the front garden.

This patch got the most sun. I planned to plant seeds here but only after I retrieved my father's body from Horrin. I refused to spend a fraction of the credits on anything else for now. All the supplies I'd collected so far—like the cleaning solutions and the spare rags and buckets—I'd found and scrounged for. The fungus pastes I'd gotten from Marr, a local villager.

"She followed him wherever we went. Her memory," I added. "And she was the one who chose a different life. A life that didn't include my father."

"But if she hadn't," Kythel said, "then he would have never found you."

"Yes," I said, giving him a soft smile. "You're right."

"And do you think he regretted that?" he asked.

Grief went through me, sharp and unexpected. It *hurt* but only because I'd loved him so much, and I didn't think that was such a terrible thing. At all.

"No," I answered, wiping at my wet eyes, unashamed to let him see. "I don't."

Kythel loomed before me, so tall that he blocked out the sun that was peeking through the canopy overhead.

*Handsome,* I thought, studying the sharp cut of his features, his dark hair, and the subtle downturn of his lips, like he was displeased all the time. *Incredibly handsome.*

This silly fascination for him was foolish, and I felt oddly guilty for it. I had no business letting my heart flip and twirl for a *Kyzaire* of the Kaalium, even if I was beginning to think of him as my friend. I had no business pining over *anyone* when I should've been wholly focused on getting to my father, on fulfilling his last wish.

I was lonely. That much was obvious. But I enjoyed Kythel's company. I believed he enjoyed mine. Our time was freely given. Was there anything wrong with that?

I didn't have the answer.

"Thank you for the *zylarr*," I said quietly. I motioned behind me toward the cottage. "Would you like to—"

But he cut me off before I could get the question out. "No, I'm needed in Erzan."

"Oh," I murmured. "All right."

He hadn't come to Raana *Dyaan* last night, even though I'd lingered in the alleyway during my break for longer than necessary, then felt foolish for doing so.

"Will you come to the *dyaan* tonight?" I asked softly.

Our gazes locked and held. I was holding my breath, my fingers curling against the splintering wood fence behind me— just one more thing that needed repairing, one more thing rotted by this place.

There was turmoil in Kythel's eyes. Indecision, though it was brief.

Finally, he backed away, and my lungs released a slow breath.

"No," he said. "No, I won't, Millie."

It felt like the firm words were in answer to another unspoken question, one we both heard.

Disappointed dismay flooded me, but I nodded.

"All right," I said, smiling, keeping my tone light. Chipper, even. "Have a good afternoon, *Kyzaire*."

He lingered, studying my features. Then, faster than I could blink, he whipped around, his strides certain and quick. He leaped into the air, pumping his wings hard and fast until he was beyond the trees.

Watching him go, I felt even lonelier than I'd been before.

# CHAPTER 16

## MILLIE

*L*ong after midnight, long after my night at Raana *Dyaan* had ended, I was cleaning inside the cottage with a bleary gaze when I heard a heavy *thump* outside.

Immediately, my eyes flitted to the closed door, trepidation rising. The Kylorr of Erzos might've stayed clear of this forest, but that didn't mean there weren't beasts living within it. Dangerous, large beasts. Kythel had said there were hunting cabins nestled within it, after all, for game. Something about *lyvins*.

All the exhaustion I'd felt left me in a single moment as I crept to the window. Peeking through the glass, I roved the front garden with my gaze before landing on—

I blew out a long breath of relief, my shoulders slumping. Then I backed away, another thread of nerves zinging through me.

Going to the door, I tugged it open, only to find Kythel already on the other side of it, filling the space of the entire doorway.

"What are you doing here?" I asked, my adrenaline still pumping. "I thought…"

He was in a foul mood. That much was clear to me when I examined his face.

"What's wrong?" I asked, watching him stride inside. At the threshold of the door, he had to turn slightly to account for his wings.

His gaze was pinned on me, and the intensity in those blue eyes should've sent me running.

"Millie Seren. Who are you really?" he asked, voice gruff. Perplexed.

Bewildered, I laughed. "What?"

He shook his head, but I got the sense it was to clear his mind. He looked as exhausted as I felt. Looking beyond me, he inspected the interior of the cottage. It didn't look like much, and yet...I'd been working every waking moment I wasn't at the *dyaan*.

Every moment I spent here, I knew I was meant to be here. I'd cleaned out its insides. I'd scraped the fungus off the walls, washing them repeatedly with *gaanyel* paste so it killed the spores. I'd polished the metal posts on the bed upstairs. I'd swept and mopped and cleaned the floors until I could eat off of them.

And yes...there were larger issues. The roof needed patching in a few places. There was a terrible draft that funneled its way from the upstairs windows. Not only that but all the frames on the windows were beginning to rot and would need replacement. The pathway leading to the house needed repair. The fence bracketing the cottage was crumbling. The table and chairs and rug might not've been salvageable, though I would try.

It was the kitchen, however, that I loved best. It was the kitchen that told me all I needed to know: That my father had been here, had *lived* here. That he'd perhaps—as Kythel had said—even helped build this cottage.

The kiln oven was modest since the room was cozy and small, but as I'd been cleaning out the black muck inside, I'd found something stamped into the left wall. A familiar swirling design made up of three intertwined circles. I recognized it immediately. It was the design on the signet ring my father had never taken off. It was a symbol he'd used almost as much as his signature—for business, for contracts.

He'd used the ring to make the stamp inside the oven when he'd constructed it. Just like the one he'd built when we'd lived on Rupon.

"I can't seem to stay away from you," came Kythel's quiet confession. Tingles ran down my arms. "It's quite infuriating. I'm at a loss of what to do about it."

I should've been flattered. A powerful *Kyzaire* of the Kaalium was admitting that I was a weakness. A tender place in his thick armor. What female wouldn't be thrilled?

Me.

In his words, this was what I'd heard: *We are too different, you and me, and our friendship is too strange to be believable.* Because I was just a girl who'd been abandoned on a space port as a baby, who'd lived in too many places that I couldn't even begin to remember, who'd never truly had a home except in her father, who was now dead.

He was an heir to the Kaalium, one of the greatest legacies the universe had ever seen.

Yet he was here. And he couldn't understand why. Because I was so beneath him in my dirtied clothes and unwashed hair when he was in a pressed vest that looked as fresh as it had that afternoon. With my unknown bloodline, when he could trace his back multiple generations. When my only concern was reaching my father before his body was burned, and his was running an entire province.

We couldn't be more different.

*But he likes that you know Ver Teracer. He likes that you know about Drovos wine. He likes the way you smell and the food you prepared him,* I thought next. *He likes your sharp tongue, but he might even like your smile more.*

"Are you not perplexed by this?" he asked, seemingly irritated, prowling deeper inside as I closed the door behind him. "Or am I the only one?"

"I've met enough people to know that nothing makes sense in this universe," I informed him, shrugging a shoulder. "I don't question it. So no. I'm only perplexed by your resistance. Are there rules on who you can be friends with? Unspoken rules that you've learned since you were born?"

He scowled. "Of course not."

My lips quirked. "I've always heard you were the logical brother. The cold one."

*That* made him still.

"I've seen traces of him," I admitted softly, approaching him, close enough to make his eyes flicker back and forth between mine. "But I've also heard it's your twin who is known for his impulsiveness. His fiery temperament. To me, you resemble *that* male more."

"You think I have a temper like Azur?" he asked.

"Yes, I see it now," I answered. "Don't we all? We had a little tiff earlier, didn't we?"

A sharp laugh barked from him, entirely unexpected. "Ah, yes. Your little claws came out. How I enjoyed them."

*I knew it,* I thought.

The warm, rough timber of his voice made me shiver.

Then we both stared. For much longer than what would've been considered appropriate in any given situation.

When my cheeks felt hot, I broke his gaze. "Well, as long as you're here, you can help me build my first fire in the hearth."

He snorted. "No *akkium* power out here?"

"What do you think?" I asked, quirking my brow. "Surely the *Kyzaire* of Erzos isn't afraid to build a little fire?"

"I've never needed to before, little one," he purred, his cantankerous mood beginning to melt away. "That's what keepers are for."

"Then let me teach you what even a child knows how to do," I replied.

Kythel shook his head but strode to the hearth without my prompting. I had a neat stack of wood I'd chopped earlier this afternoon. Not much, since I'd needed to leave for Raana *Dyaan*, but enough to last a few hours.

I knew he'd been teasing when I watched him build the fire easily, stacking the wood in a methodical way and placing the blue fire-starter paste below the mound and in the cracks. From his pocket, he pulled his *lore* pipe, long and clear, and used the sparker at the end to ignite the starter.

The blue flames roared to life before melting into gold.

I kneeled at the hearth, our shoulders brushing briefly as I leaned forward to heat my cold palms.

"Consider me impressed," I said.

Kythel sat back, leaning against the wall next to the hearth. "If this is what it takes to impress you," he said, "then I've been failing in my courtship."

I knew he was just teasing, evidenced by the wry smile that lightened up his previously somber expression, but my heart leaped at the word. *Courtship.* Like that was what he was doing. I wasn't foolish enough to believe that. I wasn't foolish enough to even *want* that.

"Are you not impressed that I own this entire province, Millie Seren?" he asked, his voice tired, though it made the words seem all the more intimate. Because who did he allow to see him like this? Not many, I imagined. "Are you not impressed of my lineage, of my family, of my wealth, of my reputation beyond Krynn?"

"I'm impressed by your Ver Teracer art," I replied, trying to keep a straight face and failing. "Does that satisfy you?"

"I think I like you because you're not impressed by me at all," he said next, shaking his head at my glib answer. I was surprised by the honesty I heard in those words. "How many wealthy, spoiled, high-handed males have you met like me? There must be a lot throughout the Quadrants."

"Oh, there are," I assured him, plopping back onto my butt, drawing my knees up so I could rest my arms on them. It felt nice to sit. My legs were sore from all the exertion of the day. "And be thankful that you'll likely never meet the majority of them."

"I want to," came his quiet reply. "Even the terrible ones."

"Why?" I asked.

He didn't answer. He leaned his head back against the freshly de-fungused walls, the sharp tip of his horns scraping the stone. Biting my lip, I studied him under my lashes, wanting to know what he was thinking.

"I'm just teasing, you know," I said. "I've never met anyone quite like you, *Kyzaire*."

"Kythel," he corrected, leveling me a long, unreadable look.

"You know I shouldn't," I said. "It's…disrespectful."

"Who's going to know?" he asked, gesturing around the empty cottage. "You said it before."

"Did I?" I asked, surprised.

"Disrespectful, you say," he murmured quietly. Another laugh rose from his throat, and I softened into it. "Disrespectful, when you make me build you fires and fetch you *zylarrs*."

"You offered."

"And trespass on my land," he added.

*That* I had no answer for.

Instead, I took a deep breath.

"Thank you, Kythel."

Those winter-sea eyes softened. He leaned his head back again, regarding me from a few feet away with a half-lidded gaze. "You're most welcome, Millie."

My belly went jittery. I rubbed my hands up and down my arms to dispel the goose bumps.

"Cold?" he asked.

"Yes," I lied.

The small narrowing of his eyes told me he knew it too.

"What does a *Kyzaire* of the Kaalium do all day?" I wondered, scooting closer to the fire. I wanted to hear his voice. The voice that made me feel like a puppet. "I've always wondered."

"Too little of the things that actually matter and too much of the things that don't," he replied. "I spent today in my office reading export contracts, met with two noble families over a dispute of their lands' borders, and then met with a group of builders for the South Road. We expect to begin construction soon."

"I know a lot of the townsfolk aren't happy about it," I commented, shrugging a shoulder.

"They think the road is unnecessary given that, oh yes, we can merely fly the distance."

Though his tone was even and careful, I still heard the bite. Me? I bit back a smile. I didn't envy him.

I thought of the caravan that we'd taken to Erzos from the port. My back still ached in one place from all the jostling. My poor father had almost been ready to strap our trunks to his back and fly us the rest of the way.

"Supplies and goods still need to be transported," I murmured. "And people *without* wings, of which our numbers are growing. A road to Vyaan would be nice considering it's the nearest travel port off-planet."

"Many of Erzos's citizens don't see it that way," he said.

"What would you want to do if you didn't do this?" I wondered.

"Do what?" he asked, gaze pinned on me.

"Be a *Kyzaire*."

His wings rustled. "It's a ridiculous game to play. I am a *Kyzaire*, and I always will be."

"Humor me."

A sharp exhale. His gaze flitted around the cottage, taking in the ceiling beams of black wood and the large crack in the stone near the door. The floor was in good shape, however—a warm, beige-colored stone that looked gold in the firelight.

"I wanted to create buildings. Homes. Even entire cities," he finally said.

"A builder?" I asked, surprised.

"No," he said. "An architect. A creator. Despite my father's wishes, when I was younger than you are now, I was training with an architect in Laras. Buildings and cities can outlast generations until they become a permanent place in history. Like great stories. Like great legends. Before Erzos passed to me, I wanted to travel throughout the Quadrants to see the great temples of the Bartu. The cathedrals of Hydroni. The undersea cellars of the Drovos. I wanted to explore the ruins of Old Earth. The sky kingdoms of the Ikkalu people. The gambling dens on Gharata, made to withstand the fiercest of storms. The Golden City of Luxiria, one of the oldest in our universe."

My heartbeat seemed to match the soft rhythm of his unexpected words.

"How many of those places have you been to?" he wondered.

"Most of them," I admitted softly. "Though not Old Earth. Or Ikka."

The fire popped in the hearth.

"The Golden City is breathtaking," I told him. "We thought about living there permanently after my father's contract ran out. Because it's one of the few places that won't bat an eye at a Kylorr *and* a human. Luxirians share ancestry with humans. Many of my kind live there or are hybrids."

"Why didn't you stay?"

"The heat," I admitted, smiling. "My father was miserable. The heat there...it can be suffocating during the hot season. So thick you can hardly breathe. The horizon shimmers with it across the sand. If you look out beyond the city, it's like you're looking at something that doesn't exist because nothing ever comes into focus. It's a mirage. Ever changing."

"Are their gods and goddesses as powerful as ours?" he asked, seemingly content to listen.

I laughed. "I didn't stay long enough to find out. But with heat like that, you do need a higher power to pray to. Or else you might not last a single season."

"Tell me what your favorite place was to live," he ordered, the rough rasp of his low voice making more goose bumps spread.

"Rupon," I said immediately.

"The small farming colony you mentioned before?" When I nodded, he asked, "Why?"

"I didn't want for anything there," I said, lifting a shoulder. My throat tightened, remembering those happy days. "We were content. Perfectly happy. We had a little house—a bit like this one actually—on the edge of town. The flowers there are unlike any you've ever seen. So bright and full, and they bloom all year. And the rolling hills. The meadows. The lakes, so clear you can drink from them. It was paradise. The best kept secret in all the Four Quadrants."

His gaze was magnetic, drawing me in. "Why did you leave?"

"My father had a restless spirit," I said, grinning even though I remembered the fight we'd had over Rupon: I'd wanted to stay. He'd wanted to return to Krynn. "He never liked to stay in one place for too long. I was used to it. He loved Rupon, but he told me that it made him miss home. Krynn. He wanted me to know Krynn, to see where he...to see the place he loved most."

Understanding dawned in his gaze.

I didn't want to talk about my father anymore. I remembered something he'd mentioned and said, "If you were training beneath an architect in Laras, then you at least believed you would become one, right? What changed?"

I wanted to understand him even though, at times, I wondered if that was even possible.

"What changed?" he asked, those eyes trapping me in their ice. "I did."

# CHAPTER 17

## KYTHEL

"In what way?" Millie asked.

"I realized that what I wanted was selfish," I told her, that familiar place in my chest pinching. "That what I desired didn't serve my duty to the Kaalium."

Aina's death had been the trigger of it all. Followed by my mother's grief, the words I could never get out of my mind, playing on an endless loop whenever I deviated from my responsibilities. I'd been hearing her voice a lot this week.

Because the truth was that my selfish desires had likely cost Aina her life in the most tragic of ways. I never intended to make that mistake again.

I couldn't.

So why was I here? In this cottage, talking with Millie Seren after midnight, when I should've been in my office finalizing the *lore*-planting schedule and the imports of stone for the South Road from Salaire?

Her hazel eyes shone in the firelight. Her hair was a mess, looped back in a low bun, though tendrils had made a valiant effort to escape.

I could listen to her talk for hours, I realized. A part of me mourned that she wasn't from a noble House on Krynn. A part of me wished she was anyone else except a human server girl at Raana *Dyaan*.

Then I felt like a cold bastard for wishing that. Because it would be so easy. It would make this courtship all the sweeter—not that this *was* a courtship. It never could be. Even despite what I suspected, why her blood called to me so enticingly. I wondered if this was what Azur had felt. This aching madness. How he must've struggled to resist his enemy's daughter, the self-loathing and guilt that must've eaten him up, gnawing and tearing at him.

Only he'd eventually fallen. Surrendered on his knees...but Gemma Hara had knelt beside him too.

"Doing what you want is a luxury that very few people have," Millie said.

"Most humans I've met would disagree with you," I said dryly. "The ones I've met believe you should pursue a life that makes you *happy*."

"Happiness is subjective," she told me. "You would do anything for your family, wouldn't you?"

"Yes," I replied without hesitation.

"Die for them?"

"Yes."

"Though you don't have to be so extreme as to die for them, serving them is still a way of loving them," she said. "And does loving them bring you peace? *Happiness?*"

My answer wasn't as immediate as the others, but I still heard the indisputable truth in the single word. "Yes."

"I've told you before," she said. "I don't envy you, Kythel. I know it must be hard, to sacrifice so much for the sake of your duty. The responsibility you know? Most cannot fathom what it's like. But this is the life you were given. You do the best with it as you can."

I thought on her words, turning them over in my mind like a Drovos wine on my tongue.

"Do you ever wonder where you came from?" I asked her. "Who you would've been had your father not found you?"

"No," she said. I was surprised by her answer. "Because it's not my reality. I've wondered about the circumstances that led my mother to give birth to me and then abandon me in a seedy travel port. Of course I have. I used to imagine that maybe I was stolen. That she was desperate to find me because she loved me so much. But the truth…is that she was probably alone. Scared. Poor. With no other options and nowhere else to turn, with another mouth to feed. I forgave her for that a long time ago."

*She would make a good* Kylaira, came the unwanted thought, sudden but clear. She had the mind for it. The disposition. The patience. The understanding. It was a rare skill not many possessed.

"And truthfully, I'm thankful. My father gave me a wonderful life," she told me, tears blurring her vision, but she made no movement to clear them away. I'd never encountered another being so unashamed of their softer, vulnerable emotions. In fact, Millie smiled through her tears. "A life not many could ever dream of having. And he loved me so much. He taught me how to love openly in a universe that can be harsh and cold and, at times, brutal. Not many can say that about their parents either. He just…he never prepared me for *this*. Being without him. I'm doing my best to learn."

"How did he die?" I wanted to know. "He was off-planet while you stayed behind?"

"Yes," she answered. "He got a contract for an ambassador dinner being hosted on Horrin—one night only. He wasn't supposed to be gone long. We had only been in Erzos for a short time, so I stayed behind, getting settled. Then I got word that he got sick right when he arrived on Horrin. He caught a *borvo* para-site from a contaminated water source at the last travel port. It was an outbreak that got a lot of people sick. My father was one of the few who died from it."

"I remember hearing about it. They shut down the port completely, opened an inter-Quadrant investigation," I said, frowning. "Millie, I'm sorry. It was a tragic accident. Something that you never imagine could even happen with all the regulations we have now."

"I know," Millie said, meeting my eyes and giving me a sad smile. One that felt like a fist squeezing my windpipe. "It was a tragedy. I'm just waiting for it to *feel* better. I don't know if it ever will."

"I can't say I have the answer," I told her, thinking of Aina, my mother. "Maybe with time you just forget how much it hurts. Maybe that's how it becomes manageable."

I wanted to ask if she'd managed to transport his body back to Krynn—for surely, his soul gem could still be created, though I knew *borvo* parasites liked to eat at bone.

Before I got the chance, however, she was rising from the floor.

"Enough talk of this," she said, making a concerted effort to brighten her tone. "It's getting a little too depressing for such a late-night conversation already."

"Do you want me to leave?" I asked, making no effort to move, hoping she would say no. I watched as she went to a familiar blue pack she'd been carrying the day before, settled on top of a wood slab next to the kiln oven. She rummaged around. I heard clinking from deep within.

She returned with a silver flask.

"This," she told me, holding it up for my inspection, toeing her boot against mine, "is the last of my father's whiskey. The *good* whiskey from the Earth colonies. He tracked down a bottle from Everton—*Old* Everton, not *New* Everton."

One of my brows rose, impressed.

"We only drank it on special occasions, and I can think of no better night than to finish it," she said, finality in her tone before I realized what she meant.

"No, Millie, wait—"

She popped the pressurized seal off the flask, a hiss filling the quiet cottage, as I stared at her in disbelief.

"Why would you do that?" I wondered softly, thinking of what she'd said about using her father's compote for the dishes at Raana *Dyaan*. "Don't you want to keep these things for yourself? They're the last remnants you have of him."

"That's not true," she argued. "I have all of him already. And it's like you said about the Ver Teracer art. It would be a waste to keep it all to myself."

A sharp huff left me. I couldn't argue with that. Familiar affection infused in my chest, especially when I saw her smiling. Not a sad smile either, like the one she'd been wearing before. This one was pleased. Excited.

"Things like this are meant to be enjoyed," she informed me, settling down next to me against the wall, closest to the fire.

I tilted my wing to block out the draft coming from the front window when I saw her shiver. Her shoulder brushed my arm, and I felt the heat of her seep through my vest. Her scent was strong. All I wanted was to bury my face into her neck, hold her to me, until I could taste her on my tongue. I struggled to keep my fangs in my skull.

"I don't believe in waiting for a perfect moment that might not ever come," she said. Our eyes met. Closer than we'd ever been before. I could see the strands of gold in her irises, the subtle lines at the corner of her eyes, and the light brown spots across the bridge of her nose. Did all humans have those? I'd never noticed before. "Tonight is the first night that there's been a fire in this hearth in a long time. I think *this* is a perfect moment. Right now. Will you join me?"

Gods, how I wished she was mine. If only for a little while. I would cherish and savor her, like that rare fruit from the Kaazor, until she was gone. A fleeting, ephemeral, beautiful thing in my life until I couldn't have her anymore.

I inclined my head. "Yes. I'd be honored."

She poured thick, amber liquid into the top cup of the flask and then handed me the larger base.

"To perfect moments," Millie toasted softly. "And to *Kyzaires* who know how to make fires and let me trespass on their land."

I couldn't help but chuckle, delighted in her grin, and we held each other's eyes as we took the first sip. I'd never had whiskey before, preferring Drovos wine or fermented brew from the southern regions of the Kaalium, and so I wasn't expecting the *burn*. It felt good, that little path of fire. It was sweeter than I'd expected.

Millie exhaled a slow breath. "You like it?"

The huskiness in her voice from the whiskey only added to that slow burn.

"Yes," I replied, my eyes catching on her lips. "I do."

Her cheeks were flushed—from the whiskey, from the fire, or from my lingering gaze, I couldn't be certain.

Selfish desire added to the heat in my belly. But Millie must've felt it too because she didn't shy away when my head dipped toward her.

*A perfect moment,* I realized.

*How many do we get in a lifetime?* I wondered next, determination rising. Not many.

The moment I kissed her, I knew it was a foolish decision. Right then, however, all I could think was that I would forever regret *not* kissing her. She was correct in her observation that I was the logical brother. The overthinker. The assessor.

Right then? All the reasons I shouldn't do this flew out the drafty cottage window as I turned more fully into her, slinging an arm around her hip and dragging her into me.

She tasted sweet like the whiskey, the heat of her slick tongue agonizingly tempting as I chased it. A small, eager gasp puffed against my lips. She pressed closer, so hot that she felt like she was burning up in my grip.

"Millie," I urged against her lips. *"More."*

Her hand dug into my shoulder as my cock hardened in a rush, the knot at the base beginning to swell and pulse. She teased her dull little teeth against my bottom lip, biting down in a way that made me groan and made my hips buck up. I dragged my free hand up her spine, pushing up her dusty and dirty tunic, encountering warm, smooth flesh.

At my touch, Millie gave a contented sigh, her kiss softening while mine hardened, becoming more demanding. Her scent was driving me steadily toward the lost realm. My mind went hazy, like a cloud of silver *lore* smoke.

Then two things happened at once.

The first...my fangs elongated in a rush and nicked her bottom lip, drawing a sweet bloom of her blood that hit my senses like a damn *akkium* bolt.

*Sublime,* I thought, groaning in astonishment.

At that first taste, all my common sense vanished. Blood rushed downward. Muscles began to swell. I could feel the aching stretch of my claws, clamoring to hold her against me, listening to ancient instincts that told me to *keep her.* That she was mine. That this was *it.* I knew what this was. I'd already suspected, but this was written in *drava* metal. It was undeniable.

Secondly, completely and utterly overcome and distracted, I dropped the oval flask. It clattered, the sound making Millie pull away and gasp, and the last of her father's whiskey spilled out onto the warm stone of the floor.

It took me a moment to realize what I'd done, chasing Millie's lips, needing another taste, only for her to place a steadying hand on my chest to keep me away.

Reality flooded back in.

"Fuck," I cursed, snagging the flask to right it quickly, hardly recognizing my own voice. "Gods, Millie, I'm sorry."

She was breathing hard, her lips swollen and red from the smeared drop of her blood. Her eyes were glassy and wild. She scrambled off me, setting her own whiskey aside, before raising her fingers to her lips, gingerly touching the small cut.

"I'm sorry," I said again. But that brief taste of her blood made my awareness of her rise to new heights. I could *hear* the throb of her heart in her chest, beating in time with my own.

"It's...it's all right, Kythel," she said in a breathless rush, eyeing the pool on the floor as I rose to my full height. "It was an accident."

That was when the grim realization of what I'd just done hit me.

Because I was meant to be distancing myself from her, and now...I'd just tied her to me in a way that I'd never be able to forget. Not for a single day for the remainder of my life.

*"Fuck,"* I breathed, running my hands over my horns, my wings beginning to stretch. I was restless. Energy buzzing under my skin in a way that felt like the beginnings of a rage. She didn't need to see that. I wasn't certain what I would do, that out of control with the tempting, lingering taste of her on my tongue. "Raazos's blood. I need to leave. *Now.*"

She licked her bloodied bottom lip, and it took everything in me not to lunge for her.

"I shouldn't have done that," I growled, backing away to the door, my tone harsh. "I shouldn't have kissed you, Millie. I need to leave. Before I do something we will both regret."

Was that hurt that flickered over her face?

"Go," she said quietly. "I understand. Just go, Kythel."

"I'm sorry," I said again. "I really am, Millie."

She didn't meet my eyes. Instead, she looked down at the pool of whiskey on the floor.

"I know," she said.

Even though I felt like the coldest bastard in the entire

universe, I left, nearly barreling the door right off its hinges once more.

Behind me, our perfect moment was left in ruins, glittering on the floor in a small pool, the taste of my *kyrana's* blood on my tongue.

# CHAPTER 18

## MILLIE

"Millicent," came Lesana's husky voice. "Kitchens with Draan tonight."

The statuesque Kylorr female took the tray I'd been carrying into the lounge before passing it off to an unsuspecting Illaira.

"Illaira, you're on duty in the lounge tonight."

"But the common room is packed tonight," she protested. "Tyaan can't serve there alone."

Lesana leveled her a hard look, one that had the other Kylorr female straightening, righting the tray on her arm.

"I'll pull one of the givers to work the common room with him," Lesana said, "until I can find Grace's replacement." To me, she repeated, "Kitchens."

Which meant Kythel was here.

A fluttering started up in my chest, nerves mingled with excitement. It had been two days since that night in the cottage. He'd avoided me since, and just this morning, I'd told myself that was probably for the best, even as I'd felt disappointment and hurt settle deep.

Now? My treacherous heart leapt at the prospect that he was here as I turned down the hallway to the kitchens. Even Draan's grouchiness wouldn't dampen the sudden lightness that took root inside me. I smiled at him brightly despite the way he grumbled and pointed wordlessly to a mound of *davrin* that needed cleaning.

Two hours later, even when my hair was sticking to my forehead from the steamy kitchen and I'd accidentally cut my finger when my slick grip had slipped from a knife, I was still feeling hopeful. I would tell Draan I was heading out for a break soon.

I wanted to talk with Kythel about that night, especially about that kiss. A kiss I had replayed over and over in my mind.

I didn't want him to think I was angry about the whiskey. It had been an unfortunate accident, but I didn't think I'd expressed that very well to him.

Illaira came into the kitchens.

"Stewed *wylden* for two in the lounge," she said.

She could've placed the order through the Com tablets, but I got the sense that she needed a brief reprieve. I watched her lean against the black metal prep counter, snagging a marinated *laak* egg I'd prepared and popping it into her mouth. Her eyes closed in delight. I smiled.

"How are you holding up?" I asked her, wiping my brow before cleaning my knife on a wet cloth.

"All the nosy gossips flooded in an hour ago," she told me.

"Because the *Kyzaire* is here?" I wondered.

"Because the *Kyzaire* is here with Lyris of House Arada," she corrected. "There have been rumors throughout the villages that an engagement is inevitable."

My stomach bottomed out. "What?"

Illaira took another *laak* egg. Through the mouthful she said, "This would mark their first appearance together, and the moon winds *are* tomorrow night. So I'd wager the rumors are actually *true.*"

I nodded wordlessly because I didn't know what else to do.

Mustering up a smile that felt stretched over my skull, I looked down at the *wylden* I was prepping and commented, "Lucky girl."

My voice sounded far away. I couldn't believe it. Why hadn't he said anything?

*He didn't need to,* I knew. It was none of my business what a *Kyzaire's* personal decisions were...even if he had given me the best, most surprising kiss of my life. Just thinking about it sent shivers trailing up my spine.

"Not luck," Illaira said. "Circumstance. Noble Houses marry noble Houses. It's always been this way. House Arada's influence stretches wide."

She glanced at Draan when she said it, but his back was turned. I remembered what Grace had said about Lesana—that she was connected to the House, that she was indebted to Hanno. I wondered how Draan felt about it all.

*Noble Houses marry noble Houses.*

And House Kaalium was the most noble of them all.

"I'm going to get some air," I informed Draan. Illaira hummed as I slung the dirtied rag into the washing pile, but she was too busy poking at a *davrin*-wrapped puffed-pastry ball to notice me leave.

I didn't go outside, however. Instead, I changed directions, heading to the storage room adjacent to the lounge, the only one that shared a wall with it. I closed the door behind me and went to the hidden viewing window, digging my fingernail into the smooth stone until I found the latch and pulled it open.

Not many knew about this. I only did because I'd stumbled on Lesana spying in here once. There was a painting on the back lounge wall that lined up with this window. No one in the lounge would ever know that Lesana sometimes spied on her guests and her servers.

I went on my tiptoes to look through the window, my heart pounding in my chest, making me feel dizzy. It didn't take me long to find Kythel. He was sitting in a private back booth, lined with black, supple *onu* leather, a goblet of Drovos wine in front of him, his long, strong fingers curled around it lazily.

Across from him sat who I assumed was Lyris of House Arada.

*Beautiful* was my first thought.

Lyris was stunningly beautiful because of course she would be.

She had dark indigo-blue hair that shimmered in the orb lighting and bright, light blue eyes that contrasted with it. Their color was similar to Kythel's. Her light gray skin was smooth and unblemished. She held herself gracefully—her lithe wings, decorated in silver cuffs along her wing joints, tucked against the booth's back. She was in a sharply cut vest that molded to her curves and blue leather pants that had silver metal running up the sides, visually elongating her strong legs, even sitting.

Hanno approached the couple. He placed a hand on Lyris's shoulder, interrupting their conversation with a wide, pleased grin. A marriage between the two Houses would be fortunate for everyone involved. No wonder Lesana had threatened me over being a blood giver for Kythel. She didn't want anyone getting in Lyris's way.

Kythel was smiling, his eyes pinned on his companion, who was chuckling at whatever Hanno was saying. He looked different tonight. More present. Maybe it was a mask, I didn't know, but all I could see was the way he *looked* at her.

*He likes beautiful things, remember?*

It was an unwanted thought but undeniable. He filled his keep with beautiful, expensive things. He'd handpicked every last detail of his home. He never had a hair out of place, a clasp undone. He held himself to a high standard for his people, for himself…

And Lyris of House Arada suited him perfectly.

A perfect Kylorr couple. A perfect match of two great Houses.

A hot streak of jealousy seared through my chest at the realization. It surprised me. I'd never been the jealous type. Not even in my previous two relationships. One had been with a human man on Qapot'a, kind but restless like me. The other had been a brief love affair with a shy Luxirian male, who I still thought of fondly.

I'd never been jealous over either. I remembered them with happy softness. Neither relationship had ended poorly. But neither had lasted because of the nature of my father's work. They'd known it. I'd known it.

And yet...

All Kythel had done was kiss me, and I was on the verge of throwing up at the sight of him with his perfect, perfect counterpart.

The jealousy was shocking. Disappointing, even, because it was such a wild emotion that I didn't understand or even have the right to feel. Kythel wasn't mine. He never would be.

Stumbling back from the viewing window, I slapped the concealed door closed, plunging me into darkness in the storage room.

This time, I really *did* need air.

But I didn't take the back entrance out of Raana *Dyaan*. Maybe I was being a little foolish and impulsive. I wasn't thinking clearly—that much was for certain.

Instead, I walked down the main hallway toward the front entrance. Lesana wasn't standing guard at her usual post, so I paused at the door into the lounge.

I was sure I looked like hell with my sticky hair and dirtied tunic and flushed cheeks—the complete opposite of Lyris, who looked as polished as the diamonds I'd seen glittering on high society ladies' fingers on New Inverness.

Across the lounge, Kythel's gaze immediately zeroed in on me. As if he could *sense* me near. And maybe he could.

I watched his smile slowly fade. He straightened in his seat, those faceted wintry eyes holding mine. But I couldn't read the expression in them, and I suddenly found that it was difficult to breathe, my lungs tightening.

Hanno turned to see what had claimed the *Kyzaire*'s attention. He caught sight of me, but I was already walking away, through the high, arched doors of Raana *Dyaan*.

I needed air. Desperately.

Because I felt my own anger rise. Not at Kythel. At *myself*. Was I really so foolish as to believe that the kiss had meant something to him? Of course it hadn't. And I hated how dependent and needy that made me feel.

I prided myself on my ability to care, albeit a little too deeply and too easily, for others. But I loved people. I loved their beauty and their ugliness and their flaws and the things that made them different and unique.

I cared about Kythel. Perhaps more than I should've.

I wasn't afraid to throw myself into someone else. Sometimes I leapt without thinking—a gift and a curse. Father had called it my soft heart. But he'd always warned me it would get me into trouble.

Maybe I needed to learn to not give my heart so freely to those who would be careless with it without a second thought.

Slipping into the darkness of the alley, I went to my tree, touching the rough bark, letting it hold me up as I breathed. I dragged in slow breaths. Already the night air was cooling me off, making my thoughts calm, smoothing out the jagged edges of my jealousy.

Footsteps. I recognized the cadence of them, the weight as they struck the cobblestones, the whisper of his wings.

"Millie."

# CHAPTER 19

## KYTHEL

"*D*o you think I look beautiful tonight?" came Lyris's pointed question.

There was a soft smile smudged across her dark lips.

It was the first interesting question she'd asked me all night, and my grin came easily, dropping into place—a familiar feeling taking hold as if I were on display at a ball or a party with noble families that we didn't truly need to impress. *They* had always needed to impress *us*. I got the distinct impression that that was what Lyris was trying to do.

She was different tonight. More…desperate. It clung to her like the perfumed oil across her neck, a cloying scent that made my nose twitch. I wondered if her father was beginning to get nervous that my proposal had not yet been given after I'd refused a meeting with him.

I held her gaze. "Every male in this room thinks that you're beautiful, Lyris."

She knew it too. But that obvious beauty, frustratingly enough, I'd begun to find bland. Her features were in perfect symmetry. Her skin was like Hindras silk. Her eyes had a tapered shape, the tilted corners giving her a sultry appearance. She had beautiful eyes and perfectly tailored clothes that I knew had cost her father a small fortune.

And yet...I was looking for the flaws. A chip in the perfect, cold marble. I wanted to see it. I craved imperfection now, like Millie's strange beauty. But I found none in Lyris.

Hanno appeared at his niece's side. His hand dropped to her shoulder. Tonight I had been ambushed by House Arada when I'd arrived at the *dyaan*, a realization I hadn't appreciated in the slightest, but I had invited Lyris to join me nonetheless, knowing it was the right step in the inevitable direction I needed to take.

"I've sent for some *wylden* from the kitchens for you both with my compliments," Hanno said. "You must try it, *Kyzaire*. I know you appreciate good food, and Draan has proven himself to be an exceptional culinarian."

I knew it wasn't Draan alone, however, but I said nothing, only giving him a small, diplomatic smile in return. Millie must've been in the kitchens tonight, and at the very least, I would consume whatever she gave me with pleasure. Because right then it was the only way I could have her.

A familiar tingle spread around the roots of my wing and trailed down my spine. I caught sight of her before I caught her scent.

Millie was standing in the hallway just beyond the threshold of the room. I straightened like an *akkium* jolt passed through me. I forgot Lyris. I forgot Hanno. The lounge seemed to melt around me, and I felt despair rise. It would always be like this, I knew. I would always crave her.

A *fucking* blood mate.

A *kyrana*.

One of the oldest and most sacred of bonds among the Kylorr, and I'd found mine in a human female who could offer me and my House nothing of true value. Necessary value in a time that might lead to war.

I'd already cursed Raazos and Alaire and Gaara and Zor for their cruel trick. Was this punishment for Aina? Punishment for Ruaala, even? Perhaps.

The look in Millie's eyes, however, had me forgetting all the reasons why she was wrong for me. I saw the hurt in them. The vulnerability. The chip in the marble I'd been looking for in Lyris.

She looked a mess. Tired and sweating from the kitchens and angry and sad. But my eyes *ate* at her like I was starving for my next meal. She felt *real*.

Hanno turned. Millie slipped away. I stood.

"I need to speak with someone," I said, my gaze still on the place where Millie had stood. "My apologies—I'll return shortly."

I left without a backward glance, striding through the lounge, ignoring the lingering looks cast my way. I followed Millie's trail until I left Raana *Dyaan* and went down the side alley.

She had her palms spread across the trunk of the bleeding tree, forehead lowered against it.

"Millie."

She turned and then forced a small smile.

"Good evening, *Kyzaire*," came her voice, oddly stilted and humorless.

I stilled for just a brief moment before I was stalking closer. Until she was just a hand's span away.

"*Kyzaire* now?" I rasped, a little burn of irritation beginning to melt the boredom I'd felt for the majority of the evening.

"How has your night been? Enjoyable, I hope."

"What are you doing?" I asked her, hunching down so our eyes were level. "What are you *doing*, Millie?"

Her chin tipped up. She'd managed to shield the soft, hurt, tender place I'd witnessed moments before across the room of the smoky lounge. Now there was a bright spark of anger.

Her scent flooded my senses, and my gaze dropped to her lips.

She crossed her arms in front of herself, and the soft material of my vest bumped against them.

A smirk pulled at the corners of my mouth.

"I see," I purred softly, stepping closer. There was a prick at the back of my neck. A warning. I knew this wasn't smart. Nothing with Millie ever was, and yet...

"You see what?" she asked, her tone equally silky.

"Her name is Lyris of House Arada," I told her. "The daughter of a noble House."

"I know who she is," Millie said, smiling. "Why would you think I care?"

"Don't you?" I asked, liking that she was jealous.

That fake, barbed smile slowly died. My own smirk died with it because I saw Millie underneath. The imperfect marble—cracked and chipped and beautiful.

"I do," she admitted, looking down at our booted feet, nearly touching, hers half the size of mine. "But even I know I have no right to care. You're a *Kyzaire* of the Kaalium. From a noble family. I've heard your legacy whispered about across the *universe.*"

I frowned, this conversation not going the way I'd wanted it to.

"Millie—"

"I do *see,*" she said. The sad smile that tipped up her lips made me want to raze my claws through the trunk of the bleeding tree behind her, a violent impulse that surprised even me. She patted her hand against my chest, the movement oddly dismissive and cavalier. "You don't have to worry about what happened a couple nights ago—the kiss. I know it meant nothing. I'm happy it happened because it felt right in that moment. But I know it was just...one of those things."

"One of what things?" I growled, losing all lingering amusement. I'd been ready to come here tonight to tell Millie everything *she* was telling me. Only she was beating me to it, and it fucking *ached* more than I'd expected it to. I didn't like it. Not one bit.

"I've kissed enough men throughout the Quadrants to know that they don't always need to mean *anything*," she informed me, shrugging. "It was impulsive and fun. Nothing more. We shared a nice moment, and that's all it will be. I understand. You don't have to worry about me following you around like some lovesick puppy after one little kiss."

*Lovesick puppy?*

Visions of her kissing *enough men* flitted through my mind, and...I didn't like the way that made me feel either.

"I know who I am," she said, patting my chest again. "I know who you are."

Why did this feel like a dismissal?

My hackles rose. Pride too, perhaps.

"It didn't mean anything to you?" I asked, snagging her hand from my chest, intertwining her fingers with my own. "Have you not thought about it? Have you not replayed it over and over and over in your mind since? Because I have."

A shuddering, surprised breath blew from her lips. She hadn't expected me to admit to that. It was written plainly on her face. I liked taking her off guard. I liked shocking her.

"I want to feel it again," I said, lowering our hands to the side so I could step against her body. Desire, frustratingly urgent, rushed through my blood. My fangs were already elongating, my mouth watering for her taste. She was so small against me, so warm. A little heartbeat against my belly.

I wanted to make a liar out of her.

So easily she thought she could dismiss me. Didn't she know? My pride burned bright, and I would not be leveled by a maddening, beautiful human woman of all beings.

A flicker of anger sparked in her eyes.

I pressed her against the tree, dipping my head. She turned her face, and my lips landed across her cheek. It didn't deter me

—I trailed my mouth down, skimming the tops of my fangs across her neck, more of a tease for me than for her. I was physically shaking with the control that took, and I knew I was playing a dangerous game, one I might not win.

"You're betrothed."

Those words drew me up short. I lifted my lips from her neck, my unfocused gaze steady on her.

"No," I said dryly. "I'm not."

She blinked. I dipped my head, skimming my mouth across the corner of her pink lip. Then I kissed the tip of her nose, across her cheekbone as she processed those words.

"You're not?"

"No."

"Oh."

"Satisfied?" I growled, trying to stop my hands from trembling. But I remembered that brief hit of her blood storming my senses. The strength. The power. The fear. I wanted it again but knew I couldn't have it. That made me all the more desperate. "Would it really matter even if I was? You want me too, *sasiral*."

That gaze burned. "Of course it would matter."

"Liar."

She gasped, but I threaded my hand into her hair, pulling so her mouth was raised up to me, her neck exposed.

I studied her like this. Her chest heaved, her back bowed into me. There was a slight edge of a glare in those wide hazel eyes, a glare that made my lips curl and my cock hard. I'd felt *feral* ever since I'd tasted her blood. My mood had been black. This moment was the best I'd felt since that night in the cottage.

"Kiss me," I ordered. "Show me how little it means to you."

I lowered my lips until they brushed hers. A taste. A tease.

Did she think me the cold, logical brother right now? Little did they all know, I was *burning up* inside the majority of the time.

"Do it, little Seren," I purred. "My little fallen star from the universe. I am a *Kyzaire*, after all, and you should know better than to disobey me. Or—"

She lifted onto her toes, her mouth crashing into mine. Immediately, I pushed her roughly back into the tree, angry and needing her and desperate for her kiss. I squeezed my fist into her short, silky hair to keep it from trembling. I devoured her just as she devoured me. Our tongues stroked together, tangling. I dropped her other hand, and my hard touch roamed, possessive and brash and shameless, squeezing her to me.

Her own hands curled into my chest. I felt the bite of her fingernails through the thick fabric, the prick making me buck my hips against her. Millie was making tiny desperate sounds in the back of her throat, threading through her lips and between mine. I groaned, my wings wrapping around us, shielding us from the chill of the night until we were cocooned together.

"Millicent," came the sharp word, piercing through our private veil.

She stiffened in my arms.

Whipping my head around, I growled, the intrusion unwelcome. Ancient instincts rose—ones that told me to protect what was mine, to keep what was mine. I was still dazed from the kiss, from the haze of her scent. My *kyrana's* scent. It took me a moment to realize that Millie was utterly frozen, her face paling in the darkness when she spied who stood at the bottom of the alley's path.

"My apologies, *Kyzaire*," Lesana said, her tone cool though she wore a serene smile that belied the sharpness in her gaze. "Millicent is needed in the kitchens. *Now.*"

# CHAPTER 20

## MILLIE

Kythel's palm was pressed to my belly, the touch oddly soothing and protective. Intimate, even. But I gripped his wrist, pulling the touch away, and slipped between the gap of his wing and the tree trunk.

I felt sinking dread when I met Lesana's eyes. Completely opposite from the passionate rush I'd experienced in Kythel's kiss, the way my heart had beat madly in my breast and I'd clamored for more. *Needed* more. A momentary insanity.

*And a costly one,* I thought next, recognizing the icy anger in her gaze.

"Millie," Kythel said, his voice a rumbling growl. Husky and dark. Different.

Meeting his eyes, I told him, "Go back to your guest, *Kyzaire.* You've already kept her waiting long enough."

His jaw tightened, that familiar mask dropping into place as he straightened to his full height. I swallowed the thick lump of regret in my throat and stepped away from him, my strides eating up the distance between Lesana and myself.

I left Kythel in the dark alley, following the seething lady of

Raana *Dyaan* inside. She wove her way down the main entrance hallway, past the lounge doors, past the bustling common room, the laughter and commotion making me feel mildly ill.

She led me to her private office, the one she shared with Draan when he was helping with the accounts and client payments. Closing the door behind her, she swung to face me.

The stinging slap that landed on my cheek made me cry out in surprise. I stumbled back, the force of her strength sending me into the wall. My hand flew up to my face. It *burned*.

What was most unsettling was that Lesana merely clasped her hands behind her wings afterward, leveling me a steady stare. Outwardly, she didn't even look angry. Only, I saw the shielded fury in the lines of her mouth, which was even quirked up at one corner.

"I trusted you," she said.

The accusatory words filled the office. I was beginning to regain my composure, my shock over being struck. I'd been struck once before, when I'd been a child. We'd been living in a wealthy household on Bartu, my father employed by the owners. I'd been friends with their son, who'd been of similar age to myself. We'd been playing. In our roughhousing, he'd broken a priceless vase, an heirloom of the family. He'd blamed it on me, and his mother had struck me with her rough, taloned hand, leaving fresh welts of red blood.

My father had been furious. I'd never seen him so angry in my life—my normally calm and serene father had cursed up a storm and smashed another vase on his way out. Despite the fact that we'd needed the credits desperately, he'd packed us up and we'd left that very moment, leaving the couple in the lurch for a large dinner party they'd been throwing the next day. I remember the Bartu boy crying black tears as we'd left, sad to be losing his friend.

That memory surfaced now. Even though the Bartu mother

had drawn my blood, it was Lesana's strike that had hurt even more.

"*I trusted you.* I took you into my *dyaan* when you had *nothing*," she said quietly. "When you were sleeping in a storage room of an inn and stealing scraps of food from the market. And this is how you show me your respect? Your gratitude for my kindness?"

She was going to fire me. I could feel it, a terrifying chill in my bones.

"I'm sorry," I said quickly, desperate and frightened at the prospect that the steady stream of credits I'd had coming in would dry up in a single moment. I was barely even halfway to my goal to get passage off Krynn to Horrin. "Lesana, I'm sorry. He hasn't fed from me! It was just a kiss. A stupid kiss. It won't happen again, I promise. Just please...*please* let me stay. I'll do whatever you ask."

"Draan warned me," Lesana continued, like I'd never even spoken. "He told me I was being too kind. Now my kindness has threatened *everything*."

"It's threatened nothing," I said, adding strength I didn't feel to my voice. I needed to reason with her. It was the only way. "Lesana, listen to me. *Please.* I will do whatever it takes to prove that—"

"You will not be the one to ruin this for my House," she said, her voice clipped but soft. "*You.* A human who doesn't even belong on Krynn. Who comes from nothing. Who has no one. And yet *you* risk it all for our great House."

Grace had said Lesana came from House Arada. Which meant that Lyris of House Arada was her family too. Lyris, who was rumored to be soon betrothed to the *Kyzaire* of Erzos, though he had assured me that the engagement didn't exist.

But Lesana certainly thought there was reason to suspect it did.

"He's fed from others here," I said softly, trying to reason with her, my cheek beginning to throb with my heartbeat. "Why have you not thrown them from the *dyaan*? I don't understand."

"You are a poison," she replied. The hurtful words flung from her lips like they stung her tongue. "You cannot stay. You will only destroy everything we have worked toward."

My lungs squeezed. I stepped forward, reaching for her hand. "No, Lesana, you don't mean that. I've worked hard for you. For Draan. I—"

"Pack your trunk and leave. I don't want to see you here ever again."

"Lesana," I said, taking a deep breath, even as wild panic infused in my very soul. "Please. I'm just trying to earn enough credits to reach my father. He died. A few months ago. His body is going to be burned soon, and I need to reach him before—"

A sharp laugh, beautiful but cutting, burst from her lips. "You think I don't know about your father?" she asked.

My eyes widened. "How?"

She tilted her chin back, observing me through slitted eyes.

"Grace told me," she said. "Before she left."

A sharp prick of disbelief stabbed at my chest. "What? No. She wouldn't do that."

"Yes, she told me all about your father and his letters. To Ruaala, was it? She showed me them herself. We laughed about them, how pathetic they seemed," she said coolly.

Why would Grace do that? Hurt and betrayal made my tongue feel like lead in my mouth. All I could do was stand there and feel like the floor was sliding up past my ankles.

"I know *everything* that happens here, Millicent. Don't make the mistake in thinking I don't. You broke your promise. You broke my trust. Now you'll never reach your father in time."

The cold cruelty in her words made my throat tighten until it felt like I couldn't breathe.

"Learn this lesson well, my love," she said softly. "Don't cross me—or House Arada—again. You won't like the consequences."

Her smile felt like it was shredding me into scraps of parchment, my skin fluttering to the floor in a heap.

Her smile sharpened even further.

"Now get out of my *dyaan*."

# CHAPTER 21

## MILLIE

*I*t seemed like I'd blinked and I was in my cottage in Stellara.

*Not mine,* I corrected. *Theirs.*

I didn't remember packing my trunk from my room at Raana *Dyaan*, but it was sitting on the beige stone floor next to the hearth. I didn't remember leaving the *dyaan*, but the thick mud on my boots and the dampness that had crept in through the worn toe told me I must've.

Pulling out my Halo orb from my pocket, I navigated to my account with trembling, cold hands. The number projected upward, a beam of blue light. I was nearly 4,000 credits short of my immediate goal, and now I had no way to make up the difference.

"Not entirely true, Millie," I whispered to myself, wiping my wet eyes though I hadn't realized I'd been crying.

There was one option left.

I didn't know what the hour was or how long it had been since I'd last left Raana *Dyaan*, but I dragged myself up from the floor. Time was a luxury I didn't have. If he said no, I needed to know as soon as possible.

I turned my Halo orb onto a yellow glow to illuminate my way and set out from the cottage, heading south. It was raining, I realized, a soft pelt that got harder and harder the longer I traveled. But I wouldn't be deterred. I needed an answer.

After a mile or so, I used the sharpened edges of the turreted keep to guide my way until I came to a stone wall that bordered Stellara's land. I followed it until I found a crumbled edge just short enough to crawl over. Then I made my way to the front entrance of Erzos's keep.

At the imposing, black arched doors, I raised my cold fist to knock but then thought better of it. Kythel likely wouldn't be near enough to answer, and I didn't need to be turned away by a bewildered, suspicious keeper. Instead, I went around the side of the keep, looking for windows that were still lit at this late hour. He was awake. I knew he was.

The north wing of the keep was glowing, illuminated like a star from within. There was one window, one that took up almost an entire wall, with a view out to Stellara. Inside, I saw a shadow move. I recognized the flicker of a hearth. My teeth were chattering, my hands numb.

Taking a deep breath, I shouted, "Kythel!"

My voice echoed in the cold night, jarringly loud, even against the rain.

A figure appeared in the window. Nerves crept up in my chest, the first emotion I'd felt since Lesana's office, banishing the strange numbness that had taken hold.

The window was pushed open, and I saw wings flare once he stepped out on the balcony. He shot down, tilting the wide expanse of those wings until he was barreling straight at me.

Kythel landed with a grim expression, his gaze raking over me, before I was swept up into his arms and he was launching us back up to the open window.

The first touch of warmth sank into my chilled bones when

we were inside the room—an office, I realized—and Kythel slammed the arched window closed. I was shaking. Violently.

"What in Raazos's blood are you doing, *sasiral?*" he asked me, his tone angry but concerned, pressing his hand to my back to guide me to the fire. "You're practically blue!"

"I-I need to as-ask you something," I said. A steady trickle of water ran down my neck. My hair was soaked. Kythel tore at my tunic when I realized my clothes were sopping wet, my nipples so hard and tight they were painful.

"It can wait," he growled, a grimly determined expression on his features. "I need to get you warm."

The laces on my pants were loosened. Kythel tugged, and they sagged to my ankles. Next, he crouched, pulling at my boots. They made a wet squelch sound as he tossed them into a corner.

I was naked before I knew it, shivering as I met his blue eyes in shock.

"Sit by the fire," he ordered me, snagging a nearby Halo orb that floated by. He tapped it, and it began to glow, radiating heat. Pressing it into my hands, he said, "Stay here."

He left the office.

The warmth from the orb *hurt*. But my hands were so cold that it felt like needles were stabbing into my flesh. I clutched the orb tighter, crouching down near the fire. My muscles felt tight and tense. Every icy slide of water that dripped from my hair, down onto my shoulders, my chest, made me shake violently. My teeth chattered, but I was too cold to be embarrassed.

This had been reckless. I should've, at the very least, tucked my father's cloak around me to keep most of the rain from soaking into my own clothes and boots.

Kythel returned. I couldn't read his expression as he tossed a large *hot* blanket around my shoulders—one that smelled like him. I nearly gasped in relief, dropping the Halo orb to clutch it between my hands, wrapping it tight. Next he placed something small on the crown of my head. I heard a whistling rush and felt a pulsing wave reverberate down my skull. Water droplets flung away in all directions. Next came a wave of heat, and to my amazement, when I lifted my hand to the strands of my hair, it was completely dry.

My scalp tingled. Kythel lifted the small device away, tossing it onto the floor as he knelt next to me.

Warmth slowly thawed the freeze in my bones. And only when I stopped shivering, only when my teeth stopped clicking together and my toes didn't feel like they were detached from my feet did I look over at him.

The office was quiet. Rain pelted the window. The fire cracked, especially when Kythel tapped into the Halo screen and increased the flame size.

He'd been with Lyris of House Arada tonight. He'd kissed me outside Raana *Dyaan*—an angry, passionate, consuming kiss that I'd craved. My reality had been upended since I'd last seen him, even though it had been mere hours earlier.

"I'm okay now," I informed him quietly. "Thank you."

"What in Raazos's blood possessed you to come here tonight?" he asked me, his voice low. It would have sounded comforting, soothing if I didn't hear the hint of a sharpened edge to it. "In this storm?"

Exhaustion mingled with my nerves. But I needed to ask the question, even if it ruined everything between us. I hated being this person, but it would be a transaction, wouldn't it? He would get what he wanted. I would get what I wanted.

"Did you mean it?" I asked. "When you said you wanted me as your blood giver?"

Immediately, his whole body stilled. Those blue-jewel eyes fastened on me with an intense scrutiny that made me feel like squirming in place.

I clutched the blanket tighter, drawing it around myself like it was armor.

"You told me to name my price," I continued when he said

nothing. Doubt began to creep into me, making me feel a little sick. "Does your offer still stand? Or have you changed your mind?"

He remained silent, and the sickening feeling in my gut intensified. I began to shake again.

"You have," I said quietly, turning my face away to hide my disappointment. My *despair*. Because I didn't know if I would get enough credits in time now. Unless I asked Grace for help...but then again, she'd betrayed me. Why would I trust her after what she'd told Lesana?

Out of the corner of my eye, I saw Kythel's hand shoot forward. He snagged my chin, turning me to face him.

"I haven't changed my mind."

Hope rose as I regarded him. Even still, I couldn't help but notice the way the words seemed to tear themselves out of his throat.

"Truly?" I whispered.

"What's your price?" he asked, just as softly.

I took in a deep breath. "I need you to secure me passage to Horrin and then back to Krynn."

Kythel's eyes narrowed, but otherwise he didn't move. "Horrin? Your father?" he guessed.

"His body is still there," I admitted. The weight of those words dragged my shoulders down, and I curled tighter into myself. "Horrin burns their unclaimed dead. There's not much time left before their next cycle. I'm afraid that he'll be lost to me. To Krynn. His soul gem... He wanted to be here. With Ruaala. That's why we came here. Because he wanted my soul to attach itself to Krynn, to your gods. So that when I...when *I* die I can find him in Alara."

I knew I was rambling, but soft realization had formed over Kythel's features.

"What's your father's name?"

"Joss."

He snagged a Halo orb when it floated near. He brought up the Com screen, and it flickered in the air between us. I studied him through the blue light, even as a figure appeared, a projection of a Kylorr male I didn't recognize.

"Setlan," Kythel greeted, inclining his head.

"*Kyzaire*," Setlan murmured, though I heard the humor in his voice. There were loud voices in the background. Laughter. Music. It sounded like he was in a club on Qapot'a, especially when I heard the warbling of their language nearby.

"I have need of you," Kythel said.

"That's a given," the other male replied, raising a glass tumbler filled with a foamy liquid to his lips. "You don't make a habit of calling me in the middle of the night on Krynn."

"Joss Seren. His body is being held on Horrin. Find him and have him transported back to Erzos immediately."

The air in my lungs seemed to freeze. I stared at Kythel, my heart pumping in my chest in disbelief. In relief so stunning that it didn't even feel real. This was a dream. Surely it was a dream. But if it were, my hands wouldn't feel like they were burning from the cold as they warmed up and tears wouldn't be stinging my eyes, blurring my vision.

"Consider it done," Setlan said before draining his tumbler. It hit an unseen surface with a metal clang, and then he was rising, wings unfurling. "I'll update you in the morning."

Kythel ended the Com call, and the blue pixels dropped away, giving me a clear, unmarred view of him.

"You see, *sasiral?*" Kythel murmured, turning those eyes to me, a hunger I recognized from the alley outside Raana *Dyaan* sparking in them. "How easy it is."

I could cry. Instead, overcome with joy and gratitude and hope, I surprised him when I leaped at him. He caught me with a grunt, a chuff of a sharp laugh following.

But I silenced it when I kissed him. I ignored all the reasons why kissing him was a bad idea. For one, it blurred the lines between us. Being his blood giver was a transaction—nothing more. A contract, the terms of which hadn't even been fully laid out. How long would he want me? Only for three feedings, his maximum? Or more? And would he want sex too? Like Grace's agreement with her noble couple?

I didn't give those intrusive thoughts any mind. Not right then. He was a friend. And he'd just given me the greatest gift of all.

"Thank you," I breathed against his lips. His hand slipped into my dry hair, cradling the back of my skull. I leaned away to kiss his cheeks, one then the other. The sharp slant of his nose. Against his forehead, I whispered, "Thank you."

After kissing his brow, I pulled away, just far enough to meet his eyes. The blanket had slipped down my shoulders, baring my nakedness, but Kythel didn't break my gaze.

It felt like there was a charge of *akkium* power in the air, raising the hairs on my arms. Kythel's eyes were hungry. His lips were still parted from my kiss. His arms were around me. I realized he was cradling me in his lap.

But then I watched a metal wall slam into place, steeling those jeweled eyes.

Kythel rose, bringing me up with him as I nervously adjusted the blanket around my shoulders.

"I'm sorry," I told him, feeling foolish for acting on my impulses. "I shouldn't have…"

"One month," he told me. "In exchange for bringing your father's body back to Krynn, I want you to be my blood giver until the next moon winds. After that, our agreement will be ended."

There was detachment in his voice. I realized what he was doing. He wanted to keep this *clean*. Neat. He wanted me to stay in a box in his mind. While that stung a little, if

I was being truthful with myself, I couldn't say I blamed him.

"All right," I said, nodding. If he wanted to keep this purely professional, I would too. He was giving me what I wanted. What I needed. For that, I would forever be grateful to him. With one hand, I held the edges of the blanket together. The other hand stretched out into the empty space between us. "This is how humans seal agreements."

Kythel took my hand. Instead of shaking it, as I'd expected, he turned my palm over in his own. Holding my breath, I felt him trace a line down the center of my palm with the tip of his claw.

Before I could blink, he swiped, so quick that it was a blur. In shock, I watched the shallow cut slowly bleed, tentative at first, as he cut his own palm.

A strange sound reverberated from his chest. Low and deep. It almost sounded like he was in pain.

With wide eyes, I met Kythel's unreadable gaze.

"This," he rasped, "is how the Kylorr seal agreements."

With that, he pressed our palms together, our blood mingling. I was in a daze. The metallic scent of my own blood floated up between us, coupled with the tang of his own. My heart was pounding too roughly, making me dizzy. All I could see were his eyes.

His pupils dilated further in the dimly lit office, blocking out the blue until there was only blackness.

His voice was rough. Guttural. "I want my first feeding now, *sasiral*."

"All right," I breathed. No use in waiting. And I would be lying if I said I wasn't curious, if I didn't want it too.

The fire popped in the hearth. The whole room felt entirely too warm as he stepped into me, our hands still intertwined, our blood slippery and hot. I craned my neck back to look up at him.

"Where—" My voice cracked, and I cleared it, though it did nothing to help its huskiness. "Where do you want to feed?"

Kythel's wings shook behind him before he jerked them inward, tucking them against his back. I was confused when I spied trepidation in his eyes, just a hint of worry. For me?

"You don't have to worry about me," I told him, reaching out my other hand to press against his chest in comfort. "I know what's involved. I've been around enough blood givers and Kylorr, don't you think?"

"I'm not worried about you," he informed me, voice blackening. My brows furrowed. His tone implied he was worried about himself. But why?

His gaze was pinned to the crook of my neck. Ah. Slowly, I reached up to push my hair to one side, baring my neck. I tilted it, staring forward at the rise and fall of his wide chest. He made a sound in the back of his throat, dark and needful.

"Kythel," I said softly, stepping into him, reaching up for his own neck to guide him down. "It's just a feeding. How many times have you done this in your lifetime? Don't worry."

I was using the words as a balm for myself—because I was on the verge of trembling like a leaf in a storm.

At my words, I heard his soft curse. A puff of hot breath trailed over the sensitive column of my neck, and I shivered when he pressed into me. He let his body go. The tension fell from him like a waterfall, and I gasped when those warm lips kissed my neck. Confused, too, when I knew he'd wanted to keep this...detached.

"I don't know how I'll react," came the rasping confession. "Don't be frightened, whatever happens, *sasiral*."

My brow furrowed. "What do you—"

A sudden prick of pain came but one that felt heavy and oddly *comforting*. Then it melted away, only to be replaced by a dizzying tug that I rose onto my tiptoes to prolong. A sensation unlike any other, one that made heat scorch a trail through my body, settling in the junction of my thighs.

"What is…" I whispered in disbelief. Realization hit. "Oh gods."

A groan tumbled from Kythel's throat, muffled against my neck.

*No, no, no,* I thought. This wasn't what a feeding should've been. It didn't make any sense. I'd worked at a bloody *dyaan*. I knew what a feeding entailed. It was a service. Nothing more. And it certainly shouldn't feel like *this*.

Unless…

An inkling of suspicion took hold, but Kythel clasped me tighter, dragging me fully against his hard, unyielding form. His tongue lapped at the bite, hot and slick and ravenous and seeking, and I felt another heavy pull, one that made my eyes roll back and my knees buckle.

He caught me as I moaned, my clit beginning to tingle and ache and throb.

"Kythel!" I gasped.

I felt the pinch of his claws prick into my hips, the heat of his blood from his cut palm seeping into the blanket. It was becoming too much. Overwhelming. I was scared. Scared of what this might mean.

*The agreement,* came the rational thought.

My father.

Kythel had given me what I'd asked for. Without even blinking. In mere moments, he had fixed a deep fear that had been plaguing me for months.

So, instead of pulling away, I decided to submit to the pleasure. I slid my hand into his silken black hair, holding him to me. He groaned, the unmistakable hard press of his cock becoming all the more evident with every passing moment.

He felt it too. This madness. I was glad I wasn't alone.

He'd suspected too, hadn't he?

*I don't know how I'll react. Don't be frightened, whatever happens,* sasiral, was what he'd said before he'd bit me.

He'd *known*. That was why my scent called to him. Why he'd wanted me to name my price. Because that was how desperate he'd been to taste my blood. It all made sense.

"Take what you need," I breathed. "Take everything you need from me, Kythel."

It was very likely that I was his blood mate, after all.

# CHAPTER 22

## KYTHEL

*H*er voice sounded both far away and too close. But there was no denying the need, the dizzying relief, the aggressive urgency that her words triggered within me.

"Take everything you need from me, Kythel."

The first taste of her blood had me spiraling. The second, third, fourth pull? The luscious, silken heat of her blood as it soaked my tongue?

I was in ecstasy. I couldn't get enough. I didn't know if I would—or could—ever be satisfied again. Not like this.

My vest was getting tighter by the second, the clasps beginning to press against the growing muscles. The seams were stretching. The flood of chemical processes triggered by the taste of my *kyrana*'s blood was something I'd never experienced before. It could hardly be believed, even though I'd seen the evidence of it within my own twin.

The aggression was rising, doubling and compounding by the moment. The edge of my control was fast approaching. I could actually *feel* it. I could actually feel that tipping point, held in suspension in the ether of my mind, a decision I had to actively fight against in fear that I would hurt Millie. In fear that I would cross a boundary I wouldn't be able to return from—not without losing something irreplaceable.

Resignation and grief mingled with desire and possession.

My claws bit into the swells of her hips, clutching her to me tighter as I drank more greedily. Pinning her against my body as my cock pulsed, the knot at the base of my shaft throbbing. I felt like I was held on the edge of release. Just one more buck of my hips against her might get me there. A maddening sensation. One that only made me more ravenous.

Her moan spurred me on. I drank deeper. Harder. Mindlessly.

*I could drink her dry,* came the stray, dark thought.

"*Vaan,*" I cursed roughly, muffled against her throat.

*That* thought made me retract my fangs and pull myself away from her with a guttural growl. Millie's hand flew to her neck. I saw the bite marks drip maroon.

I pressed the pad of my thumb to my fangs, drawing out venom. "Come."

She approached on wobbling legs, the blanket askew, and I reached forward to swipe my finger over the wound, my blood mixing with the clear venom. The bleeding stopped. Almost instantly, the skin began to close up, mending, repairing.

"You…" She trailed off, her voice husky. Her eyes were glassy, her cheeks flushed. "You knew."

I turned away from her, stalking toward the window behind my desk. The blood beneath my skin felt like it was buzzing. I wanted to scratch at my flesh until it stopped. The exhaustion I'd felt earlier was gone. I could fly to Laras and back and not feel winded. This power, this strength…it was incredible.

And it also meant I was fucked.

Truly fucked.

"I thought…I thought it was *rare*. Really, really rare. I never even thought that…" She trailed off.

What in Raazos's blood had I been *thinking?*

*That's because I hadn't been thinking,* I thought, anger rising though I held it at bay.

Already I was hungering for more. Over my shoulder, my gaze fastened on her pulse, zeroing in on it. Venom flooded onto my tongue, and I swallowed down the sweet taste of it, forcing myself to look away. Her scent was clinging to me. Every breath I took, all I could smell was her. Her blood, her skin, her need, her warmth.

"Kythel, will you look at me?" came her softened voice.

I turned. I clasped my arms behind my back, though it only stretched my vest tighter across my chest. I felt constricted. Suffocated. I wanted to tear off every stitch of clothing I had because only then would I be able to breathe.

"What does this mean?" she asked, finding the strength in her voice. She peered at me carefully. "For us?"

She knew what a *kyrana* bond was, that much was clear. I wondered if her father had told her. If her father had been bonded with Ruaala and that was why she'd done what she'd done. It would make sense. Losing a *kyrana* would make anyone slowly descend into madness and grief.

"Our agreement won't change," I informed her. "You will be my blood giver until the next moon winds. Then we are done."

She didn't frown or scowl. Instead, she peered at me harder, and I had the urge to scratch at my skin again because I felt like she was burrowing beneath it with that piercing look. Did humans feel the bond as strongly as the Kylorr did? I couldn't be certain.

"Yes?" I prompted, tone hardening, needing to hear her say it.

"Yes," she finally said. A part of me wished that she were ignorant of the *kyrana* bond. A part of me knew that if she were, it would make the end of this all the easier.

"Wait here," I told her, striding past, holding my breath as I did so I wouldn't smell her. She stayed facing the window, her back to me, when I reached the threshold of the door. "I'll have a keeper take you back to Raana *Dyaan*."

"No," she said.

I stiffened. This was what I'd feared. She'd start making demands of me, things I knew better than to entertain. Would she want to stay in the keep now? My own bed? It didn't matter that my fangs dripped at the thought. It was a matter of duty, and I knew better than to entertain such things with a female without a drop of noble blood in her.

"Have your keeper take me to the cottage, please," she said. Millie turned to face me, catching my scowl.

"I don't like you being there so late at night, especially in this storm," I said, the words out before I could stop them. As if on cue, I heard the clap of an *akkium* strike in the distance. "They will take you to Raana *Dyaan*."

"Then I'll walk," she shrugged, going to the wet pile of clothes on—still—trembling legs.

"What in Raazos's blood do you think you're doing?" I asked quietly, watching as she plucked up the soaking tunic I'd taken off her. She reached for the small device I'd placed into her hair, fumbling with it.

"Drying my clothes," she said. "How does this work exactly? Can you show me?"

Clothes? I wouldn't call them even that, I thought, glaring at the hole in her boot.

"The keeper will bring you new clothes," I growled, an unexpected irritation rising. "Now that you don't need to travel to Horrin, I expect that you'll purchase items that are more durable to wear as you trek through Stellara. Ones without holes and popped stitching. Lesana pays you well enough, doesn't she?"

Millie blinked at me. A sharp ache pinched my chest when I realized she looked slightly embarrassed, but I was too on edge to apologize.

She cleared her throat. "How often do you usually feed?"

"What?"

"I'll need to start taking *baanye*," she said, changing the subject entirely, clutching the blanket tighter around her shoulders. "Won't I? I'll need to know how much I should take, depending on your preferred feeding schedule."

She made it all sound so…clinical.

"I'll feed when I please," I snapped. I needed to fly. To stretch my wings and let the punishing rain wash away this buzzing under my skin. I detested it. How did Azur stand it? "Take *baanye* daily."

Millie's nostrils flared. Gently. But I knew my black mood was beginning to wear on her.

As evidenced when she said, "Yes, *Kyzaire*."

Her tone was sweet and soft, but there was warning in it when she said my title. Had I been in a better mood, I would've smirked in amusement at her little claws coming out to play.

"Wait here," I ordered.

"Yes, *Kyzaire*."

I nearly tore the door right off its hinges when I shoved through it. I heard her sigh behind me. Then came the scurry of her footsteps.

"Kythel," she called after me. "Wait."

I stopped at the banister, prepared to leap over the edge so I could fly down to the ground floor of the atrium. My fist squeezed the metal before I regarded her over the edge of my left wing.

She was standing just underneath the arches of my office doorway. The nape of her neck was bare, her cheeks were flushed, hair shining from the firelight. She made an intimate portrait, and I thought of the way I could draw her, just like this, my eyes skimming her lines, though I didn't think I'd ever be able to capture the softness in her gaze.

"Thank you," she said.

Such simple words. There was no bite to her tone. She looked at me steadily. Relief swept through me. The buzzing under my skin began to dissipate, melting away into a thrumming awareness. Of her. I could hear her breath, the gentle throb of her heart. I felt tethered to her, which was both a comfort and a worry.

"Thank you," she said again.

She meant her father. Horrin.

I inclined my head.

"I'll keep in contact with Setlan," I told her, turning away to peer down at the darkened atrium below. "I'll have an update for you soon."

"Tomorrow?"

"Yes."

With that, I stepped from the edge, flaring my wings wide.

I needed to get away from her before I did something I truly, truly regretted.

# CHAPTER 23

## MILLIE

The apothecary in Raana always smelled like the lavender fields from the small town outside of New Inverness. Fishshire, I believed the town was called. I'd always thought it strange that a town would be called Fishshire when it was so far from any type of water—lake, sea, pond, or otherwise. Especially when it was known for its lavender fields.

The apothecary was packed this afternoon. Well, as packed as a quaint little shop could be with Kylorr, though I spied a slim Hindras female standing near a body oil display.

I knew where the *baanye* was located, and I did a quick sweep of the shop to make sure Lesana wasn't here—or any givers from Raana *Dyaan*, which was just down the road. I knew a Keriv'i male owned the shop, but it was a Kylorr female who tinkered with the bottles behind the counter.

"Good morning, Eriaan," I greeted when I stepped up to the polished stone, the slab cutting into my belly.

"Ah, Millie," Eriaan said, focused on positioning the bottles of *baanye* just so. "Did Lesana send you for more *baanye*? Already?"

"Yes," I lied, smiling at her wings. "A couple bottles will do."

Eriaan plucked them from her display and finally turned. Her green eyes were kind, but there was a distant coolness in them that I recognized in many Kylorr. They weren't known for being a warm, inviting species, after all. Most Kylorr were raised in the belief that restraint would elevate them. Control over one's baser impulses was pushed as an ideal state of being.

I'd always thought that fascinating, given that the Kylorr, at their cores, were berserkers. Unable to control their battle rages once unleashed. In a way, it made sense. Control would be viewed as an ultimate strength, considering the beastly power that lay dormant in them all.

Eriaan slid the red bottles, slim and tapered at the top with a wax seal, across the counter. "I'll add it to Lesana's account."

"I'll pay for these today," I told her quickly. When she cocked her head, I said, "One is for a friend who doesn't work at the *dyaan*."

Eriaan inclined her head, and I transferred the credits to her, silently mourning their loss, feeling a little thread of anxiety pull through me, like puppet strings.

*I don't need them anymore,* I thought. Well, not entirely true. I had a little nest egg of credits I'd been saving for the journey to Horrin. Now I could use them on things for the cottage, *baanye* for the feedings, new clothing that didn't have holes. Still, I wondered if every purchase would feel like a small defeat.

"We expect his proposal tonight," came the voice, pouring into the shop from the bustling street. "At the moon winds celebration."

"Lyris," came a sterner voice, a warning. "Enough."

A small sniff. "My apologies, Mother."

When I turned, there she was, in the corner of the shop, perusing through selection of off-planet imports, expensive balms, and bathing salts, which glittered gold in the high morning sun.

"Eriaan," Lyris called, and I turned quickly, facing forward. "Where are these from?"

"Hydroni," the other female said, not even looking up. "Just received them this morning."

I heard a bottle pop open. Then I heard, "It smells *awful*. Why do Hydronis have such terrible scents?"

"It's for muscle aches and strains," Eriaan answered. "It's not perfume."

"It should be. They would sell more of it, certainly."

"I need to retrieve something from the clothier," came Lyris's mother's voice. "I'll return shortly."

"Yes, Mother." Lyris waited a beat for her mother to leave the shop and then turned to her friend, a young Kylorr female whose father frequented the *dyaan*. A noble House, I believed the family helped with the *lore* production once it was harvested. "Once the contracts are drawn up, I expect I'll be moving into Erzos Keep by the next moon winds."

A tug in my belly. Kythel hadn't lied. He wasn't engaged to Lyris of House Arada...yet. But would likely be soon. That was what he hadn't told me.

He must've made his intentions quite clear if the female in question was going around Raana bragging about it so openly. When I glanced up at Eriaan, Lyris's words had caught even her attention.

The memory was unwanted, but it rose nonetheless. Kythel's hot breath on my neck, the lap of his slick tongue. The way he'd pressed and rocked his hips into me, as if unable to stop. And me? I'd been just as desperate, clawing at him to drag him closer. Never before had I ever experienced something like his feeding. I likely would never again, if what I suspected was true.

A blood mate.

A *kyrana*.

I shook my head, a sharp breath puffing out of me.

And he would marry another. Not that I wanted to marry Kythel of House Kaalium. That was not a life I envisioned for myself—not that I even had the right to imagine it. When I thought of my future, I thought of...Rupon.

Of that perfect summer in our small cottage on the edge of a meadow. Of herbs drying on the windowsill, fragrant bread baking in the kiln, and sunlight dappled across my cheekbones. I wanted a family, children. I wanted a soft, quiet life, unburdened and simple.

Only...I'd promised my father I would stay on Krynn. I'd promised that I would tether my soul to this place so that in the after realm, I could find him again. Rupon was lost to me and whatever life I might've had there. My father was more important.

Looking up at Eriaan, I smiled. "Thank you."

"Give my regards to Lesana," she said, nodding.

I forced a small smile and backed away from the counter.

"So soon?" asked Lyris's friend. "Why the rush for a marriage?"

"Now that the business with his aunt's death has been settled and with his own brother married to that human noble, he probably feels the pressure from his father to secure Erzos," Lyris answered, her tone distracted as she settled on a new display. "War is coming, you know. That's what my father is saying."

War?

His aunt's death?

His brother had married a human? I hadn't heard that. Then again, I wondered which brother. His twin?

I felt discomfort settle, knowing I was eavesdropping, and so I slipped from the shop without another moment of curious hesitation. I tucked the two bottles of *baanye* into my pants, hitching my pack higher onto my shoulder, filled with food I'd purchased from the market. I wondered about Setlan, who he was and if he'd found my father. If he was on his way here, even now. Kythel had promised he would have updates for me, but when would I see him next?

*Not tonight obviously,* I thought. I'd forgotten about the moon winds, but there had been a familiar, energetic buzz in the market, hadn't there? I just hadn't connected the dots.

Kythel might be engaged to Lyris of House Arada by tonight.

I wondered what that would mean. For us. If I could allow the feedings to continue, knowing what I knew.

*It doesn't matter,* I thought, steeling my shoulders, and I walked down the cobbled road. *We made an agreement. He has me until the next moon winds.*

Then he would likely be married.

Down the road, I caught a maroon flash at the entrance of Raana *Dyaan.*

My heart stilled when I saw Lesana, accepting an order from a delivery for the kitchens from a lanky Kylorr with a torn wing. Across the courtyard, her eyes narrowed on me. My cheek still felt tender from her slap. This morning, there had been a faint blue mark from the decorative metal band around her middle finger.

Breaking her gaze, I slipped into Stellara, heading south. Only when I couldn't see the road anymore did I feel like I could breathe again.

---

I'D ALWAYS ENJOYED THE MOON WINDS ON KRYNN. I LOVED THE bright moonlight, the way it cast everything a blue-tinged silver, and the ferocity of the winds, so wild and violent that you could scream into them and it would get carried away, unheard by anyone.

The Kylorr felt pulled, lured by the moon winds, something a human like me couldn't understand. My father had described it as a freeing experience. He said that it was when a Kylorr was most likely to be on the edge of a rage, while at the same time having the most control over it. I could never quite understand the duality, and it was one of the few times in my life where I felt completely disconnected from my father.

But tonight...

Tonight was the first moon winds I'd spent at the cottage. And I could admit that I was frightened.

The trees of Stellara funneled the winds toward the cottage, which broke into the clearing like a violent wave in the sea, crashing against the front and back and sides of the house until I feared it would blow down completely. The windows rattled. A crack had appeared in the glass of one, and I just prayed that it lasted through the night, or else the interior would be a complete disaster come morning.

The cottage creaked and groaned. The front door rattled as if some restless spirit was trying to force its way inside. The draft coming from down the stairs kept blowing out the fire I'd created in the hearth.

Not only that but I kept feeling the icy touches of souls all around me. I was beginning to feel claustrophobic, and I jumped, gritting my teeth, when I felt something pass through me, scraping against my bones and making me shiver.

*I need more* zylarrs, I thought. Kythel had been right. The moon winds were a night where the veil between the realms was at its thinnest, but I'd never experienced this much activity from Alara or Zyos at once.

All the more...I kept remembering that Kythel was with Lyris this night. Possibly making plans with his future bride. His perfect, beautiful, noble future bride.

I wasn't used to being alone, I realized. Even when my father had been working, I'd always been surrounded by others. In the homes we'd lived in, in the villages, on the space ports. Being alone made me feel restless, afraid.

A pounding came at the door. At first I thought it was the wind jostling the wood in the frame again, but then it never stopped.

"Millie," came the growl. "Open the door."

Relief pulsed through me, and I pushed up from my crouched position next to the hearth. I'd been working on patching a hole in the thick blanket I'd purchased from the junk vendor at the market, but my hands had started shaking too much and I'd kept pricking myself with the needle with every window rattle. I still needed to re-stuff the mattress upstairs regardless, so I would sleep on the floor of the kitchen again, where it was warmest.

Fumbling with the bolted lock, I slid it open, and then Kythel was pushing inside like the gust of wind behind him. He slammed the door closed again, but before he could say a single word, I was pressing against him.

I wanted to be touched. I hated this weakness in myself, but right then, I didn't care. I didn't want to be alone and afraid in a moon-wind storm, and Kythel was *here*. He was here when he was supposed to be with Lyris. That must've meant something.

Or maybe I was just desperate enough to want it to mean something.

"You're shaking, *sasiral*," came his gravelly voice, one of his warm palms spreading against my lower back, the other gripping my hip. "Are you cold again?"

I shook my head, leaning my cheek against his chest. "Any news of my father?"

It was a question I'd been bursting to ask him all day.

His hand stroked a line up and down my back. "Setlan reached Horrin this afternoon. He's located your father and is filing the appropriate permits to transport him back to Krynn."

"They didn't cremate him, right?" I asked, needing to be sure, my heart pounding in the cage of my chest.

"No," he said, and I made a little sound against his chest. "Setlan will personally accompany him to Erzos. He will be on Krynn within the week."

Everything I'd wanted...

I nearly couldn't believe it.

"Thank you," I breathed, forgetting how quickly he'd gone cold on me last night. Detached. I didn't care. He was right. We'd made an agreement. He was holding up his end of the deal, and I would hold up mine.

"You weren't at Raana *Dyaan* tonight," he said.

I could hear a gust of wind roaring toward the house, coming from the North, and instinctively, I took a step back from the door, though I tugged on Kythel's vest to take him with me.

He followed, matching my steps. Looking up at him, I saw his gaze was fastened on me. My heart twisted. So maddeningly handsome. And the intensity, the need in that gaze? It sent a thrill through me. That this powerful, beautiful, complicated male wanted *me.*

My back hit the wall next to the stone stairs that led up to the bedroom. Above me, Kythel loomed, his eyes dropping to my lips, his head dipping.

"You didn't answer me."

"You didn't ask a question," I replied, feeling more like myself. Gleeful and relieved after the news of my father. Even the moon winds couldn't dampen my spirit...though something might've been able to.

Unconsciously, his lips curled, but then he remembered to look stern and disapproving again.

The question was out of my mouth before I could stop it. "Are you and Lyris engaged?"

Kythel stiffened. "I already told you—"

"I overheard her in the apothecary shop today," I told him. "She expected a proposal tonight."

Kythel was quiet above me as his hands trailed to my hips. His wings braced against the wall behind me, bracketing us in until all I could see was the glow of his eyes. Even the intensity of the storm outside seemed to lessen in the comfort of his wings. I waited with bated breath, wondering how I would feel if his answer was indeed yes.

"No," he said. "I made no such proposal tonight. I cut my dinner with House Arada short."

A sharp stab of relief made me smile. He scoffed when he saw it, which only made mine widen.

"Why?" I fished, though I thought I knew already.

"Don't act coy, *sasiral*. You know why," he told me, narrowing his eyes on me, though his small glare held no true bite. "What is this mark on your face?"

He took my chin in his grip, turning it to inspect it in the dwindling firelight. Lesana's ring. The bruising that had begun to bloom overnight.

"It's nothing," I lied, jerking my face out of his hold.

But I felt a thrum of tension vibrate through him.

He took my chin again, tilting my face to the side. He blew out a sharp breath, and when he spoke, his voice was blacker than it'd been before: "Don't lie to me. There's a marking here. Like it was etched in metal. Did someone *hit you*?"

I didn't answer. I didn't know what to say, but I was becoming wary of his growing anger. The way his shoulders seemed to bunch, muscles growing, just like they'd done last night after his first feeding. A physical response from a flood of chemicals, rarely seen among species outside of the Kylorr. It was what made them so dangerous.

"Tell me who struck you."

I shook my head, my tongue glued to the roof of my mouth.

He cursed, a long drawn-out thing.

I knew he wouldn't hurt me, so I placed my hands on his chest in an effort to calm him. If I truly *was* his *kyrana*, his blood mate, he never would. Not that I believed he would regardless.

"Why weren't you at Raana *Dyaan* tonight?" came his next pointed question when I didn't reply. "I went there to see you, but I couldn't sense you there at all."

Sense me?

One of us had to tell the truth, or else we would end up a big tangled jumble of half-truths and unspoken wants.

"Lesana…asked me to leave the *dyaan*," I confessed.

He stiffened. He was crouching, his face so close that if I blinked he would feel my eyelashes brush his jaw.

"When?"

I swallowed, turning my face. "Last night. Before I came to see you."

"So she did this?" he asked, his voice deceptively quiet and soft. The backs of his fingers brushed the bruise on my cheek.

I caught his wide wrist in my palm. In an effort to distract him, I brushed my lips over his thumb.

His smile was feral, those eyes pinned to my lips. "I will ruin her."

My chest squeezed. "No."

His eyes narrowed dangerously. "No?"

"You can't," I protested. "There are so many who work there, Kythel, who rely on the pay. Please don't. It's not a big deal."

Kythel's nostrils flared. His wings vibrated around us, rippling.

"She was upset that she saw you with me? In the alleyway?" he wanted to know.

"Yes," I answered. It was obvious.

"I'll speak with her," he said, his tone entirely too bloodthirsty.

"No," I said, steeling my voice. I could still see the coldness in Lesana's gaze. It had been chilling. I'd never been afraid of her until that moment in her office. It wasn't the slap that had shaken me—it was the look in her eyes when she threatened me. "I don't need your help. I'll be fine."

"I cost you your work," Kythel said. "I will make it right. Even if I'll grind my fangs into dust looking at her, knowing that she struck you. But I can play nice, *sasiral*. You know who my brothers are, yes? You know the kind of self-discipline it takes, dealing with them?"

My lips couldn't help but quirk. All the same, I said, "Don't interfere. Please. I know it's hard for you, but...let me handle this, all right?"

"How many credits a night did you make at Raana *Dyaan?*"

My eyes narrowed, exasperation rising. "Enough."

"You'll have me guess?" he asked, tilting his head to the side. Leaning forward, he pressed his lips against mine, and I hated the way my body seemed to melt at that small kiss. "I'll pay whatever I cost you."

*That* made me stiffen, even if it made me a hypocrite. I'd been prepared to be his blood giver for credits after I'd lost my only source of income. Only, Kythel had bypassed everything and given me what I'd truly wanted.

"No, I don't want your money," I said, my tone stern. "You're already giving me my father. That was all I wanted. That was all we agreed on. Nothing else matters to me but him."

Plus, knowing he was paying for my father's way back to Krynn—and this Setlan's journey too, whoever he was to House Kaalium—made me feel uncomfortable accepting credits from him on top of that. It made me feel like a...like a kept mistress. Especially considering the inevitability of our blood-giver relationship and where it would lead. A *kyrana* bond was proving to be surprisingly...erotic.

And we both knew it.

"Lesana told you to deny my original offer, didn't she?" Kythel asked. "That first night, when I wanted you as my blood giver."

"Yes," I whispered. "I was prepared to accept it, but I think she suspected...that maybe..."

"I know what she suspected," Kythel said, stroking his thumb over the bruise on my cheek. I watched his jaw tick as he inspected it. I would be lying if I said it didn't warm me in some way, knowing he didn't like seeing the mark. He did care for me. Just like I cared for him. As strange as our friendship was to an outsider looking in, we did care about each other.

I only feared that I would care *too* much by the time he was done with me.

And he would be done with me. Eventually.

"She was right to be nervous," he added.

My breath hitched. "She was?"

He inclined his head, those blue eyes glowing.

His voice roughened when he asked, "Did you take your *baanye* today?"

"Yes," I whispered, anticipation rising.

"Good. That's my good *sasiral*," he praised, and my hands gripped his vest tighter, a thrum of desire making the room feel entirely too hot. "Take off your cloak. I need you again."

# CHAPTER 24

## MILLIE

It felt like flying, that exhilarating rush pumping my blood, fluttering my belly.

I moaned, "Kythel."

His feeding wasn't urgent tonight. It was a slow, gentle thing, but it was steadily driving me mad.

He was sitting with his back to the wall, his wings gently tucked around us. I was straddling his lap with his fangs lodged deeply into my neck, that sense of heavy fullness a comfort. Every lap of his tongue made me jerk and twitch and squirm. Every greedy suck made me wetter until I feared I was soaking through the material of my new pants.

I didn't know what the rules were between us. The rules of a *kyrana* feeding. We hadn't discussed it. Kythel wouldn't tell me, but I sensed that he was trying to push me to the brink. That he was trying to make me shatter in his lap, testing the limits, curious about how I would respond to this.

Did he think I wouldn't come in his lap? Was this a game between us, to see who would succumb to the pleasure first? Because Kythel's cock was unmistakably hard beneath me and every moan that escaped my throat made him buck up into me—

that sweet, perfect pressure hitting all the right places between my thighs.

"*Ohhh*," I breathed, feeling my clit pulse. Even with his fangs in my neck, I was entirely too empty. I'd missed sex. Missed the feeling of a heavy, needful body against me. I'd enjoyed it with my past partners—all two of them—but with Kythel, I knew it would be different. Much, much different. It would feel like a brand. One I'd carry with me through the remainder of my life.

Was I ready for that?

My nails bit into the back of his neck, holding him to me. I felt his deep, desperate groan reverberate into my skin before I heard it.

I was going to come. This had gone on much too long. Kythel was thick and hard beneath me. Every pull of my blood made the edges of my vision spark, little stars bursting. I felt an icy chill pass through my hair—another soul on the moon winds—but it was a welcome distraction, to cool the impending heat.

Kythel's muffled curse pressed into my neck as I rocked my hips. I was too far gone to care anymore. I *needed* to come with every thread of my being, held together by the tether of his fangs. My head lolled, tilting back as I trapped his cock against my clit. Desperate little sounds escaped me. My nails dug into him so hard I wondered if I drew his blood as the crest of pleasure rose and rose.

"Don't stop," I gasped. "*Gods*, please, don't stop, Kythel. More!"

He fed harder, pulling deeper. My breath hitched. I ground my hips down, wantonly seeking what I needed most, consequences be damned. I'd said I wouldn't like being a kept mistress? *Look at me now,* I thought.

"*Raazos*, Millie," I heard.

When the orgasm hit me, my whole body froze, held suspended as Kythel took over, rocking between my legs, prolonging the pleasure. Distantly, I wondered if he could feel me coming. If he could taste it. Did an orgasm sweeten the blood?

*It should,* I thought, a breathy laugh escaping my throat as the pleasure stretched on and on.

I made sounds I didn't recognize, but I needed this. Desperately. When was the last time I'd come like this?

*Never,* I knew. This was too intense to be believed.

I heard his rough growl, felt an unmistakable throb between my thighs.

"Fuck," came his disbelieving curse, *finally* releasing his fangs from my neck as his wings twitched and shuddered against the wall. His nipping bites trailed around the marks he'd made, deep groans filling the little space between us as the violent winds continued to howl outside.

His arm moved. He pressed the pads of his fingers to his fang, catching venom but not breaking his skin. When he spread it against my flesh, I shuddered. It was the venom, I knew, that caused such a strong, physical reaction inside me as he fed. Only his venom.

"I thought myself immune to such things," he murmured, his voice relaxed and deep despite the bulging strength and tension I felt in his body. "But I quite like seeing my mark on you."

He didn't heal the skin, only stopped the bleeding. I would have twin fang marks in my neck for days. Our eyes met and held. I felt a flush starting to spread up the sides of my neck, a giddy shyness that felt new and unwelcome. I didn't want our odd friendship to change because of this. But I didn't see how it couldn't. Not now.

Looking down between us, my flush only deepened when I saw a wet patch spreading against his too-tight trews.

"I can't find it in me to be embarrassed," came his amused comment when he saw where my gaze had dropped.

I sighed. Kythel didn't seem worried about what had just happened, and so I told myself to *relax.* This was a natural response between blood mates. It would happen every single time. So there was no use working myself up about it.

"Let's not overthink it," Kythel murmured, seeming to read my thoughts. "Yes?"

"Yes," I replied, attempting to slide off him, only to be held in place by the bracket of his arms. They came around my hips, tethering me to him, so I didn't fight it. Still, I couldn't help but tease, "You get awfully clingy after an orgasm, you know."

His deep laugh felt like a warm caress. I savored it, found myself smiling in return.

His eyes weren't blue anymore. They were flooded with black. Peering at him, studying his tightened clothing, I began to unclasp his vest. It couldn't be comfortable.

Kythel seemed content to watch me as I worked the silver catches, one by one. I felt his cock pulse under me, but I ignored it.

"How does it feel?" I wondered. "Do you feel like it'd be easy to go into a rage right now?"

We'd beaten around the bush, as the old saying went, but we both knew what this was. We both knew the physical effects a *kyrana* bond would have on him.

"Yes," he confessed. "And no. It's like the moon winds. I feel like I'm on the brink of it, and yet I could trigger it at will too. For the first time in my life, I feel like I have full control. It's…addicting."

I'd never seen a Kylorr in one of their infamous berserker rages. Only through paintings and sculptures in the archives and through my own research throughout the years.

I nodded. "I never knew that a human could be a *kyrana*."

There it was. The word—out in the open, between us. To his credit, Kythel didn't so much as flinch, though his jaw did tick.

"My brother's *kyrana* is human," Kythel admitted softly. "It happens."

"She is?" I asked, incredulous. At his nod—though he didn't elaborate on his words—I blew out a sharp, surprised breath.

"My father was half-human, but I suppose…I just always assumed that it was the Kylorr in him that bonded to Ruaala."

"So they were blood mates?" Kythel asked after a brief moment. "I had wondered."

I nodded. "That's what he told me. Why he could never forget her."

Kythel *did* stiffen at that, and I realized what I'd said. Implying that *we* would never be able to forget one another. Maybe that would hold true.

Outside the winds battered at the door, but I wasn't frightened anymore. I felt safe in Kythel's arms. I wasn't even worried about the cottage blowing off its foundation, as if his mere presence wouldn't allow that.

"Do you know where Ruaala's soul gem is?" I asked. "Which shrine? Is it here in Erzos?"

I'd checked them all but hadn't found a trace of her in the records.

"Is that why you're doing this?" he asked. "Why you're trying to rebuild this cottage? Why it was so important to reclaim your father's body from Horrin and bring him back to Krynn? Because of the soul gems? Because of Alara?"

Alara was the after realm. Where they would meet again in the afterlife. Where I would see my own father again, should the gods and goddesses accept my soul here on Krynn.

"Of course," I said. "They couldn't be with one another in this realm. I promised him that I would do everything in my power to bring them together in the next."

"And if Ruaala's soul is in Zyos?"

The lost realm.

"If her soul gem was made, don't you think that's unlikely?" I asked. "She has a tether here."

Again, I got the sense that he knew more than he was letting on, especially when it came to Ruaala. But I had time. I didn't want to press too hard, considering that Ruaala was tied to his own family's legacy. Were there things he *couldn't* tell me? Noble houses were always tight lipped about their private matters, their secrets held together tightly like a tapestry. But maybe with time, Kythel would learn he could trust me.

I would let it go for now. Instead, I listened to the rush of the storm outside and the steady thud of Kythel's heart.

"Do they not call to you? The moon winds?" I asked, changing the subject.

"You called to me more this night. I'm content to miss them," came his unexpected reply.

"Oh." It was all I could think to say, as a pleased smile stretched itself over my lips.

Kythel watched it unfurl, his blackened eyes dropping to my mouth. When he met my gaze again, he asked, "What will you do now?"

"Now that I don't work at the *dyaan* anymore?"

He inclined his head, but I got the feeling that he hadn't meant that at all.

I *did* need to speak with him, since he owned the cottage and the surrounding land.

As if reading my thoughts, he stilled and asked, "You can't mean to live *here*, Millie."

It shamed me to say it, but it couldn't be helped. "I lived at the *dyaan*. I have nowhere else to go, Kythel."

I couldn't even afford to rent a room at an inn or common lodgings in the village either. Not until I found steady work again. Before Lesana had taken me in, I'd seen how difficult that could be for a human on Krynn. I'd been rejected more times than I could count. My only skills were cooking and talking. Both had proven necessary at Raana *Dyaan*, but where else could I go now?

"Then you'll live at the keep."

"No," I said quickly.

He rose a brow. "No? You find my keep *abhorrent*?"

I rolled my eyes, knowing he was being extra prickly about this. "Of course not. But that's not a good idea. And you know it."

Kythel licked his bottom lip, the flash of his black tongue making me remember the way it had made me tingle from his feeding. My body tightened as he shifted beneath me.

"Then I'll place you in a house in one of the villages," he said. "Would you prefer Raana or Erzan?"

Again, that would make me feel like a kept mistress.

"No," I said quietly. "I want to stay here. If you'll allow it."

"But I won't allow it," he answered, his tone infinitely patient, setting my teeth on edge even as I smiled.

"No?" I asked, leaning forward. He seemed to stop breathing when I pressed my lips to his. I kissed him once, twice until his hands were gripping my hips tighter. Softly, I said, "It's important to me. To be here. I feel connected to my father here. I know that he built this cottage with her. I found his marking in the kiln. *Please*, Kythel. Allow me to stay here. It won't cost you a single thing, but it will mean everything to me."

"It's not safe," he argued. "There is no living soul close by. There are still *lyvins* in these woods."

"I've not seen one," I argued. *Lyvins* were large wolf-like creatures. I'd seen pictures of them in the universal databases. I thought them quite cute, actually, if I could look past their sharp fangs. *And* their penchant for entrails.

"It doesn't mean they aren't here. They used to be all over this region of Stellara," he said firmly. "No."

I pressed my lips together.

"There's not even a bed here," he argued when he noticed my look. "Where will you sleep?"

"There is," I replied. "And it's perfectly suitable."

"Show it to me, then," he challenged.

Damn him. I'd taken out all the stuffing from the mattress already, so it was practically nonexistent. Only the frame was intact right now.

"Even if I stayed in the village, it wouldn't prevent me from coming here," I told him. "I'd be traveling through Stellara more, if anything."

"Then you'll stay at the keep," came his reply. "One of my keepers will take you here every morning and return you in the evenings. Not that's it up for discussion—I've already decided."

A small exhale of disbelief left my lips. I was reminded that Kythel *was* a *Kyzaire*. Sometimes it was easy to forget, especially when he was relaxed. But this was a male who was used to giving orders and getting exactly what he wanted.

"It will be a convenience," he continued, nodding to himself, "for the feedings."

"Is that the only reason?" I couldn't help but ask. Truth be told, I was a little hurt by his flippant words, that he only wanted me at the keep for *convenience*.

"No," he said. My breath hitched in surprise. His gaze turned molten. "It's not the only reason."

Tension thrummed between us. I was all too aware that his come was drying stiffly in his pants right underneath me and that the bite marks on my neck felt hot and tingly.

"You'll have your own room in the north wing," he added. "I'll even give you free reign of my kitchens whenever you wish."

"I don't think your culinarian would appreciate that," I said, distracted, actually entertaining the idea.

"You'll find that Telaana is not like most culinarians you've met," he replied, piquing my interest.

"But you'll allow me access to the cottage during the days?" I asked quietly.

"Yes," he said. "But once night falls, you need to return to the keep."

Because *lyvins* were nocturnal hunters?

"Millie," he said. "Do this for me, yes? And once the cottage is finished, I'll file a new deed in the Erzan archives. I'll put it under

Ruaala and Joss Seren's names, relinquish my own control and House Kaalium's control over it and the surrounding forest."

"What?" I breathed. My heart fluttered, warmth spreading. "You will?"

"I vow it to you," he told me, inclining his head. And my heart filled with want. With joy so bright that my eyes filled with unexpected tears. His features twisted briefly, appearing sad but also curious about the tears. "So easy to please you, *sasiral*."

Leaning forward, I embraced him tight, grinning into his neck.

"Are we in agreement?" he asked after a moment.

"Yes," I said. "Yes."

"Good. Then gather your things," he rasped. He shifted, a short, impatient breath leaving him. "I need to get out of these pants and soon."

My laughter filled the cottage.

I felt a soul trail against my left arm. But this time, instead of icy tendrils, it felt warm. Like the heat of the sun. Like a warm kiln.

And I knew, deep in my own soul that this must be Ruaala. She was here.

*Soon,* I vowed to her as I crawled off Kythel's lap. *Just a little while longer. I promise.*

# CHAPTER 25

## KYTHEL

*A* week later, I was watching as the builders broke ground on the South Road.

Situated in a less populated area of Erzan, just between the larger inn and a nearby *dyaan*, the road would begin and would run south, cutting through a portion of Stellara, running between the twin peaks of Vakaan Pass, the forests of the Lorin just beyond. A new bridge would be constructed over the Black River, where a contingent of builders were already working, before the road would join up with the North Road, leading from Kaldur's province of Vyaan.

Just before the Vakaan Pass, I would build the village of Sorn, a half day's flight from Erzos.

Lingering on the edge of my vision, I saw Marr. Saw her speaking with other onlookers, though she didn't dare approach me. As a whole, the commotion was drawing quite the crowd. The energy was a mixture of excitement, trepidation, and thunderous disappointment.

When I finally came over to Marr, she said, "Congratulations, *Kyzaire*. Your project has been the talk of Erzos. Did you hear that a raiding party took the North Road straight into Vyaan two days ago? Paved it for them, didn't you and your brother? Four villagers were injured in the attack."

I crossed my arms over my chest. "You heard wrong, Marr," I informed her. "There was an attack on the builders. Far from Vyaan. They never reached any village."

She harrumphed, but it didn't matter. Nothing I said would sway her opinion. "Doesn't mean they won't. A road will only make it easier for them to reach the villages. I wouldn't want to live where a road ends."

Over her shoulder, I stilled when I saw Millie pushing her way through the crowd, curiosity obviously spiking her interest. She'd known I'd be here today. She'd known today was when the road would break ground, and yet she shouldn't have been *here*. I'd dropped her off at the cottage this morning, bright and early, as she'd requested. After my morning feeding, of course, one that had had her gasping and squirming in my hold, one that had had me thrusting against her covered cunt, the scent of her arousal and blood filling my senses until I'd thought I'd drown happily in both.

My pulse jumped at the mere sight of her, venom flooding over my tongue in anticipation. Even as irritation made my gaze narrow on her. If she was in Erzan, it meant she'd trekked through Stellara again. And she knew I didn't like her roaming about in the forest, even if most *lyvins* were sleeping in their dens this time of day and stayed far away from the bustling activity of Erzos.

I would have to arrange for a keeper stay with her throughout the days, I realized. If she needed to journey to the village for supplies, at least a keeper would be there to act as her guard and escort. At least then I would have the peace of mind that she was safe.

"Good afternoon, *Kyzaire*," Millie greeted when she saw me, flashing that secretive, knowing smile that made me want to find the nearest private spot so I could kiss it right off her. Madness. This female would be my downfall—I already knew it. I could already *feel* it, and she'd only been within my keep for a week. What damage could she do to me before the next moon winds?

If I was being truthful, it was terrifying to think about.

"What are you doing here?" I asked, my tone stern.

"Seeing what all the excitement is about," she replied, her smile never leaving her face. "And to get some jars of paint."

For the walls in the upstairs room at the cottage, I knew. She wanted to paint them a light blue, her father's favorite color.

"Hello, Marr," she greeted, turning to the Kylorr female I hadn't realized she knew.

"Millicent," Marr said, sniffing, nodding stiffly. Though she still held a stern glare in her gaze for me, it softened when she turned to Millie. "How did the *gaanyel* paste work out for you? Did you get the fungus off whatever you needed it for?"

"Yes," Millie replied, reaching out a hand to squeeze the older female's shoulder. "Thank you. I never would've thought about using that, but it worked perfectly. You saved me so much time and effort."

Marr grinned, obviously pleased. "Good. It was a trick my mother taught me. Growing up, we used to live in a little cottage by the coast. The sea fungus grew on everything. My mother discovered *gaanyel* after we'd tried everything else. We were constantly mashing it up to make a paste."

"Well, your mother must've been a genius."

"I certainly tell her so at the shrine every moon winds," Marr said. Her eyes returned to me, and the spark in them dropped. "It's a good thing she cannot see what's happening to Erzos."

"What worries you about the road, Marr?" Millie asked, cocking her head to the side. "Roads are good things, you know. Throughout all species and cultures, they're the mark of civilization. It will make it easier and safer for the outer villages to access Erzan and Raana. The *Kyzaire* placed stretches of road out to them in the plans," she said, turning to me, "did you not?"

"I did," I answered coolly.

"Erzos has always been a quiet province," Marr said next, her voice rising, obviously upset. "We take pride in our fields, in our cliffs, our forests, our mountains...our sea. To cut through them with machinery, with metals, with noise and pollutants and people...it will change them forever."

"Machinery and metal and noise and pollutants and people made the province you love so much, Marr," Millie pointed out softly.

"The road will not cut through the coast," I informed her, a thought occurring to me. She was worried for the village where she'd grown up, a village she still lived in to this very day. "It runs through Stellara and comes out near Vakaan Pass. It never even gets close to the cliffs, to Savina. None of the existing villages will be within its path or even remotely near it."

Marr sniffed but said nothing.

"I admire your tenacity, you know," Millie said, grinning, a hand reaching out to squeeze the other female's shoulder again. "Wherever did you learn it?"

"My father," Marr grumbled, though I could see the little flicker of brightness Millie's compliment brought to her. "He always said I could rival his hard head."

"I believe it," Millie said. "Look, Marr, I think it's fair to say that the South Road will be built regardless, don't you think? But maybe your tenacity and determination can be used to help it rather than hinder it."

I cut her a sharp look, brow raising, wondering what she would offer.

"How so?" Marr asked slowly, pursing her slim gray lips.

"Why, with a South Road committee, of course!" Millie exclaimed, her eyes wide, as if it were obvious. "The travelers and merchants will need assistance when they arrive to Erzos. The caravans bringing all the beautiful and new imports from the South will be needing direction and guidance to the markets and to the shops in Raana. Who better to lead it than you, Marr? You grew up here, you know and love Erzos, yes? Who better to share its beauty with the southerners who travel the road...and who better to ensure that all Erzos customs are adhered to?"

This cunning little creature...

"I see your point." Marr sniffed primly. "We *will* need such a service, or else it would be chaos."

Chaos? I nearly snorted in exasperation, but I knew when to stay silent. Especially when it came to Kylorr like Marr.

"Think on it," Millie encouraged, squeezing her shoulder one last time. "But I'm sure the *Kyzaire* would approve a committee for such a thing, wouldn't you, *Kyzaire*?"

Marr turned her mistrustful gaze to mine, but for the first time, she was actually waiting for me to speak.

My gaze flitted to Millie, promising punishment later—but only the kind she would enjoy.

"I'll think on it," I said, knowing my answer would drive Marr mad. But at least it would give her something else to obsess over. Already I could see her making counterarguments in her head. "If you draw up plans for a committee, Marr, I will look over them and see if one would be necessary. We can meet at my keep to discuss it."

That flustered her a little. Because I didn't think she'd ever expected to be invited to the keep. But Millie was right. It would be better to have her on my side than against me. Not that I was worried a Kylorr female would cause serious problems for the South Road in the long run...but it was true that she was an anchor within Erzos. A familiar face who most Kylorr respected.

"Perhaps I will," Marr said, her tone all pomp. She turned away from us without another word, likely already going over all the points she would lay out in her proposal.

"You might've created a monster," I said quietly when Millie and I were alone. I studied her, my gaze running over her features, delighting in the dark brown spots dappled across the bridge of her nose and the way the corners of her eyes crinkled up when she smiled.

She leaned forward, and I took a step closer.

"Sometimes people just need to feel involved in something they fear. That way it makes that fear a little less frightening and they feel like they have some sense of control over it," Millie told me conspiratorially, giving me a small wink. "Marr would make a better ally than an enemy for you. She might not be from a noble House, but her influence stretches throughout Erzos. I haven't been here long, and even I can see that."

I chuffed out a sharp breath, affection building in my chest, something I was becoming more and more wary of with every passing day.

"You see everything, don't you, *sasiral*? You see more than most," I told her gruffly. "Things that I cannot. Things that I would not think to look for."

Then that stray, unwanted thought returned to me—that Millie would make a good *Kylaira*. Just thinking it made my skin feel too tight, made my blood buzz underneath it.

My words pleased her, and she grinned up at me. In the small space between us, I could scent her. Only this time, my own scent mingled with hers. Throughout the week, I'd kept my distance from her at the keep. I'd *behaved*. She had her room down the hall, as far away as possible within my own wing, and I'd never stepped inside it. I'd mostly kept our feedings to once a day— though sometimes I fed from her twice when the need became too distracting—and kept my hands to myself beyond those feedings.

We took our evening meal together, however. Something I hadn't expected, though something that had just fallen into place naturally.

This last week, I'd felt *focused*. With her blood fueling me, I tore through my work faster than I could've imagined. I needed less sleep but had more energy. I flew to the ports in nearly half the time. I'd come to rely on the feedings because they allowed me to do what was necessary with the most efficiency. *Vaan,* some evenings I even had time to spare at the end of the day. To spend on plans for Sorn Village, to pack a pipe of *lore* up on the roof of the keep and enjoy the view of the North Sea, to thumb through a few pages in my library.

The most worrying thing, however, was that I wished Millie was beside me for all of it. It was taking more and more self-control to keep my distance. Especially when our feedings were becoming more and more…needful. More and more intimate.

*Only a matter of time,* I knew.

"I have news for you," I said when silence dropped between us. She'd asked me nearly every day, but today I could finally give her the answer she'd sought. "Setlan will arrive with your father on Krynn tomorrow evening. They arrived to the last travel port."

"Really?" she asked. She didn't smile, but I knew she was relieved. I knew it was a strange mixture of relief, grief, sadness, and acceptance for her. Because now she would finally make her peace with her father's death and she could begin to make plans for what would come next. "Thank you."

She reached out to squeeze my hand, holding on to it. A comforting, intimate gesture that she did all the time when we were alone. But when I saw a familiar figure standing at the edge of the crowd over her left shoulder, I knew it wasn't appropriate when there were others watching. I released her hand, stepping away. Millie frowned.

"I'll see you at the keep later tonight," I told her, catching Kaan of House Arada's gaze across the crowd. He inclined his head at me stiffly, his eyes straying to Millie for a brief moment before he was turning his back.

Before she said anything, I was striding after him, leaving her in the crowd.

I caught him near the edge of Erzan.

"Kaan," I called out. He stopped in the road, turning to face me.

"*Kyzaire*," he greeted. "My congratulations on the South Road. If House Arada can supply any additional *drava* than we already have, know that we are at your complete disposal."

The words held a double edge. A barb that I sensed just beneath the surface. I knew it had been a slight against him when I'd left the moon winds celebration. I knew that he'd been expecting a proposal to join our two Houses together.

"I'll keep that in mind."

Kaan's gaze went back to the crowd, zeroing in on one person in particular. When he looked back at me, I could tell he noticed the larger cut of my vest and pants.

"May I speak plainly, *Kyzaire?*" Kaan asked, dropping his voice.

My lips pressed. I inclined my head.

"Have your amusements with the human female. Keep her, if you wish—I'm sure Lyris will not protest." I stiffened. "But don't forget that your own father wants our Houses to be joined together. Don't forget the value that we will bring. No other House has more value to you than Arada does. *I* want my daughter married into House Kaalium. *I* want our legacies to join at this place in time. If that's not something you can offer me anymore, then let me know. And soon. Give me the respect of your honesty at the very least. That is all I ask."

With that, he left, heading back toward Raana.

I blew out a sharp breath, watching him go. He was right. He deserved an answer. In my mind, I knew the answer that I should give him. The only one.

When I turned, I saw Millie, standing in the crowd. She'd been observing the exchange, and she likely knew who Kaan was, as inquisitive and curious as she was. She watched Kaan leave, then her eyes came to me.

There was a question in them that I thought she already had the answer to.

Then I watched her turn back toward Erzan, a jar of blue paint held loosely in her grip.

# CHAPTER 26

## MILLIE

"*Sasiral*," Kythel prompted quietly. "Would you like to be alone?"

I looked up from my father's face, focusing my gaze on Kythel, who stood a respectful distance away. Beneath the shrine in Erzos, down two flights of stairs, deep into the earth was where the bodies and bones were kept, awaiting their soul gem creation.

My father was still sealed in a hydrosack. The cerulean fluid inside tinged his gray skin blue. His dark horns pressed into the lining of the clear sack, made of a stretchy material that settled around his body like a blanket.

Other than the hydrosack, my father looked like he was sleeping. His body had been preserved all these months, and seeing him broke a little piece of hope inside me. That maybe this nightmare would end. That I'd been lied to. That he wasn't truly dead.

The material squelched when I reached out to touch it, but I pressed my fingers into his hand. His claws had continued to grow, the sharpened tips pricking the material until I thought they might pierce through it. But his hand was solid. Cold.

"No," I replied to Kythel. My eyes were bleary and burning.

How long had I been standing here? Though the vault was underground, it was well lit by Halo orbs and *akkium*-powered crystals perched on thin, decorative columns. The walls were made of a stone, a warm cream. "No—I'm ready to leave."

"You're certain?"

I squeezed my father's hand, running my thumb over the top of it, hating the slick glide of the hydrosack material. I hadn't cried once. I'd expected to be a bawling mess the moment I saw him. Instead, all I'd felt was a calm grief.

My father's body had been waiting for us the moment we'd stepped into the vault room, spread out on a stone slab made from the same material as the walls. Next, Kythel told me, his body would be cleaned. The proper rites would be performed. His body would be burned, his ashes collected, purified. On the next moon winds, his soul gem would be created.

Longer to wait. But it gave me time to find Ruaala.

"Yes, I'm certain," I told Kythel, turning from the stone slab.

This was only my father's body. His soul was in me already. It had never left.

I found soft comfort in that knowledge, and it gave me the strength to walk away, returning to Kythel's side.

The *Kyzaire* was watching me closely. When I walked into his arms, he smelled like summer spices, and I breathed him in deeply. He was warm. *Alive.* A steady, solid, breathing, living thing against me.

"Take me back to the keep," I requested. "Please."

Since I'd seen him with Kaan of House Arada yesterday, Kythel had been distant. Distracted. But right now, I had all of his attention.

"Whatever you need, *sasiral.*"

---

THREE DAYS LATER, I WAS SITTING IN THE KEEP'S KITCHEN WITH MY morning meal, swirling my spoon in the thickened *rusk* oats, which Telaana had told me had been milled in Salaire.

Telaana, the culinarian of Erzos Keep, was singing at the prep block, a whispery, ethereal voice pouring out from her. Haunting in its beauty. I smiled as Kelan, a keeper who oversaw the north wing, entered.

"Good morning," I chirped.

He shook his head. "Humans and your greetings."

He was a bit of a grump, but I quite liked him.

Or maybe I liked him because he was one of the only keepers who didn't treat me any differently than how he treated everyone else. I wasn't a fool. I'd poked and prodded around. Kythel had never had a permanent blood giver living within his keep. Only me. Moreover, his strength was plainly evident after our feedings. They all knew what I was to him. Because of that, many keepers gave me a wide berth.

Even so, I was settling in at the keep nicely. Perhaps too nicely. I found myself spending more and more time at the cottage in Stellara because it frightened me how easy the last couple weeks had been.

"What's for eating today?" Kelan asked Telaana, peering over her shoulder at whatever she was chopping, trying to snag a shriveled root that still needed rehydrating.

I smiled into my porridge, spooning out the last few mouthfuls before standing. Strangely, I took comfort in its blandness. My father had always told me that you couldn't truly appreciate great food if you had it constantly. Most mornings, our breakfasts had consisted of simple fare, just like this porridge, only seasoned with a pinch of blue salt.

I washed up, enjoying Kelan's grumbling as Telaana made him his own bowl of porridge. I slipped out the side door, hitching my pack up over my shoulder, and made my way to the keep's border.

It was a beautiful day, and though Kythel would surely protest, I wanted to walk to the cottage this morning.

———

THE DAY PASSED SWIFTLY. TODAY I'D WORKED ON TEARING OUT THE crumbling fence of the front garden. I had plans to expand it, to plant seeds for vegetables and herbs, since the sun shone more brightly there than it did toward the back of the house during the mornings and afternoons.

But the fence was in the way. The path leading to the front door also needed replacing, and I'd started prying out the loosened, heavy slabs of stone, finding thick, wiggling grubs and worms beneath each and every one, which burrowed into the damp earth upon discovery.

I'd only cried once, thinking about my father that day. But now that he was returned to Krynn, I knew that my search for Ruaala was pertinent. The black book that Kythel had given me, all those weeks ago, still lay within the cottage, sitting face up on the table I'd repaired, sanded, and sealed. It had a permanent place within my blue pack, and I told myself that I'd read the passage on Ruaala's history with House Kaalium every day…only to avoid it.

Truthfully, it frightened me. What if I never found her soul gem? I'd already searched the shrines in Erzos. Kythel had said her previous husband now lived in Vyaan. Had Ruaala lived there when she'd died? Was that where her soul was rooted in the Kaalium?

If so, I'd need to journey there. But with my agreement with Kythel, I would need to wait until after the next moon winds.

My heart gave a dull little pang. I *liked* Kythel. I cared about him more than I probably had a right to. Every moment I was with him, those feelings only deepened. Stretching softly, sinking heavily in my body until I felt brimming with contentedness and hope. Every stray thought—of which there were many—had me smiling, a flutter of awareness and anticipation building inside me.

All while knowing that he would likely break my heart. That he would shatter it so completely.

It was a strange duality, constantly fighting inside me. The need to fall into him, damn the consequences. The need to let him hold me, to quiet the grief and anxiousness that had been my constant companions these last few months. He was my centering point of calmness in a storm. He was a stable pillar to cling to when all I wanted was to sink into the earth. He made me feel safe. Protected. Cared for.

A part of me feared that I couldn't stand on my own. I'd realized that I'd relied on my father for much too long. I'd felt lost when he'd passed. I worried that I was doing the same with Kythel, letting him support me when he was a crumbling, decaying column that would be gone from my life within a few weeks.

In the end, as I tore the pickets of the fence from the ground, I decided to let it go. It wasn't in my nature to dwell on something so ephemeral. Growing up as a child of the universe, moving from place to place, experiencing dozens of different lives in the span of one, I knew that nothing ever lasted. Why not enjoy it while it was here, right in front of me?

I wanted Kythel. For now he wanted me. *That* was all that mattered.

*If only he wanted me enough,* I thought next. I'd been taking marroswood for the last week, purchased from the apothecary with blushing cheeks, though Eriaan hadn't batted an eye as I'd paid for it across the counter. It would prevent me from conceiving a child should Kythel lose a smidge of his frustratingly fierce control.

It was only a matter of time, but I was becoming more and more determined to nudge him over the edge. We were *alive,* warm blooded and lustful creatures. Sex should've only been an added benefit to our arrangement, one I was more than prepared for.

If only Kythel felt the same.

As the day grew longer, the sun stretching across the moss until it disappeared behind the canopy of the purpling trees, as night deepened the sky to an inky blue, I realized how easy it was to lose myself in this forest. Was this how Father and Ruaala had felt? Why they'd called it their own realm?

It didn't take me long to realize my mistake because Kythel came thundering down outside the cottage, the angry flap of his wings sounding like the crack of an *akkium* strike right above my head.

I swiped at my brow, straightening. I was a mess, covered in dirt. But the plumbing worked upstairs in the washroom, connected to a fresh well I'd cleaned the other day. Only cold water, though. The *akkium*-power source needed a replacement tube from the market that I didn't want to pay for quite yet.

An idea popped into my head. A devious one, though I would delight in testing just how far Kythel's control stretched.

"Hello," I greeted, giving him a small smile. I knew I was in trouble, judging by the disapproving scowl on his face, the small jump just underneath his jaw, and the way his icy eyes pinned me into place as he straightened to his full, imposing height. "How was your day?"

"It's after nightfall," he growled.

I looked pointedly toward the sky and beamed. "I see that."

When he glared, I approached, placing my hands on his chest and going up onto my tiptoes to press my lips to his tight jaw. His chest rumbled beneath my palms. I pressed another kiss to his cheek, feeling its surprising softness against my lips. I sensed when his shoulders loosened. Just a little.

"I'm sorry," I said. We *did* have an agreement, after all—I was to return to the keep before nightfall. "I lost track of time. Forgive me?"

He didn't mention that I'd lost track of time just two days ago too. We'd already had this argument before, and he likely knew that I'd find a creative way of distracting him. But perhaps it was a game he wanted to play, considering his glare never left his features.

I bit back my smile, licking my bottom lip instead.

"I'm going to wash up before we return to the keep," I informed him, turning. "You can feed afterward, if you'd like."

"Wash *at* the keep," he ordered. "I have an export contract from Gharata that I need to review tonight."

"I'll only be a moment," I said, looking at him over my shoulder as I retreated back into the cottage. The warmth from the fire made me smile, made nerves of excitement and glee spike in my belly. The stairs leading up to the washroom were in direct line of the front door. Leaving it open, I tugged up my loose, green tunic, a chill making its way across my exposed back and belly. I pulled it over my head, dropping it onto the floor behind me. The supportive band around my breasts joined it, my nipples pebbling tight.

From Kythel, I heard…loud silence. I grinned at the stairway, my fingers dropping to the laces of my trews, toeing off my boots before I began the ascent up. My pants were discarded on the top step, giving Kythel a flash of my bared backside before I rounded the corner and disappeared into the washroom.

My heart was thundering as I turned on the taps to the bathing tub manually. Down below, I heard the front door slam closed as I twirled up my hair into a loose bun on the top of my head, securing it with the pin I'd used earlier, tangled in the wild strands. It put the two bite marks on display, decorating the column of my neck. Kythel liked to see his mark on me. I quite liked it too. It made me feel like his. It made *him* feel like mine.

Kythel still hadn't appeared by the time I sank down into the chilly water. I sucked in a sharp breath, though it did nothing to dispel the heat building between my thighs, a gentle throb that seemed commonplace these last weeks.

Then I heard it. Steady, heavy steps on stone, ascending the stairs. He paused on the landing, however, and I held my breath, wondering what he would do, what he was doubting. To distract myself, I scrubbed at a muddy patch on my arm and cleaned underneath my fingernails, shaking out the soap crystals from the jar next to the tub and lathering them in my palms, smoothing them over my body.

I was shivering when he appeared, looming in the doorway of the washroom, my tunic hanging from his clawed fingertip. He'd seen me naked before—the night of the storm when I'd showed up at his keep, when he'd rapidly stripped me of my soaked clothes and sunk me next to the blazing hearth.

This felt different, though. Kythel watched me, his blue eyes glued to my hand as it trailed over my slick skin. Above the line of the water, my breasts were bared, the pinkish brown of my nipples puckered tight in the chill.

I was no great seductress, not like the dancers I'd seen on Qapot'a or the high-paid escorts at the travel ports, and yet I didn't feel shame as Kythel's gaze swept over me. And when my hand trailed below the water and washed between my legs, when my fingers lingered against the heat of my sensitive folds, those eyes practically *scorched* me. My tunic dropped to the ground. He stepped into the washroom that felt five times as small with him in it. His wings banged into the jar of soap as he crouched at the side of the tub, sending it scattering to the floor.

But neither of us flinched or moved. His eyes were stuck between my legs, watching my movements become gentler, more purposeful. My pussy clenched, my clit pulsing with excitement.

I didn't know how to be more obvious with my invitation without resorting to begging.

*Well, I could be a little more obvious,* I thought, reaching for his hand, which he had draped over the lip of the tub.

He hissed in surprise at the icy water when I led his hand beneath it.

"Why doesn't your *akkium* generator work?" he asked, voice thick. Disapproving.

I smiled, drawing his hand between my thighs. "I'll have it repaired soon."

He hissed again but for an entirely different reason, his thumb brushing the heat of my sex.

"Aren't *kyranas* supposed to satisfy their mates?" I asked, the question tumbling out of me, though I never broke his gaze.

Disbelief flashed over his expression, but then it clouded with dark desire. It was a taboo thing, what I'd just done, wasn't it? We'd never said those words before in this context—in reference to *us*. *Kyrana*. Or *mate*. It felt forbidden.

"Do I not?" he asked. A thrill pulsed through me when he didn't protest, when he played along. "Do I not ensure your pleasure every time I feed?"

"You do," I said, cheeks heating, thinking of the way he hummed every time I came with his fangs lodged in my neck. "But you aren't giving me what I really want. *This.*"

He grunted, his eyes turning dangerous as he shifted forward, pressing over the tub to grab my jaw with his free hand. Hard. My breath whistled in my throat, molten desire flooded my veins. I loved when he was demanding, when he handled me a little roughly, like he knew I wouldn't break but that instead I would bloom with his touch.

The backs of his filed, dulled black claws traced my folds, a gentle tease that made my need spark bright.

"This is what you want, *sasiral*?" he asked.

"And more," I said, breathless. "I've been taking marroswood. You don't have to worry."

A rough curse left his lips. The water was heating by the

second. I wondered if the water was vibrating around my heart—making little ripples and waves across the surface—because it certainly felt like it was trying to pound its way out of my chest.

His fingers curled, and I gasped. His touch was purposeful against my clit, making small, soft, intentional circles. The muscles in my legs tightened under the water, beginning to shake. My hips bucked against his touch, greedy and needy.

"Kythel, *please*," I begged. "You've made me wait long enough."

"So impatient," he commented. Despite the otherworldly glow in those eyes and the subtle tightness around his slim mouth, I would say his control was still very much in place.

Moaning, I closed my eyes when his hand moved, when a long, thick finger pushed into me. I clenched around him, eliciting a groan, low in his throat. Crack by crack, I saw his control begin to fracture. His shoulders were bunching, his wings beginning to twitch behind him.

"Imagine how good it would be," I said, my hips beginning to move, icy water sloshing in the tub. "Imagine feeding from your *kyrana*, your fangs deep in my neck while your cock is deep inside me. Right here. Right where you want to be."

"Millie," he growled in warning. Another fracture fissuring right before me, the cracks of ice shooting out in all directions. Another finger joined the first in my tight, clenching sheath, and I moaned. His hand was a steady pump between my legs now, growing more powerful by the moment. "Be careful, my little *sasiral*. Be very careful about what you're asking for."

"I am," I said, grinning at him, my cheeks flushed. The water lapped at my nipples. I wondered if he would bite me there. How utterly sinful and delicious his mark there would look. "I know exactly what I'm asking for, Kythel."

# CHAPTER 27

## MILLIE

Kythel said nothing to my words, only continued to fuck me with his fingers, the pad of his thumb coming up to stimulate my clit as I rocked desperately. My hips snapped and rolled. Kythel's grip on my jaw never loosened. He forced me to keep his eyes as I moaned and thrashed, the tension and pressure building...and building...

"Oh, I'm going to—" I whispered, eyes widening.

The orgasm took us both my surprise, as quick and fierce as it was.

"I'll feed by the fire downstairs, to get you warm. Stand up so I can dry you off," he commanded, voice husky and guttural and clipped. *Impatient,* I knew, fighting back a triumphant smile.

My laugh sounded choked. But I was still coming, still squeezing around his fingers, pleasure pulsing and stroking through me...and he was giving me orders.

*Impossible male,* I thought, delight thrumming through me, affection settling deeper than it should've.

Kythel didn't wait. The moment my body went slack in the washing tub, he pulled me up to stand on trembling legs, reaching for the large drying cloth slung over a metal rack tucked in the corner. He frowned at the piece of material, as if he hadn't used a towel to dry off in years. Remembering the device he'd used on my hair, I figured that was likely the case.

Though his movements were impatient and jerky, he was gentle, scooping me up into his arms and carrying me from the washroom. I shivered. Between my legs, I was still tingling. As he descended the stairs, I clung to his warmth, stray droplets of water chilling on my skin.

Leaning forward, I heard the rumble of his groan when I brushed my lips against his neck. I kissed and licked the strong column. A roughened sound tore from his throat when I bit down with my dull teeth, his whole body jerking in surprise, making me grin.

"Does it bother you that I can't feed from you?" I asked, the thought crossing my mind for the first time.

If he had a Kylorr for a *kyrana*, she would be able to feed from him. Her venom would give him pleasure, the same way his gave me pleasure, wouldn't it?

"No one has fed from me before," he replied, his voice unrecognizable. He didn't answer the question, however, in true Kythel fashion.

"I would," I whispered against his neck when he stood in front of the fire, the flames beginning to lick at my back. "If I could."

The fucked-up thing was that I believed it. A sudden dark impulse overcame me, one I'd have to explore later in private. The thought of biting him, breaking his skin, lapping at his black blood, taking a part of him into me in a way that no one else had with him before? The thought made me feral. Possessive. I was surprised by how much I wanted it.

Kythel had me whipped around in his arms in a single moment, the drying cloth dropping to the ground with a quiet *whoosh*. He hitched my legs around his waist, wrapping them tight, my breasts pressed firmly into the stiff, structured material of his vest. One of my nipples rubbed against the silver catch against his chest, and I let out a breathy moan, that startling coolness making me want *more*.

Wrapping my arms around the tops of his shoulders, I continued to kiss and nibble at his neck, just as I felt the warmth of his breath drift over mine.

"Yes," I breathed when I felt the familiar, sharp prick of his fangs against my neck. When I felt that first dizzying suck as a heavy heat flooded into the wound. His venom. So sweet that it made me ache. It made my pussy clench, and I bucked my hips against him, feeling the tendons in his arm beneath my ass tighten to keep me in place, steady. "*Yes.*"

I bit at his neck harder, squeezing the flesh between my teeth, hearing his responding feral growl. His cock was like steel. I could feel the head of it against the bottom of my thighs.

The only way I could describe Kythel's feeding was ferocious.

He was *feasting.*

His grip on my hips would likely bruise. Every deep pull of my blood made my teeth clamp down harder, which only seemed to spur him on. Even though he'd made me come on his fingers in the tub upstairs, I felt another orgasm begin to crest, my clit pulsing helplessly with every dragging lap, with every new infusion of his venom.

My body felt hot, so hot I wondered how he didn't drop me in fear of me scalding him. My blood was rushing in my ears, drowning everything else out. If he'd been talking to me, whispering delicious, dirty things against my neck as he fed, I wouldn't have heard him. The buzzing in my veins was a thunderous symphony. It was all I could hear.

When I came for the second time that night, I bit hard enough to draw his blood. I felt the vibration of his shocked, deep groan, a steady ripple against my neck. His blood was surprisingly sweet, unlike the coppery tang I'd expected.

The taste of him lingered on my tongue long after my orgasm faded. It took me a moment to realize his fangs had withdrawn from me, that he was breathing hard, his shoulders vibrating with every deep inhale he took.

"Kythel?" I whispered, leaning back so I could look into his eyes. I took his face between my palms, but he was lowering me down onto the floor, holding me steady until he was certain I wouldn't fall. My hands fell away. "What's wrong? Should I not have…"

"You know why we can't do this, *sasiral.*"

Frustration and hurt pricked at me.

"No, actually I don't," I retorted. But if he didn't want to have sex, I would accept that. I wouldn't push anymore. He'd made his wishes clear. "Why do you call me that? Fallen star?"

His gaze fastened on me. I was acutely aware that I was naked, and so I clasped my arms around me.

"That's what *sasiral* means, doesn't it? I asked a vendor at the market."

Kythel didn't answer me, and it made my shadowed doubts creep in again, peeking around corners I had tucked them safely in, trying to forget them.

Fallen star?

I was still trembling from my orgasm with the taste of his blood on my tongue. It made me bold. It made me demanding.

"Is it because you think I'm lacking in some way? Do you pity me? Because I had a different life before I came to Krynn, filled with travel and experiencing new places and meeting interesting people, and now I have nothing?"

"No," he rasped. His eyes were gentle, however. "No, that must be what you think about yourself, Millie. That thought never crossed my mind once."

I couldn't help but flinch.

Kythel straightened his bulging vest, shifting it so it sat more comfortably, though the seams had to be cutting into his flesh after his feeding.

"I'll be waiting outside once you dress," he said next, not

waiting for me to respond, stalking to the front door of the cottage.

I watched him leave, heard the gentle thud as the door shut behind him, leaving me standing next to the blazing fire.

His words gave me pause. *Was* that how I saw myself? Had I read into the name all wrong?

"Kythel," I called out, knowing he'd hear me.

"Get dressed, Millie," came his growl through the door. My hurt softened when I heard the irritation in his voice. It only took me a moment to realize...he didn't like what I'd said. About myself.

I waited, my heartbeat slowly beginning to tick up when I heard him pacing along the last remaining stones of the pathway leading to the front door. Growing more and more restless.

I still hadn't moved, my eyes pinned to the door, when he came barreling back through it.

"I call you *sasiral*," he started, stalking toward me, glaring, "because I think your resilience is admirable. Do not make the mistake of thinking it means otherwise."

An ember slowly began to burn within me, casting warmth into every vein like a spell until it felt like I was lit up from the inside out.

"You do?" I asked softly.

And even though he was still glaring daggers at me, he came close enough to grab the back of my neck, pulling me into him. His kiss was fierce, stealing my breath.

"My little fallen star," he rasped against my lips as my hands reached up to clutch his shoulders. "The universe dealt you a tragedy, but you didn't let it break you. You fell hard on Krynn, dusted yourself off, and then you smiled as you moved forward. That's what I admire."

His shoulders were trembling with his sudden need. The effort it took him to not give into what we both wanted...it was on full display, and I was only now realizing the extent of his control. Kythel was logical. An overthinker, an intellectual, whereas I was the opposite. I acted on what *felt* right, not if it was the smart decision.

This time, it was Kythel who gave into me. Who silenced that voice in his mind that told him this would only lead to hurt. I'd long silenced mine…because I liked his kiss. I liked his hands on me, the way his eyes gleamed when I smiled at him and the gentle gruffness in his voice when he teased me.

Kythel of House Kaalium might eventually belong to another. A female from a respectable, ancient bloodline like his, with deep ties to his nation and its people.

But for right now, Kythel of House Kaalium was all *mine*.

"Get this damn vest off me," he ordered roughly, his touch morphing, becoming eager, demanding, impatient. "I'm not waiting a single moment more, *sasiral*."

If a heart could sing, mine was doing it right at that moment, hearing my new favorite word fall from his lips.

# CHAPTER 28

## KYTHEL

This was a fucking terrible idea, and yet I grinned as Millie tore at my clothes.

Was she hurt about what I'd said? There was quiet determination in her features, her brows lifting with her rising desperation and need. I couldn't tell if she was angry or solemn or lustful. But did it matter? She could be all three, and it wouldn't change the fact that we'd have sex tonight.

This would only further deepen the ties I already had with her. A weaving, tangled tapestry of millions of threads that would be difficult, if not impossible, to tear myself from when the time came.

That was what fueled my anger. Because I knew she would never be mine. Not the way she was intended to be.

I made the effort to soften my grip on her hips so I wouldn't bruise her in my eagerness. My hands joined hers, tearing at the clasps on my pants as she pushed my vest off my shoulders, ripping off my heavy boots, which clattered to the floor like weighty stones.

The vest got tangled on my wings so I shredded the material, throwing it away. At the first press of our bared bodies, I sighed, a harsh breath whistling from my throat. My neck was still throbbing from where she'd bitten me, and it made my cock harden like steel, prodding into her belly, greedy.

When I felt her grip drift between us, her small, warm hand wrapping around the length, I bucked, a hoarse cry bursting from my lips. I ducked my head, capturing her lips as I backed her up toward the single table in the center of the room. The slide of her firm hand was a tantalizing tease because it wasn't enough. It never would be. Even though I felt like the membranes of my wings tingled when she rubbed her thumb under the head, sparking the sensitive nerves.

She squeaked when I pushed her up onto the table, when I disentangled her hand from my cock and sank to my knees on the stone floor.

"You don't think I've thought about this, *sasiral?*" I murmured, wings stretching wide, which she tracked with a flitting gaze. They felt like they were buzzing. I itched to fly, to pump them hard to dispel the crazed sensation building in my belly. "You don't know how much control it takes. You'll never know."

"I have an idea," she said, biting her lip as she watched my head duck. She moaned when I licked a line up the crease of her inner thigh. Her scent was driving me wild, clouding my head.

Unable to withstand it, I trailed my tongue to her cunt. The sharp point of my tongue parted her pink folds, and I groaned against her, the taste of her delicate, musky sweetness making my knot swell at the base of my cock. Millie's head dropped back, her eyes sliding shut. Lips parted in a silent moan, she was a work of art.

I'd only ever drawn buildings—stark, cold, unyielding lines. Black ink on parchment. And yet I wanted to try my hand at drawing her in perfect color. The soft curves of her breasts, the pinkened brown of her nipples which perfectly matched her lips. The light scar on her arm. The shadowy hollow of her belly when she sucked it in with her gasp. The wild tendrils that escaped the pin in her hair, the ends still damp from the bath, curling against her neck.

*Beautiful,* I thought, unable to keep my eyes off her as I sucked and laved and licked between her thighs. Her moans filled the cottage, rising higher and higher. I'd never met a creature so singularly focused on their pleasure, so unashamed of it.

Millie had surprised me at every turn.

"Enough, Kythel," she rasped when I lapped at her clit. Her legs squeezed around my ears to keep me in place, and I growled, my own hands tightening around her hips in warning. The heady, intoxicating look she was giving me however made all protest die in my throat. "Before you make me come." I smirked, lifting my head. "Again," she amended.

Swiftly, I tugged her off the table, making a husky, delighted laugh fill the warm cottage. She was smiling, teeth shining in the firelight, when I pulled her to lie on top of me, her legs straddling my hips. Her legs were spread wide to accommodate my size, likely uncomfortably so, but she made no complaints.

"Take what you want from me, *sasiral*," I commanded. "Take what you so desperately want, my needy little mate."

Her eyes flared at the word. That forbidden word. My cock jumped with it, bouncing on my belly as she shifted over me.

"Say it again," she whispered, leaning over. Her lips brushed mine. "Please."

"Mate," I said. I hesitated. But then she was kissing me harder, her tongue stroking against mine. The weight of her against me, the warm softness and slide of her body, the wet droplet that landed on my cheek from her hair…it made me lower my guard. "*Kyrana.*"

Her breath hitched. When her eyes slowly opened, our gazes locked and held. How was it possible that she was most the exquisite, beautiful creature? I liked beautiful things. Once, I hadn't thought her beautiful at all. Now? I couldn't look away. I reveled in every sloping, unsymmetrical line of her face, in every gleam of gold in her hazel eyes.

"Again."

"*Kyrana,*" I murmured more gruffly, sliding a hand up the back of her neck, into her hair, cradling her skull as I shifted my hips. Millie pushed forward, seeking. I blew out a sharp breath when the head of my cock met her heat. And when she slid down with a slow pump of her hips? I groaned, "*Vaan.*"

Millie's eyes were wide though determined. Obviously we were mismatched in size, and it took everything in me not to selfishly demand more of her, to keep my hips still, pinned in place as she adjusted herself over me.

When she sank down even further, another muted curse fell from my lips. I gritted my teeth, another strenuous test of my control descending upon me. From her neck, my eyes fastened on a bead of dark red blood trailing from the wound I hadn't closed. Leaning forward, I lapped at it before latching my fangs into her.

A desperate moan tumbled from Millie. Her hips bucked as my venom flowed, as I lapped at her delicious blood, as it coated my tongue. Both a comfort and a curse.

She was moving more purposefully over me, sinking down, stretching herself wide with my cock. One of my hands was in her hair, holding her in place as I fed. The other was pressed into the floor, grappling for control. I heard the shrill scratch of my claws when they curled, when she sank down as far as she could, the swell of my knot the only thing preventing her from going farther.

"Gods, your cock feels so good, Kythel," came her breathless moan. Another dizzying blow to my control.

"Millie," I said against her neck. "*Cease speaking.*"

"Why?" she laughed, rocking her hips. A gentle grind that made me hit places inside her that made her gasp.

"It's taking everything in me not to flip you over and fuck you the way I need to," I growled. "So cease speaking until I can—"

"So grumpy, even when you have a naked woman on top of you," she teased, kissing the edge of my jaw. She swiveled her hips in small, maddening circles. Under my breath, I prayed to Alaire, the god of mercy. I didn't need to embarrass myself at the hands or hips of my *kyrana*. "It's a good thing you feel so perfect inside me, or else I might not put up with you."

A unrecognizable sound rose from me, my tight control snapping at her flirtatious teasing. Before she could blink, I had us flipped, using my wings to help push me off the floor, one of them banging against the table, but I paid the dull pain no mind.

Millie was breathing hard, staring up at me in delighted surprise and anticipation. A drip of her blood ran down the back of her shoulder from her neck, plopping onto the stone underneath her. It took everything in me not to lick it up. It took everything in me not to consume every part of her, as greedy for her as I was.

"Put up with me?" I asked, grabbing her legs swiftly and tugging them open obscenely wide. I grinned down at her, gaze running over her bared body, humming when I brushed my fingers over the pink folds of her slick cunt. Positioning my cock at her entrance, I pushed forward, a ragged cry escaping her when she found herself filled so suddenly. "You'll do a lot more than that by the end of the night, *kyrana*. That I promise you."

I caught the flutter of a smile on the edge of her lips, even as her walls clenched around my cock.

"Looking forward to it," she said. "Now, Kythel?"

I grunted, sinking more deeply into the cradle of her thighs. Her scent was all around me, but it was her smile that made me want to do anything she asked.

"Make good on your threat," she told me. Her arms trailed up my wrists, stroking up my forearms, my shoulders. "I'm yours."

# CHAPTER 29

## MILLIE

*A*s if my words sparked a challenge, Kythel became like a male possessed.

A switch flipped. His winter-sea eyes morphed into a color so deeply blue that they appeared black and endless. His hips drew back. He pushed forward, and all the breath was wrung from my lungs. Another powerful thrust made me moan before I could even recover from the first. And then he wasn't stopping.

A tumble of rough, deep sounds tore from him as he fucked me.

"Is this what you want?" he asked above me, his face flickering with the licks of the flames from the fire. Half in shadow, half illuminated. "Is this what you've been craving, *sasiral?*"

"Yes," I breathed, letting my thighs widen even further for him.

I'd had sex before…but then there was *this*. This consuming, otherworldly, intense act that made me wonder if I could ever be normal again after it.

Every slide of his cock made me see stars, bursting bright in my vision. Rough sounds tumbled from his throat—small, huffing, erotic moans that made me clench tighter around him, as if afraid he would pull away.

My fingernails bit into his back before sliding down, encountering the joint of one wing. Stroking the rough skin there, I heard another groan, and I smiled.

"Sensitive?" I wondered, fascinated. All the places I ached to explore.

He didn't answer me, but the burn in his eyes and the rattle of my teeth on his next particularly deep thrust was all the answer I needed. I continued to pet and touch that place. Kythel's head dropped into the crook of my neck. Though he didn't feed from me, I felt the slick heat of his tongue lap at the wound, sending sparks of awareness flurrying out from the bite.

When he rolled his hips, trying to get *deeper*, I felt the burn of his knot at the base of his cock. I huffed, determined to take it, though I knew it would only grow after he orgasmed. And he would. That I knew with the utmost certainty. He was already beginning to shake with his restraint.

Every time his knot teased the entrance of my pussy, he groaned and snapped his hips harder before retreating, as if he believed he couldn't—or *shouldn't*—give in to his desires.

"Deeper," I breathed into his ear, wrapping my arms around his neck, holding him in place. "I want all of you."

His breath hitched. When he lifted his head from my neck, there was disbelief in his gaze but also that deep, deep want that made my belly flutter. Every grind of hips stimulated my sensitive clit. My own orgasm was climbing higher and higher. I held my breath, my legs beginning to tighten, my pelvis beginning to lift to meet his thrusts, which were becoming more wild.

"You're going to make me come, Millie," he told me. "*Vaan*, I'm going to come so hard."

I snapped my hips, and I felt the burn of his knot begin to stretch my pussy. Slight pain that mingled with the pleasure. I was surprised by how exquisite it felt. Kythel bellowed—a deep, hoarse, desperate cry. My movement had been unexpected, catching him by surprise as he bucked his hips forward, further seating himself inside me.

"Oh gods," I breathed, biting my bottom lip hard, my gaze flying up to his in disbelief as I began to come.

My back bowed against the warm stone, my hands digging into his shoulders, using him to anchor me into place as the orgasm whipped through me like a violent lash. Dimly, through the rushing in my ears and the wild pound of my heartbeat, I heard his guttural groan, felt the powerful thrusts between my legs, the stretch of his knot, and the satisfying burn as he sheathed himself fully inside me.

If I'd thought his bellow had been erotic before, it was nothing compared to the sound that shredded itself from his throat, reverberating out in ribbony rasps and growls.

Through the haze of heat and pleasure, I felt his knot swell, stretching me to my very limits. He ducked forward, capturing my lips in an uncharacteristically wild, feral kiss. And I met it with enthusiasm, clenching around him, that burn of his knot prolonging my pleasure as I felt heat flood me, as Kythel shallowly pounded his hips before seating himself fully.

I felt his heart thud maniacally against my sticky skin, lost in the abandon of his kiss. When he pulled back, his gaze captured mine and we looked at one another silently for long, breathless moments as our orgasms finally began to ebb.

Not knowing what to say—what did you say after something like *that?*—I only smiled like a loon. Kythel gave a deep groan of exasperation, but I saw the corners of his lips twitch.

There was a sensation of fullness and pressure between my thighs, though not distracting enough to pull my gaze away from Kythel. My hand reached around his slick back, to stroke my finger between his wings, as far as I could reach. For a brief moment, his eyes shuttered closed, the simple pleasure on his face making my throat tight, and I wondered how long it had been since someone touched him as freely as I did.

Beyond Krynn, the Kylorr had a fearsome reputation. They were portrayed as cruel and selfish with uncontrollable rages should you cross one. But I knew better. My father had dealt with his own obstacles—being a Kylorr and a traveling culinarian —but he'd had his reputation to open up doors.

I knew that most believed the Kylorr weren't a particularly affectionate race…but I knew better.

My father had been deeply affectionate. I'd grown up used to touch, to warm embraces, to ruffled hair and obnoxiously loud, peppered kisses across my cheeks when I'd said something amusing. Even when he'd been angry with me, my father had never withheld his affection. If anything, when he'd been angry with me, he'd given me more so I wouldn't doubt.

Instinctively, I knew that Kythel might not have had the same experiences growing up. He was closed off, cold. He kept himself so tightly leashed that I wished I could just snap the cord and free him. Earlier on in our friendship, he'd always seemed surprised when I'd touched him, to the point that I wondered if it was considered rude to touch a son of the Kaalium so freely.

"Do you like when I touch you?" I whispered in the quiet between us.

"Yes," came the rumbled word, his eyes flashing open, as if surprised by his own honesty.

I chuckled softly, my smile so big that it felt like it was splitting my face.

"What is it?" he wondered.

"You're hesitant to admit that," I commented, looking between our bodies pointedly, "even after this?"

His knot was starting to recede because I felt his come begin to trickle between my legs. Instead of embarrassing me, it made me clench around his cock, eliciting a ragged breath from Kythel.

I continued to trail my fingers up and down his back. He was supporting his weight off me, but I wished he would relax, just a little. He wouldn't crush me. I wanted him boneless and sated. I wished we were in a bed and not on the kitchen floor because I wanted to cuddle up against him, lay my head on his chest, and listen to the sounds he made.

"Will you relax?" I teased, shifting under him. "Lie here." I slid my hand over to the floor next to me.

He grumbled. "Have you always been so demanding with your lovers?"

My lips lifted, but Kythel was watching me carefully, even as he turned us so we lay side by side. His knot was still lodged tightly when he gave an experimental thrust, making me jerk and wince.

"*Vaan*, I'm sorry, *sasiral*," he murmured, concerned, lifting his hand to my cheek to smooth his thumb there.

"It's okay," I assured him. Then I admitted, "It's been a long time for me."

"Since when?"

"Since Luxiria," I said. "Nearly three years ago."

Kythel stiffened lightly. "A Luxirian?"

"Yes," I said.

"Luxirians are possessive. I find it hard to believe that he would let you go."

A small chuckle left me. "You're being sweet now?"

Kythel grunted. "Never mind. I don't want to talk about your past lovers when I'm still inside you, Millie."

"Jealous?" I asked, quirking a brow, my limbs feeling like jelly, and I nudged closer to his chest, savoring the heat that poured off him in waves. His body was always bigger after feeding, the muscles so pumped I wanted to dig my fingers into them and squeeze, never letting go.

"Yes," he answered.

"I get jealous when I think about you and Lyris," I admitted, wondering whether it was wise to. But he was being honest. So would I.

Kythel exhaled a long breath, but I ignored the disappointment when he didn't say anything on the matter. Instead, he trailed his fingers down my shoulder, holding my gaze all the while. His expression was almost…imploring.

Forcing the dismay away, not wanting to ruin the night if I made demands of him I knew I didn't have the right to make, I tested the stretch of his knot.

Kythel growled when I slid down, popping it out of me, and I felt a rush of his come, slick and thin.

His cock was still hard, and it stirred, bouncing once, twice, when he saw the mess between my thighs. He *liked* that, I realized.

*And he thinks the Luxirians are possessive?* I wondered, biting my lip when he trailed the backs of his claws against my sensitive, overstimulated pussy. My breath hitched when he circled the swollen bud of my clit, coating it in his silvery come. It shimmered in the firelight against my thighs, making a pool on the floor that I'd need to clean.

"Kythel," I whispered, snagging his wrist, though my palm only wrapped around half of it.

"Sensitive?" he asked.

"Yes."

"I'll give you a brief reprieve."

"Only brief?" I asked, quirking my brow.

Kythel rose to his full height, and I craned my neck to see all of him, enjoying the sight. He truly was a gorgeous male—all dark gray skin, broad shoulders, thighs like columns, and a cock that made me see stars. I stared longer than I should've. Impossibly thick with a wicked, wicked curve, dark veins, and a smooth, bulbed head…I marveled that he had fit inside me at all.

And his knot…

It had gone down already, but I remembered the sizzling stretch of it. I remembered going wild as it had sealed itself into place, every small hitch of his hips making it rub against places I'd never known even existed. The pressure had been delicious. I craved it again.

"Millie," he said, his tone edged in warning.

I grinned, arching my back in a stretch as he retrieved the damp cloth he'd used to dry me off after my bath.

I hadn't expected him to clean me up, but he did, wiping gently at his come before wiping up the floor. He dropped the cloth and then touched around the tender bite at my neck.

"I'm sorry," he murmured, swallowing. "I was rougher than I wanted to be."

I watched him slide his thumb against his fangs, a bead of blood mixing with his venom, which he smoothed over the bite. It felt like a bruise. It didn't hurt, was just tender, but slowly, even the tenderness began to melt away as it healed itself.

"Forget *lore*," I told him. "Kylorr venom is like magic."

He pulled me against him when he lay down again, and I savored his embrace, knowing he wasn't one to show physical affection.

Looking between our bodies, I caught the edge of something black, slumped on the floor next to the table.

"Oh," I whispered.

"Hmm?"

"The book," I said. We must've knocked it off when Kythel had laid me back on the table.

He lifted his head. "You still have the book?"

Drawing in a steady breath, I admitted, "I still haven't read the passage on Ruaala."

"Why?"

"It's silly," I said. "And it doesn't even make sense. But I'm scared of what I might find."

"I've read the passage myself, Millie," he said. "There's nothing frightening. There's not a lot of information in there regardless."

"That's what I'm scared of," I admitted. "That it will be another dead end in finding her."

Kythel stiffened.

"That it will be one more disappointment. I won't feel like I made good on the promise I made to my father until I know where her soul is tethered. Sometimes I feel like it's *here*—because sometimes I swear I can feel her, though we've never met. That makes me worry. It makes me worry that she's in Zyos. That she's lost."

Kythel was quiet. I hadn't meant for the admission to bring an air of sudden solemnness between us, but I felt it drop like a heavy stone nevertheless.

"Sorry," I said, mustering up a smile. "Let's not talk about it. I just want to lie here with you, all right?"

But he was pulling away from me, rising from the floor again.

"Kythel?"

He reached out his hand, and I took it without hesitation.

"Get dressed," he murmured, pulling me up from the floor, my legs still a little wobbly.

"Why?" I asked, incredulous.

A deep sigh escaped him. His blue gaze went out the window, the sill of which I still needed to repair.

Finally, he said, "There's something I need to tell you. And show you."

# CHAPTER 30

## KYTHEL

There was an eeriness about Stellara, especially late into the night. It was why I didn't like the thought of Millie out here past nightfall. I'd blamed it on the *lyvins*, but even I knew those creatures stayed far to the northeast of the forest, that one hadn't been seen near Erzos in years.

Millie was holding my hand, her warm grip keeping me anchored, though I wondered how she would react to what I was about to confess. Would she be angry? Disappointed? Melancholic?

*Likely all three,* I thought. I could have saved her a lot of time and worry if I'd just been honest from the beginning, when she'd asked me about Ruaala in Erzos's archives.

But no one knew what I'd done. Not even Azur, which was illuminating in itself. I'd buried the truth so deep because it was what Ruaala had wanted, what she'd asked of me in her letter, though we'd barely known one another.

Guiding Millie around the back of the cottage, I pulled her closer when she shivered. There was no wind tonight, so it was likely a tendril of a soul, tracing its way across her skin. She seemed more sensitive than most, and I inspected the *zylarr* when we got close, already noticing it needed to be replenished with another crystal. The souls were hungry here. I would likely need to install another within the clearing to keep them satisfied.

"Ruaala went a little mad," I told her, my voice quiet in the silence of the back garden as we came to stand beneath the bleeding tree, "toward the end of her life. Truthfully, she was lost after her child died. She never recovered from that. And if your father and she were blood mates, it would have only added to the grief."

Millie jolted. "What do you mean? She had a child?"

I peered at her in the darkness, the confusion on her face slowly morphing into understanding.

"I knew you'd been keeping something from me. I knew you knew more than you were telling me," she said quietly. I felt shame settle deep, but Millie never pulled her hand out of my grip. Instead, she squeezed it, stepping closer. "Tell me now. Please."

Taking in a deep breath, I said, "The child died in her womb. A mere month before she was due."

"Oh gods," Millie whispered, her brows scrunching, dismay stretching over her expression. "Was...was the child...was the child my father's?"

I shook my head. "Unlikely. She had been married to my uncle for a year by then. Unless your father was still living on Krynn."

"When was this?"

"Twenty-six years ago," I answered.

"Then no," she said. "That was around the time my father found me. He had been working on Genesis prior to that."

"Then the child was my uncle's," I said. A child of House Kaalium.

"She went mad, you said," Millie prompted.

I gestured to where we stood, eyeing the way the silver flashed in the moonlight.

"The trees," I told her. "Every day, it was like she was

possessed. Carving them up. Hammering metal into the trees. Like she was marking her way. Or marking someone else's."

"My father," Millie guessed.

"Likely," I told her. "She barely ate. Never fed on blood, choosing to survive on food alone when she could stomach it. She rarely slept. For years and years, she looked like a ghost. Once, I saw her standing in this very clearing, and for a moment, I thought she was a soul. A soul casting their previous form before me. She looked like she was dissolving around the edges. Like she wasn't even there. It appeared as if she was stretched between all three realms."

I still remembered that moment, clearly imprinted on my mind. I felt guilt now, whenever I thought about it. Another shameful, guilt-ridden memory that I wished I could take back.

"I was around your age then," I told her gruffly. "I'd been in Erzos for a short time. I knew Ruaala, knew she'd left the union with my uncle, but I hadn't seen or heard much of her in the years after. But as I explored Stellara, I discovered the trees. I found her here. But by then, she was a shell. She didn't want help. She just wanted me to leave."

"She lived here, all this time?" Millie wondered. "But the cottage looked as if it had been abandoned for decades."

"I tried to convince her to leave this place," I told her. "She was of House Kaalium, after all, despite the circumstances. She would always be our blood. I wanted her to live in Raana. I told her I would secure her a home, make her comfortable, get her a helper from Erzan. But she refused to leave. She told me that she was too deeply rooted in this place, that the trees had hold of her ankles, her wings, and she didn't want to disappoint them."

Millie frowned.

"She said she was waiting," I confessed to her. "She told me she was waiting for a quiet place."

She stilled.

"You said that to me before—a quiet place," I said. "It took me a while to place it. Until I came here, until all those memories came flooding back."

"It was in my father's letters to Ruaala. He...he always called the cottage their quiet place. He said it was a realm of their own making. I assume it was because they couldn't be with one another elsewhere. Here they were hidden. Safe. They could forget that she was meant to marry into the most powerful family on Krynn."

My heart twisted, like a tangled branch of these silvered trees.

"Where is she?" Millie asked, looking at me steadily. "You know, don't you?"

"A letter came to the keep," he told me. "Eight years ago. She didn't sign her name, but I knew who it was from."

"What did it say?"

Swallowing, I said quietly, "She asked me to bury her body. To let the trees take from her. To wait quietly beneath the earth for the day that her love returned for her."

The hand not gripped tightly in my own flew to Millie's mouth, her eyes widening. "But the Kylorr...you don't bury your dead. It's *wrong*."

Because in burying one's dead, you would be condemning their soul immediately to Zyos. No soul gem to anchor them into place in Alara. It was a desecration of a body to be buried—the flesh slowly rotting away beneath the earth, insects and roots feasting, the bones laid bare.

I nearly shuddered at the thought.

"When I received the letter, I flew straight here from the keep. But she was already dead," I told Millie.

Tears pushed in her eyes, luminous and shining, her whole body stilling.

"She'd dug herself a grave," I said, the words rumbling from me hollow because I could still see her in my mind. Right here. Her thin, tangled light hair spread wide. Her face peaceful, the wrinkled lines smoothed. She'd cleaned herself, the streaks of dirt across her cheeks and the wood shavings in her hair gone. "Do you know what *saanor* is?"

She shook her head wordlessly.

"I found a vial of it next to her. It's a poison. *Saanor* is a concentrated extract from a bleeding tree's sap."

"But I thought the sap was used to make soaps and oils," she whispered.

"It's usually harmless," I assured her. "But Ruaala had been concentrating the sap down for months. It's instant death for a Kylorr upon consumption."

"She poisoned herself," Millie said softly. A whistled breath flew from her, and she shook her head, her brows furrowing in an expression of sorrow. "It's such a tragic tale, Ruaala's life. Her path was chosen for her. She lost her mate, her child, her parents, her future. It must've been such a lonely existence out here. I just...I want to know *why*. Why are some punished so thoroughly, Kythel? Why do some people's hearts take merciless beatings without reprieve? I don't understand it."

I thought of Aina right then. Of my mother. I could still hear her wails in my mind, the anger in her voice when she'd blamed me, though she'd later been horrified by what she'd said.

But the truth always rang clear in my mind. My mother had been the one to say the truth out loud, when no one else had dared.

"I don't know," I told Millie. Gently. Quietly.

"Where is the grave?" she asked after a long moment.

In front of us was the bleeding tree, its trunk winded with silver metal. I gestured to the base of it.

"Here," I told her. "She's been here the entire time."

Millie stared down at the moss-covered earth, struck and still. Then, slowly, she turned to face me. "Why didn't you tell me?"

"Because I was ashamed," I confessed. "*Am* ashamed of what I'd done."

"Because you buried her?"

"Yes," I growled. "And a part of me was relieved that she was dead! That's the ugly part of me I cannot hide."

Millie didn't pull away as I'd expected her to. She came closer, reaching up to press her hands to my jaw and cheek. "Tell me."

"It was clear to anyone that she was suffering," I admitted. "I feel that I should've done more to help her. Instead of letting her waste away in Stellara, all by herself."

"She wasn't your responsibility," Millie reasoned. "She was her *own*. She made her own choices."

"She was still of House Kaalium," I said. "So yes, she was my responsibility."

"You can't take care of every extension of your House, Kythel," she said. "That would drive anyone to madness. It simply can't be done."

She didn't understand. She couldn't. But after Aina's death, I knew my duty and responsibility to my family better than anyone.

"I was relieved when she was no longer suffering," I continued.

"That's understandable," she whispered.

"Are you angry with me?" I wondered. "For keeping it from you? For allowing you to believe that she had gone?"

"I won't say I'm happy about it," Millie answered, peering up at me, sighing. She looked down to the grave beneath the tree. "But what's done is done. I understand why you did it. Now I know where she is. I have all the answers I wanted, though the truth is more horrible than I ever imagined."

"Millie," I said, clasping her face between my palms, forcing her to meet my eyes. "I'm sorry. I truly am."

She held me gaze for a long moment and then said, "I know."

It felt like both a weight off my shoulders but also a deepening of my shame. I imagined a new root of that shame crawling down my limbs, threading around muscles and veins and organs, like the seeking root of a tree. I would never be free of it. I knew that.

"I'll dig up her body myself," I told Millie.

"No, Kythel—"

"I must. I should have done it long ago," I said, my tone allowing no argument. "I'll dig up her bones and take them to the shrine. Her soul gem can be made alongside your father's. I think that's what she would've wanted, don't you?"

Millie's shoulders dropped slowly, the longer she stared up at me.

Finally, she said, "Yes."

She took my hand in her palm, pressing a kiss to its center. I marveled at her ability to forgive. How easy it was for her. Me? I could hold grudges for a lifetime.

I was falling in love with her. It was like another wiggling root inside me, growing stronger every day. But instead of invasive, it felt like an embrace. Comforting. Warm.

All while knowing I would have to tear it out of me soon. Would I survive it?

"Yes, I believe that's exactly what she would've wanted," Millie said, nodding.

# CHAPTER 31

## MILLIE

When I woke, I was warm and comfortable. It felt like I was sleeping on a cloud, my limbs suspended in nothing and yet cradled perfectly.

Kythel shifted behind me. One of his wings twitched where it was draped over the side of my body like a blanket, and I smiled sleepily, shifting around to face him.

His eyes were closed, but I knew he was awake. His stroking touch along my hip had woken me…unless I'd dreamed it.

I felt his claws skim my flesh and knew I hadn't. Morning was breaking over Erzos like a *laak* egg, spilling out its creamy lilac yolk.

For a week I'd slept beside him. In his bed. In his private rooms within the keep. Ever since the first night we'd had sex, ever since he'd told me the truth about Ruaala, I thought we both knew how futile it was pretending to keep our distance from one another.

With every passing day, I'd begun to hope more and more than maybe the moon winds didn't have to be our end. That perhaps Kythel could open himself up to me, allow me to slip inside the thick barriers he had stacked, high and impenetrable, where we could explore wherever this might lead us.

The moon winds were fast approaching, a little over a week away, but we hadn't spoken about them—unless it was in connection with my father's and Ruaala's soul gems, and even then, mentions were fleeting.

I'd begun to breathe a little easier this last week. I'd begun to allow myself to grieve for my father now that I'd nearly fulfilled my promise to him. Of course, the cottage still needed many, many repairs, but I felt like I could take my time with it. I felt like I could *enjoy* the process of it. Uncovering and caring for all the little details of the home. No longer did it feel like a burden with a time limit. Both their soul gems would be together. They'd be rooted in Erzos. That was all that mattered.

"Good morning," I greeted Kythel. "You slept the whole night. Well...nearly," I added, flashing him a teasing smile.

"I woke in the middle," he confessed, his voice a gravelly rumble. "Azur wanted to speak on the Coms."

Azur. His twin brother, I knew.

"What about?"

Kythel's answered, "We spoke about Sorn Village—my plans there. He wanted updates on the South Road."

"In the middle of the night?" I asked pointedly.

Azur had a human *kyrana* too. Gemma of House Kaalium, the daughter of a disgraced war hero from the Collis, Rye Hara, who was now sitting in a prison cell awaiting trial.

Kythel said nothing. He was keeping something from me.

"Kythel?"

"Stop," he rumbled, but there was no bite in the word. "We spoke of another matter, but beyond my brothers, we think it best to keep it between us. So I will not speak of it. Not with anyone."

"All right," I said, trying not to be hurt when he was only being honest. "I understand."

"Are you angry with me?"

"No," I said, sighing, pressing closer. When my legs straightened along his, my breath hitched as I felt the stiffness of his cock, already hard and hot against my belly. I should've been used to it by now. "Sometimes it's easy to forget who you really are."

"And who is that?" he teased.

"Kythel of House Kaalium," I answered. "Son of Thraan. High Lord of Erzos. Heir to the Kaalium."

He sobered at his title, his jaw tightening, and I regretted bringing it up at all. To distract him, I leaned forward and brushed my lips against his. I liked when we were lying side by side because it made kissing him all the easier. And I liked kissing him very, very much.

Reaching between us, I caught hold of his cock. He sucked in a breath, holding it as I dragged my fist up the thick length, unable to wrap my hand fully around him. Gently at first.

"*Sasiral,*" he murmured. "I have a meeting with House Nyra this morning."

It was strange—in my last two relationships, the sex had been nice. It'd felt good. It'd felt comforting. I'd liked feeling connected to my partners. But I'd never *needed* it. I'd never been ravenous for it, never felt like climbing out of my skin to escape the pinching need of it.

With Kythel? I couldn't get enough. Case in point, when I shifted, I felt a dull ache between my thighs. Kythel had woken me up in the night—perhaps when he'd returned from his call with Azur—and had been insatiable. Then again, so had I.

"It can wait," I told him, squeezing the underside of the crown. "Can't it?"

He said, "It can't."

Sighing, I released his cock. "All right."

I knew his responsibilities weighed heavily on him. There was something driving him to be the best *Kyzaire* he could possibly be. At first, I'd wondered if it was competitiveness with his brothers. But Kythel wouldn't care about that, so I'd struck it from my mind. He'd told me before that he hadn't always wanted to inherit Erzos, that he'd studied to be an architect in Laras, a creator of cities.

So what had changed?

We lay in silence for a brief moment, Kythel's chest heaving. The blanket was pushed down to his upper thighs, and I admired the lines of his body in the purple-toned morning light. I took in the way his cock dripped with the beginnings of his come, the way it pulsed from my brief touch.

He was watching me watch him.

Then he growled, and I smiled, though I tried to hide my smug triumph as best as I was able. I squealed before it turned into a husky laugh as he pulled me on top of him.

"Make it quick, my needy little female," he rasped. "*Vaan*, I want you so much. All the fucking time. It's madness."

"You don't want it quick," I teased, though I gasped as I settled into place on top of him, straddling his hips, my legs spread wide. "You want it nice and slow so you can feel every part of me."

And he did. Kythel liked to *savor*. He liked to take his time with me, especially during the night, when he had no duties to attend, no meetings about the South Road to catch, no contracts to sign, no requests from the villages to deliberate over, no *lore* reports to analyze.

The searing heat of his cock head met my entrance when I lifted up, but I evaded the powerful thrust of his hips.

"Millie," he bit out.

I grinned, watching the tendons in his throat tighten with his restraint. I was wet already, throbbing for him...and yet I liked to see him lose a fraction of that tightly held control. Nothing made me hotter.

I teased his cock between my thighs, sinking down an inch

over his crown, watching his eyes close in relief, until I bucked my hips back up, sliding off.

The flickering fire in his eyes promised retribution.

"Enough, *kyrana*," he said. And when he said that word...I knew he wouldn't allow any more teasing. "Fuck me now, or I'll bend you over the side of the bed and take what I want."

That was intriguing, I'd admit, sending a pulsing flutter spiraling straight to my clit.

Who knew that Kythel of House Kaalium, with a gaze like ice and a hardened demeanor to match, had such a dirty, dirty mouth?

"Yes?" he asked, the demand in his voice unmistakable.

"Yes," I whispered, feeling his grip on my hips tighten. Biting my lip, I sunk down onto his cock with a quick slide, and I heard a murmured, strained word tumble from his throat, though I didn't know its meaning.

*I changed my mind,* I thought, moments later when I was gasping and sweating, feeling him pull me up and down on his cock with his unfathomable strength as if I weighed nothing. *I like when he's impatient too.* He was *using* me, and I loved it. I couldn't get enough.

The room filled with the sounds of sex—slapping flesh and breathy moans and gasps.

My fingernails were biting into his chest, anchoring me to him as he pounded between my thighs. He leaned up with a growl, capturing one of my nipples between his lips, nipping lightly at the bud, making me gasp, before sucking hard.

My hands dove into his hair before one curled around one of his horns, holding him to me.

"Yes, Kythel," I breathed, my legs beginning to tighten up, feeling my orgasm begin to creep up on me.

"Beautiful," he purred, leaning back to meet my eyes. "You're so beautiful, *sasiral.*"

My throat went a little tight at his compliment. My first

impulse was to deny his words. When I'd been younger, I'd always been self-conscious of my features, knowing they weren't considered classically beautiful by human standards. Now? It didn't truly bother me as much as it used to. I liked that Ver Teracer himself had said I had an interesting face. I would never be beautiful like Grace or Lesana or Lyris.

But I liked who I was, and so my beauty rarely bothered me. When it came to Kythel, however? I'd been more and more aware that we made an odd pairing. He was sinfully gorgeous, so beautiful he could make me ache just looking at him. And me…well, I was short and small and strange looking.

Hearing Kythel call me beautiful, it made old insecurities rear their heads. But then I reminded myself that Kythel would never lie to me about this. Never about this. If he thought I was beautiful…it was because he truly thought that.

That realization alone made my heart sing.

"You think so?" I asked, grinning.

He kissed me, hard and quick. Against my lips, he answered, "Yes."

We kissed as I began to come. His tongue tangled and stroked against mine, and he groaned when I tightened on him. He changed his pace, grinding against me, stimulating my clit, and that alone flung me over the edge.

I gasped, my eyes screwing shut, my hand squeezing around his horn as I rocked wildly over him.

"Millie," he groaned out, releasing my lips, his mouth trailing down my neck until it hovered just over my breast. "*Raazos*, you feel so fucking good."

I cried out when he slid his fangs into the side of my breast, his venom flooding the bite, prolonging and stretching out my orgasm until I felt like I could snap.

Kythel drank but not because he was hungry for my blood. It was more of a comforting act, given he was more than well supplied on my blood. Over the last week, his bite had begun to feel more like a kiss or an embrace than an act of feeding and a source of nourishment for him.

It made me feel closer to him, and so I held his head against my breast. And when I felt him begin to come, his pumps becoming shallow and quick? I squeezed my inner muscles and reached between us to tease his swollen seal at the base of his cock. On a particularly rough squeeze, he gave a hoarse cry and a sudden jerk of his hips. I felt the hot lashes of his silver come flood me, and I savored every drop.

As he came down from the high of his orgasm, he gave a gruff laugh, a sound in which I delighted because I didn't hear it that often. He was much too serious, so when he laughed, it felt like a small victory.

He released my breast, smoothing over a bead of venom to close the wound, but he didn't heal the flesh. Later, I knew he'd drag his hot, thick tongue over his bite, territorial and possessive, despite the fact he didn't believe he had such base impulses.

*I know otherwise, however,* I thought, biting back a smile.

"You'll be late for your meeting with House Nyan," I whispered as he kissed me, lingering and savoring as his hands traced lines down my back. Between us, I felt his come begin to drip since he hadn't knotted me.

"House who?" he grunted, making me laugh. "What I wouldn't give to lie here with you all day."

Affection slid down my chest like a sweet, warm glaze.

"You like me, don't you?" I teased.

Kythel didn't miss a beat. "Yes—too much."

"For the record," I said quietly, giving him a small smile, "I like you too much too."

It was moments like these that gave me hope. Tiny little moments that made my heart swell so much it felt like bursting.

Then I could feel him retreating, as he always did. He seemed to realize what he'd said, as I'd figured he might, but I merely pasted on a smile and pretended. Which I was becoming very good at these last few weeks.

"You'll be late," I reiterated, offering up an easy escape route on a silver platter.

"Yes, I will be," he said softly, helping me dismount off his lap. As he swung his legs over the edge, rising, I knelt on the bed, clenching my thighs together so I didn't make a mess of the blankets.

"I'll go wash," I said, maneuvering on wobbly legs to the attached washroom, which was the size of my entire cottage in Stellara. "See you this afternoon?"

He shook his head when I turned to regard him, and I watched him request a specific outfit from the Halo tablet in the wall. A moment later, he opened up the hidden dresser, which tucked into the black paneling seamlessly, and pulled out the perfectly pressed vest—dark maroon today, gray pants with silver stripes running down the seams, and soft leather boots.

He usually always stopped by the cottage at some point during the day. To check in on me, even though it took him away from his duties.

"It will be a long day," he said. "I'll see you tonight."

I hid my frown and nodded. Smiling, I said, "See you tonight."

Then I disappeared into the washroom, closing the door behind me. I washed leisurely, trying to ignore the dread in my gut that told me this would not end well, that told me Kythel of House Kaalium would absolutely crush me into a million pieces in a week's time.

But I must've been a masochist because the thought of walking away from him now—even if it was the logical, smart move—hurt even more.

After I washed and dressed, Kythel was already gone. Sighing, I made my way out the door of his private rooms to a quiet north wing. Passing a few keepers on my way to the kitchens, I nodded at them in greeting, giving them bright smiles that they didn't quite return. No one knew what to make of me, I realized. I was a blood giver to the *Kyzaire*, but all of them would know by now that I was warming his bed too. They would all know what I was to him. His blood mate. But not his wife.

Pushing that thought away, I saw Telaana mixing a thick soup at the stovetop as I joined her.

"Good morning," I chirped.

"Ah, Millie," she said, distracted as she poured in a little too much *kanno* spice into the soup, in my opinion, but I bit my tongue. "A message came for you from the markets."

I perked up. "Oh?"

"About an off-planet delivery?" Telaana asked, confusion written on her features. "Did I hear the messenger right?"

"Yes," I said, excited, surprised the ingredients had arrived so quickly, though I might have implied in my order that they were for a *Kyzaire* of the Kaalium. "I'll go right now to pick everything up."

"What are you up to?" she asked, shooting me a conspiratorial but insanely curious look across the kitchen.

I snagged a seasoned *laak* egg and a puffed piece of circular bread I'd helped Telaana prep last evening, showing her a kneading technique I'd learned from a culinarian on Jobar.

"It's a gift for the *Kyzaire*. But promise you'll keep that a secret," I added, throwing her a small wink.

The culinarian of Erzos Keep didn't make me that promise, but I walked toward the side door of the kitchen anyway, already munching on the pillowy softness of the bread, pleased they'd turned out just as I'd remembered.

"He's different, Millie," Telaana called out suddenly. "He's different with you here. I know it's not my place to say, but we've all seen a change in the *Kyzaire*."

I stilled, hand still on the cool handle of the door that would lead out to the back gardens.

"He is?" I asked quietly, around a mouthful of sweet bread. "How?"

She seemed hesitant to say. Then again, Telaana was an interesting soul. Just when I had her pinned, she did something to surprise me.

"I won't say he was like a cyborg," she said, raising a shoulder. "But well...he was. He wasn't natural."

A laugh of disbelief left me.

"And I'll keep your promise about the gift if you promise me to never tell the *Kyzaire* I said that," she added, pointing her metal spoon at me, splattering soup onto the floor.

"I won't say a word," I vowed.

She turned at the stove, perching her hip perilously close to the flame.

"Telaana," I said, my eyes nervously watching it dart near her tunic. She'd already set her pants on fire earlier in the week. "The burner—"

"But after his aunt's murder, his mother's death, and his father shoving all the responsibilities onto his sons and *leaving*, I wouldn't want a single *tun* of that family's problems. No matter how noble or wealthy they are."

"Telaana," I said softly, quietly processing her words. "Maybe we shouldn't be discussing these things."

It struck me as improper, gossiping about the *Kyzaire* behind his back, as I reeled over what she'd revealed. I'd known none of that. Kythel had mentioned his aunt but not that she'd been murdered. He rarely spoke of his mother or his father—only brief mentions in passing.

"All I'm saying is that he actually seems happy. *Relaxed,*" Telaana continued, her expression fixing into a serious expression. "I've known him long enough to know that I've never seen him like this before. And I think—no, I *know* it's because of you."

My heart softened at her intent. "Thank you for saying that," I said. "He's a good friend to me. I hope he's happy."

She nodded, studying me carefully, opening her mouth as if to say more.

But just then I saw a bright spark, and I watched as her tunic caught fire. My muscles tensed, preparing to dart over to her, but she laughed, slapping at the flame, extinguishing it completely with her wide palm. The only evidence that it had ever been was a small burn mark on her tunic, and I wondered how in the world this clumsy culinarian who set herself on fire on a regular basis had started working at Kythel's keep.

"Oh!" Telaana said, turning back to the stove. "Do you mind picking up a bunch of cower's roots when you're at the market? I need them for the evening meal tonight."

I shook my head, my heart still going after the fire. But for Telaana, that was likely a normal occurrence.

"I will," I said, turning back toward the door to the gardens. "And Telaana?"

"Hmm?" she asked, already absentminded, stirring the soup.

"Thank you. For what you said."

She nodded but said nothing in reply.

# CHAPTER 32

## KYTHEL

"Couldn't stay away, could you?" Millie singsonged, flashing me a smug, maddening, but genuinely pleased grin when she saw me land in the clearing.

My wings flared, itching from the uncommonly warm weather this afternoon. A beautiful day. Clear skies, gentle winds, and the perfume of ripening *syaan* berries in the air. There must've been bushes of them nearby.

"Where are you going?" I asked, eyeing the brown leather pouch she had looped with a frayed, braided cord around her shoulder. I glared. "I know you're not going out into the forest."

"Well, I am," she said, pausing at the threshold of the clearing, her path set southeast. "Now that you're here, would you care to join me? Protect me from all the scary *lyvins* that will be sleeping right now, far from here?"

I stalked toward her, grumbling. When I reached her, her smile changed. Morphing from teasing to soft. I felt a wave of affection roll through me. That was the thing about Millie. I always knew what she was thinking, what she was feeling. She was open and vulnerable with her emotions—the complete opposite of me.

It was so damn easy being with her. Even when her temper reared its head—which, admittedly, wasn't often enough for my liking. I liked when her claws came out. I liked when she nicked me with them.

*Maybe I'm more like Azur than I thought,* I mused, watching Millie's hand reach for mine. A gentle squeeze came as her soft palm wrapped in mine, fingers entwining. A strictly human form of physical affection, but one I found I didn't mind.

"Hello," she said quietly, rising onto her tiptoes to press a kiss to the underside of my jaw. My spine tingled. "I really didn't expect to see you here this afternoon. I thought you had a long line of meetings today."

I had. Meetings I had pushed off so I could be here, but I didn't tell Millie that, knowing she'd be displeased. But I'd felt like I was going insane. If I went a few hours without seeing her, I needed her scent, her smile, her touch to ground me again.

Was this how Azur felt with Gemma? I hadn't told him about Millie during our Com call because, truthfully, I hadn't known how to admit the truth. That I'd found my *kyrana*, a rare feat in itself, that the eldest twins of the Kaalium had both found their mates in the form of human women.

I didn't know how to tell him that I would still choose the Kaalium over Millie if it came down to it.

Because he would try to dissuade me. He'd found happiness and peace with Gemma. He would want me to have the same. And with my twin's influence, it would only be too easy to forget my duty.

"One meeting fell through," I lied. "I was just heading back to the keep when I thought I'd check on you. And good thing I did. How long have these trips into Stellara been happening?"

She rolled her eyes, pulling away. I followed when she began walking into the forest, guided by our clasped hands. "You act like I do this all the time. I'm searching for *davrin* roots. Telaana said they grow in Stellara but only near water. I thought I heard a running stream the other day, so I thought I'd check."

"Why do you want *davrin* roots? There are plenty at the keep, I'm sure. Or at the market."

"I need them. I'm planting a garden of all my father's favorites and need to get the bulbs in the ground while the weather is warm," she said. Then added, "Plus, I have a surprise for you."

"Oh?" I asked, raising a brow, intrigued. "What surprise?"

"You'll need to wait and see," she said. "Your nights are free, yes?"

"Yes," I said slowly. Well, no, but I could shuffle things around should the need arise. Except for one very important meeting that I could not miss later this week—a meeting I had yet to even tell Millie about, even though I would be gone for a few nights at the very least. "What are you up to?"

"So suspicious," she commented, grinning as she walked under the purple leaves of the bleeding tree. With the sunlight streaming through them, it cast the forest in an ethereal glow, soft and otherworldly.

Just then, my ears ticked, and I snapped my head to the side, my eyes scanning the empty forest. Millie stilled when I froze, and she watched me, stepping closer for protection, but wisely remained silent.

There was a buzzing. A gentle whirring, like an insect, but the sound was much too smooth. I recognized it, my brows furrowing in confusion as it bounced off a nearby tree. I released Millie's hand, squeezing her wrist to keep her in place as I approached the tree.

A small black metal tracker scout was clinging to the edge of a nearby bleeding tree. Fortunately, tracker scouts weren't programmed to successfully evade a motivated pursuer, only to be discreet. Most wouldn't even notice them, but I'd been trained from a young age to be watchful and wary of them after a handful had gained entrance to Laras's keep when we'd been children, recording private meetings between my father and the Kaazor.

Aina had trained us to detect their low frequency, that dull buzz that sounded like a quiet ringing in your ear.

When the tracker detected me close, it went limp, falling from the tree trunk to land in the moss. Crouching, I picked it up, holding it by its four translucent metal wings, pinched between my claws. The black body was small, no bigger than the tip of my finger.

The issue with tracker scouts was that they couldn't be traced to their programmers. Which made them excellent tools for cowards and spies. So I crushed the tracker between my fingers, black dust from the body mingling with the minuscule tech inside. It wasn't inexpensive tech. Whoever used it had the credits to spare. Then again, most who spied on House Kaalium did.

Would Zyre, the king of the Kaazor, do this? If so, what was he playing at, requesting a meeting with the heirs of the Kaalium at the border between our nations in just a handful of days, only to be spying on us? The Kaazor had used tracker scouts before. While this one looked like it was of Kaalium make, I wasn't foolish enough to believe that the Kaazor didn't keep spies within our nation.

Maazin of House Laan, after all, had slipped into my brother's keep, undetected, and worked there for years. We'd believed him to be a spy for the Kaazor, until it had been discovered that he might've been of Thryki origins. Zyre had sent his head to us as if it had proved he wouldn't kill one of his own, but could we really trust Zyre? Perhaps he was playing us all for fools. The scout must've followed me from Erzan. They could fly at startling speeds to keep up with a Kylorr.

"What is it?" Millie asked, the serious note in her voice breaking me from my thoughts.

"Nothing," I lied, meeting her eyes as I wiped the black dust off on my pants. "I thought it was a tracker scout, but it was just an insect."

The truth in reverse. Would she believe it? Or would she see right through my lies?

"A tracker scout?"

I smiled, approaching her. "During the last war with the Kaazor, tracker scouts were all over the Kaalium, used to spy on noble Houses and my own family. Aina taught us how to detect them relatively easily. I thought that was what the sound was, but I was mistaken. Still, I wanted to be sure."

Millie's brow furrowed, but I was relieved when she nodded.

"Shall we continue to the stream?" I asked, my mind replaying the conversation between us that the scout would've caught, but I knew it had been nothing of consequence. Still, it worried me that the scout had seen her at all. "It's not far."

That was a mistake. Her gaze narrowed on me, likely catching on my eagerness to usher her away from this area.

But she didn't comment on it. Instead, we continued walking. Then she asked, "Who is Aina?"

My hand flattened on the small of her back, a small spasm that I hid with a gentle caress up her spine.

"My aunt," I said. "My mother's sister."

"Oh," she said. "The one you told me about? The one who gave you the fruit from the Kaazor?"

"Yes," I said, thinking that conversation with her felt like years ago already when it had only been a few weeks. "Yes, that was Aina."

"So you were close with her?" she asked.

My throat tightened. *Yes.* And then I'd turned my back on her when it had been my duty to join her on Pe'ji. I would live with that shame, that guilt for the rest of my life.

"Yes, we were close," I replied quietly. "The new village, along the South Road, will be named Sorn. House Sorn was my mother's line. And Aina's. Though you would know that if you would only read the book I gave you."

She slapped me on the arm, and my chest loosened. That was another thing I liked about Millie. She had a talent for reading a conversation, for reading the body language of another and knowing when to push and when to weave. That talent had come with time, no doubt from her travels, from the way she'd grown up, a child of the stars, jumping from one galaxy to the next.

"Maybe you should read it to me," she suggested. "It's your family, after all."

"And you should know them," I said without thinking.

"Why?" she asked.

I blew out a rough breath.

*Because my family will be your own* was what I wanted to say. But it was wishful thinking, a fantasy that might never come true, and I didn't want to give her false hope. That wasn't fair.

"It would be useful," I replied instead. Clearing my throat, I added, "If you intend to remain in Erzos."

Millie nodded, but I knew the answer disappointed her.

"Maybe I'll travel again," she said quietly, not meeting my eyes. "Once I'm done with the cottage, once my father's and Ruaala's soul gems are joined. Traveling again might be nice."

I jerked, frowning, my heart beginning to race at the thought of her slipping away.

"You would leave Krynn?"

"No," she said, which was a dizzying relief. "But even if I did, it wouldn't be for long. I promised my father that I would try to root my soul here, with your gods and goddesses. But there are other provinces I'd like to see. I've thought about living in Laras, seeing the Silver Sea. Or journeying to Vyaan because I heard they have an eatery for humans. With my experience in kitchens, it might be easier to find work there."

It pinched harder than I'd expected that she was making plans to leave Erzos. Then again, I had given her no reason to stay. Our agreement, no matter how entangled, ended at the next moon-wind storm—which was not that far away, I realized with a panicked squeeze in my chest.

It made sense she would want to travel. It was in her blood.

"You've never stayed in one place for very long, have you?" I commented, my tone harsher than I wanted. In an attempt to lighten it, I said, "I just thought you'd want to be near your father."

"I'll return for the moon winds, no matter where I am," she told me.

"You've given this a lot of thought, I see," I grunted.

We both felt the tension rising between us, the unspoken thing we couldn't say.

"It would be hard to stay here, Kythel," she said quietly. There was tendril of melancholy in her voice, but she hid it with a small smile.

"Why?" I demanded.

But we both knew why. It was selfish of me to make her say it.

"Never mind," I said, shaking the thought from my mind. The week we had left already felt entirely too short, stretched and strained, and I didn't want to spend it arguing. "Let's not speak of it."

Millie nodded, looking down at her booted feet—worn, secondhand boots likely purchased at the market, but at least these didn't have holes in the toe. Still, looking at them made me feel restless. Regardless of what happened between us, I would always take care of her. She never had to worry that she'd need to sleep in a storage room or scrounge for food or wear clothes until they disintegrated into threads. Ever again.

Did she not understand that?

*No, because you've never discussed it. You've never given her assurances,* I knew.

She wouldn't accept my help. She'd only accepted my assistance with retrieving her father from Horrin because she loved her father more than she valued her pride. But otherwise? Millie Seren would never accept a single credit from me.

I'd asked her to visit the seamstresses shop in Raana to have a new wardrobe made when I'd noticed her *lack* of one...and she'd laughed in my face.

When I'd bought her a glittering set of culinarian knives I'd had Setlan secure for me last week, she'd balked even as she'd stroked them lovingly, telling me they'd been crafted by the Kimnians and that she couldn't possibly accept them. Later, when I'd researched the Kimnians, I'd discovered that only a handful of knife sets were made every three years and that culinarians from across the Quadrants clamored to get their hands on one. As such, they were outrageously expensive, though truthfully I didn't remember the price Setlan had quoted, only that I'd thought Millie would like them.

As such, she'd shoved them back into my hands like they'd been on fire even though I'd seen the *want* and awe in her gaze, as if she'd never expected to see a set in person.

She'd done the same with a new mattress I'd purchased for the cottage, one of the best in the Kaalium, stuffed and hand-quilted with *nerkkya* feathers from a tradesperson right in Erzan. We'd argued that afternoon. I'd called her stubborn. She'd called me high-handed when she'd seen the mattress situated into place in the bedroom. And then we'd fallen onto the new mattress and made love until even Millie had known we couldn't possibly send it back after that. I'd been smug the rest of the evening but had known better than to show it.

I'd thought that perhaps she didn't like gifts. But then when I'd given her a crystalline blue vase filled with starwood blooms from my own gardens—my mother's favorite flower—she'd nearly split her face in two with a grin so wide. She'd placed the vase in the center of the table at the cottage, fussing over it endlessly. I'd often caught her rearranging the blooms or making sure the vase was well filled or shielding it from streaks of sunlight should they creep too close.

Just thinking about her simple joy made all the frustration loosen from my chest. My shoulders relaxed, determined to enjoy the afternoon with her before I needed to return to the keep.

"The stream isn't far," I told her, shaking off the tracker scout and thoughts of Zyre and of Millie debating leaving Erzos. "Do I get a hint about this surprise?"

Millie blew out a long breath, but when she turned her face up to me, her smile was bright and open, no lingerings or traces of her previous melancholy. She seemed to have made the same decision.

"Let's just say it's out of this world," came her cryptic reply.

I grumbled. "That tells me nothing."

Grabbing her waist, I tugged her into my side, my wings flaring out behind her like a shield.

"You'll enjoy it," she said, chuckling. She turned her head to regard me as we walked. "I promise."

Unable to resist, I lowered my head and caught her lips. Millie stilled, her hand winding around my wrist when I cupped the back of her head to deepen it. And perhaps I poured my need and frustration and desire for her into that kiss, trying to tell her all the things that went unspoken between us. Because by the end, both of us were gasping and Millie was clinging to me, the only thing keeping her standing being the support of my wings at her back.

"Looking forward to it, *sasiral*," I rasped against her lips.

# CHAPTER 33

## MILLIE

Three nights later, nervous excitement made it hard to sit still as I waited for Kythel to arrive. He'd had plans to meet with Vadyn tonight, the head keeper, as they did on a monthly basis. But he'd promised to come to the cottage straight after, and I hoped he arrived soon, since the first course was ready and waiting.

I'd been preparing the food all day—and truthfully had started yesterday evening to allow the yeast in the dough to ferment properly. Some of the meal I'd had to prepare at Erzos's kitchen, Telaana allowing me free reign as long as she got to observe my process.

I'd planned five courses in all, sourcing ingredients from Erzos when I could but ordering the others I couldn't get from the off-planet merchant at the market. I had been hesitant to spend the credits on the expensive ingredients—that gut-wrenching anxiety as I'd watched the subtraction from my Halo orb was a feeling I wished I'd never need to feel again.

Yet…it was for Kythel. I wanted to give him something only I could give him, especially when he was a son of the Kaalium, who had nearly the entire universe at his disposal.

269

I smoothed my new dress down my sides—another purchase I'd been loath to make, though I thought the lilac color complimented my skin nicely and it made me feel *pretty*. Kythel hated my clothes, evidenced when he'd nearly forced me to the seamstresses to acquire new ones at his expense. I'd refused, though the insecurity that the way I dressed might embarrass him had stayed.

When I'd seen this dress at the market, tucked underneath other mismatched patterns and fabrics and colors at the vendor stall, I'd known it would be an upgrade. I wanted to look nice for him tonight. Even if I hadn't worn something so impractical in what felt like years.

I'd brushed my hair until it was silky, noticing that it was getting long. I'd decided to forgo perfume oil since I knew Kythel went wild for my natural scent. I'd never be a great beauty, but I smiled at myself in the gilded mirror regardless before I'd gone downstairs to the kitchen.

The cottage was beginning to feel like a home, and it had never felt more complete than this night. Just a few nights, I knew, before the moon winds, which only added to my nerves.

A familiar thump came from outside, and I grinned, going to the front door, hand already outstretched for the handle. I hadn't seen him all day and—

He was there in the doorway before I could reach it. Kythel's eyes darkened when he took me in for the first time. The thin-strapped dress was like a waterfall of silk, hugging to my small curves and leaving very little to the imagination considering I was entirely naked beneath it.

Kythel seemed to freeze on the threshold, for the first time seemingly at a loss for words as he took in the sight of me.

Then, ever so slowly, he closed the door behind him before prowling to me with a measured gait. Eyes pinned to me, bright in the warm firelight. I'd made it romantic tonight. Floating Halo orbs, dim lighting, a meal I'd lovingly labored over for a full day, and this damn dress.

And he liked it.

A lot.

I'd wanted to give him something special, and it looked like I'd made the right call.

I grinned when he tugged me into him, his hands already skimming my sides to grip my hips hard. Breathless, I met his deep, deep kiss, my hands going to his broad shoulders, digging into the muscles there to keep him against me.

He groaned, his palms running from my hips to my ass, where he squeezed. The possessive touch made my knees shake.

"So beautiful, *sasiral*," he purred. "I love my surprise. Where did you find it?"

"The dress isn't your surprise, Kythel," I said, chuckling, even as my cheeks heated, pleased by the compliment.

He pulled away, confused. I gestured at the small table behind me, the one I'd restored. The flowers he'd given me still looked in perfect health. The first course was already set into place, a decanter of Drovos wine sitting beside the platter.

"I'm giving you the universe tonight," I said, taking his hand and leading him to the chair, the back of it straight and narrow, specifically made for a Kylorr to accommodate their wings. "Four dishes from four different Quadrants. And a fifth of my own creation."

Kythel's lips parted. His head tilted down in a quiet, assessing expression, his eyes flickering back and forth between mine. "You're giving me the universe?"

"You said you had dreams of traveling throughout the Quadrants," I said. "I thought I would bring a portion of them to you here on Krynn. One of the recipes is my father's, two we worked on together. One I learned from a Tirutian—from the party where I met Ver Teracer actually. But the last I made for you. Only for you. Inspired by Stellara."

The intensity in his gaze was making me a little emotional. Not the response I'd expected, but when tears sprung in my eyes, he blew out a sharp breath, tugging me into him more fully, kissing me again. This time more restrained but no less passionate. Soft and deliberate, the way he kissed me made my throat tighten with the sweetness of it.

"You are unlike anyone I've ever met, Millie Seren," he whispered against my lips, his forehead resting on mine when he broke the kiss. "Thank you, *sasiral*. I love my surprise."

I laughed, dashing away the tears that threatened to fall down my cheeks, though I wasn't embarrassed that he witnessed it. "You haven't tasted anything yet," I reminded him. "I'm a little rusty, you know."

"Whatever you give me will be perfect," he replied, "because you made it."

I flushed until I was certain I resembled one of the bright red berries I'd used in one of the compotes. Kythel's gaze went to the prep counter, where the other dishes were sitting under hydro-warmers. Telaana had let me borrow the clear domes for the night. They would keep the individual platters at the ideal temperature, and then I would add the fresh garnishes as I served Kythel.

"No peeking," I chided, ushering him into his chair. When I took a seat in the chair just next to him, I tucked a strand of my hair behind my ear and said, "This is inspired by Bartu. You said you wanted to see the great cathedrals there, right? This is a dish from Inru, which has the largest cathedral dedicated to a deity in all of the First Quadrant, perhaps even the entire universe."

Kythel couldn't take his eyes off me, and they drifted back and forth between my eyes and my lips as I spoke, flustering me, though all I wanted to do was grin. But I kept my composure, always nervous about a first course, especially considering I hadn't made this particular dish in years. But the Bartutians and the Kylorr enjoyed similar levels of spice in their food, so I thought it would be a good choice.

"They sell something similar on the streets right outside the cathedrals," I explained. "It's simple food, meant to be eaten after they sing their long chants. It takes a lot of energy, I'm told. But the Bartutians begin to sing at sunrise, and to hear them sing is hauntingly beautiful. And so when my father and I created this recipe, we used all the same ingredients as the original we had that day, but we added an orange glaze made of *ojun* fruit to brighten up the smokiness of the game. And little popping *alcui* berries because they snap on the tongue, and the sound reminded us of the clicking chorus of the Bartutians' chants. That's what those little spheres are," I explained, gesturing down to the plate.

The plates were mismatched because I'd bought them second-hand at the market. Mine had a chip in it, but I thought they were both a pretty blue, each complimenting the other. The Bartutians served *buno* on a skewer, but ours sat in a pretty orange glaze, the color of the sunrise that morning on Bartu.

"I'm not boring you, am I?" I asked, laughing a little when I realized I'd been rambling and the dish was getting colder by the second.

"Not at all," Kythel rumbled, leaning forward to capture my chin in his grip, giving me a lingering kiss. He admitted, "This is a side of you I haven't seen much. You think you're boring me? It's quite the opposite. I promise you, *sasiral*, I could listen to you talk about faraway places all day and night."

I swallowed, feeling a lump rise in my throat.

Falling in love with him had been much too easy, I realized. Hadn't it?

"I hope you're hungry," I told him quietly.

"Ravenous," he replied, throwing me a secretive smile I recognized, one that made me squirm in my seat. Kythel pulled back, picking up his two-pronged eating utensil and using the sharpened side to cut through the Bartutian game—which had taken a week to source—like it was warm butter from the New Earth colonies. He popped the bite into his mouth, making sure he got a bit of everything, which pleased me.

I watched him with bated breath, watching his jaw work, though I knew the game would melt on his tongue. When he said nothing, I worried I'd messed up the recipe and quickly took a bite of my own.

The flavor was mild at first—the protein lightly spiced—but then I got a hint of the tart but sweet glaze, followed by the surprising spark of the berries. *Delicious.* Just how I remembered making it with my father.

Kythel said nothing, only peered over at me, the corner of his mouth quirking upward in a decadent smirk.

"What do you think?" I asked, though I was confident in the first course, a hint of triumph entering my tone. "You're in love with it, aren't you?"

"Yes," he said, those eyes pinned on me. "I am."

I didn't read too much into his words or the intensity of his expression as he said them…though it was difficult.

"Like your dishes at Raana *Dyaan*," he started, "I've never had anything quite like it, Millie."

That was a high compliment coming from a *Kyzaire*, who'd no doubt had only the best throughout his life. Which made me think of Telaana, setting her clothes on fire on a regular basis, and I let out a small chuckle.

"What?" he asked, going in for a second bite, his movements eager.

"How did you meet Telaana?"

"A random question," he commented, licking a stray drop of glaze off his utensil, and I followed the lap of his tongue with bated breath.

"I—I was just thinking that she seems an odd choice for someone like you. You, who likes everything in perfect order, everything running efficiently and smoothly."

His eyes lit up in understanding.

"Oh, don't get me wrong," I said hurriedly when I realized how my comment sounded. "Telaana is a talented culinarian. The *wylden* roast she makes? It's the best I've ever tasted. But she's..."

"Absentminded?" he guessed.

"Yes," I said, shoulders sagging, a sheepish smile crossing my face. "It's not usually a trait that you see often in a professional kitchen. So I just wondered if there's a story there."

"Yes and no," he replied. "She's an old family friend who fell on difficult times. I had an opening in my kitchens, and she had a mother who was well known for her *wylden* roast."

My lips lifted slightly.

"Don't get me wrong," he quoted, repeating my words with a gentle quirk of his lips. "I expect everyone to do their assigned duties within the keep and do them well. But for Telaana...I am more lenient than I likely would be on anyone else."

I...liked that. Most wouldn't guess that the *Kyzaire* of Erzos with his icy gaze and grim expression had a soft spot. Most wouldn't guess that it was bigger than they could imagine.

Kythel noticed the goblet on the table and swiftly changed the subject with, "And Drovos wine? You spoil me, *sasiral.*"

I grinned.

The night continued on, soft and slow. We took our evening meals together often since Kythel was away or working in his office most mornings and afternoons. But tonight's meal felt different. It felt...significant. In a way that I couldn't quite pinpoint.

Kythel's eyes gleamed with every tidbit I told him about my travels, with every course I served where I gave a backstory on its creations, its inspiration, where I'd been living at the time, what my life had looked like then.

We had to take a break between the third and fourth courses because Kythel came up behind me as I was garnishing the plate of spiced Luxirian fillets, his hands gripping my hips as he nibbled along my neck. I gave a breathless moan as his fingers dragged the hem of my dress up, and he found me wet and aching, already turned on by the heady looks he'd cast my way over the rim of his goblet throughout the first half of dinner.

He wordlessly bent me over the prep counter, shoved my dress up until it was bunched around my waist, and took me from behind. His hands dipped into the front of my dress, pinching and tugging at my sensitive nipples as I cried out around his thick, searing cock, stretching me to my limits.

It was fast and raw and quick and uncontrolled, both of us needing a little relief. And when it was done, after I washed his dripping come from between my legs upstairs, we sat back down at the table and I took a long drag of wine to soothe my parched tongue and hoarse throat.

When it came time for dessert, I went to the icebox tucked under the prep counter and took out the final course. The Kylorr didn't typically have a course reserved solely for dessert, which I thought was a shame.

The tart I'd made was beautiful. The pastry crust was perfectly golden, the lilac-colored cream silky and smooth, flavored with ripe *syaan* berries from Stellara, and I'd sugared and candied the various New Earth fruits I'd fanned out on the surface. Deep and ripe figs, seeds bursting, the inner fruit as red as blood. Fat jewel-like blackberries the size of old coins. Edible white flowers I'd foraged in Stellara, which I found cut the sweetness perfectly. A smattering of frozen blueberries I'd dipped in a citrus glaze were tucked between the other fruits, like hidden treasures.

It was perfectly beautiful and neat, sweet but sophisticated, deliberate, with a bit of an icy bite. Just like Kythel, I thought.

When I served it to him, I said, "When I visited the New Earth colonies for the first time, it was to New Inverness with my father. While he was prepping the kitchen during the day, I would explore the city, and I came across a little patisserie that served these beautiful tarts, bursting with fresh fruits. So I made one for you. The base cream is with the *syaan* berries in Stellara. The other fruits are from New Earth."

Kythel shook his head in amazement. "How did you get all these ingredients?"

"I have my ways," I said with a small smile.

"You also have a talent for making things beautiful," he said next, dipping his spoon into the tart, breaking off the crumbly crust before sliding it into his mouth.

"That's because of my father," I said.

"Ah, because culinarians focus on presentation of their food?"

"No, because he didn't," I answered. "My father didn't like fuss. He believed the beauty of food happened on the palette, in the brain, in the heart. His best creations were also ridiculously ugly. Brilliant but ugly."

Kythel chuckled around the groan of delight as the flavor of the tart burst on his tongue, and my smile widened, watching him.

"Until I grew older and realized that the wealthy families that brought him into their grand households *wanted* beauty. For their parties. For their friends. Or even the people they hated."

Understanding dawned in his eyes. "You were the mind behind the beauty."

"Yes, while still maintaining his intended flavor profiles, which proved difficult at times," I admitted. "But...we make a good team. *Made*," I corrected, clearing my throat.

*My little artist*, he'd call me, pride shining in his voice, admiring the way I'd plated his food. A stray stab of grief and longing ached when I thought of that memory, but I pushed it from my mind. Food was the best way I knew to celebrate and remember my father. I thought he would've been proud of what I'd done here tonight.

Kythel's gaze was gentle, and he reached across the table to take my hand. "I know how much you miss him, Millie."

"It's more than that. I miss *this* too," I confessed, sweeping my other hand at the table. "Food…the culture of it all…it was such a big part of my life. These last few months, it's hardly been a blip. It feels like a missing limb. I don't know how else to describe it."

"Is that why you did this for me?" he asked. "To remember?"

"No," I said, softly. "Of course not."

"Then why? Why did you do this for me?" he asked, his thumb smoothing along the back of my hand.

A loaded question. Our eyes locked and held.

"Isn't it obvious?" I asked quietly, and then I held my breath, my heart thudding hard and loud in my chest.

*Because I love you and I wanted to give you something that you will always remember,* I thought silently.

His hand tightened on mine. His eyes flashed in knowing. Even still…he slowly pulled his hand away.

Trying to force down my disappointment, I gave him another out. For him. For me, to try to salvage a little bit of pride.

"Though, maybe tonight…this was also for *me.* Because I wanted to share who I used to be with you."

"It's not who you *used* to be, Millie," he said, inclining his head. "It's who you are—just another facet of you."

I nodded. Silence dropped between us, and I felt a miserable little curl of dread begin in my belly. I didn't mean to push. But I wasn't used to holding my feelings back. With Kythel, however, I needed to be careful. I still found it incredibly difficult to navigate.

We ate the dessert in near quiet, the only sound the gentle whoosh of the fire in the hearth. The change was palpable. The tart began to taste like nothing on my tongue.

Finally, Kythel cleared his throat and said, "I'll be gone the next few nights."

My head snapped up. "What?"

"I have a meeting with my brothers," he informed me. "In the North."

"In Laras?" I asked, confused. "I thought Laras was to the west."

"It is," he said, leaning back in his chair to regard me over the table. "We're meeting with the Kaazor."

"Oh," I said, uncertain how to respond. "I see."

I wondered if this had anything to do with the call he'd made in the middle of the night to Azur.

"It's nothing terrible is it?" I asked. "I mean…you won't be in danger, will you?"

"The meeting is a formality only. There will be soldiers on both sides of the border, I'm certain," he said.

"A meeting about what?"

Kythel deliberated a long while before he finally said, "About a Kylorr we believed was a Kaazor spy, one who'd gained access to Azur's keep. Only for that information to be false. It's not often we speak with the Kaazor, but both nations agree it's in our best interests to convene."

"So you'll be careful?" I asked, needing to be absolutely sure.

His expression softened slightly. He took in a deep breath and then hesitantly reached for my hand again. I accepted his touch without the hesitation he had, threading my fingers between his. Did it make me pathetic that I longed for his touch? That after the distance between us during the last course, his touch made me feel better? Reconnected?

"I'll be careful, *sasiral*," he told me. "You don't have to worry about me. I'll return the night before the moon winds."

I tensed. He felt it too.

Forcing myself to relax, I nodded. "All right."

Because I could say nothing else.

# CHAPTER 34

## KYTHEL

*I* hadn't seen Zyre since we'd been children, but I remembered him accompanying his father into our keep during the war, to negotiate a treaty of peace with House Kaalium. I remembered the legion of soldiers they'd brought with them, stationed outside the keep's gates.

I remembered my mother's pinched face. Aina's calm demeanor. Azur had tracked Zyre with his eyes, but it was me who'd spoken to the other young Kylorr boy first.

Just as I did now, on the border between our lands, marked by nothing but a thick line of trees—the beginning of the Kaazor's forest—that looked out onto the open meadow of Kaalium land. I always hated meeting here because it was difficult to determine how many Kaazor Zyre had brought with him. How many Kaazor were lying in wait in the darkness of the forest?

"Zyre," I greeted, stepping past my twin's imposing form, his wings spread wide whereas mine were tucked.

The king of the Kaazor was not like how I remembered. Back when we'd been children, there had been something weak about him. He'd been lanky, though his wings had been large. As such, he'd been a clumsy child, not having yet grown into his wings.

His legs had been like sticks, making me wonder if the Kaazor had been starving their children, as had been whispered through the keep, and his eyes had held a feral wildness that made me wary.

But I remembered him being quiet. *Polite* even, which had struck me as strange.

The Kylorr male before me now was not the boy I remembered.

The areas around his eyes were darkened with black ash, making his vibrant gray eyes appear even more luminous and chilling in the evening light. His indigo-blue hair was gathered and tied back with a silver clasp. Gone was the clumsy, lanky boy. In his place was a male who appeared even larger than Kaldur.

Overhead, a *kyriv* roared, the rider on his wide back making circles over the small legion of soldiers we'd brought, some from each of our territories. We had made a small base camp nearby but well hidden, with even more soldiers lying in wait should the meeting turn ugly.

But I didn't think it would.

"We agreed on no *kyriv*," Azur growled at Zyre.

"Did we?" Zyre asked, cocking his head to the side. "I don't remember that. I'll have the rider land."

Bringing his fingers to his lips, he let out a shrill whistle that made my ears twitch and the inner drums throb. A moment later, the *kyriv* circled down, landing with a heavy thump to our right, making the earth shake. I could smell the beast's musk. I could hear its rough pants. It felt restless.

I thought of Millie, asking me if I would be in danger here. I'd assured her I wouldn't be. And yet...

"You put us in a difficult position, Zyre," I said, hardening my voice. "We aren't fools. Your *kyriv* could take us all out with a single breath of fire."

"You don't know much about *kyriv*, do you, *Kyzaire*?" Zyre asked, tilting his chin down, though his eyes never left mine. "If you did, you'd know this one has no such ability."

My jaw tightened.

"Get rid of him," I said, keeping my voice even. "Or this meeting is over."

"Her," Zyre corrected, giving me a grin that revealed elongated incisors. "The *kyriv* is a female."

"Get rid of her," Lucen said. Zyre's gaze turned to my younger brother, narrowing on him. My brothers made a long line, the soldiers at our sides and backs. "And stop playing games. We came to this meeting of good faith, at your request. Every moment you delay makes our patience grow even thinner."

Zyre stared at Lucen before flicking his eyes down the line of my brothers. Azur, myself, Kaldur to my right, then Lucen, and Thaine at the end. We'd thought it best to keep Kalia back in Laras, though Zyre had requested all the heirs of the Kaalium. We wouldn't unnecessarily endanger our only sister. She was much too precious to us all.

Another sharp whistle sounded. Azur was glaring at Zyre, and I reached out to bump his wing. He shot me a sharp look, but I merely raised my brow. He settled, likely thinking that once he got this meeting over with, he could return to his wife.

At the beckoning of Zyre's whistle, the *kyriv* took flight again, the gust of wind stinging my eyes, before it circled overhead and rode high above the Kaazor's forest, flying north. Flying back to its home.

Zyre spread his arms wide. He had no weapons. No gauntlets, no blades. And oddly enough, I could see no soldiers present with him, despite the *kyriv* and its rider. It made us look like fools, a line of Kaalium heirs with a legion of soldiers at our backs. Or cowards, standing down a single Kylorr male, even if he was an enemy.

Kaldur's order mirrored my own thoughts when he gruffly told the soldiers to fall back. Without hesitation, the guards sheathed their blades, the synchronized thuds of their boots falling on the compact earth as they retreated too.

Zyre stepped forward, away from the line of the forest, coming out into the open meadow. His clothing was made of thick leather, rough but durable, covering the barrel of his chest. Deep scars ran down the length of his arms, scars he certainly hadn't had as a child.

After another shared look with me, Azur stepped forward first to meet him. The rest of us followed suit.

"What do you know of the Thryki?" Azur asked, wasting no time. "You claim that Maazin of House Laan, though we now know no such House exists, was not a Kaazor. But do you have the proof?"

Maazin had been the spy, working within Azur's keep and supposedly funneling cheap *lore* to the Kaazor for exorbitant profits, should the records be believed. Gemma, Azur's wife, had discovered the discrepancy herself, but by the time she'd told Azur, Maazin had already disappeared from the keep. The last we'd seen of him had been his head, sent to us from Zyre himself.

"He told the leader of the village he lived in that his name was Maazin Zor Koreen," Zyre said, sliding his arms across his chest, leveling us a hard stare. "That he had grown up in northeast of Kaazor, in a small village named Loreena. The village exists—I know it well. But no one remembers him living there."

It was Zaale, Azur's head keeper, who had traced Maazin's journey to a port in Salaire from across the seas. The vessel had come from the Thryki's territory, though it had been a patrol. They weren't supposed to pick up any passengers.

"We believe he was a Thryki," I told Zyre. "But he must've had contacts within Kaazor. He disappeared from the Kaalium for a year. We assume it was because he was living in your nation."

Zyre said nothing.

"No one knew him?" I pressed.

"There was a group he was close to," he finally revealed.

"And where are they now?"

"Dealt with," Zyre said, flashing a quick smile.

"I want to speak with them," Azur said lowly.

"That will be quite impossible, *Kyzaire*," Zyre answered with infinite patience.

Meaning, he'd had them killed. Fuck.

"You must've questioned them before," I said, narrowing my eyes on him. "What do you want for the information?"

Zyre's held tilted back to look up at the stars for a brief moment, pondering the question, exposing the line of his light gray throat. He had quite a wide jaw, sharp and cutting.

"Let me savor this moment," he said, blowing out a sharp breath as Kaldur tensed beside me. "It's not often that an heir of the Kaalium makes me an offer on the precipice of war. I must think very hard and very clearly on what I will do next."

"You know exactly what you want," Thaine finally said, speaking for the first time. "You've had it planned for a while. Because you're not like your father, are you? You're calculated. You're intelligent. Both of which your father was not."

Zyre stilled, leveling Thaine a dark look. His voice was clipped, humor gone as he bit out, "My father was a great leader. Can you say the same about yours, Thaine, son of Thraan?"

A dark rumble rose from Azur's throat, but I stepped in front of him before he could do anything that would bear conse-quences. Because, despite the circumstances, we *needed* Zyre. And I believed he needed us or else he wouldn't have suggested this meeting. We might actually be able to negotiate a strong peace between the two nations with a war looming across the seas. This was the best position we could be in. I wouldn't have my twin brother doing anything to fuck that up, even though a bloody brawl might make him feel better in the moment.

"What did you learn from the group that Maazin was meeting with?" I asked, walking toward Zyre, my strides eating up the distance between us. I was right. Though we were a similar height, his build resembled the bulk of Kaldur's. Brute strength, forged in the nation of Kaazor.

He must've learned something vital to call this meeting. If there was one thing I knew about the Kaazor, it was that they were *proud*. They didn't yield, they didn't bend—unless absolutely necessary. Their hardheadedness was held in the highest honors, and it had nearly sent our nations to war after Aina had negotiated the peace treaty.

But Zyre Draakan was different. More dangerous than his father, yes, but I believed he wanted the best for his people, and that didn't include a bloody, endless war.

"I want a quarter of the *lore* yields for the next ten years," Zyre said. "From all the territories in the Kaalium."

Azur laughed, loud and humorless. "You're out of your mind."

I gritted my jaw. Millions in credits, if he sold the *lore*. "What else?"

"Two hundred *tun* of *drava* metal, sourced from the Three Guardians itself."

Kaldur scoffed. But I tensed, my nostrils flaring.

"You want us to supply you with millions of credits and material for weapons when we all know Krynn is on the verge of war?" I asked softly and slowly. "Do you see what kind of position that puts us in? Do you think we're foolish, Zyre?"

"It is nothing for you, *Kyzaire*," he argued, shrugging one of his wings. The membranes held silver ink. Tattoos, I realized.

"You think two hundred *tun* of *drava* is nothing?" I asked.

"For you? Yes. But it is everything for my people. You cut us off of our own land. The Three Guardians was once ours. Remember that, son of the Kaalium?" he questioned.

I did everything to hide my own glare until I knew there was a solid wall of ice over my features, revealing nothing. Zyre only observed my reaction, eyes narrowing. I realized he hadn't said that to make me mad. He'd only wanted to see what I would *do*.

*Dangerous indeed,* I thought, taking a step away from him.

"Blood was shed on both sides in that war. Both sides made decisions they might've regretted. Your ancestors *and* mine."

"But only one side got the ultimate reward," Zyre finished. "The land."

"Are we here to debate ancient history?" Lucen asked. "Or are we here to negotiate?"

"To negotiate, of course," Zyre answered, never breaking my gaze.

"Yet we don't even know what we're negotiating for," Azur said, stepping up to my side. Zyre was only an arm's length away. Azur could make a quick strike with his gauntlets, and Zyre would bleed out at our booted feet. "Because you've told us nothing. Maybe because you have nothing and you're trying to squeeze the Kaalium for whatever you think you can get, still bitter over a war that ended centuries ago."

"Azur," I said, feeling my twin's temper rise.

Zyre only smiled. "The Dyaar and the Thryki have made a war bond with one another. Sealed in the blood of their kings. Two months ago."

Azur and I both stilled. I heard a soft curse leave Thraine behind us.

"My own spies within Thrykan confirmed it. I received their report two weeks ago."

"You don't have spies within Thrykan," Azur scoffed. "Not even *we* can get spies into Thrykan."

"I have my methods," Zyre said, cocking his head to the side. "In all your arrogance, do you honestly believe that just because *you* cannot do something, it cannot be done? In all your arrogance, have you ever considered that the Kaazor might offer you something that you cannot get yourself? Hmm. Perhaps I *am* negotiating with the wrong nation in this war. As my advisors have told me repeatedly."

His implication made my shoulders tense.

"If you truly believed that, you wouldn't be here," I said quietly, keeping his eyes.

War *was* coming. We all knew it. Zyre's information only confirmed it if the Dyaar and the Thryki were making war bonds. And I believed him. I didn't think he would lie about this.

"We will need to see those reports before we agree to anything," I told him. "But we both know that you want more than *lore* and *drava*. And you know that the Kaalium would benefit from your armies. You know that we would not want your numbers against us, coming from the North, while the Dyaar and Thryki land at our shores from the South and the East."

It was Azur's turn to reprimand me with a sharp look.

I was only being honest. We all needed to hang our cocks out and spread our wings wide if we were going to come to an agreement that mutually benefited *both* nations.

"So what are we really doing here?" I asked Zyre. "We all know the best path through this war is to bind our nations together. You benefit from our wealth and supplies. And your armies would help shorten a war that would save thousands and thousands of lives across the Kaalium *and* Kaazor. That's what we are truly negotiating, is it not? You don't want a war. Just like we don't. That's what we have in common."

"A war bond," Zyre murmured, a smirk twitching at the corner of his lips. "I'll take your offer back to my advisors. But even if I do, I don't think you'll like the terms I set."

"Beyond the *lore* and the *drava*, what else do you want?" Azur growled.

His eyes were glinting. "I want one more thing. But I won't ask for that quite yet. War is not here, but we can start discussing the terms in the coming months. I've always wanted to return to Laras. Such beauty. Tell me, how is your sister?"

Lucen rumbled behind us. "Keep her out of this, Zyre."

He and Kalia were closest in age. They'd been attached at the wing from a young age, and naturally, both were more protective of the other.

"For now, I will," Zyre said in reply. Then he was walking backward, like a shadow sinking toward the safety of the dark forest. "I'll send you the report. It's obvious to me that the Thryki were trying to cause trouble on the mainland between the Kaalium and the Kaazor with their band of spies. There are more. And there will be more. But if you need the proof, then you'll have your proof. Me? I don't need to see what is plainly written in blood before us all."

With that, Zyre turned his back on us, flaring his wings wide and disappearing into the darkness of the forest. A shrill, familiar whistle sounded. Then the trees seemed to vibrate, a gust of wind funneling toward us. A *kyriv* shot up from the forest, the glint of the silver wings of its rider gleaming on its back.

Bastard. He'd had his own *kyriv* nearby, watching us the entire time.

All of us watched Zyre until he and his *kyriv* faded from view, melting into the night.

Then we turned to regard one another.

"What do you think?" Thaine asked. "Can he be trusted? Or will he try to cross us and ally with our enemies across the sea after he takes our resources?"

"Are we going to ignore the obvious?" Lucen growled. "War bonds are made in blood *and* in marriage. He knows there's a lot more to gain from House Kaalium. Fuck him. We have enough wealth, soldiers, and supplies to take on the entirety of Krynn. We have allies off-planet. They will come if we ask for their aid. We don't need Zyre."

"Lucen, enough," I said, nostrils flaring. "This isn't about our family. This is about preserving the lives of our citizens. Citizens we're duty-bound to protect!"

Our youngest brother glared. "We all know what he wants. What he's wanted for years. I won't allow it."

"It's not up to us," Kaldur pointed out grimly.

Lucen scoffed, stalking away to go clear his head. He only ever got riled up about one thing. Kalia. And Zyre knew how to poke at that tender place.

"His first demands we can meet," Azur said. Now that Zyre was gone, my twin was calming, the fire in his eyes dulled. He turned to regard me. "Can you secure the *drava* from House Arada? Two hundred *tun* is a lot to ask of them. But it's necessary."

*I can secure it,* I thought, my gut churning with the inevitable.

But it would cost me Millie, wouldn't it?

*Duty always comes first,* I thought. Though for the first time, the thought felt mocking. It made fury burn in my throat. I had given everything for the Kaalium. When would it be *enough*?

Would it ever be enough?

I thought of Ruaala. Of the trees' roots feeding from her body, in the cold, hard earth. Sometimes I felt like that. Sometimes I felt like I was being consumed until there would be nothing left but my bones.

Though the words felt like stones dropping from my tongue, I said, "I can get the *drava*."

I pretended I didn't see the shared, concerned look between Kaldur and Thaine. And I walked away from my brothers before I tore the entire forest apart in my grief.

# CHAPTER 35

## MILLIE

Starlight shone brightly overhead, illuminating the silver metalwork Ruaala had hammered into the trees. It appeared like they were glowing, little rivers of metal flowing within the blackened trunks.

My arms ached. My legs throbbed. My whole body felt sore and tired. Since Kythel had left, I'd worked endlessly at the cottage, mostly in the front garden, digging out stones and fencing, hacking at the overgrown foliage, tearing out the rotted panels from the windows, foraging for stones from Stellara to make a new pathway, lugging them all the way back to the cottage.

Truthfully, I felt grateful for the distraction. The physical exertion felt good, especially considering the *baanye* I'd been taking made it feel like my blood was throbbing beneath my skin. An endless reminder that Kythel hadn't fed from me in days.

The moon winds were tomorrow. He told me he'd be returning to Erzos this afternoon, but I hadn't seen him, though I'd been scanning the sky at regular intervals, seeking his familiar figure silhouetted against it. All day, I'd had this gut-churning feeling I couldn't dispel. So I'd thrown myself into my work, hardly breaking, even to eat.

And though it was after nightfall, I couldn't bring myself to return to the keep.

Just as I finished scrubbing down the outside of the window panel and coating it with *gaanyel* paste to dry overnight, I heard the *whoosh* of his wings approaching from overhead. Anticipation and nerves rose within me as I swung around, tilting my face up to the sky. Though it was dark, I'd be able to spot him anywhere, and I put the jar of paste down, setting my brush inside, and hurriedly went to meet him.

*Maybe my nerves are for nothing,* I thought, heartbeat quickening. *Maybe he'll wrap me in his arms and kiss me long enough that I'll know I worried for nothing.*

But when Kythel landed in the clearing and rose to his full height, I saw an expression on his face that I hadn't seen in a very long time. It froze me right in my tracks, a hesitant smile spreading over my face, hoping I was just imagining it.

"You're home," I said, a warm breeze picking up. It had been windier all day, heralding the start of a strong moon-wind storm. I should've been relieved. Because tomorrow my father's and Ruaala's soul gems would be created. "When did you get back?"

Kythel inclined his head. "Just now. Vadyn said you were still here."

He appeared tired, and the frown pulling at the edges of his mouth made him appear like he was in a foul mood. But it was the coldness in his gaze, that detachment, that *wall* that made me feel sick to my stomach.

"Yes," I said, not stepping toward him. "I know it's late but…"

The distance between us felt like it was slipping underneath my rib cage like a blade. When just a few nights ago, he'd been looking at me across the dinner table like I was all he ever wanted to look at again.

"Millie," came my name, the word clipped but strangely vulnerable. "I—"

I closed my eyes briefly. "Please, Kythel."

Please what?

*Please...don't? Don't do whatever it is I see in your eyes?* I thought. *Please don't break my fucking heart, even though I'd expected you to all along?*

"What...what happened with the Kaazor?" I asked.

What had happened to make him decide *this*?

"I can't say," he said after a long moment, finally beginning to close the distance between us. My neck tilted back with every step he took so I could continue to look into his eyes. "What I can say is that I...I wish it could be different, Millie. I wish I could be anyone else but who I am. Because that's the only way I could have had you."

My heart gave an ugly twist in my chest. My lungs wrung out all the air. I felt like I couldn't breathe.

"No," I choked out. "You just wish it wasn't *me*."

Silver light from the moon cut his face in two when, in this moment, I needed to witness all of him, every cold line, every unyielding decision he'd made without me. The ancient trees of Stellara—dark, towering, starving guardians that had long kept the forest's secrets in—witnessed us both, and I wondered what they saw. I wondered what they thought. If they could feel the way I began to tremble, if they could feel it vibrating their roots beneath my feet.

Did their gnarled roots tangle together under the damp earth? Could one tree pass on my budding misery to the next? Did they feel and drink the bitter ache of it?

"You think I'll weaken your House. That I'll shame your family. Your territory. Your people."

All thoughts I'd had before. All thoughts I'd wished weren't true. I'd moaned for him, burying those truths deep, even as he'd fed from me, distracted by the smell of his sweat, the addicting heat of his roughened palms, the copper tang of my blood on my eager tongue as he'd kissed me.

His brows furrowed. I heard his swallow and his rough growl as he said, "When did I *ever* say that?"

"You didn't have to," I told him, focusing on the faceted ice of his moonlit eyes. I wanted to sink into the earth, clasping my hands with the roots of the trees, sharing in their memories, their judgments. "I already know."

Instead of sinking, I remained within this pinching, aching realm. Behind him, I spied the glittering windows of the north wing of Erzos's keep. I smelled the sweet, pungent rot of *syaan* berries on the warm breeze as it funneled through the clearing. I heard the creak of my open door behind me, the pop of the fire as it sparked violently in the freshly cleaned hearth.

"The truth is that you wish it had been someone else to spark the bond," I said, my voice wavering, my gaze sliding past him to the blackness of the forest beyond. "A Kylorr female, of noble ancestry, who would bring you pride whenever you looked at her. But instead you got me. A human woman, found abandoned at a travel port, with nothing and no one, with no true home anymore. And you believe I am beneath you, *Kyzaire.*"

"That's not fucking true," he rasped, angry now, those eyes shooting blue fire in the darkness. "Don't even say that, Millie."

"If it weren't for my blood, you would have never even noticed me," I said. "But I didn't care. And there's a part of me that will always feel pathetic because of that."

My shoulders were slumped, and that same pathetic part of myself I feared was feeling sorry for myself. Rejected. Cast aside for another person I could never, ever be.

"Are you going to marry her?" I whispered. I didn't need to specify who. We both knew.

Kythel's jaw tightened. "I have no choice. It's been decided."

His words felt like a hammer against an anvil, striking my heart.

"There's always a choice," I argued, hating the pleading note I heard in my voice. "You just don't see it."

"And *you* don't understand, Millie," he said sharply. "It's not always so simple. Especially for someone like me."

I felt like I was making a mess of this, but Kythel looked hardly affected. Tears were dripping down my cheeks, and my throat felt unbearably tight.

"I love you," came my miserable confession as I wrapped my arms around my torso. "But you already know that, don't you?"

Kythel shook his head, his jaw tightening as if I hadn't spoken at all, willingly ignoring the words that I had kept bottled for much too long. "Millie. *I told you.* I told you that I could only give you until the moon winds, then our agreement would end. I haven't lied to you. I haven't made you promises I couldn't keep."

"Is that how you justify it?" I breathed, thinking that was cruel. "Is that how you walk away with a clear conscience? Because you always knew that this would be temporary? That it wouldn't matter how I felt about you, only that you were honest that you could never return my love?"

When he didn't answer, I let out a sound that was a half sob and a half laugh. My brow furrowed, a spring of fresh tears blurring my vision even though I felt...*lost.* I didn't know what to do. My chest ached. My body felt numb.

"Well, then...an agreement is an agreement," I said, the words hollow. "You have me until tomorrow night. Would you like to feed now, *Kyzaire?* It's been days, so you must be hungry."

"Millie," he said, his tone anguished. For the first time, my words seemed to break through the thick shield of ice, striking hard enough to make him jerk. "You must think that I'm a monster if you think I would do that to you."

But when he reached forward to cup my cheek, I nearly fell in my haste to get away. If he touched me, I'd crumble. I didn't consider myself a proud person, not like he was, but right then I felt like I needed to save what little dignity I had left or else I truly wouldn't respect myself come morning. When the fresh rays of sunlight brought clarity and shame.

"You know what I think?" I asked softly. "I think you're afraid, Kythel. Just like me. I think you're afraid to let go of your tightly leashed control, to disappoint your family, to do what *you* want to do. Because you've never done what you want to do, isn't that right?"

"Once," he said, eyes burning. "And it cost my family more than you'll ever know."

"But that's another secret you'll keep from me, right?" I said before I thought better of it. Then my shoulders sagged. Suddenly, exhaustion weighed on me heavily. "Please. Just go, Kythel."

"I'm not leaving you here. Not like this," he said, shaking his head slowly.

"If you care for me at all, then you'll leave," I said, lifting my eyes to his. Though it took every ounce of self-control I possessed, I kept my voice even as I reasoned, "This was always going to end. We were always going to go our separate ways, weren't we?"

His silence was answer enough.

A sad smile quirked my lips, and I looked past him, into the depths of Stellara, wondering if this was how Ruaala had felt. In these woods. Alone. Broken hearted. Angry.

"Did you think you could ever love me?"

The broken, whispered question was out of my lips before I could stop it. But I didn't take it back. I needed to know.

When he shook his head, it felt like a blade to my gut, slicing me into pieces. I wanted to sink into the earth like Ruaala and stay there.

"Not like this," he said quietly, stepping forward. "I was never free to love you, Millie. I could never allow myself to. Not like this."

Silence descended as I processed the words, tears dripping

down my cheeks, landing on the moss below my feet. He needed to leave. I didn't want him to see me break down.

"Leave," I pleaded softly before a sob broke from my lips. "*Please.* Please, Kythel."

"If you intend to stay the night here, I'll send a guard from the keep," he finally rumbled. Out of the corner of my eyes, I saw he was watching me, hand outstretching briefly before his fist curled and he pulled it back.

"No," I said.

"What do you mean *no?*"

I wiped at the tears on my cheeks. I needed to get through these next few moments. That was all I needed to do. *Just a few more moments,* I pleaded with myself. When he was gone...then I could crumble.

*You knew that this was coming. You felt it,* I knew. That knowledge centered me. Strangely enough, it helped give me calm and peace when I needed it most.

"We made an agreement," I said, proud when my voice didn't waver. "At the end of it, you would place the cottage deed and the surrounding land into my father's and Ruaala's names. Unless you've changed your mind."

"The cottage is yours, Millie," he told me. "I would *never* take it away from you. You don't have to worry about that."

My shoulders loosened. "Then send a guard tonight if you wish. It's not the moon winds yet, after all. But beginning tomorrow night, this land doesn't belong to you anymore. Besides...I'm not your responsibility, Kythel."

"Yes, you are," he replied.

"You can't protect me forever."

"I can try," came his determined words.

"Stop," I said, a throbbing headache beginning to pound at my temples. "What you're doing isn't fair to me! Can't you see that? Do you know how confusing and hurtful it is to me?"

"Millie—"

"You want to end this. *Us,*" I said, locking eyes with him, and though it took everything in me, I held his gaze, even when it felt like daggers in my chest. "So end it. Don't make this harder than it needs to be. Don't drag me along and give me hope for something that will never happen. *End it.* Right now. And leave!"

"All right," he said. Sudden and sharp. He was a frozen statue in the front garden of the cottage, cool like marble and just as perfect. His head dropped to glare at the ground, but when he looked up, his expression was smooth. Softly, he said, "All right. I will. I'll leave."

I took a stumbled step away, closer to the front door of the cottage.

My safe haven.

My quiet place.

My back met the door, and Kythel's eyes glowed in the darkness, watching me.

"Millie," he said. His lips parted. Then closed. His brow furrowed, and I watched his wings lower behind him. Whatever he was going to say, it died in his throat. Our eyes held until every passing moment severed whatever calm and control I had left. "I'm sorry."

My throat was beginning to burn. My hands beginning to tremble at my sides.

Saying goodbye felt too final.

Instead, I said, "Me too."

Then I walked inside the cottage on numb legs. And shut the door behind me.

With bated breath, I waited until I heard him take to the sky. Only then did I allow myself to sink down to the floor of the cottage and cry.

I felt a warm touch on my shoulder, but I knew that nothing was there. Only Ruaala, perhaps, her soul rooted to this lonely, quiet place too.

# CHAPTER 36

## KYTHEL

*E*ven Vadyn was giving me a wide berth these last couple days, evidenced by the hesitation in his gaze when he entered my office that morning.

"What is it?" I growled, not bothering to look up. I kept the privacy screen down on the outside window. Though I could see out, none of the sunlight could stream in, and the only illumination were the Halo orbs floating above my desk silently. Over the course of the last two days, there had been times when I hadn't known if it was day or night. My neck felt tight, my legs fatigued, though I'd been at my desk or staring unseeing out into Stellara.

*I can't keep doing this,* I thought for the hundredth time. *This will kill me.*

And yet...I continued on, not stopping my work. There was always something that needed to be done. Always another problem that needed to be solved.

Vadyn started, "There's a letter here—"

My head snapped up, heart speeding for the first time in two days. "From who?"

His expression was careful. "Marr from the coastal village of Savina."

Disappointment made my hands shake, but I swiped at the next *lore* contract on my Halo screen to hide it. Marr?

Right.

The committee. Millie's idea.

"Leave it there," I said, gesturing to one of the empty places at the very edge of my desk. "What else?"

Now he was *really* hesitating, shifting from foot to foot.

"Vadyn," I growled, already impatient.

"Your father wishes to speak to you."

"*Vaan*," I cursed under my breath. "I'll call him."

"And Kaan of House Arada wishes to arrange a meeting this evening."

"Tell him no," I said. I wasn't ready to meet with Kaan. Truthfully, I didn't know if I'd ever be, with Millie's tear-streaked face still haunting my every waking moment and every sleepless night. I'd ended our relationship, cast away my fucking *kyrana* to marry into the House that controlled *drava* production. And yet...I hadn't made a marriage offer to Lyris.

The mere idea made me feel sick.

"I'll inform him," Vadyn said.

As he was turning to leaving, I called out gruffly, "I'm sorry, Vadyn. I know I've not been myself."

"I know," my head keeper replied. "But I'll always be here, Kythel. For whatever you need."

My chest tightened at the genuine words and the meaning behind them. I met Vadyn's gaze across the room, inclining my head at the male who'd always felt more like family than a keeper to me.

"Thank you." Then I hesitated. "Vadyn?"

"Yes?"

"How is she?"

He let out a sharp sigh, turning to face me. "She's working on the cottage, day and night. Telaana went there yesterday to bring back whatever she had here at the keep, from your rooms and hers. Telaana was gone all night. She said they made dinner and just...kept one another's company."

I nodded, rubbing at the ache in my chest, one that wouldn't leave.

"Good," I said gruffly. I didn't want Millie to be alone. She didn't like to be alone. "That's...good."

"The credits were deposited into her account as you requested."

My lips pressed together. Millie wouldn't like what I'd done when she found out. "Thank you."

"Anything else?"

"Not for now," I answered.

Shortly after, once Vadyn had left, I took in a deep, steadying breath and called my father through the Halo Com. I stood when the full projection of his body illuminated the darkness of my office—every detail of him, from his wings to his horns, traced in perfectly colored pixels, becoming solid lines. So solid and real that it felt like my father had never left the Kaalium after my mother's death.

"Thaine told me about your meeting with Zyre," Thraan of House Kaalium said. No greeting. No warm regards. I couldn't tell where my father was. Only his body was in view, not his surroundings.

"Did he?" I asked. There was resentment built up between us, only mine was tinged with the bitter taste of guilt. I was the peacemaker of our family...and once, our relationship had been solid. Not so much anymore.

I felt like he'd abandoned us when we'd all been riddled with grief. I would never forgive him for that. Just as he would never forgive me for what I'd done.

"Yes," Thraan said.

He was a handsome, imposing, intimidating male. Large like a god statue in the gardens of Raazos in Laras. Even with his wings tucked behind his back, he still took up a substantial amount of space within my office, cast in perfect proportions by the Halo Com.

"Kaan of House Arada contacted me too."

I stiffened, my nostrils flaring wide. "He did *what?*"

"I'm having a difficult time understanding why you have not yet made the bond announcement," my father said, his tone even but firm. The same tone he used to take with us as children when we'd misbehaved.

My father had been a different person when our mother had been alive. *Well, when she'd been healthy,* I amended quietly.

"House Arada has been an ally of our family for years," my father argued. "Make the tie and present your marriage offer to Lyris immediately."

I bristled at the order, but I hid it well, smoothing my expression. My head was pounding with irritation, and my heart felt caged in, battering its way against the walls of a *drava*-encased prison.

"Do you think I have respect for a noble who would go over a *Kyzaire*'s head and run instead to his father, who hasn't stepped foot on Krynn in over five years?" I asked.

"This is no time for your pride, Kythel," Thraan growled, sweeping his arm out like a slice of a blade, as if to cut off whatever I was going to say next. "Kaan said he's tried repeatedly to have a meeting with you."

"There's been a lot to do in Erzos."

"Including this human mistress you've been keeping?" my father asked.

I stiffened.

"Yes, I imagine that takes up a lot of time," he spat. "I never expected this from *you*, Kythel. Your brother, yes. Obviously. Kaldur, perhaps. But not from you."

"She's my *kyrana*," I said, the words slipping from my lips before I could stop them. But I didn't want to. "Not my mistress."

Whatever my father was going to say died. His wings

twitched behind him, and then he smoothed a hand over his left horn, as if to calm himself.

"You have a responsibility to the Kaalium," he finally said, and a little flame of fury and hurt stoked in my belly, becoming hotter and hotter. Searing me from the inside out. "Your mother and I were not fated. Our marriage was arranged. And we made our own fate, and I loved her with every drop of blood inside my body. I would have bled out every last drop from my veins if it meant I could save her. Having a *kyrana* means nothing."

"How can you say that?" I asked. "You never had a *kyrana*. You don't know what it feels like."

"You will build a life with Lyris, and you will come to love her, just as I did your mother. A marriage that benefits Erzos and the Kaalium," Thraan said.

"I love my *kyrana*," I informed my father. For the first time, those words escaped, as shackled and restrained as they'd been. And it felt like a *relief*...only I'd said them to the wrong person.

He scoffed. "Don't be a child, Kythel. We *need* the *drava* when war comes."

"And what do you care if war comes?" I asked.

My father's nostrils flared.

"Maybe you would like to see the Kaalium burn," I said, wanting to hurt him. "Maybe you want to see the memories burn too. It might make it hurt less."

Whatever restraint my father possessed, I saw it play over his face in a flash. But I refused to take back my words. A long stretch of silence lapsed. For all his flaws, my father could hide his emotions like a shield of ice. Just like me.

"You will make your marriage bonds within the week," Thraan ordered me. "You owe it to your mother. Don't you?"

It felt like a blade slid deep into my lungs, robbing me of breath.

"Marry Lyris of House Arada not because of the *drava* but because you owe it to Aina...and your *mother*. You promised her that you would always put duty first, didn't you? I heard you say it. Are you going back on your word now? Are you breaking the promise that you made to her as she was dying?"

"You're a bastard," I breathed, staring across the space right into my father's eyes. "I have given everything for the Kaalium!"

"Not everything," my father said, his tone hardening. "I am not blinded. You are. If you saw things clearly, you would do what is right. Protect the Kaalium. Do your duty to your people. Fulfill the promise you made to your mother. *That* is what's important. Not your human whore."

A swipe of my claws whistled out, shredding the Halo Com screen in two. The projection of my father disappeared, the call ended with violent finality. Rage was building, clamoring and clawing its way up my throat until I felt like I would *fucking* choke on it.

There was a sound echoing in the office. Rough and raw and angry. And it took me a moment to realize it was *me*. Bellowing out my fury and my grief and my hatred and my exhaustion. The realm of the living slowed. I felt the painful pound of my heart-beat. Shreds of paper were falling like snow around me. I was tearing at everything, my claws bleeding. Glass shattered, the window gone. A warm breeze slid over the nape of my neck, sunlight flooding in, blinding. The shattering of a priceless vase, and I grinned at the sound. Nothing would calm me down. I wouldn't stop until I tore this entire keep apart.

*No.*

I knew what I wanted.

All I wanted was Millie.

She would calm me. She would soothe and bandage this oozing, gaping, stinging wound inside me, one that had never quite healed. Even now, after what I'd done, if I went to her, she would still open her arms and embrace me. Because her heart was warm, not covered in ice so cold it burned like mine. I didn't *fucking* deserve her. I never had.

She was everything I was not, everything I wanted—and needed—to be.

And I'd turned my back on her, choosing what I'd perceived as my *duty* over her. Was this who I was?

This monster, tearing apart every single thing I could get my claws into? Was this who was best for the Kaalium? For Erzos? For my family? Was this who would lead us in a war against the Kylorr across the seas?

Was *this* who Millie loved?

*Enough,* I thought, the word clear, stopping me in my tracks after I toppled my desk over, sending everything I hadn't already destroyed flying to the ground.

Enough.

When reality returned, my office was utterly destroyed. Bits of parchment were still floating in the air, the breeze coming in from the smashed window carrying them toward the door.

I raked my hands through my hair and stumbled back against the wall, my boots crunching in glass. When I slid down, I felt a jagged edge of the pane scrape against my wing, scratching against bone and sensitive membrane, but I welcomed the pain.

---

"What in Raazos's blood…" came a familiar voice.

My brow furrowed, and I raised my head from my hands.

"What are you doing here?" I rasped, though there was no bite in my words. They felt hollow. They felt like I wasn't even here. They felt like this was a dream, a nightmare. Me, sitting in the shattered fractures of glass, my father's words repeating over and over in my mind, all while thinking about Millie. Because she never left. I was aching for her—for her blood, for her warmth, for her smile.

It was becoming more and more apparent to me what I'd done. What I'd lost.

"Vadyn sent for me," Azur said, stepping into the dark office. It was night now, I realized. Just how long had I been sitting here? "For good reason."

"He heard?" I asked, not even caring enough to be embarrassed.

"Who didn't?" Azur asked. "All your keepers look spooked."

I closed my eyes.

"I am too," my brother admitted softly, approaching me, his boots treading over fabric and filling and broken Halo Com parts and light orbs I didn't even realize I'd gone after. "I've never...I've never seen you like this, Kythel. But I felt something today—I knew something was wrong. I flew straight here. Did you go berserk?"

"I don't know," I admitted. I had cuts on my hands and arms, I realized, though the blood had long dried. "I don't think so."

Azur crouched down next to me, and I leaned my head back against the wall, regarding my twin with a tight jaw. He looked concerned. Usually, it was the other way around.

"Why didn't you *tell me?*" he asked, his tone softly aghast. "Kaldur and Thaine knew, but you didn't even tell *me* that you'd found your *kyrana?*"

"They were there when I first saw her," I said, tired.

"What kind of excuse is that?"

"It's not one," I said. "I didn't know how to tell you."

"It's quite simple," Azur said.

"Is it?" I wondered.

He went quiet. Then asked, "What happened?"

"Father."

"*Vaan,*" Azur cursed, letting out a deep sigh and sitting in the glass, back leaning against the upturned legs of my desk. "Tell me."

So I did. I told him everything. About Millie, our agreement, Kaan and Lyris of House Arada, Raana *Dyaan*, and what had happened in the last few days, including my conversation with our father.

Every word I spoke felt like a scab being picked off a deep, infected wound, letting it drain. It felt *good*.

And when I was done, Azur was regarding me with a solemn expression.

"What is it?" I asked, my throat raw and guttural from speaking so much when I'd barely spoken in the last few days.

"You need to forgive yourself," he said, making me flinch. "For Aina's death. Mother had no right to say what she said to you that night. She was grieving and angry. She had a broken heart. But you've taken those words and you've swallowed them so deep I don't know if you'd ever be able to purge them from you now. They're etched into your very bones, Kythel. You've punished yourself ever since."

I dragged in a deep breath.

"You think you're the only one who blames himself for what happened to Aina?" Azur asked. "For so long, I dreamed of her. Tortured myself over the image of her in Zyos, lost and wandering. It ate at me. Constantly."

"But *I* was supposed to be there with her," I said. "On Pe'ji."

"And Aina was outnumbered," Azur reasoned. "Would anything have changed if you were there? If any of us were? You weren't going to be with her every waking moment. Stop blaming yourself. It's been years. It's past time you moved on. And what Father said today? He *is* a bastard. He'll see that with time, and he'll regret his words, just like Mother regretted hers."

I stared unseeing into the space that separated us.

"And since I am your elder brother and the *Kyzaire* of Laras..." Azur started. I scoffed, but I caught his small grin. "I will not allow you to marry Lyris of House Arada. Not for *drava*. Not for anything."

"Since when do you have a right to tell others who to marry

and who not to?" I asked, the question pointed, considering his own history with his wife.

Azur's expression turned serious. "It would ruin you, Kythel. I'm sure you already feel the distance, the craving for your *kyrana*. It only gets worse. Trust me. Knowing the happiness and peace I feel with Gemma now? It truly frightens me how close I was to losing her. I won't let you do this. House Arada is still bound in duty to yield to our House. There are other ways to secure the *drava* that don't include you shackling yourself to a female who isn't your mate."

"You should have seen the way Millie looked at me that night. She won't forgive me," I told him, the truth ripped from my throat. "I was so cold to her. She told me she loved me, and I said I was *sorry*, Azur. I've never seen her like that before—the realization slowly coming onto her face. Whenever I close my eyes, it's her face I see. I don't deserve her. I don't fucking deserve her."

"Then tell her the truth and give her time," my brother told me. "That's all Gemma wanted from me."

*Would she look at me differently if she knew the truth?* I wondered. Would she think me a coward? Selfish?

No. The answer came easily.

I needed to learn to restructure the way I thought about Aina. Azur was right. We had *all* blamed ourselves in some way for what had happened, my mother more than anyone. But the truth was that it had been no one's fault. It *was* a tragedy, a war crime.

But it was difficult to unlearn years of guilt and self-loathing. For Millie, though, I needed to try.

Azur and I both stood from our places on the debris-ridden floor.

He smirked as he looked around the office. "You're more like me than you realize."

"I'm not proud of this," I informed him, though it had felt like a large weight had released itself from my shoulders. A start. I needed to speak with Millie. Immediately.

Azur rounded my desk and bent to right it, pushing it into the correct position, though the legs crunched on the broken shards of the vase I'd shattered. When he straightened, his gaze went out the window, toward Stellara. He stiffened, his eyes pinned on something in the distance.

"What is that?" he asked, rounding the desk.

I swung around to peer into the darkness of the night. A red glow was illuminating the tops of the bleeding trees. Something dark was winding up from the forest.

"Is that smoke?" Azur asked, incredulous, concerned.

I was leaping through the window, my wings scraping on jagged glass, before he could say another word.

Millie's cottage was on fire.

# CHAPTER 37

## MILLIE

When I opened my eyes, I thought it was morning. The orange glow of the sun was flickering along the walls of the bedroom. I thought that was strange, but then again, I had been tired lately. Perhaps I'd slept the entire night.

Then I smelled the acridness of smoke, funneling up my nostrils. When I gasped, shooting straight up in the bed, I choked on smoke and loud, hacking coughs racked my body. My eyes watered, stinging.

It wasn't sunlight flickering on the walls. They were flames.

I scrambled from the bed, my breath hitching in fear, which only prompted more coughs. Smoke was beginning to billow up the stairs in waves, dark and gray, and I pulled up the hem of the tunic I'd been sleeping in, covering my nose and mouth. Heat, unlike anything I'd felt before, was funneling up toward me.

I needed to get out of here and *fast*.

Instead of freezing, the terror pushed me into action. I scrambled down the open stairs, my feet falling onto the hot stones. Pain registering, I hissed but kept going. Adrenaline pumped through me. When I reached the bottom floor, I saw the walls were on fire. The prep counter, the table, the chairs.

The smoke was so thick here that I could barely make out the door, and even through the cloth covering my nose, I hacked. Deep, wrenching coughs. The heat was *searing*. I tasted blood on my tongue. I would burn my lungs if I didn't escape. It was too hot. I'd never felt *anything* this hot.

Stumbling my way to the front door, I tugged on the handle… but then released it with a cry, my palm burning. Draped over the back of the kitchen chair, my father's cloak wasn't yet consumed in flames, and I tugged it off, patting off the embers that had begun to eat at the hem. I used it on the handle of the door, pushing with all my might—

But it wouldn't budge. Not a single inch. As if something heavy was blocking it from the outside. I cried out, gritting my teeth, throwing my entire weight into the frame. Metal was beginning to melt—Ruaala's designs—sliding off the wood like condensation on a glass. It burned my exposed flesh, but I continued to slam my body into the door. My heartbeat was a fluttering, wild thing in my chest, and as I tried to catch my breath, smoke wound down my throat so deep I couldn't get air.

Dropping to the ground where the smoke wasn't as dense, I dragged in violent, rasping breaths. Tears dripped down my cheek, but it wasn't because I was crying. The smoke was stinging them until they felt bloodshot and raw.

*I might die here,* came the sudden realization.

The stone floor was burning my kneecaps and shins where I was kneeling.

*The windows.*

Pushing up sluggishly from the floor, I kept low, keeping my tunic pressed to my nose. When I flicked the latch open and pressed at the glass, the window wouldn't move. Brow furrowing, I banged at the pane, thinking it was stuck…until I saw large bolts pinned on the outer ledge frame—a frame I had just repaired yesterday. Bolts I didn't recognize, that hadn't been there this morning.

Using my father's cloak to protect my fist, I pounded at the glass, though I knew that it was impossibly thick. I didn't think I could break it, and my damn tools were outside in the front garden. I only had knives in here, and even the sharpened blades wouldn't be able to puncture glass.

Just then I heard a loud *crack*, the ceiling giving a mighty shake, dust falling from the wood beams overhead.

*Oh gods,* I thought. How long until they burned?

"*Millie!*"

A guttural roar nearly shook the cottage.

My breath hitched, hope and desperation mingling tightly together.

"Kythel!" I called back before I dissolved into body-wracking coughs once again. My voice was too weak. I felt like I could barely hear it over the blood rushing in my own ears. "Ky-Kythel, I'm here!"

I screamed when I heard another thunderous *boom* from above, when one of the wooden beams cracked and fell to the ground. Shaking, gasping, I eyed another beam as the ceiling began to cave in, the falling debris shooting the flames even higher as they lapped at the fresh material.

"Millie!"

So close. He sounded so close. But I felt sluggish, trying to crawl back toward the door. I couldn't get enough air.

The door gave a sudden violent rattle.

Then it was practically torn off its hinges, and I heard the whistle of oxygen just before the fire seemed to explode in size and intensity.

Kythel was a blur, snatching me up into his arms quickly as another wooden beam crashed to the ground. He shot us both out of the cottage just as the rest of the ceiling caved in on the ground floor, feeding the ravenous fire below.

The clean, cold air that rushed down my throat made me hack until I felt like I would cough up both of my lungs. Kythel took us nearly to the edge of the clearing, leaning me back against one of the bleeding trees.

"Are you hurt, *sasiral?*" came his roughened demand. "Where are you hurt?"

He was running his hands over me in the darkness—*trembling* hands, I realized when I was finally able to control my cough—and I hissed when he encountered the burns on my legs.

"Azur!" Kythel yelled into the clearing. Azur? His brother was here? "Go to Erzan and get the healer!"

But then I heard the whistle of wings as another Kylorr took to the sky.

Kythel's voice sounded different. Deeper. Gruffer. And when I finally blinked away the tears from my eyes, I saw he was changed too. His vest hung off his body in tatters. The blue of his eyes were so bright they were almost glowing. He was barefoot, his seams at the sides of his pants popped open.

His horns were straight, no longer curving along his skull. And a deep growl was rumbling constantly from his chest.

*Berserker,* I reminded myself. Sometimes it was hard to remember that at their core, that was what the Kylorr were. Berserkers. It was what made them so dangerous. With my father, I'd never seen him go berserk. I couldn't imagine him hurting another living being.

Kythel, however?

There was a madness in his gaze, unleashed and furious. He *was* dangerous. So why wasn't I afraid of him?

*Because he went berserk for me,* I realized.

*He is scared for me,* I realized next, especially when he batted a trembling palm the size of my head along my cheek, smoothing away my tears. His whole body was shaking.

"I'm okay," I rasped out, my voice raw and husky from the smoke. It hurt to talk. I wondered if the insides of throats could be burned because mine felt like it. "I'm okay, Kythel."

His shoulders shuddered, and he dipped his head. His forehead met the side of my face, holding himself there as if to assure himself that I was speaking the truth. The small movement brought a fresh wave of tears to my eyes, and then I began to cry. I'd cried so much over the last few days for this male. I'd thought I was fresh out of tears, but I supposed a near-death experience changed that. I could still feel the heat of the flames, and through the strands of Kythel's dark hair, I watched as my cottage burned.

My father's letters. The last of his stores. All my belongings. They all might be gone.

His cloak, however, was still wound around my fist.

I closed my eyes, not wanting to believe it.

This was a nightmare I *needed* to wake up from. Only, I never did.

# CHAPTER 38

## KYTHEL

"You need to rest," I urged Millie quietly, trying to catch her bandaged arm, though I avoided the burns caused by the molten metal from the front door of the cottage.

"No, I need to see what's left," she said, not quite meeting my eyes as she stepped forward in determination.

"Millie," I growled, catching the small wince on her features when she stepped over a charred beam, when she landed on her blistered feet, though the healer had bandaged and padded the wounds as best as he was able. Humans healed more slowly than Kylorr, but I'd mixed in some of my blood and venom into the burn paste to help speed it along.

"I'm fine," she insisted. Only she wasn't. Her skin was still covered in soot and ash, making the tear tracks that ran down her cheeks all the more obvious. Her arms and right hand were bandaged in thick cloth, as were her knees, shins, and feet. The stone had been so hot that it had burned her exposed flesh. She was still dressed in a tunic that ended at her mid-thighs, and she looked so vulnerable and sad, picking through the rubble of the cottage she'd worked so hard on.

My fists clenched at my sides. Just recalling the fear I'd felt and the desperation I'd heard in her screams...I felt the rage building. Right now, I needed to keep it at bay. I'd never experienced anything like this before, but with my *kyrana*'s life having been threatened, it took everything in me to keep from going berserk again.

*I almost lost her,* I realized. If I had reached her even a few moments later, she might've been crushed underneath the beams of the ceiling.

When all I wanted was to hold her against me, to keep her pressed close to my side—since my heart was a living, breathing thing outside of my body now—Millie was keeping me at arm's length, with good reason.

It was morning now. Dawn was breaking over Stellara, spilling soft-hued purple and pink streaks across the sky like watery paints. The clearing was filled up with more Kylorr than I'd ever seen it hold—Telaana, Vadyn, various keepers who had woken in the middle of the night to help put out the flames. Azur stood with the healer, speaking in low tones, across the clearing. I watched as a solider approached him, who I'd ordered to comb every inch of the surrounding area, and I watched him hand my brother something.

The fire had been no accident. Millie had insisted she'd put out the fire in the hearth before going to bed. There had been a black metal brace against the door, locking her inside, and bolts nailed against the frames of the front windows, barring all escape. Someone had wanted her dead. House Kaalium had many enemies—the Kylorr across the seas, for example, who Zyre had warned had spies throughout the Kaalium. And while Zyre wasn't quite an enemy, he wasn't an ally either. He had every reason to try to strike against us where it would hurt most.

Even still, I thought the assassins were much closer to home. Especially when Azur approached me, observing me watch Millie poke through the blackened ash of her beloved cottage.

Azur pressed something into my hand. When I felt the cool metal, I knew what it was without looking down, and I was impressed that the solider had found it all, though they'd been trained to have keen eyes and ears.

A tracker scout. The same model as the one I'd found nearby not that long ago.

"Where?" I asked.

Azur gestured to the tree I'd buried Ruaala under. "He heard it over by the tree. Then it wiped itself."

Someone had been watching. Just now.

"I thought they had been watching *me*," I said quietly, looking back up at Millie, my eyes tracking her every movement, however slow. "But they've been watching her this whole time."

"You found another one?"

"Last week," I informed him. "It followed us as we were walking in Stellara."

"Someone knows she's your *kyrana*, then," Azur said.

"Everyone in Erzos knows by now," I said, scoffing. "I wasn't exactly *subtle*. It's not like I could hide it."

"Do you know who would want to track her?"

"House Arada," I replied, my jaw tightening.

They had the most to lose if I chose Millie over Lyris. Kaan had told me himself that he wanted his daughter to marry into House Kaalium, to have our Houses tied together in history. His call to my father had been a desperate action. And when yet another moon winds had gone by without my proposal to Lyris... it must have tipped his patience over the edge.

Eliminating the only obstacle that stood in House Arada's way would have been a tempting option. The only question was who'd given the order. Or had it been all of them?

"You're certain it wasn't an outsider?" Azur asked, knowing the implications of what I'd said if it were true. "Zyre? The Thryki?"

"It's possible," I allowed. A blood-mated Kylorr was a

dangerous thing, especially one who was an heir of the Kaalium with legions of soldiers at their beck and call. "But why not go after Gemma too? No, it doesn't make sense."

I stared down at the tracker in my hand.

"The brace against the door was *drava*. The bolts too," I said. "They were builder grade. Not everyone has access to materials like that."

"What are you going to do?" Azur asked, his tone grim. "To threaten the life of your mate bears grave consequences indeed. Death, even. But..."

"I know," I growled.

We still needed House Arada.

And the bloodlust I felt at the thought of confronting Kaan— or perhaps Hanno or even Lesana—should have made me pass the responsibility onto my brother, who'd likely have a cooler head in a situation like this. When I envisioned it, after I got the confession I sought, I would likely rip them in two. For *daring* to threaten Millie, to try to burn her alive in the cottage that mattered so much to her. Her screams still echoed in my mind, and I felt the pierce of my claws into my palms, black blood beginning to drip.

The *only* thing giving me pause was Zyre's request. And despite what I *wished* to do as a mated Kylorr...I was still the *Kyzaire* of Erzos. Murdering the heads of an entire noble family— or even stripping them of their possessions—set a dangerous precedent, one that mirrored a darker time that hadn't been all that long ago.

Even if I wanted to...I couldn't.

*But I can still make House Arada bend to my will,* I thought, watching Millie pick her way through the rubble. *And I can still punish them for daring to harm my mate.*

I made my decision right then, another path opened to me.

I would make House Arada pay for every burn and scratch on Millie's body. I would make House Arada pay for every tear she'd shed, every ragged cough that shook her shoulders, every scream and cry that would haunt me for the rest of my life.

But first, I would win Millie back.

This time, I wouldn't be the biggest fucking fool in the entire universe and let her go.

No matter what it took, no matter how long it took, I would not rest until she was mine once more.

Crushing the tracker in my hand, I strode through the burned wreckage of Millie's cottage, heading straight toward my mate.

I saw her watch me out of the corner of her eyes, and my gut gave a harsh twist. What I wouldn't give to have her *look* at me again, to smile at me warmly, openly, in that special way that made me feel connected to her. But I knew that I'd cut her deeply. That she felt rejected, tossed away, abandoned. And how could she not feel that way?

"Don't tell me to rest," she said.

"I won't," I said, even though all I wanted to do was take her back to the keep, back to my bed where she fucking *belonged*, and keep her there until every wound healed on her body. I hadn't realized how vulnerable humans were. How easily their skin could blister. "What do you need? What are you looking for?"

Millie still didn't look at me. On the ground, she toed over a charred...blanket? The fabric crumbled into ash.

"A trunk from the bedroom," she said. "The inside was lined with Jobarrian metal, so I hope..."

She hoped it hadn't burned.

"I'll find it," I promised. Without another moment's hesitation, I strode over to the back portion of the house, knowing that the quicker I located it, the sooner I could convince Millie to sit back down.

It didn't take long. The whole second floor had burned, and I found the trunk buried beneath the washing tub, though I'd had to climb up a small mountain of rubble to reach it.

Millie let out a relieved sigh when I procured it for her, and my chest puffed with pride when she *finally* met my eyes.

"Thank you," she said, holding them for only a moment before they flitted away. The handle was burned, and the material covering the front was half-charred. When she crouched right where she stood and opened it, I saw the inner metal lining had held up well.

Her shoulders relaxed. Familiar pressurized bottles, jars, and flasks were nestled inside. Her father's preserves. Along with a stack of neatly tied parchment.

"What are they?"

"Letters," she replied softly. "Letters my father wrote Ruaala. And one he sent to me. Before he died."

My chest tightened. "What did he say in your letter?"

"I don't know," she admitted quietly. "I haven't read it."

She pulled out the letter in question. I saw that the silver wax seal was unbroken. Her hands were trembling, and she struggled to hold it when her right hand was bandaged, as her left hand tried to break the seal.

"And all I could think this morning is that it might have burned and I would have never known what his last letter said… because I'd been too much of a coward to read it," she continued softly. "Now it just feels so silly."

"*Sasiral…*" I trailed off, my heart beginning to ache at the sorrow in her voice. But I heard determination too. "I imagine you didn't want to read it because then his death would feel final. That doesn't make you a coward."

She paused to look up at me, her eyes going a little glassy.

"May I?" I asked, gesturing toward the letter.

She nodded.

Reaching out, I swiped my claw neatly under the seal, the flap of the letter popping up. I wiped my hands on my torn pants so I wouldn't dirty the parchment as I unfolded it for her. Keeping my eyes averted, I handed her the letter.

Millie took a deep breath and then read it, staying silent for a long time, her eyes skimming the page over and over again. Reading. Then rereading.

Voices drifted through the clearing from the others, but crouching in the rubble of the cottage, it was only Millie and myself. No one else could reach us here. And so when she began to cry, gentle little sobs that broke my damn heart, I reached out and she fell against me, needing the support. Repositioning us to a sitting position, I brought her into my lap as she cried.

"*Laraya,*" I whispered into her hair, my throat closing up at the sound of her grief and sadness. "*Laraya,* I'm here."

*And I always will be,* I added silently.

If she knew what that word meant—*heart's blood*—she didn't respond to it. Only pressed her ash-streaked face into my vest harder and soaked whatever remained of the fabric with her tears. Carefully, I folded up the letter and placed it back into the safety of the trunk, closing the lid. I didn't read it. It was private, only meant for Millie from her father.

One day, if she wanted to share it with me, I would be there. But not like this. Not like this when I knew that Millie only sought comfort in her grief and her shock, the events of the night stressful and overwhelming. I was familiar, even though I'd been reckless with her heart. Her trust.

The night had brought clarity for me, when it had only brought confusion for her. Her whole world had upended. Again.

With time, I would prove that Millie could trust me—could love me without fear. Because I would make sure that she never felt this way ever again.

# CHAPTER 39

## MILLIE

"The *Kyzaire* won't be happy about this," Kelan grumbled, setting me down in the very center of Erzan's square, the archives to my left. It was the notice board I was interested in, though I might pop into the archives building, if only to have a little quiet.

I was still limping, but I'd had the bandages taken off my feet this morning by the healer.

"This doesn't concern him, so he doesn't need to know," I said, my eyes already on the board.

"What are you even looking for?" Kelan wondered.

"I can't stay in the keep forever," I informed him. "I'm looking for a room or an inn in Erzan while I get back on my feet. I need to find work and then start saving for the cottage rebuild."

"Millie," he said, shaking his head, his wings rustling in protest. "The *Kyzaire really* won't be happy about this."

I ignored what he'd said about Kythel and limped forward toward the notice board. There had always been one on every travel port I'd come across, though they'd usually been projections. The Erzan board had actual parchment nailed to it with handwritten scribbles.

"I'll find a way back to the keep," I promised him. I knew this put him in an awkward position, considering he was one of the only keepers assigned to the north wing—Kythel's private wing. "I don't know how long it will take."

"You think I *want* to get murdered by the *Kyzaire?*" Kelan grumbled. "No, I'm not leaving your side."

"Suit yourself," I said, shrugging a shoulder.

It would still be another week until my father's and Ruaala's soul gems were finished. The shrine master had told me they were "settling," though even after his lengthy explanation about the three realms and the nourishment of the souls, I wasn't quite sure what that meant. He'd assured me everything about the process had gone smoothly, which had been the one blip of good news I'd had this entire week.

It had only been two days since the cottage had burned down. But I'd decided that I wouldn't dwell on it, that I wouldn't be angry about it. Well…more than was healthy. I had a healthy dose of anger, but I also realized that my anger didn't *change* anything. It had happened. The only way forward was to move on. And I'd decided that I wouldn't be at peace until I restored the cottage entirely, though it would be a long process. It would mean that I'd likely need to stay in Erzos—within viewing distance of Kythel's keep—for longer than I'd anticipated, for longer than would be comfortable.

On the notice board, I noticed one advertisement for extended stay rooms at the Erzan Inn, which was the one closest to the South Road construction, the cheapest rate per night and further discounted if I paid a month in advance.

*Probably because of the construction,* I realized, imagining waking up to the sounds of machinery and the cutting of rocks. But I didn't have a choice. I was right back where I'd started, saving every credit I could for the cottage, being frugal and obsessive over every little thing I bought.

*Though, thanks to Kythel, at least I* have *my father this time around,* I couldn't help but think.

For that, I would forever be grateful. No matter how much it hurt to look at Kythel, no matter how much it hurt to be near him. And since the fire, he'd been a constant presence at my side.

Being in Erzan this morning, away from the keep, away from Kythel, it felt like I could finally get my head on straight.

"Erzan Inn it is," I declared softly, catching Kelan's frown when he peered at that particular advertisement.

"No one in their right mind would stay there longer than necessary," he protested.

"Then it's a good thing I'm not in my right mind," I said, shooting him a self-deprecating smile as I turned and hobbled across the square, heading toward the road that would lead south. I'd pay the month in advance, I decided. I'd pay it today, and I could have Kelan bring my trunk and the meager amount of clothing I had left. I could be away from the keep tonight.

*Away from Kythel,* I added.

The thought brought a small thud of dismay and grief. Because even though Kythel had made his decision about us, it wasn't as if my ridiculous heart had gotten the message.

I had just stepped away from the cobblestone square when I heard, "*Millie?*"

Stiffening, I turned. Grace stood there, dressed in a beautiful emerald-green dress that hugged the curves of her waist and flared out over her generous hips. A basket was hanging from her arm, filled to the brim with brightly colored wildflowers and a bundled parcel tied in silky red ribbon. She looked as beautiful as ever, her cheeks flushed a healthy pink, her eyes bright. She looked happy.

"Oh gods, it is you!" she exclaimed, beaming, coming forward. "I've been trying to find you, but I was told that you'd left Raana *Dyaan* and…Millie? What's happened to you?"

She finally took in the wrapping I still had covering both my arms. The molten metal from Ruaala's door during the fire would likely leave rivers of scars down my flesh. The healer thought to keep them moisturized with burn paste and bandaged for as long as possible. My hands and feet and legs were healing well enough, however, spurred on by Kythel's blood and venom, which he'd added to the burn paste whenever the bandages had needed to be changed.

I couldn't forget that Grace had betrayed my trust. She'd showed my father's letters to Lesana. *Laughed* about them. I'd thought we'd been friends.

Kelan stepped between us when Grace approached, and she looked taken aback for the first time, peering at him in bewilderment.

"Millie?" she asked.

"Kelan, it's okay," I said, touching the bone of one of his wings, and he stepped away. Even though I wanted to, I couldn't find it in me to ignore her completely. I greeted, "Grace. How have you been?"

She blinked. "That's the greeting I get after over a month of not seeing you?"

My temper snapped, but I kept my expression neutral. "No, it's the greeting you get after betraying my trust."

"I'll..." Kelan trailed off before saying, "wait over there."

The keeper, who Kythel had assigned as my guard, strode away, giving Grace and me a little space as her eyes practically bugged out of her head.

"Excuse me?" she asked. "Betrayed your *what?* What in the world are you talking about, Millie?"

She looked genuinely puzzled, which made me falter for a brief moment. For all her flaws, Grace wasn't a liar. Or, at least, I hadn't believed she was. Then again, she'd hidden her relationship with Vraad and his wife at the *dyaan* for who knew how long.

"The letters," I said. "My father's private letters. Lesana told me you showed them to her—she knew all about my father and Ruaala. That you both thought they were pathetic and that you laughed about them."

Grace's lips parted and then closed. Parted and then closed.

Then she exploded, her cheeks burning a bright red. "Are you fucking kidding me, Millie? You know I hated that bitch. Why would I show your letters to *her* when *you* were my friend? I would never do that!"

More doubt crept into my mind. Freezing, I asked, "You... didn't?"

"*No*," she bit out sharply. She crossed her arms over her chest, one of the wildflowers escaping her basket with the agitated movement. "Of course not."

Now she was mad. Angry at me for thinking the worst of her, for believing Lesana over her.

"Then how did she know about the letters?" I asked, my shoulders dropping. I supposed it didn't even matter now. Lesana and Raana *Dyaan* seemed like ages ago. Just like the cottage, I would need to move forward. "Gods, I'm sorry, Grace. I don't know why...I don't know why I believed her."

"Because she has a way of sounding very convincing. Believe me, I understand how she can be. It's why I never trusted her. I've known females like her my whole life."

Crouching down, though the tight, tender skin around my knees protested, I gathered up the fallen wildflower, a corn-flower-blue bloom, and tucked it safely back into Grace's basket.

"I'm sorry," I said, taking in her pressed lips and flickering eyes. "I'm sorry, Grace. Please forgive me. For thinking the worst, for not even *considering* that she might have been lying."

Grace's shoulders dropped, and she let out a harsh sigh.

"Like I could ever stay mad at you, Millie," she finally said. "Even when I wanted to, I couldn't."

Hesitantly, I reached out my hand, and she took it, squeezing softly, which made me wince a little, considering it was still healing.

"Oh, I'm sorry," Grace said, ire already forgotten, concerned. Stepping forward, she gingerly touched my shoulder and asked quietly, "What happened, Millie?"

"Long story," I said, giving her a tired smile.

"I'm free all day," she offered, casting a look over at Kelan. "Are you?"

Erzan Inn could wait, I supposed.

And I'd missed my friend, even though the guilt at thinking the worst still pricked in my mind.

"Yes, I am."

"My home isn't too far away," she said. "I have your favorite steam cakes."

I smiled. "As if I could say no to those."

---

GRACE LEANED BACK AGAINST THE WALL OF HER WINDOW SEAT, which looked out over a small patch of meadow, filled with blooms. She made a beautiful portrait, her dress hanging loosely, her knee drawn up, flashing the side of her smooth calf. I spied small bite marks along her throat—two on both sides.

Her home was everything I wanted myself. Something small, cozy, safe. The inside was comfortably furnished with feminine patterns and materials and soft colors that made the front room feel bright and airy.

I was sitting at the table, decorated in intricate white lace, a small platter of steam cakes sitting perched in the very middle, though as I'd recounted the last month of my life to Grace, they'd hardly been touched.

With my good hand, I cradled a warm cup of flower-stem tea, the taste pleasantly sweet, and I couldn't help but think it would go wonderfully with a small dash of *kanno* spice and a squeeze of *syaan*-berry juice.

"My gods, Millie," Grace said. She wasn't smiling. She was... thunderstruck. And that wasn't an expression I'd witnessed on her features often. "Do you know who did it?"

The cottage had been burned down because of my relationship with Kythel. Of that, I was certain. And I couldn't help but remember Lesana's threat that night in her office when she'd slapped me, when she'd lied to me about Grace, and when she'd threatened me.

*Don't cross me—or House Arada—again. You won't like the consequences,* she'd told me.

I hadn't even told Kythel of my suspicions about who was responsible. But the more I thought about it, the more certain I was.

"Whoever it was, too bad they didn't realize that Kythel had dumped me before the fire," I tried to joke, though the words landed hollow and dull. "It'll take a lot to rebuild."

"And you're living at the keep now? With him?" she asked.

"Yes, but..." I trailed off. "I'm going to live in Erzan Inn, I've decided." Grace made a face. "I was heading there before we stumbled across one another."

"Gods, why would you want to live there?" she asked. But she knew—because it was cheap. Out of everyone at Raana *Dyaan*, I thought that Grace understood best about worrying over every credit. "No, you'll live here with me. And I won't charge you a single credit, if you promise to cook me dinner every now and again. I miss your fruit pastries. The ones you made for my birthday."

I straightened in my chair. "Grace, I couldn't impose on you like that."

"Nonsense," she said. "If you're worried about my, um, clients, they don't come here. I go to their residence for all feedings, and

I usually stay the night when they request me. You'll have time to yourself—it's only me, and I have another bedroom."

Longing went through me. Hope too.

"You can stay as long as you need," she assured me.

Tears pooled in my eyes, her generosity and kindness making me feel even worse for having thought the worst of her.

"Don't," she said, rising from her window seat, as if reading my mind. She took the chair next to me, taking my hand—my *good* hand. Outside the window, I watched Kelan walk through the meadow, waiting for me. "Don't, Millie."

"She knew about the letters," I tried to explain again. "Do you think she went through my belongings when I wasn't there?"

"One of the reasons why I left," Grace said quietly, "was because I believed she was spying into the private rooms. Bugging them with tracker scouts. And you know she had that window in the storage room, the one that looked into the lounge."

"Tracker scouts?" I asked, knowing I'd overheard a conversation with Kythel and Azur about them.

"Vraad was being threatened," Grace told me.

"He was?" I asked, my brow furrowing.

"He got a letter delivered to his residence. In it, they said they would tell his wife about me, about what really went on between us in the feeding rooms. It made me think that whoever was watching didn't track us all the time because then they would've known that Lynara and I were intimate too. Nevertheless, he was threatened. They demanded credits. He never paid because it wasn't an issue. No one ever contacted Lynara, and we all had quite a laugh over it. But someone knew what was happening at Raana *Dyaan*."

"I didn't tell her about Vraad, I swear," I said, wondering if she thought it had been me.

"No, I know. I know you wouldn't," Grace said. "I never thought it was you. But I do think Lesana was responsible. And if what you said is true about Kythel's involvement with House Arada, then I wouldn't be surprised if they were the ones responsible for the fire. They had everything to gain if you...disappeared."

My chest tightened, but I nodded. I'd come to the same conclusion myself. To think that a person could so easily attempt to murder someone, to burn them to death...it made me sick to my stomach.

"Do you think he knows?" Grace asked.

"It's possible," I said, lifting my shoulder in a small shrug. "Which puts him in a difficult position, considering he's still planning to marry Lyris."

"He's not," she said, her tone dry. "You cannot believe that, Millie. Not after what you *are* to him."

"It doesn't matter anymore what I am to him," I said, hating the defeat I heard in my tone. "I'm just trying to move on."

Grace was silent momentarily.

"You don't think there's a chance that you'll find your way back to one another?" she asked gently.

"You've always been a romantic, Grace," I said, giving her a sad, soft smile. "But no. He puts his duty before everything. He serves his people and his family before all else. Me? I'm only a distraction, an obstacle in his way. And maybe it's selfish, but I don't think I can be with someone like that. I don't want to always feel like I come last to him."

"That's not true," she told me. Her hand tightened on my hand.

"I can't even say I blame him. He's a *Kyzaire*. It must be hard to never get what you *really* want in life, to always sacrifice for others, for the greater good. That was a part of why I fell in love with him in the first place," I admitted. "Because he's selfless. Because he cares about Erzos. He protects his family. He's a *good* male. But it doesn't mean that he loves me."

"If you believe he doesn't love you, then maybe *you* are

blinded, Millie," Grace said, sighing, though there was no malice in her words. "Without ever having met him, just from what you've told me, I think it's clear that he cares about you."

"I never said he didn't care about me," I said. "I know he does. Just not enough to choose me."

She gave my hand another soft squeeze. "Like I said, you're more than welcome to stay here for a long as you need," she told me. "But don't give up on him quite yet, Millie. Will you promise me that at least?"

"Why do you care so much?" I asked her quietly, trying to understand.

"Because you're my friend. One of the best I've had, though we haven't known one another for long," she added, quirking her lips. "But I know you're a genuine and kind person. That's rare. And I want to see you happy. I want to see you cherished. Loved. As you deserve."

"Oh, Grace."

"And maybe one day, it'll prove to *me* that I can have those things too. So you see?" she asked, giving me a mischievous smile, bumping my shoulder with her own. "We're all a little selfish in the end. Who knows…maybe your Kythel will prove that he can be selfish too. Maybe he'll get his head out of his family's ass and snatch you up all for himself."

The peal of laughter that escaped me made me feel better. A lot better.

"Now, eat these damn steam cakes," she ordered me, smiling, pushing the platter forward, "before I do."

# CHAPTER 40

## KYTHEL

"You were supposed to be at the keep hours ago," I told Kelan, though my voice sounded more tired than irritated. I landed on the soft grass of the meadow and peered around, my gaze landing on a warmly lit single-level cottage on the outskirts of Erzan. "She's in there?"

"Yes, *Kyzaire*."

"Get some rest," I ordered him. "I'll return her to the keep."

He hesitated. "She was looking at renting one of the rooms at Erzan Inn today."

My shoulders stiffened. I'd wondered when she would try to put distance between us. I just hadn't expected it to be so soon.

I inclined my head at Kelan before striding toward the front door of the cottage, intent on collecting my mate and getting her back to the keep. I heard my keeper leave, taking to the skies, just as I reached the door, pounding on the wood with the side of my fist.

A human woman with red hair answered the door. I thought I recognized her. It took me a moment to place her as a blood giver at Raana *Dyaan*.

Her eyes didn't widen in surprise. If anything, they narrowed at seeing a *Kyzaire* on her doorstep.

"Millie," she called out.

I heard movement inside. I only needed to wait a moment before my shoulders relaxed and I caught the scent of my *kyrana* as she came into view. Her hazel eyes peered up at me.

"I was wondering when Kelan would snitch on me," she said, crossing her arms over her chest before remembering that her skin was still tender from the burns. She seemed to be in good spirits. Had she been *drinking*? I wondered, catching the scent of wine perfuming the air and observing her pink cheeks.

"I'll be inside if you need anything," the human woman said, squeezing Millie's shoulder as she passed.

My mate joined me outside. Over her shoulder, she said, "Thank you, Grace."

When the door shut, it was just the two of us in the warm night.

"Are you ready to return to the keep?" I asked. "You need more salve for the burns."

She shook her head.

I tried a different tactic. "It's a nice night. Will you walk with me?"

*That* caught her attention.

"There's a small forest beyond the meadow," I said, tilting my head to gesture to the darkness. Chirping insects with flickering light trails illuminated the edge of the clearing. They left a luminous pink powder in their wake from their wings, which dissipated in the gentle wind. "I'll carry you."

"No," she said quickly. "I've been sitting all day. I'd like to stretch my legs."

It was better than her shutting me out, I supposed. "As you wish."

We walked together in the quiet, her feet swishing softly

through the short grass, peppered with wildflowers, though their blooms were closed up in the moonlight.

"Grace has offered to let me live with her here," Millie said suddenly. I didn't react, my pace steady, though my jaw tightened at the declaration. "I've decided to take her up on it."

"No," I said.

Millie froze. "*No?*"

I turned to face her. We'd only made it to the middle of the meadow before we'd started arguing.

"Someone threatened your life, Millie. Until I know for certain who that person is, then you'll remain at the keep, where I can protect you myself."

"I'm not a prisoner there," she argued, her brow furrowing. She wasn't *angry*, I realized. Because she'd expected my protest?

"Do I make you feel like a prisoner?" I wondered. "You're free to go wherever you please. If you want to go into town, you know you only need to take a guard."

"That's not what I meant."

"I almost *lost you*, Millie," I exclaimed suddenly, cupping her cheeks with my palms, needing her to understand. She blinked as she peered up at me, her expression somber. "I will *never* go through that again."

It still haunted me. The *possibility* of that night. If I had been moments too late. If Azur hadn't journeyed to the keep, if he hadn't seen the fire in the distance. If I had continued to feel sorry for myself, sitting in the wreckage of my office as my *kyrana* burned to death, crushed by a falling ceiling or suffocated by smoke.

It had shaken me to my very core.

I'd thought Aina's death had changed me? Even Ruaala's death? Those were nothing compared to what I felt now.

"So until I find whoever was responsible for the fire, for your attempted murder," I said, catching her flinch, "because that is what it was...I need you to remain close, Millie."

"You can't protect me forever, Kythel," she said.

"You already told me that," I said. "And I nearly failed you. I will not make that mistake again."

Our eyes held.

"I've made too many mistakes with you already," I told her gruffly.

Her gaze shuttered. I mourned the loss of her when she stepped away.

"Yes, you've made that perfectly clear."

I scowled. "That's not what I meant, Millie."

"Let me speed this up for you," she said, straightening her shoulders. "I believe that House Arada, perhaps even Lesana, had something to do with the fire. And believe me, I wouldn't lob an accusation around like that, especially against a noble House, unless I was relatively certain."

When my expression didn't change, she shifted on her feet, looking down at the grass that separated us.

"But you already know that," she said quietly. "Which puts you in a very uncomfortable position, considering you're marrying Lyris."

"I'm not marrying Lyris," I growled out. "I had decided that even before the fire."

She stilled. Softly, she asked, "You did?"

"I've made a mess of things, *sasiral*," I said, softening my tone. All I wanted to do was pull her into me, feel her heart thud against my skin, breathe in her scent, though it would send my venom pooling on my tongue. But this wasn't about feeding or sex. I missed those things with her, obviously...but I missed *her* more. "I swear on Raazos, on Alaire, that I will do everything I can to be worthy of your love again."

Millie's hitched breath never released as she stared up at me in shock. Mistrustful shock, I noted.

"I've been a fool. A blind fool," I confessed. "I made a choice that I thought would best serve the Kaalium, but it turned out to be the worst decision of my life. I see that now. There will not be a single day where I don't regret it, even if you choose to forgive me. Because I see now that *you* are what's best for the Kaalium."

"You're wrong," she said, though it was fear that made her bottom lip tremble. "I'm just a human. I have no great ancestry I can trace back generations. Not a drop of Kylorr blood in my veins. I have less than three thousand credits to my name."

Had I really make her doubt *this* much? I wondered, every word she spoke like a whip strike.

"You are what's best for the Kaalium because you are what's best for me," I told her. "And if you give me another chance, *sasiral*, I will prove that I am what's best for you. No other male will love you like I do. No other male will protect you, will cherish you as much as I will."

She didn't believe me, I realized with a sharp pang. It would take time to earn back her trust.

"You asked me why I call you *sasiral* once," I said softly. "I told you it was because I admired your strength, your will, your determination. And that was all true."

I stepped closer, reaching out to trace her soft cheek.

"What I didn't tell you was that I call you my fallen star because you landed right in my hands," I said, my tone gruff, filled with longing. Her lips parted. "A gift from the universe—a beautiful, bright treasure, unlike anything I'd ever known before. You landed on Krynn, and against all odds, we found one another."

"Kythel…" she said, her voice strained.

"I intend to care for you as one would care for a rare gift from the gods. Because that is what you are to me. I won't let you forget that. Never again, *sasiral*."

Tears shimmered in her eyes, but she quickly blinked them away.

"I love you, Millie Seren," I said, the words landing softly. Words I'd never said to a lover before. A small gasp left her. "My biggest regret is that I didn't tell you that night at the cottage. I knew even before you gave me the universe." That dinner and the special meaning behind it, I would never forget. "But I'm telling you now that I love you. That I want you—and only you—as my wife, as the *Kylaira* of Erzos. There will be no one else for me, *sasiral*. You are everything I've ever wanted. You are everything I've ever *needed*. I'm sorry it's taken me this long to realize it."

"Why are you doing this *now*? You're not being fair," she breathed, crying again, tracks of clear tears tracing down her cheeks.

"I know," I said, my tone ragged, my throat tight. I pressed a kiss to her cheek, tasting the saltiness of her tears. Against her temple, I admitted, "I cannot promise that I will be fair as I try to reclaim your love, Millie. But I will promise to be patient."

When I leaned away, her hazel eyes were luminous. Sad. Confused. But I thought I saw the lingerings of *hope*. Or maybe I just wanted to see it.

"I'll be patient," I vowed. My eyes slid to the cottage. "And while I would prefer if you remained at the keep, you're free to live wherever you please. If you wish to live with your friend, however, I will be posting a guard rotation here at all hours of the day and night."

A compromise. But I couldn't tie her to me. Millie wouldn't like to be bound and tethered.

"I'd like to stay with Grace," she decided.

Disappointment speared through the ever-present ache in my chest, but I hid it well and nodded.

"I'll have your things brought over tonight," I promised her.

"Thank you," she whispered. Sliding me a careful, hesitant look, she asked, "What...what are you going to do about House Arada?"

"What would you like me to do?" I asked.

Her brow furrowed. "Me?"

I nodded again. She said nothing about my confession. Taking a step away, I knew that she didn't want to discuss us. *This*. That would come with time, I hoped. For now, I'd decided to keep nothing from her. Azur had told me that Gemma had only wanted the truth from him.

Millie deserved the truth, and she could make her decision about House Arada's fate.

"House Arada controls the Three Guardians," I told her. "You know it?"

She nodded. "The mountain range to the north. Filled with *drava*."

"It was a gift to their family from my great-grandfather. They were loyal to House Kaalium during the winter wars against the Kaazor, long ago."

Millie watched me carefully.

"They alone control *drava* production," I said. "An expensive export, it's made their House very wealthy. In times of war...*drava* can decide a victor. Unbreakable weapons, armors, shields, those are all crafted from *drava*. Which is why I was going to marry Lyris.

"An arranged marriage to help take back some of the control for an invaluable resource—one I think was foolish to give away to begin with," I admitted. "But nations are not built by a single legacy. I need to remember that. Without House Arada, the Kaalium might not be what it is today."

Understanding settled in my mate's eyes.

"War is coming, Millie. Zyre, the king of the Kaazor, has agreed to make a war bond with the Kaalium. But he has his own demands, and they include a steady supply of *drava*. Even still, I want to burn their House to the ground for what they did to you."

Millie's lips firmed. "You can't."

Whatever she saw in my eyes made hers widen.

She stepped closer. "Kythel, you can't. This isn't about me."

"You are still my *kyrana*. Any Kylorr in my position would

seek to punish whoever threatened your life. You don't *understand* my need for retaliation against all those who hurt you, Millie. Every scratch, every burn, every fear, every cry…I *need* to punish them for what they did to you."

"But you're not just any Kylorr," she argued quietly, meeting my eyes. There was a calmness in her gaze, a steadiness in her voice. "You're a *Kyzaire*, responsible for every single life throughout your nation. You can retaliate against them without bloodshed. You can make them bend to your will without destroying their House. I don't envy you for the politics you need to juggle, Kythel. But I've been around enough nobles and politicians to know that nothing is ever truly fair and that power is attained through ignoble means more times than not."

"Is that your answer for me, *Kylaira?*" I asked.

Her whistled breath sounded quickly. "Don't call me that. That's not what I am to you."

"Not yet," I said. "I said I wouldn't be fair, and I meant it. But I've always thought you would make a good *Kylaira*."

Her gaze slid to the ground. Embarrassed? Pleased? She hid her expression, so I couldn't be certain.

"Because you're right," I added. "Nothing is ever simple. Nothing is ever clear. But I can tell you one thing—this will be *easy* for me. That is almost never the case."

"What are you going to do?" she asked.

"What you suggested, *sasiral*," I said. "I will make them bend to my will. And make them regret ever hurting you. That I can promise you."

# CHAPTER 41

## KYTHEL

*T*here was a smug expression on Kaan's features when he entered my bare office.

The window had only recently been repaired, the artwork that had hung on the walls destroyed beyond saving. My desk had escaped the worst of my fury, however, and it was where Azur sat while I stood at the window, looking out over Stellara.

I caught Kaan's surprise in the reflection when he spied Azur sitting in my usual place.

"*Kyzaire*," the head of House Arada greeted. "I hadn't expected to see you here. What an honor it is to meet with you again."

"No need to sit, Kaan," I said, keeping my voice steady, when he moved for one of the chairs opposite of my desk. Azur was here to ensure I didn't throttle the other male with my bare hands, though I'd insisted that he had nothing to worry about. I would only draw a little blood, after all. "This won't take long."

Even still, having a witness to this meeting wasn't a terrible idea. It had been Kaldur's idea actually.

The first crack in Kaan's confidence splintered across his expression. It had been three days since Millie had left the keep.

And in that time, I had worked on breaking down Hanno and then Lesana, gathering my evidence to use against House Arada.

Now that I had my proof, it was time to bring Kaan to his knees.

Kaan's gaze zeroed in on something perched on the edge of my desk. His wings stilled.

"Recognize it?" I wondered, turning to face him, walking around to the side of my desk and leaning my thigh against it. I crossed my ankles, then my arms, before flashing him a small smile.

"Well, of course," Kaan said, gaze flitting to me, confusion on his face. "It's a tracker scout."

"It was found outside my *kyrana*'s cottage in Stellara. After it was lit on fire, burned to the ground—my mate trapped inside, considering the door had been barred and the windows had been sealed shut."

"I heard," Kaan said, his tone morose. "My deepest apologies, *Kyzaire*. I hope the female is all right."

"You know she is," I said, "considering it's your tracker scout."

Kaan blanched, his mouth falling open in shock. "You cannot possibly be suggesting that I had anything to do with—"

I tapped a button on my new Halo screen, and before us, a projection of Lesana appeared. On the opposite side of the room, I projected the recording of Hanno for good measure, so Kaan was trapped between members of his own House.

The recordings began to play simultaneously. The words were a jumbled blur. Their voices, their pleading, panicked, melancholic tones made bile rise in my throat. Sickening. Perhaps I had suggested execution wasn't out of the realm of possibility when I had questioned each of them. Perhaps I had played into my rage, my fury, my bloodlust a little too convincingly. Because it hadn't taken long for both of them to turn on Kaan.

*"I never wanted to hurt her,"* Lesana said, fat silver tears tracking down her cheeks. *"But Kaan insisted it was the only way to secure the*

*proposal for the House. A* kyrana *bond is too powerful—that's what he said. He knew I had access to tracker scouts. I've used them before...in the* dyaan. *But—but I never wanted to hurt Millicent, Kyzaire. I didn't have anything to do with the fire. Kaan only ordered me to monitor her location. I had no choice. Hanno controls Raana* Dyaan, *and Kaan controls Hanno. I would have been left with nothing. Draan and I have worked too hard to be left with nothing."*

Behind Kaan, Hanno's recording sounded. His voice was quieter, not as desperate as Lesana's, and his expression was drawn tight. *"Kaan said it was best for someone within the House to do it—the less that knew, the better. He asked me to do it. He went to House Kraan's social event that night, to be seen, whereas I went to the cottage. Lesana told me where to find it. There were these trees lined in silver that guided the path. It was almost too easy. I didn't expect it to burn so quickly."*

Azur shut off the recordings. Lesana's and Hanno's projections fell away. The silence was almost too loud, and Kaan's fear smelled acrid, like smoke.

"They're lying," Kaan said, eyes bulging. "You must believe me. They're lying, *Kyzaire.* I had no part in this. They've always been jealous that I was the head of the House. Now they're trying to blame this—this *heinous* act on me!"

"That's the difference between House Arada and House Kaalium," I said quietly, watching him fall apart in my office, unraveling like a tapestry. He realized that he wouldn't be able to lie his way out of this. This had his stench all over it. "Because I know my own family wouldn't sell me out, even in the face of death. That is true loyalty. You? House Arada is weak and greedy. You have no true allegiance to one another."

Kaan's wings were beginning to tremble, a reaction I'd only ever seen in a child. Good. Fear made a great motivator.

"What was it, Kaan?" I wondered. "After you tried to go behind my back to my own *father*, you realized that I still wasn't going to join our Houses? Did that thought make you desperate?

Did it make you afraid that you would lose everything you desired, everything you had maneuvered toward for years because of one human woman?"

He said nothing, smartly.

"If he'd done the same to my *kyrana*," Azur murmured to me casually, staring Kaan down, "I'd pluck his head right off his shoulders. I'd give it to my wife as a gift."

Kaan's wings gave a mighty quake.

"Luckily for you," I said, "my *kyrana* has asked me *not* to do that."

"*Kyzaire*," he said, his tone turning pleading, his reality upended in the span of mere moments, stepping forward quickly. He would kneel if I asked him. "I beg you. I had nothing to do with this and—"

"Stop lying," I clipped out, the first of my rage beginning to rear its head. I was on edge already, only managing to get through the day on blood rations that tasted like mud in my mouth. "Tell me the truth, and I promise I won't slaughter you where you stand. *Tell me the truth.* Now!"

"All right!" Kaan burst out, his jaw tight with horror but his fear more palpable. "I—I did it. I told Lesana to track the girl, and I ordered Hanno to kill her." His tone quickened. "But they were in support of the idea—both Hanno and Lesana, despite what they tell you. We *all* were to benefit from the marriage, not just me."

It took him a moment to realize his confession hung in the air like a thick, suffocating haze.

He crumbled in a heap on the ground, his shoulders curling in. I'd never seen a more pathetic sight. I'd never wanted to kill someone more than I wanted to kill Kaan of House Arada right then.

*But things are never simple,* I reminded myself, my conversation with Millie from that night in Grace's meadow returning to me.

CRAVING IN HIS BLOOD

"What..." he started, his voice breaking. "What are you going to do?"

"Your family was once loyal to House Kaalium," I said, gritting my teeth because it took everything in me to choke out the words. "You were given the Three Guardians as a gift, as a sign of respect for that loyalty and friendship."

"If you take the Three Guardians away, it will ruin us," came Kaan's hollow words.

Azur laughed, the sound cutting.

To Kaan, I said, "You have already ruined your House, Kaan. I didn't need to do it for you."

Rounding the desk, I crouched in front of the male who had nearly taken Millie from me.

"The Three Guardians belong to you," I continued, which finally made his head tilt up toward me. "But as way of apology, to show your obvious remorse for the actions you've taken against me and my House, you will give back two of the Three Guardians. You will sign them back into House Kaalium's name. Tonight."

Disbelief went through his gaze. This was a mercy. A great mercy. Because I'd needed to remember optics and perception. I needed to remember my own ancestor's bloody rule in Erzos a hundred years ago. Of Jynaar, my great-grandfather's brother. Where blood had flowed quickly in the streets of Erzan for all those who'd opposed him.

We had evolved. Though I wanted to make a bloody example of Kaan, a warning for all those who threatened House Kaalium, I couldn't. We would settle this the diplomatic way...but I would ensure that I cut him off at his knees so he would always remember what he'd done.

"You can save face among the nobles," I nearly spat. "You can keep your House. You can keep one Guardian, so that you will always remember the loyalty and honor of your ancestors, to give you something to strive for again, considering how low you've fallen." He flinched. "But if you *ever* think to rise against House Kaalium again, I will take everything from you and destroy your family's name so that no living soul of our future generations would even dare to speak it. Do you understand?"

"Yes," Kaan choked out softly. He didn't meet my eyes. He kept his head lowered, his jaw tight. "Yes, I understand."

One Guardian would allow him to retain appearances among the nobles, but his abundance of wealth would dry up. Most importantly, one Guardian wouldn't give him enough power and influence should he try to sell *drava* to our enemies, especially when war came.

"Where is the deed?" Kaan asked quietly.

Azur shoved two copies over the side of the desk, and I unsheathed the blade at my hip. The contract was already drawn up. Simple in its wording but thorough. Kaan's unseeing, vacant eyes scanned the words. I handed him the blade, and he took it without hesitation.

"There is a clause at the end," I informed him cooly. "Should you betray House Kaalium again, the Third Guardian will be forfeited to my House. You would lose everything, and we would expose your crimes publicly."

Kaan's lips pressed together, but he only inclined his head in acknowledgment. He didn't have a choice. He knew it. The clause had been added in as insurance. While I didn't think Kaan would try to make deals with our enemies for *drava* behind our backs, I certainly hadn't believed him capable of trying to assassinate my *kyrana* either.

Slicing his palm, he dipped the tip of the blade into the droplets of blood before using it to sign his name at the bottom. He did the same with the next one, the contract identical to the first.

"What will happen to Hanno and Lesana?" he asked.

"Nothing," I said, rising swiftly from the floor and rolling the deeds, careful of the drying blood, before handing them to Azur.

He would make sure one was filed within the public archives and one was deposited within our own family's vault in Laras. "As long as you adhere to your end of the contract. But know that House Kaalium will be keeping a careful watch on the third Guardian and on Raana *Dyaan*. Yes?"

"Yes," Kaan rasped.

"Good," I growled. "Now, get up and get out of my sight."

The male didn't need to be told twice.

When he was gone—likely being escorted out by Vadyn, who'd been waiting in the hallway outside my office, I found Azur studying me.

"I like this change in you," he commented casually.

"What change?" I asked, narrowing my gaze on him.

"She makes you more bloodthirsty. It suits you."

# CHAPTER 42

## MILLIE

"*W*hat is this?" I demanded from Kythel, pushing the device I'd had clenched tightly in my hand since the market close to his face.

Kythel's jeweled gaze briefly dipped down before his eyes caught mine. If he was surprised to see me at his keep, he didn't show it. Vadyn had told me he was out in the gardens, and I'd found him walking among the hedges and blooms that evening, though he wandered in a restless way. It twisted my heart when I had the stray thought that he looked a little *lost*.

"That appears to be a Halo orb, my love," he said smoothly. It didn't matter if my heart stuttered in my chest at *my love* or if there was a part of me that enjoyed when he was being facetious. "One incredibly out of date."

"Don't get smart with me," I warned. "What's this number here?"

His lips pressed together when he finally peered at the flickering number projecting up.

"When did you do this?" I breathed.

"Before the fire," he answered, not denying it.

"Before the…" I trailed off. He had deposited nearly a quarter million credits into my account, and I'd not even realized it until today in the market, when my eyes had nearly bulged from my skull when I'd gone to pay for a bucket of old tools from the secondhand vendor.

Kythel waited, crossing his arms over his chest as he studied me. The sunset was beautiful tonight, casting bright streaks of lilacs, ceruleans, and fiery oranges through the sky.

"I don't want your money," I finally said. "I never did. Do you have any idea how this makes me feel?"

"I only wanted to ensure that you wouldn't want for anything, Millie," he said, his voice tired. "I didn't want you to feel like you were trapped, like when you were trying to reach your father. No one should have to feel that way. Even if I couldn't be with you, I still wanted to take care of you. That's why I did it."

"Because that's what you do, right?" I couldn't help but ask. "Everything becomes your responsibility, your duty."

"That's not what it was," Kythel said quietly, shaking his head. "I *want* to take care of you. I crave it. You're not my duty, you're my *kyrana*."

"Did it make you feel better?" I asked. "Did it assuage your guilt, paying me off because at that point you had chosen another female over me?"

*Maybe that was a little too harsh,* I told myself, especially when he flinched. It didn't make me feel better, hurting him. It made me feel worse.

His jaw tightened, and he stepped closer, taking the Halo orb and tossing it away so it hovered above our heads. He took my face into his cold hands. "If it meant giving you the freedom to do whatever you wanted to do, then yes, it did make me feel better. Was it influenced by guilt? No. I only wanted you to be happy, Millie. But that was then, and this is now."

"What does that mean?" I asked, flustered by his nearness. "You don't want me to be happy *now*?"

"Are you looking for an argument, *sasiral?*" he said, but his tone was almost *affectionate*.

Was I?

*Perhaps,* I thought.

"If you want to send back the credits, you can," he added. "I would prefer that you didn't, in case you ever have need of it, but...it doesn't matter anyway."

"Why?" I asked, my suspicion piqued by something I heard in his tone.

"Your name has been added to my accounts," he informed me. "Every shop, vendor, marketplace throughout the Kaalium will send the bill for whatever you purchase directly to me."

I couldn't help but gape at him.

"How do you feel about that?" he wondered, brushing his thumb across my cheek, back and forth. He looked like he wanted to kiss me. I could see the hunger in his eyes.

"I—I don't know," I answered truthfully.

"I think you like it," he declared softly.

"Oh? How so?"

"It doesn't make you weak to want to be taken care of, Millie. You've had to shoulder a great burden these last months. Alone. You're frightened to rely on me, to put your trust in me again after what I did to you. I understand that. I understand your hesitation. But I wish that you would believe me when I say that I'll always take care of you. That I will *always* choose you."

I *wanted* to believe it. That need felt like it was buzzing with energy in my chest, making me jittery and frustrated. But there was something holding me back. There was a barrier I couldn't breach with Kythel.

He was right—I was scared. Scared that he would shut me out again, that I would have no say in a decision that involved both of us. We'd had an agreement until the moon winds, yes. That I would be his blood giver and then we would go our separate ways.

But neither of us had expected to fall in love. And even knowing that we had, he'd still walked away as if it didn't matter. As if *I* didn't matter.

"You've been awfully honest lately," I bit out, my throat tight.

"Would you prefer that I lie to you, Millie?" he wondered. He shook his head. "I won't. I've decided that there will be no more secrets between us. I won't lie to you about anything."

That…was a start.

"Ask me anything, and I'll tell you," he said. "You were always so open with me. You had no fear sharing your memories, your thoughts. How you felt. I'm striving to be more like you, *sasiral*. I'm not saying I'll be perfect. I can't unlearn a lifetime of control and restraint and mistrust. But with you, I don't want *you* to ever doubt that I will hide anything."

I could ask him anything? And he would tell me the truth?

"Do you love me?" I asked.

His eyes flashed. "Yes."

"When did you know?"

"Before I broke your heart," he answered. "I knew for certain when we had dinner that night at the cottage. I knew for certain that you loved me then too."

"You pulled away that night," I pointed out. "Because you were scared?"

"Yes," he answered, his lips pressing.

"Why?"

He blew out a harsh breath. "There's something you need to understand. But I hardly know where to begin."

"Try from the beginning," I suggested. "I'll be here."

Kythel didn't say anything, not yet. But he did lower his hands from my face, clasped my hand in his own, and tugged me through the garden. I didn't know where he was taking me, but I had explored his gardens, the extravagant maze of them, and had a guess.

Lush, fragrant perfume from the various flowers greeted us as we passed. The warm season was blooming, a gentle breeze winding its way through the maze, guiding us, leading us. Hidden between two tall bright purple shrubs was an alcove made of stone, a bench carved from it.

Kythel sat me there, but then he retreated, walking a little ways to the left, pacing back to the right, his arms clasped behind his back. It took me a moment to realize he was *nervous*.

"Tell me," I ordered quietly. "What do you fear?"

"It's not quite fear," he admitted. "But I've never recounted this story. Not once. Not ever. But I must. For you. Because in doing so, I hope that you will have a better understanding of why I am the way I am. Why I did what I did."

"Then help me understand," I said simply, shrugging up one shoulder.

Behind him, the sky was deepening into dramatic shades of purples and inky blues.

"My aunt Aina was a peace ambassador during the Pe'ji War," he started.

"I remember it," I murmured quietly. Though I'd been young, it had been all over the news coms throughout the Quadrants.

"You know that the Pe'jians lost that war. We came to their aid, but it was much too late. Since we were allies of theirs, my aunt was brought in to negotiate on behalf of the Pe'jians in the aftermath. But she was murdered, assassinated by a team of United Alliance forces. A human unit."

My throat went tight.

"The human leading that unit was Gemma's father," Kythel added.

"Azur's wife?" I asked, lips parted in shock. "The *Kylaira* of Laras?"

"Yes," he said. "But we can discuss *that* later, if you wish. There were other circumstances surrounding their marriage, none of them…ideal. But it has nothing to do with my part in this."

Hesitantly, I nodded. I remembered what Lesana had told me once, that House Kaalium had many demons. Was this one of them?

"Go on," I urged quietly.

"I told you that I had been studying under an architect in Laras. That I wanted to follow in his footsteps, to *create* for the Kaalium, not rule a territory of it. You were right. You wondered once if I had even *wanted* Erzos. The truth, at that time, had been no. I didn't want Erzos then. The thought of coming here, serving my life here, it was suffocating. Before Pe'ji, I told my father that I had no intention of coming to Erzos. That I wanted to travel the Quadrants to expand my studies, to become an apprentice to a master architect who lived on Cron'yu, whose training was said to be rigorous."

"He didn't like that, I'm guessing," I said, my heart twisting in my chest.

"No," Kythel said softly, holding my gaze. "He didn't. It was the first fracture of our relationship—one that hasn't quite mended, even to this day. What happened on Pe'ji made it all the worse.

"Aina was the mediator in our family. She reminds me of Kaldur, actually, because she was brash and strong and outspoken. But she was incredibly diplomatic. She could sell anything to anyone, and she was a talented negotiator."

"You said she had negotiated peace with the Kaazor," I remembered.

"Yes," Kythel said, inclining his head. "She saw the discord that my...*rebellion* had caused within our family. She came to speak with me. The war on Pe'ji was in its final stages by then. She knew she would be leaving soon, and she asked me to come with her. I wanted to travel to see other planets, other cultures...what better way to get perspective than to help prevent the complete destruction of one?"

My brow furrowed. I thought...I was beginning to understand.

"She thought my temperament would be well suited for peace negotiations. She asked me to join her on Pe'ji, to accompany her, to aid her, and I accepted," he said, his voice ending on a rueful note.

"But you didn't go," I guessed softly, my chest twisting with realization. And Aina had been assassinated on Pe'ji. "Oh, Kythel."

"The master architect on Cron'yu wished to meet with me, to discuss an apprenticeship. I was eighteen years old then," he said, his tone wistful. "The call came in a couple days before we were set to leave for Pe'ji...and I chose to go to Cron'yu instead. Aina was disappointed in me. That's what still cuts me the deepest— remembering her face when I told her that day. I'd been excited. Now it makes me sick. Because she was leaving to help an entire race of people reclaim a fraction of the home that had been stripped away...and I'd never even given a single thought to them. Going to Pe'ji had been a burden to me. I had been so consumed in what I wanted that I couldn't see what was happening. I never got the chance to apologize to Aina for that. Our last meeting had been tense. Her last words to me..."

Kythel shook his head, his voice drawing tight. Catching his hand when he paced in front of me, I pulled him down to sit next to me on the bench, turning my body to face him.

"She told me that the Kaalium was built through loyalty and sacrifice and blood but that I was too selfish to see that," he finished quietly. "I had just made it to Cron'yu, had just landed at the ship depot when Azur called me to tell me about Aina. That she was missing. That no one knew what happened to her."

"I'm sorry," I whispered, tears pooling along my lash line.

"But my mother knew that Aina was dead. They were twins, like Azur and me. You can...you can feel it. Your souls will always be connected. I would know if something happened to Azur," he told me. "My mother was a different person after that. So consumed in her grief, it ate at her. During one of those uglier moments, she blamed me for what happened to Aina."

I squeezed his hand tighter.

"Just like Aina had, my mother called me selfish. She called me heartless to turn my back on my family. She said if I had been on Pe'ji like I'd promised, I could have protected Aina. That she was dead because of me."

"Kythel," I breathed, hardly able to process what I was hearing. What mother would lay that kind of guilt and blame on her child? Even in her grief? It was shocking. It was unfathomable to me, and I didn't even have a mother. "You know that's not true."

"Later, she was horrified about what she said," Kythel added, meeting my gaze. "She begged for my forgiveness, said that she didn't mean it...but I knew the truth. I knew that at least some part of her believed it. And I had already made my decision. That I would put the Kaalium first, my family first. My duty. My responsibility. Because if I had done that, Aina might still be alive.

"My mother died eight years later of blood sickness, but I think it was the loss and the grief and the obsession with finding her sister that really killed her in the end. We didn't even find Aina's body until Rye Hara, Gemma's father, confessed to the crime, only a few months ago. For eighteen years, her soul wandered in Zyos. For eighteen years, we didn't have closure. My family finally has that now, but...I could never forget. I never forgave myself."

"You punished yourself," I said softly, processing the words with something that resembled horror and sympathy and sorrow. "You threw yourself into Erzos, into serving the territory and the people you hadn't asked for, working yourself to the bone because you thought it was how you could repay Aina? Your mother? You were punishing yourself, Kythel, for something that was a tragedy—but not one that you caused."

"Punishment and duty were one in the same to me," he

confessed, and that nearly broke my heart all over again. "I couldn't have one without the other."

My brows drew together. "And now? Do you still feel like Erzos is your punishment?"

"No," he answered. "No, I've made this place my own. I've come to terms with my birthright, Millie. I accepted it a long time ago. I'm not the child I was then. I *care* about Erzos. Deeply. I care about its citizens. I want to prevent war. I only want peace. I want to make Erzos greater than it's ever been before—*that* is my purpose now. I was born into this family with my future already mapped out for me...and that is my fate. But it's a fate I've embraced."

"It was your sacrifice," I said, my voice strained and quiet, looking between us at our clasped hands. His gray skin gleamed against mine. "The sacrifice you believed you had to make."

"No," he said. "That sacrifice would have been you."

I jolted.

"Azur had married Gemma of House Hara, a human noble from a New Earth colony. Though it hadn't begun that way, in the end he married for love," Kythel said. "As the second eldest, I knew I would have to marry for purpose. A war bond was made between the Thryki and the Dyaar—Zyre told us at our meeting, and I believe he is telling the truth."

"What?" I breathed.

"War is closer than we think. *Drava* is a valuable resource in war. I saw it as my duty to marry Lyris so that House Kaalium could gain back a little control over its production and its export."

My heart was pounding, quick in my chest. I'd known all this...and yet I hadn't truly understood, had I? I hadn't understood the guilt, the pain, this driving need with Kythel, had I?

Now that I did, it *hurt*. It hurt me to think of the pressure that he'd placed on himself, the overwhelming burden.

"You were in an impossible position," I said softly. "You had to choose me or what you believed was best for the Kaalium."

"Yes," he said, his voice guttural and harsh. "When I came to you after the meeting with Zyre…it *was* the ultimate sacrifice, Millie. There was a part of me that believed if I gave you up, my *kyrana*, the female I'd fallen in love with, then I could finally be free of that memory of Aina. I could finally stop hearing her words in my head. My mother's words. I could finally be *free* of that sickening guilt."

"And did it?" I asked. "Did it help?"

"No," he rasped. "It made me furious."

"Why?"

"I asked myself…when would it be *enough*? What else would I have to give? Did I have to bleed out on the streets of Erzan, give my life blood to the Kaalium for it to be enough? Because that's what it felt like when I didn't have you anymore. It felt like I was bleeding out, Millie. I was furious because you were everything I wanted. And I didn't think I could have you. I wouldn't *allow* myself to have you because I didn't think I deserved you."

My breath whooshed out of me, tears dripping down my cheeks at the ugly truth I heard in his voice.

"So that night, when you said that you were *beneath me*," he rasped. I flinched, remembering the ugly words. "It couldn't be further from the truth, Millie."

"And what's the truth?" I whispered.

"That I'm fucking miserable without you," he exclaimed, tone harsh, his shoulder slumped. He was breathing hard, but he made an effort to lower his voice as he said, "That you're all I want, and that I would give anything to go back to that night and tell you that I loved you too. That's the truth, Millie. It took almost losing you to make me realize that I can't live without you."

I was stunned speechless, his honest words lingering between us like the beautiful fragrance of the garden blooms.

"But I know it's a lot to ask, *sasiral*," he finished, bringing my hand up to his lips, brushing a kiss across my knuckles. "I know being with me will not be easy. This is not a life that many will choose, despite how it appears to outsiders. You know that. You know how difficult it would be—to marry into a family like mine."

I did know. I'd told him many times that I didn't envy him.

"You've chosen me," I murmured softly. "You want to know if I'll choose you."

"I'll be patient," he said, skimming his fingers over my hand. "I promised you that. Until you decide."

"Thank you for telling me. About Aina," I said. "I do appreciate that, Kythel."

He inclined his head. "I should have told you a long time ago."

I was worried about him. There was a tightness around his eyes that hadn't been there before.

*Because he hasn't been feeding,* I knew. It was obvious to me. My father had sometimes grown weaker, more on edge when it had been too long. Food would only sustain a Kylorr to a certain point, especially a full-blooded Kylorr.

"You need to feed, Kythel," I said softly. Even if I wasn't certain about where we stood, I didn't want him to suffer. I cared about him. I loved him. And he looked worn down. "It's been too long."

When I went to move my hair away from my neck, he rasped, "No."

"No?" I asked, frowning.

He wanted it, and I wanted to ease some of his strain. He went still, the sudden hunger in his gaze dizzying when he looked at me.

"I'm fine, Millie," he told me, smoothing my hair back into place, shielding my neck from his view. "I've been feeding on blood rations. I just haven't been sleeping."

I didn't want that either. He needed the rest. Deep down, I knew it was because of me.

"It's getting dark," Kythel said. I had the impression it was to change the subject away from feeding. "I'll take you back to Grace's cottage."

But for the first time since that night before the moon winds...the thought of leaving him filled me with disappointment and longing.

"All right," I said quietly.

# CHAPTER 43

## MILLIE

*L*ong after Grace had gone to bed, I was sitting at the table in the front room, listening to the quiet—the creak of the window shutters from the gentle breeze, the brief musical chirping of nocturnal insects in the tall grass outside, the hum of my Halo orb as it twirled around my head.

I was listening to the quiet when I heard a heavy thud land outside in the meadow. Anticipation rose, an automatic response. I thought it might be Kythel, and I was hurrying to the door, opening and closing it carefully behind me, intent on meeting him.

Only it wasn't Kythel.

"Azur?" I asked, my eyes widening in surprise. "I mean...*Kyzaire*. I apologize—I didn't..."

"None of that, Millie," Azur cut in, shaking his head, peering at me with an expression that reminded me of Kythel. Enough to make me jolt. It was an observant, assessing look, as if he could see to my very bones, all of me exposed. "I know it's late, but I won't be long."

I crossed my arms over my chest, tucking my shawl around me tighter.

"I didn't realize you were still in Erzos," I commented, nervous.

Azur was just as intimidating as I'd remembered. I'd only spoken to him briefly the morning after my cottage had burned in Stellara, but I'd still been half in shock then, not really processing that he was the eldest son of House Kaalium and Kythel's *twin*. He'd been there in the aftermath, but I'd gotten the same impression I had now: he was trying to read me.

"I'm worried about my brother," he confessed. "I left from Laras this morning, but I wanted to see you first."

"What is it that you want from me?" I asked softly.

His lips slid in a half smile that reminded me, stunningly, of Kythel. "Astute," he commented. "Perhaps I just wanted to see how you were doing after the fire. Because I would not be here if I didn't want something from you?"

"No, I don't believe you would be," I said honestly.

"My brother loves you," Azur said, as easily as Kythel had said it earlier this evening. I wondered what Kythel had told him about us. "But more so, you're his *kyrana*. My wife is mine. And that's why I'm worried about him. Because I know the strain of being parted from her. The ache."

"He didn't want to feed earlier and—"

"I'm not talking about feeding," he said. "That can be always dampened. Suppressed. I'm talking about the *bond*. Because at this moment, your bond is an uncertainty. A lingering doubt. *That* would eat at him. It already has. I can see it. I can feel it."

"I don't know what you want me to say," I confessed quietly. "It was Kythel's decision. He's the one who chose to walk away."

A sharp exhale left him.

"You say it was his decision," he said. "But now the decisions is *yours*."

I started. I understood that, of course, but to hear it spoken by Azur...

Rubbing a hand over his horn, he peered around the darkness

of the meadow. Even the insects I'd heard earlier were silent in the presence of a *Kyzaire*.

"I suppose I just wish to know if you're going to choose him. Or if I need to be there to pick up the fragments of him left in your wake."

I frowned. "I don't want to hurt him. That's the last thing I want. I still love him, Azur. It hurts me to see him like this too."

"But you don't know if you want him."

*No, I do,* I thought. My instinctive answer was surprisingly loud, pounding out a beat inside my withered heart with finality. That want had never left me, even when he'd broken my heart. I believed I'd already made my decision in the gardens this evening. Perhaps I'd even made it when Kythel had confessed his love to me—openly, honestly.

I'd just needed time to make sure it was what *I* truly wanted. Patiently and carefully. Kythel had been right. Marrying into a family like House Kaalium…it couldn't be taken lightly.

But I loved him enough that I didn't care, that I didn't fear what it would bring.

It was a surreal experience, speaking with a virtual stranger about love of all things in a dark, dark meadow. Especially knowing the *power* of this Kylorr, his influence.

Azur said quietly, peering at me, "No, you know your decision. But he hurt you enough that you're wary to trust him."

"We spoke this evening," I admitted quietly, meeting his red gaze in the dark. "He told me about Aina. About…about what your mother said to him. The guilt he's carried for years."

He closed his eyes briefly, shaking his head. "I know the pain it's caused him. But we *all* shoulder the blame for what happened. Raazos's blood, I married my wife, intent on making her life a living hell, obsessed with destroying her family, destroying *her,* because of Aina."

The guttural emotion I heard in his voice…I hadn't expected such vulnerability from Azur.

"In the end, she forgave me. Sometimes I still don't believe I deserved her forgiveness. Sometimes I still don't believe I deserve her," Azur said. "That's what Kythel told me about you the night your cottage burned. He told me he didn't deserve you."

"He did?" I asked, my throat tightening.

"Do *you* believe that? That he doesn't deserve you?"

"No, I don't," I said truthfully. "I've traveled the Four Quadrants, and I've never met anyone like him. I doubt I ever will."

He inclined his head. There was relief in his expression. What was it that he saw? What was it that he heard?

"I'm going to return to Laras, Millie," Azur said slowly, watching me with every careful word. "Return to my wife. I don't think my brother will need me after all."

*Because he will have you* was what we both heard, unspoken.

"Will you do me a favor before you go?" I asked softly.

"Anything."

"Will you take me to him?" I asked. "The keep is a far way to walk this time of night."

---

KYTHEL WASN'T IN THE GARDENS OR THE ATRIUM OR THE KITCHENS or the library or his office—which was strangely bare, deep claw marks raking down the walls that had me frowning.

He was in the last place I thought I'd check within the keep— his bedroom. Asleep in a chair by the hearth, his wings half-crushed beneath him, as if his body had finally given into his exhaustion. At the sight, my heart battered against the bones around it, and I softly closed the door before approaching him.

A dark lock of hair had fallen across his cheek, his neck slumped in an uncomfortable position, and I brushed it away. When he didn't stir, I touched the back of his hand, entwining my fingers with his.

He woke.

"Millie?" he rasped, eyes bleary.

"Come to bed," I whispered softly, tugging on his hand until he rose. He pressed close, lowering his head until he inhaled the scent of my hair deeply. My breath hitched, longing for his closeness, missing it.

"Is this a dream?" he murmured against the crown of my head.

"Come to bed, Kythel," I repeated, luring him forward through the open doorway at the far end of the front room. His bed lay in the darkness, the tall floor-to-ceiling arched windows streaming moonlight across the floor. A couple spears of silver cleaved the base of his bed in two.

He tumbled into it, and I followed after, making sure the covers were drawn up around us.

"Must be a dream," Kythel decided, his eyes already closing.

"Sleep," I whispered, cuddling closer, placing my hand on the firm wall of his chest, laying my cheek against his bare shoulder. His warmth was comforting. It was everything I'd missed and more. "I'll be here. I promise."

# CHAPTER 44

## MILLIE

Kythel was awake when I finally blinked open my eyes, seeing blue, hazy dawn light filtering through the bedroom. He was curled around me, every inch of my backside pressed against his front, one arm wrapped below me in the crook of my waist and one arm above, his dulled claws tracing my hip, spreading goose bumps up my spine.

"Not a dream," he murmured into my hair, pulling me tighter into him when he realized I was awake. "Please tell me it's not, *sasiral.*"

"It's not a dream, Kythel," I told him, snuggling deeper into his warm embrace. There was a pressing ache between my thighs, heady and distracting, stirred by his closeness, his scent, and my decision.

"You're in my bed. In my arms."

"Yes, I'm in your bed," I answered slowly, reaching behind me to cradle the back of his head, one tip of his horn pressing into my forearm. "In your arms. Kythel?"

"Hmm?"

I angled my neck up and pulled his head down. "Enough, now. *Please.*"

His sharp huff blew across my skin. I closed my eyes when his warm lips brushed the sensitive skin of my throat.

"No," he rasped. "I need to know that—"

"We'll talk after," I promised. "It's been too long, Kythel. Do you want me to beg?"

He paused. "You want this?"

"Yes!"

I pulled on his head again and sighed in relief when he kissed my neck, when I felt the tips of his fangs press into me, though he didn't break my skin.

"Don't you want it too?" I whispered.

"Always," he growled. "Missed you, *sasiral*."

"I'm here," I said, but the word ended on a gasp when I felt the familiar pinch of his fangs. The heat of his venom flooded into the small wound, and the ache between my thighs became a violent need.

Reaching behind me, I tugged at the laces of his pants. While I was in a sleeping tunic—one that slipped easily up my thighs, leaving me bare—he was still fully clothed from the night before. It had to be uncomfortable. He groaned when my hand found his hot, hard cock, and he further stiffened in my grip, pulsing when I squeezed.

He was too lost in the feeding. It had been over a week since his last, when he had fed from me a couple times, if not more, a day. He was *starved* for me, and he was greedy.

"Yes, Kythel," I breathed. "Take everything you need."

*I want to be everything you need,* I thought.

His grip tightened around me, beginning to lose control. When his wing came over my body, enveloping us, I knew some deep-rooted instinct within him was fearful I would try to wiggle away.

I lifted my thigh, feeling a dizzying wave of pleasure spiral up my core, my clit pulsing wildly. The heat of his cock was searing as I pressed the broad head to my pussy. A guttural groan reverberated up his throat, vibrating against the column of my neck, as I sank down on him, holding him inside.

It wasn't so much about the sex. It wasn't about the pleasure I knew I would find in his bite, in his touch, in his kiss. It was *this*. It was about feeling connected to him when we had been apart and distant for so long. Azur was right—it was about the bond, the *kyrana* bond.

When his cock slid as deep as his fangs, I cried out, bucking against him. *Sublime,* I thought. The thickly corded arm under my waist slid up, cradling my head against him. His hair tangled with mine. His left wing felt like a comforting weight on top of me. All around me, I could smell his spicy, musky scent. I could feel his heartbeat thundering at my back. I could hear his quick gasps and the erotic slide of his tongue as he lapped at my blood.

*Perfection.*

"I love you," I gasped out. Kythel's breath hitched, his hips never stilling as he thrust between my thighs. "I love you, Kythel."

Our lovemaking felt slow and endless, and yet we both came in quick succession, the room filled with our cries and groans as we both rushed to the peak. The heat of come inside me was familiar, as was the burn of his knot when Kythel thrust particularly deep, seating himself until every drop of him was sealed in.

Helplessly, I groaned when his hips never stopped, the stimulating rub of his knot almost *too much.*

"Kythel," I gasped.

Finally, he ceased. His fangs retreated, though he continued to lick the wound at my neck, and I slumped in his arms, boneless and sated. He was still clasping me tight to him, as if afraid I'd leave.

The sweat was drying on my skin, the sensation cooling. The erotic stroke of his tongue was making me flutter around his knot, and when his cock finally slipped from me, long moments later, Kythel finally healed the wound on my neck.

I could feel his strength returning. His muscles growing, the tendons running down his arms and lengths hardening like steel. I stroked my fingertips over whatever flesh I could reach as he shuddered against me, his breaths still coming fast. But I knew it must feel like a relief. Because it felt like a relief to *me*.

Turning in his arms, I locked eyes with my mate for the first time that morning.

"You don't feel real," he murmured, voice dazed in disbelief. I was relieved to see the lines around his eyes from his exhaustion had disappeared. He'd needed the sleep. He'd needed my blood.

Leaning forward, I pressed my lips to his, soft and slow. I tasted my blood on his tongue, but it wasn't unpleasant, just a reality of being mated to a Kylorr.

"You came here last night?" he murmured. "But how…"

"Azur brought me."

"Azur?" he asked, incredulous. "Is he still here?"

"No, he left last night. He came to Grace's cottage. He wanted to talk, and afterward, I asked him to bring me here."

"What did you talk about?" he asked softly, intensely curious, his gaze piercing.

"Nothing I didn't already know myself," I said, sighing. The comfort and safety I felt in his arms…I'd missed this.

He tensed. "And what is that?"

Sliding my fingers against his lips, I traced the curve of them as I said, "I'm here, aren't I?"

"Yes."

My tone was soft as I pointed out, "Our issue was that it was a matter of trust, Kythel. Could I trust you not to walk away again? And you were right. You didn't make me any promises beyond what we had agreed on. You didn't lie to me. You were very careful about that."

"Millie—"

"No, let me finish, please," I said, touching his lips. "I need to get this out because it's so incredibly simple, Kythel. And then we can move forward. I needed to make the decision if I could trust you with my heart again. If I could trust you not to break it. If I could trust you when you said you love me."

I took a deep breath, a small smile quirking up the corners of my lips.

"And my answer was simple. I felt it in my gut," I said.

"And what did you decide?" he asked, his tone solemn, though it shouldn't have been.

"Yes," I said, that simple word filling the space between us. "Yes, Kythel. That's my answer."

He exhaled a sharp breath, his arms sliding around me tighter, as if he was still afraid I'd slip away.

"My father told me once that life is just a series of answers. I think about that a lot," I admitted. "Because answers are knowledge. And knowledge comprises a life, at its core. Life is memory, and memory is just…your answers to life's questions. How you respond. How you persevere. How you love.

"So when my father died, I asked myself a question. What was I going to do? And my answer to that question? It was to bring him back to Krynn, just as I promised him. And that answer ultimately led me to you."

Kythel's fingers traced up my spine, and I shivered pleasantly against him.

"And when I found the cottage in Stellara? I asked myself what I was going to do. That answer? I was going to restore it to what it once was, the last gift I could give my father in this life. I took one day at a time. One answer bleeding into the next. It kept me focused, gave me comfort because it made it seem like these large, insurmountable things were manageable. And one day, they would just become memories. That's a beautiful thing."

I didn't know if I was making sense or not, if the jumbled mess in my mind translated on my tongue. But Kythel's gaze was soft. He was looking at me the way he had the night I'd made him dinner at the cottage. As if I was the only one in this universe for him.

"So," I started softly, swallowing, giving him a sheepish smile, "maybe that wasn't as simple as I thought, but…what I'm trying to say, Kythel, is that *you're* my new answer. Me and you. Together. And I think I'm your answer too."

"You are," he rasped quietly, without hesitation.

"I want all the memories this life has to offer with you," I told him. "And I know you said that this life isn't for everyone, but I want you to know that I'm not scared. With you at my side, I'm not scared of anything anymore, except maybe losing you. So yes. My answer is and will always be…yes."

Kythel was shaking, I realized. Perhaps the tension, the last week of an untethered bond, the exhaustion, the doubt was leaking out of him. Once it was purged, only then could we begin fresh, to begin to build a life together—not bound in duty but bound in understanding and love and *choice*.

"*Vaan*," he cursed softly. "I love you, Millie Seren. My little fallen star, my gift from the universe. What did I ever do to deserve you?"

"You deserve everything, Kythel," I told him, and I knew he heard the truth in my voice.

"I'm sorry, *sasiral*," he said. "You don't know how many times I've relived that night. Of watching you—"

I kissed him, silencing whatever he was about to say. He sighed against my lips, finally beginning to relax.

"We're moving past that," I said against his lips. Pulling back, I smiled and said, "I forgive you. I already forgave you. You did what you thought was best. I can never fault you for that, knowing what I know now. All right? Let's not speak of it anymore."

Kythel said gently, "What about the credits? Are you still angry with me about that?"

I chuckled. Had he been worried about that, this high-handed male who had deposited nearly a quarter million into my account?

"Yes," I teased. "I've already rejected the transfer, you know."

He sighed. "It won't matter. When you become my wife, you'll need to get used to it. The Kaalium will open up to you. You'll have access to everything."

"Was that a proposal?" I asked, zeroing in on that bit of information and ignoring the rest. We'd cross *that* bridge when we got to it.

"I'll marry you right now if you'll have me," he told me. "I want myself tied to you in every fathomable way in this life and the next."

"Would you marry me? In this bed? With no witnesses?"

"Yes," he said honestly. "But I think it would be better to wait for the next moon winds. That way you'll be able to feel your father. Would you like that?"

My throat went tight. "Yes. Yes, I would."

"It's settled, then."

"High-handed indeed," I whispered, though I was grinning through my sudden blurry vision. My whole body felt like it was lit up from the inside out. "Tell me you love me again."

"I love you, Millie Seren," he said.

"Again."

His voice softened. "I love you, *sasiral*."

He kissed me, dipping his head, and I sighed. Perfectly relieved. Perfectly happy.

Against my lips, he said, "You're the answer to the question I never even thought about asking."

# EPILOGUE

## KYTHEL

*Two moon winds later...*

---

"We're going to be late," I growled down to my wife, who was currently licking my cock from the very base of my pulsing knot all the way up to the slick broad head, lapping happily at the pre-come that wetted the tip.

"Everything's already prepared," she retorted, dragging in a deep breath before teasing me with a swirl of her tongue in that place she *knew* drove me wild. "I just need to garnish the plates."

I bucked, a deep groan falling from my lips. That groan became a curse when she swallowed the head of my cock, and I hissed when it hit the back of her throat.

"*Millie.* Gods, yes. Fucking *perfect.*"

When she pulled back, gasping, she grinned up at me, triumphant.

"Don't give me that smile, or you'll end up on your hands and knees," I warned, a gruff laugh stuck in my tight throat.

"Already on my knees," she teased, the words a whisper over

my cock as she dragged her pretty lips up the sides. She bobbed her head down half the length of my cock, sucking until her cheeks hollowed.

"Don't sass me," I hissed, though the words held no bite.

She pulled back. Another grin.

"That's it," I rasped, her squeal of delight filling my office. I tugged her up and bent her over the edge of my desk, her arm cutting through the Halo screen I had projected, a blur of pixels, the plans for Sorn Village, coming to life.

Shoving her dress up around her waist, I pressed my cock against her slick sex, leaning over her back to keep her in place, my wings folding around us.

"Anything to say, my love?" I purred, nipping at her jawline with my teeth. Millie only laughed, that husky, seductive sound making me surge into her until it ended on a shocked gasp. I groaned when I slid out, gathering my wife's hair in my grip.

"No, not at all," she breathed.

When I thrust back into her, seating myself deeply, enough that the stretch from my knot made her squirm beneath me, I told her, "Oh, we will most certainly be late now, *sasiral.*"

---

THE MOON WINDS OUTSIDE WERE BUILDING TO THEIR PEAK, BUT I was content to be inside the Stellara cottage, seated at the long table, built by a skilled hand in Savina, with my wife beside me.

She, Gemma, and Grace were chatting across the table about foods they missed from the New Earth colonies. Gemma had fallen in love with the dessert Millie had prepared tonight, a *syaan*-berry cake, the sponge sticky and springy, drizzled in chocolate ganache imported from New Inverness and garnished with *kanno* spice.

Piper and Mira, Gemma's sisters, and Kalia were in attendance too, but they were outside in the clearing, watching the meteors shoot across the sky. Falling stars, they called them, which made me grin at my wife. But the moon winds and a meteor shower were fighting over the night. Through the window, we could hear the three of them gasp in delight, a spark of light brightening up the sky like an *akkium* bolt.

Over my goblet of Drovos wine, I met Azur's eyes. Next to him was Kaldur, the only one of my remaining brothers who could join us tonight.

"When do you break ground on Sorn Village?" Kaldur asked after taking a long swig of brew, courtesy of Millie, though the rest of us had wine.

"Next week," I answered.

Though truthfully, I wasn't certain if we should delay it. Zyre had sent over his reports from his spies in Thrykan. It appeared he'd been telling the truth about war bonds being made between our two most contentious enemies across the seas. We'd sent over ambassadors already to the Thryki and Dyaar, though the journey was long. It could be a month or more before we got our own reports back. But we would try to stop a war before it ever took root.

"One project after the next," Azur commented, looking pointedly around the cottage. "You both did well."

I nodded, slinging my arm around Millie's hips, sliding her closer along the bench we were seated at. Her hand found mine, but she didn't pause in her conversation with Gemma.

"The plans were easy for the cottage," I said. "It was just a matter of rebuilding what was here, expanding certain rooms. With a few upgrades, of course. *Akkium* power, for one."

"And a Halo network," Azur said, quirking a brow.

I shrugged. "Millie spends plenty of time here. It was a precaution, in case she needed to reach me."

"As if the guard you have shadowing her isn't enough," Kaldur joked, but Azur and I exchanged a look. He understood. Gemma had a guard wherever she went within Laras too. Especially now, with Zyre's warning running in our minds about spies throughout the Kaalium.

"Maybe when you find a mate, you won't be so quick to judge," Azur said lazily.

Kaldur snorted into his brew, taking another swig, but remained strangely silent on the matter.

Azur leaned forward, clearing his throat. "The South Road progress has been promising. I've been thinking we should connect it to Laras once it stretches toward Salaire."

Kaldur chimed in with, "Let's finish it between Erzos and Vyaan first before we discuss expansion. It'll be another few months, if the builders keep at their current pace. We're already pushing them too much."

"Agreed," I said. "And I think we—"

"Hey," Millie suddenly cut in, pointing an accusing finger at each of my brothers before it landed on me. "You know the rules. No talking about work at the dinner table. Especially during the moon winds."

Across the table, Gemma pressed her lips to Azur's cheek. "Just can't help yourself, can you?"

I'd never seen Azur look sheepish before, but it certainly made Kaldur let out a booming laugh.

"Come on," Millie said, tugging on my hand, nearly sloshing what remained of my Drovos wine onto the table.

We'd expanded the front room of the cottage during the rebuilding process so we could host dinner parties. Millie liked cooking here, but oddly enough, she hadn't wanted to expand the kitchen. Just the seating area for a larger table.

"Where are we going?" I wondered.

"We're going to go watch the falling stars, of course," my wife said with a small wink.

LONG AFTER OUR DINNER GUESTS HAD LEFT THE COTTAGE—
Kaldur opting to fly the moon winds after dropping off Mira and
Piper back at our keep, where they were all staying for the night
—Millie and I were cleaning up in the kitchen. Something I'd
never done until meeting my wife, but now I could say these
quieter moments were some of my favorite ones.

Her arms were covered with warm, soapy water, and she
flung suds at me whenever I sidled up behind her, nipping at her
neck.

"Have I told you how beautiful you look in this dress
tonight?" I purred against her. She was wearing the same dress
she'd worn when she'd made me my "universe dinner," the image
of her that night forever imprinted in my memory. She *knew* the
things this dress did to me, and she wore it tonight, exactly one
month after our wedding.

"Only a couple dozen times, but I never mind hearing it once
more," she said, lobbing me a small smile over her shoulder. "Stop
distracting me and bring those plates over, *Kyzaire*."

She liked to boss me around in the kitchen, like a true culinarian's daughter. She thought it was amusing when she used my
title while doing it too.

"Yes, wife," I rasped into her ear.

The wedding had been just the two of us, performed in the
old tradition—a few spoken vows during a moon-winds night,
our palms sliced and pressed together, blood mingling and dripping onto the earth beneath us.

It was the first night that Millie had felt her father in the
realm of Alara. Two soul gems had been placed in the small
shrine I'd had built on the grounds of the cottage, very near
Ruaala's tree and the *zylarr* I'd placed. Last moon winds, on the
night we'd married, those two soul gems had lit up for the first
time. Millie had been so happy, staring at them in quiet awe, as
I'd felt the touch of a warm soul, skimming its fingers across my
cheek.

"I can feel him, Kythel," Millie had breathed, her eyes shining with sudden tears, our hands still clasped tight, the warmth of our blood between them. "*Gods*, I can feel him. He found his way here."

It was the first time I'd seen *her* truly at peace, like a heavy weight was lifted off her. She'd fulfilled her promise to her father and then some. That same night, she'd buried the letters her father had written to Ruaala at the base of the shrine, though she'd kept the one he'd written to her. A letter she'd let me read.

In it, her father had written that Millie had been the love of his life, that he'd never known the extent with which he could love another. Millie had saved him in his darkest moment. She'd given him purpose and hope again the moment he'd laid eyes on a small bundle at a crowded travel port. He could never imagine a better life than the one he'd shared with her.

Millie very rarely read the letter. When she did, every single time, she broke down in sobs that made my heart twist in my chest as I tried to soothe her. But she kept it close to her. All the time. It was one of her most treasured possessions, and I'd learned that my wife didn't like many material things.

"Oh!" Millie said suddenly. "I had a thought for Sorn Village today. I was thinking that the market should actually be situated on the west side of the village. Those winds that funnel down from the pass? It would be like a wind tunnel if we kept the market on the east bank. The report came in from the surveyor this afternoon while you were in your meeting."

I smiled, handing her the dirtied platter and taking the clean one from her hands to dry. "And you accuse us of working all the time."

She laughed. "*Please.* I was the one who had to *entice* you to leave your office this evening just to make it here on time for our guests."

"We were late," I pointed out with a roguish grin.

"Who even are you?" she grumbled, scrubbing at the last

platter before handing it to me. She wiped her sudsy arms on a clean cloth as I dried the dishware, placing it on the neat stack. The fire in the hearth popped and crackled, and she stepped into my embrace. "Kythel of House Kaalium, proud to be *late* for his own dinner party?"

"My wife, Millicent of House Kaalium, was proving to be... distracting. Who can blame me?"

Millie looked up into my eyes, her arms resting on the tops of my shoulders.

"I saw Lesana in the market today," she confessed softly, though she didn't sound angry about it. Whereas me? I tensed. She smoothed her hands over the sudden knots and rippling tension beneath my skin, as if she'd expected it.

"Was Kelan with you?"

"Of course—like you'd let me go anywhere without him close by," she pointed out.

"Did she see you?" I wondered.

Millie nodded. "She nodded at me. But then we passed right by one another without saying a single word."

"She shouldn't even look in your direction," I growled softly, steadily growing at the thought. "I should have put *that* in the agreement with Kaan."

House Arada had come to heel. *Drava* production was well under way, and we were working to meet the agreed supply for Zyre as a precaution.

"Calm down, my love," she said softly, cupping my face in her hands. "She kept her distance."

It didn't make me feel any better. It didn't make me feel any better knowing that the noble House responsible for attempting to *kill* my wife were still walking around my province like nothing had happened.

But that was the price I'd paid. It was what Millie had sacrificed too, after all. Me? If I'd had the choice, I'd strip House Arada of the Three Guardians and let them rot in the streets of Erzos.

"I'm calm," I rasped.

Her expression told me she didn't quite believe me, and I forced myself to relax.

"I need to be more like you," I said quietly. "You forgive. You don't hold grudges. That's something I've always struggled with."

"Especially when it comes to forgiving yourself," she pointed out, her tone turning serious.

I frowned. "Yes."

"But you're getting much, much better," she added, pressing a kiss to the corner of my lips. "Probably because you have such a good influence in your wife."

"Likely," I said dryly, making her laugh. I exhaled, most of the tension from the mere mention of Lesana on Millie's lips draining away with that laugh. "Thank you for telling me you saw her."

It would've been easier not to say anything at all.

"I promised I would," she said.

She distracted me with a long, deep kiss, and the remaining tension loosened from my shoulders. My wings lowered, the tips dragging on the ground as my hands dug into her hips, pulling her closer.

Against her lips, I murmured, "And thank you for dinner tonight."

"You think everyone liked it?" she asked, pulling away and nibbling on her reddened lips, uncertain.

I shook my head, still amazed that she had doubts her food was anything less than spectacular. "Everyone loved it, Millie. You didn't hear, but Kaldur was only half joking when he said he wanted you to be his personal culinarian in his keep."

Millie laughed, flushing, the compliment lighting her up. "Oh. Good. What did you say?"

"That you are *my* culinarian and to keep his greedy little claws off you," I said, my tone playful. "On Raazos's blood, my brother gets absolutely feral whenever you make those *kanno* tarts."

Her laughter brightened up the cottage, and I held her close to the still-warm kiln oven. The only thing that had survived the fire. The only original piece of the cottage that was here before. Her father's engraving was still stamped on the inner wall.

"I'll send him home with some," she teased. "That should keep him satisfied for a little while."

"At least until he comes slinking back at the next moon winds," I grumbled. "When do I get you all to myself?"

"Only every night," she pointed out, quirking her brow.

"I do, don't I?" I asked, grinning shamelessly.

"Yes," she said. Her breath hitched, and she beamed up at me. Each and every day, she somehow got more beautiful. "And I wouldn't have it any other way because I'm a little possessive of you too, husband."

"Good, *sasiral*," I purred.

My eyes caught on something sitting on the opposite end of the room, something I'd received just that morning. I'd been waiting for a quiet moment to give it to her. Right now was a perfect one.

Pulling away, I crossed to the window seat I'd built into the updated plans of the cottage, carefully picking up the leather-bound bundle from the cushions there, careful not to bend it.

Returning to Millie, I took in her curious expression when I held it out to her. "A gift."

"What's this for?" she asked, suspicion lacing her tone, though she was smiling. She was only a *little* better about receiving gifts, especially the expensive kind, though I hadn't paid a single credit for this one. I didn't know how she'd react to it, truthfully, but it was the meaning behind it that I thought might make her want to keep it. Or, at least, allow me to display it within the keep. My office, perhaps, or the library.

"Open it and see."

When she untucked the flap of the leather and slid the

encased parchment from within, I watched her brows furrow in confusion…and then her lips parted in shock.

"Is this…?" she breathed.

"Yes."

"I'm…I'm holding Ver Teracer's artwork in my hands right now," she exclaimed after she squinted at the telltale gleaming, sparkling blue signature in the corner. Her tone made me chuckle, especially when she turned those dazed eyes up at me.

"Yes," I said. "*You.* His portrait of you, Millie."

The female in the drawing was achingly beautiful with her imperfect symmetry—her sloped, wide nose, her dark, defined brows and joyous eyes. I'd been attempting to draw Millie just like *this*, but somehow Ver Teracer had captured her perfectly, effortlessly.

"This isn't me," she said, frowning. "She's…*stunning.*"

I pulled her into my arms, pressing my lips to her forehead, though I was careful of the priceless parchment between us.

"He did indeed draw you," I informed her. "Just as he said he would."

"How ever did you find it?" she asked, awed surprise still filling her tone.

"Tracking him down wasn't easy," I admitted. "But Setlan managed to connect us. I spoke with him. I told him about you and asked about a drawing he might've done. He remembered you, Millie. Immediately. He saw something in you that he couldn't forget. He gave us this piece. As a marriage gift."

"Truly?" she asked.

"Yes," I said, giving her a lazy grin. "You don't think this looks like you?"

She chuckled, her shoulders finally loosening as she glanced back down at the portrait. "I…I don't know. All my features are mirrored here. It's not how I see myself though, I suppose."

"It's how I see you," I told her.

Her gaze softened. I watched that beautiful smile light up

again, and I marveled that she *couldn't* see herself the way Ver Teracer had portrayed her—this stunning, imperfect creature, my chip in the marble.

"Thank you, Kythel," she finally said, carefully setting aside the drawing on the table to loop her arms around my neck. "That is an incredibly, incredibly special gift." She laughed. "I never thought he *actually* drew me."

"You have that effect on people, Millie," I told her. "Your kindness, your warmth, your vulnerability, the connection you can have with strangers, even. It *is* special. You are special. A rare treasure in this life."

She beamed, her eyes going glassy.

"My gift from the universe," I finished, brushing my finger across her soft, pink cheek. I smiled. "My *sasiral*."

Her arms tightened around my shoulders as I dragged her closer, our lips meeting in a soft, gentle kiss as we swayed to the music of the night.

"Thank you, my love," she whispered against my lips.

The stars were still falling outside, and the moon winds were howling, beckoning.

Yet I didn't want to be anywhere else but right here.

Want to hear about new releases, exclusive giveaways, and get access to **bonus content,** like extended epilogues and character art?

**Sign up for my newsletter:**

www.ZoeyDraven.com/newsletter

---

**If you're already subscribed to my newsletter, access all bonus content here:**

www.ZoeyDraven.com/bonus-content

# ACKNOWLEDGMENTS

To my editor Mandi, as always, thank you for all your hard work and enthusiasm for this series. You make my books better, simply put. Thank you for putting up with my overused commas and my inability to use the correct tense of *"to lie."* (But, seriously, which one is it?)

To Naomi, Trev, Elizabeth, April, and Meg, thank you for being *fantastic* beta readers and friends. Your support has meant so much to me over the years, and I can't wait to meet many of you in person in 2024.

To Marcio, we talked almost every day while I was writing this book, and I see a lot of you in it. Thank you for bringing me into your recording booth and for being a good friend—even if you do pronounce Azur's name wrong, especially in your Romanian accent.

To all my readers, THANK YOU. This community is one of the most supportive communities out there. Thank you for your comments, emails, and messages...I appreciate each and every one of you.

# ABOUT THE AUTHOR

Zoey Draven has been writing stories for as long as she can remember. Her love affair with the romance genre started with her grandmother's old Harlequin paperbacks and has continued ever since. As a Top 100 Amazon bestselling author, now she gets to write the happily-ever-afters—with a cosmic, other-worldly twist, of course! She is the author of steamy Science Fiction Romance books, such as the *Warriors of Luxiria* and the *Horde Kings of Dakkar* series.

When she's not writing, she's probably drinking one too many cups of coffee, hiking in the redwoods, or spending time with her family.

Website: www.ZoeyDraven.com
Facebook group: Zoey's Reader Zone

Printed in Great Britain
by Amazon